LUINA

James Hand

A Beth Duncan series:

First published in Melbourne, Australia by Ashby's Place,
PoBox 392, Carnegie, Vic, 3163 for James Hand
Publishing, 2022 ©

The right of James Hand Publishing© to be identified as the
author of this work has been asserted by him in accordance
with the Copyright, Designs and Patents Act 1988.

A catalogue record for this book is available from the
Amazon and Kindle account Ashby's Place.

Publisher: Ashby's Place
Design/Photography: Brett Ashby
Cover Photo: Mia Sciacca

ISBN-13: 979-8-4211-8351-8

Printed in China by Amazon AU

ACKNOWLEDGEMENTS

Many thanks to Brett Ashby for continued help in publishing and direction. Judy Rankin for initial editing. Stewart Handasyde for storyline advice. Joan Hamilton, Wayne McQuilton, Maria Donato, Christine Smith, Mia Sciacca.

All deliberate distortions of reality are my own. Big thanks to Beth for being such a positive force of energy.

PROLOGUE

Beth Duncan is lounging on the sofa, the TV half capturing her attention. As her father Christian descends the stairs he calls over his shoulder.

'Norma, hurry we'll be late.'

'Coming,' is the muffled reply from upstairs. Tapping his foot impatiently, he turns to Beth.

'Oh, Pumpkin Pie, we'll be at the Newman's but only about four hours, their number is...'

'On the pad next to the phone,' interjects Beth, then turning grins at him, 'I've done this many times, you know.'

'Hey I was just being cautious, it's my job prescription you know.'

'Ha,' she laughs, 'and you're so good at it.' Smiling with confidence, he observes "his little girl is really growing up, yep she's sure something, a chip off the old block." Norma in a pattern dress and a mustered coloured wrap enters the lounge-room and begins.

'I'm here, let's go, now Beth the phone number...' Raising her eyebrows Beth forces Norma's voice to trail off.

'Yes, well, you know all that.' She moves forward and kisses her on the forehead.

'We won't be late.' Christian also moves to Beth and kisses her on the cheek.

'Later but not to late Pumpkin Pie, love ya, bye bye.' Exiting through the front door they throw a flying comment.

'Don't forget to lock the door.' The car's engine is

heard as it backs down the driveway, then the sound gradually disappears. Beth grins to herself, thinking.

'My parents are such daggs but fun for their age.' Rising she snips the door then energetically jumps back onto the sofa, flicking through the channels she finds New Asian Pop Video Hits, as the various pop bands ply their trade on the screen, she takes it in analysing their movements. Many appeal with their slick dance choreography, after an hour so she resorts to a previously taped show, "Bring It On." The show ends, with a yawn she switches off the TV and ascends the stairs. Entering the bath-room she fumbles for the toothbrush and cumbersomely squirts tooth-paste on it, finishing that and other ablutions she heads for her bedroom. At the doorway she stops and pricks her head, thinking a sound was heard. Pausing and listening more intently she hears it again, it sounds like someone is knocking on the front door. Descending the stairs, she notices the sound becoming clearer, someone is definitely knocking on the door, unsure what to do she hesitantly calls out.

'Who's there?'

'Police,' is the firm reply. She's smart enough not to immediately open the front door but rather moves to the window, easing the curtain slightly to see outside, a police-car is visible in the street, moving back to the front door she unlocks and opens it. In front of her is a police-lady and a man standing behind her, the lady seems a tad tense and asks.

'Is this the home of Christian Duncan?'

'Yes,' is Beth's searching reply.

'And you would be?'

'I'm Beth, his daughter… umm I live here, why?'

'Right,' is the considered reply.

'Ahh, can we come in please?' Anxiety starts to invade Beth's psyche, she controls herself.

'Well yes, I guess, what's this about?' The police-lady

continues.

'I'm afraid I've got some bad news, you see your parents have been involved in a car accident.'

'Mum, dad are they alright?' The lady glances at the man then re-focuses on Beth.

'They've been taken to hospital.'

'Hospital,' gasps Beth. 'They're injured?' Taking a breath the lady continues, 'No Beth they're not injured, they... umm didn't make it.'

'To the hospital?' Beth is slightly confused.

'Yes, but well, ahh... I'm sorry to have to tell you this but they were killed, your father died instantly and your mother on the way to the hospital.'

'Died!' the words hit Beth like a sledgehammer.

'But they went to the Newman's for dinner.'

'It was on the way home, we think that drugs might have affected the other driver, not sure yet, tests have to be done, I'm sorry.' Beth stares blankly trying to organise her thinking.

'Mum, dad, accident, police here... oh my god!' The enormity of the situation hits her.

'No, no... please no!' she pleads. The police-lady grabs her hands.

'I'm so sorry Beth,' the touch of her hand accentuating the reality of the situation.

'Is there someone you can stay with?' Beth's in a daze, the best she can do is shake her head, no.

'Well do you have a relative we can call?' 'No, only an uncle, he lives in another state.'

'Well I'll organise another person to stay with you tonight.'

'No, umm... no please, I'm used to staying here on weekends by myself.'

'I'd advise against that, I think you need someone.'

'No, not really, I'd prefer my own company tonight.' The lady is worried but realising the young girl seems sensible reluctantly agrees.

'One thing Beth, you'll need to come down to the hospital and identify the bodies. Can you come tomorrow? We can arrange someone to pick you up.' She doesn't want to be anywhere near the police now.

'No, no, I'll get an Uber, where do I go?'

'Here,' the police lady hands her a card. 'It'll be quick, can someone come with you?' Beth thinks, 'Umm, I'll call the Newman's they'll help.' The lady stares at Beth trying to analysis her, doubt lingers but her gut feeling is that the young girl probably needs to be alone, she stands.

'The information's there, just take your time, anytime tomorrow. I'm sorry to have to bring you this sad news, please call us anytime, we're here to help.'

'Thank you,' whispers Beth. The police move to the front door, open it and exit, the lady turns.

'Anytime, okay?'

'Yes, thanks,' mumbles Beth as she slowly closes the door. As they walk to the car the lady gives an aside comment to the man.

'This is one part of the job that I hate.' He nods in agreement, 'The poor young girl.'

Locking the door Beth walks like in a mist, glancing into the lounge-room she sees the photo of her family, Dad, Mom and her, it was taken only six months ago and stands proudly on the side-table. She wanders over to it, picks it up and places it under her arm then ascends the stairs. Entering her bedroom, she lays on the bed clutching the photo to her chest, turning on to her front she places it in front of her face and stares at it.

Her stare continues for minutes only broken by her mumbling the words 'Pumpkin Pie,' and touching her image in the photo, then 'Dad,' and touching his image, finally 'Mum,' then running her finger over the image. Tears well in her eyes, she calls, 'No...no...no...!' The calling accelerates in intensity, 'No...no...no...!' Tears flow, she starts screaming, 'No... no... no...!'

Luina

CHAPTER 1

She was the most attractive young girl seen on the
Tasmanian North West Bus for some time. Like the other
passengers seated on the old 80's custom bus she sat separate,
in that unique habit of strangers herded together. Unlike the
other passengers, however, she showed enthusiastic interest
in the emerging landscape outside the window. Her athletic
appearance and honey blonde wavy hair falling just off her
shoulders put her at odds with the other more weather-
beaten rural types stationed in their seats, her gaze actively
alive taking in the rural vision, unlike the disinterest shown
by the other passengers. The picturesque scenery tickling her
interest as it would to one travelling through any new town
or country. The alluring scenery of various gums, wattles and
black peppermints with occasionally cleared sections the result
of logging twigging her senses. The overcast clouds slightly
diminish the sight, still she radiates youthful enthusiasm
towards the scenic view. The occasional deft flick of her hair
draws glances from the other passengers who obviously see
her youthful attractive presence more pleasurable than the
monotonous rural landscape that they are accustomed to..
Unaware of the glances directed in her direction she continues

to study the images presented to her thru the window.

A narrow sweeping bend is navigated, the passengers notice buildings below them. The bus has been carefully descending the mountainous route for some time, more buildings come into view. In a vacant paddock on the town's outskirts, a car can be seen racing round an old bare paddock, seemingly performing wheelies. The descent starts to even out and the town identification board stands forlornly at the side of the road advertising the fact that the bus has entered the township of Luina pop 413. Old fibro cement houses dominate plus some weatherboard houses, the outskirts have a variety of small factory and commercial premises, but the overwhelming image is one of drabness and disrepair.

The bus doesn't deviate, just rolls into the main street finalising its motion at the stop just in front of the local General Store. The street is boarded by a smattering of buildings, a man with an apron is sweeping the front porch, he glances at the bus showing little interest. Taking out his mobile phone, he glances, it appears there is no reception, he pockets the phone and continues with his porch cleaning. Further down the street a man and a young lad are busy digging at the front of a building, an old weatherboard garage with a corrugated tin roof has an old eighty's Ford pick-up out the front with a mechanic bent under the bonnet The hairdressers is a tiny weatherboard cottage similar to a miner's cottage, an old lady exits the entrance, a few other buildings make up the commercial section of the main street, however they don't seem open. One is a weatherboard building with a plaque sitting on the front naming "Dwyer and Ass", with the door shut and the blinds down, it looks uninhabited, other buildings show no sign of being open for business.

Stopping at its designated spot, doors creak open and passengers start to disembark. They step with an older person's caution onto the main sidewalk showing the effects

of the longish trip on their old bones. The last passenger out is Beth Duncan, standing about 175cm tall with good build, she alights with the flexibility and vibrancy of youth, wearing jeans, sneakers and a grey "Stussy" hooded jumper. A large overnight bag is slung across her shoulder, standing on the sidewalk she glances around the street then extracts a piece of paper out her jeans pocket, concentrating on it she again glances up and down the street, with uncertainty she moves down the street. As she walks a few of the town's people pass her by taking no interest in this new person wandering around. The storeman sweeping his porch glances at her without saying anything, no smile or polite "good morning", she moves on, "obviously the welcoming committee is in recess here", she thinks. The man she saw digging the hole with the young boy walk past, he at least is polite, giving a nod and smile with a soft but distinct 'mornin', she is relieved to be in the presence of at least someone with manners and smiles back, the young boy traipsing just behind him is closer to her age and also gives a nod and a smile but with a slightly reserved manner, she smiles back but slightly shyly, as they move off towards the General Store.

Continuing on her way, an oldish 1980's grey Holden Commodore cruises past. A youth around twenty wearing sunglasses is driving, next to him in the passenger side is a younger looking weedy spotty faced boy in the back seat are three youths, two similarly weedy types and a girl, slightly overweight with a round face, pale complexion and dirty stringy mousey coloured hair. She has a spider tattoo on the side of her neck. As the car passes it slows, they all stare sullenly out the windows at her in a disinterested manner, Beth glances at the car but ignores it and continues on her way, the car moves off. Arriving at a minor street intersection she again stops and consults the piece of paper.

The man and his young helper are returning from the General Store, they walk past then noticing her unsureness stop.

'Are you alright Miss?' he asks.

'Not really' she reply's, 'I'm looking for Reg Duncan's house.'

'Old Reg,' he exclaims in a slightly surprising way.

'Yes, he's my uncle and I've come to live with him for a while.'

'Old Reg has a niece, I didn't know that, come to think of it we don't know much about him at all. Oh well, fair enough I suppose, I'm Geoff and young Rod here is my nephew and he lives with us.' The girl looks at Rod and smiles with youthful shyness. He smiles back and mumbles 'Yeah, It's okay.' Remembering her manners, she introduces herself.

'Oh, yes, I'm Beth.'

Geoff continues, 'Well to get to Reg's house go down here to the second street, turn left, go down a block then hang a right, continue for another block and his is on the right, number twenty-eight.'

She looks relieved, picks up her bag, smiles and says,

'Right, thanks so much, I'll find it now, bye.' Slipping the bag across her shoulder, she saunters off following their directions, Geoff moves off crossing the road, Rod follows but has a quick glance over his shoulder at the departing Beth.

Walking down the street, she inspects the dwellings. Most are fibro-cement or weatherboard, occasionally there is a brick-veneer house, but mainly they all fall into the same category. Two-window front with a front porch, driveway down the side to a garage or car-port, a small front yard with garden beds either at the front or along the side of the fence. Many front fences are wire strung across wooden or steel posts, some have plain timber palings nailed to the wooden posts, a small mesh front gate with a letter-box stationed next

to the gate. In all an unadventurous and uninspiring façade, not a white picket fence to be seen. She thinks to herself, "people round here are not very house proud." Moving past vacant blocks, the impression is open, bleak and unassuming but although rather uninviting it still captures her curiosity, eventually after negotiating the directions she arrives at number twenty-eight. It's the same as the others if not a little more run down, the lawn hasn't been mowed for a while, and the weatherboards are in desperate need of a fresh coat of paint. Hesitating she surveys the house, it's not very inviting, the dullness of the exterior is reflected in her facial expression but with a lift of her head, shrug of the shoulders and sharpening of disposition she readjusts her attitude and opens the front gate. Closing the wire-gate she walks up the concrete steps to the wooden front door, knocks and waits, no sound is heard. A second round of knocking still brings no response. Standing at this bleak house, repeatedly rapping the front door envelopes her with the feeling that she is an intruder, this exacerbates her uneasiness, with no other option she picks up her bag and moves off the porch down the driveway to the rear of the house.

CHAPTER 2

An oldish man with thinning grey wispy hair is working with a shovel in a back-yard vegetable patch. He is probably about sixty years old but looks at least ten years older, he's fiddling with some fencing wire, walking up to him Beth brightly introduces herself.

'Hi uncle Reg, I'm here, I'm Beth.' He does not startle but slowly raises his head like a Sergeant Major inspecting a new private.

'Humph… so you worked your way around the town, did you?'

'Well, not really, some people had to give me directions.'

'Directions! The town's not that big, obviously geography's not your strong point, well you're here now, better come inside and have a look at the place, it's not much, follow me.' He drops a wire with a cantankerous flay of the hand and walks towards the house, leaving her to quickly pick up her bag and follow. Moving through a rickety wooden back door they enter a kitchen, it's old and worn, linoleum on the floor is faded and dirty. An aluminium one-tub sink is on the side with a window above it, enabling view to the back yard. Small

floral curtains adorn the window, but they also have seen better days. There is an old retro fifty's table with aluminium legs and a Formica top with two chairs either side of it sitting in the middle of the kitchen. Green painted cupboards are along the back wall and under the sink, a small bench space adjoins the sink plus there is a meter and a half of extra bench space sitting at ninety degrees to the main bench. Behind the extra bench is an alcove with two old arm-chairs in it, an old television set on a small wooden table stands against the far wall. She captures the uninspiring view but returns attention to Reg as he points out another door at the back of the kitchen next to the back door.

'Laundry and bathroom… now down here.' With that, he moves away from the kitchen through another door, which is opposite the back door, the corridor moves away from the kitchen, heading down the passageway he slows at the door on his left.

'My room, don't go in.' They continue on to the next door on the same side.

'Here, this one.' He opens the door for her to enter, squeezing past him she enters a dark room, he brusquely comments.

'It's not much, but it's yours.' With that, he forcibly shuts the door with enough effort that causes her head to spin round, it's closed like a finalised full stop at the end of a sentence. Turning her head, she gazes around the room, just a bed, a bedside table, an old wardrobe and chest of draws. A simple forty-watt light globe with a brown tasselled shade hangs down from the middle of the roof. The switch is next to the door, moving to it she flicks it on then sits on the bed and again surveys the room, feelings of dejection sink in. A thought crosses her mind, "Is this what it's like in jail?" The pondered thought is again flicked away with a shake of the head and the shrug of the shoulders. It's her subconscious

manner of ridding herself of negativity and getting "On with the job," pondering finished, she unzips the bag and starts to unpack. Opening the wardrobe, the musty smell of unused wafts across her but there's nothing she's able to do about that at the moment. Various dresses and skirts are hung, other blouses, singlet-tops, t-shirts and underwear are carefully placed in the drawers, shoes are deposited in the bottom of the wardrobe. A bathroom bag is left in the bag, the last items are taken out of the bag and placed on the bed, are sports gear, aerobics style, shorts, half singlets, crop tops, short bike pants, leggings and sneakers. She stares at them with a forlorn look, thinking "Will I ever use these again?" A pause of reflection holds her then they are stowed into the bottom drawer, the final item taken out is of the photo in a frame of her not so long ago with her mum and dad either side and her diary. It's a happy family photo, she places it on the bedside table with her diary next to it, gazing at the photo a tender smile delicately emerges. Changing her direction of sight from the photo to the room's surrounds various emotions are reflected, after a pause she flicks her hair and throws the empty bag on top of the wardrobe and exits the room. Reg is sitting at the kitchen table having a cup of tea, he looks up as Beth enters the room.

'Pot's still warm if you want a brew.' The comment is more to a fellow worker than to a newly arrived niece.

'No thanks, uncle Reg, I'll have a glass of water,' she politely replies, heading towards the sink, she pauses.

'Top cupboard,' he growls.

'Oh, thanks.' With the water filled in the glass, she sits at the table and attempts polite conversation.

'Thanks for having me uncle Reg, I guess it'll be a bit of a change having someone else in the house.' He doesn't answer immediately but holds her with a long deep gaze then judgementally expounds.

'Guess so, but you wouldn't be if young Christian had

kept himself in check more, flashy living, that's what brought him and his wife's end, now I'm lumped with you.' She fights back but tactfully.

'But it wasn't their lifestyle or their fault they got hit by a drugged driver.' He's on his pedestal now and continues preaching.

'Doesn't matter, city living will do that to you, an honest day's toil, fresh air, country living, that's the way.' She can see that this discussion will only antagonize him, so she carefully generalises.

'I can see what you're saying, but I think both have their good points, anyway, I'm here now, and I'll do my best to get used to it, I think I'll take a walk around the town and try to acclimatise myself.' She walks to the sink and puts the glass in the drainer and starts to exit, as she moves to the door, he gruffly announces another order.

'Tea's at six,' Turning, she smiles, nods and politely answers, 'Thanks.' Stepping out of the front door she breathes a sigh of relief, this is obviously going to be hard work acclimatising herself here, she'll have a tricky job of getting him onside. He really is dogmatic about various aspects of living, and very interestingly he was a tad negative towards her farther. Remembering what her father said regarding his older brother, there was never any antagonistic comments or off-hand remarks, his attitude is puzzling. These thoughts envelop her mind as she starts moving off down the street.

CHAPTER 3

Returning to the main street she moves down taking in the lay of the land more accurately. There's the General Store, further down a Hotel interestingly named "The Sunshine Hotel" even though it's built from drab grey bluestone plus heavy dark timber. Continuing on she passes a Café, Nic Nac Shop, a second hand Book-shop and the Garage, there were the Hairdressers and the other couple of commercial buildings up the other end of town she noticed on her arrival, a scattering of people are moving around aimlessly, a number of other dwellings seemed closed, "Not an overly exciting advertisement for living in the country," she thinks. Instead of traversing her steps to the other part of the main street she decides to continue on to the part that the passengers all saw from the bus as they descended into the town.

It doesn't take long to meander a few blocks to where the buildings are of a more industrial style, however, they follow a similar pattern to much of the housing. They also seem in various states of disrepair or low functionality. One has a sign "McClough's Iron Foundry", another "Collins Engineering Works", there are others but no hub of activity, as she passes the last building, she hears modern music quietly emanating

from it. Intrigued she moves to the window, stretching on tip-toe she tries to peer through the glass, but there is a curtain or a hessian bag strung across the inside thus preventing anyone from seeing in. Perplexed but stimulated that there may be something alive in this town she moves around the side of the building to a side entrance that has a car-park in front of it, it seems to be the side entrance that is used most of the time.

Trying the door, it opens, curiosity overrides politeness, so she deftly enters. In front of her is a small passageway, a room that looks like an accounts room is on the left, another door is at the end of the passageway. Discretely, she tip-toes to the end, on her approach the music reverberates with more volume, not overly loud but definitely discernible, very carefully she inches open the door. Inside is a room that might have once been a storeroom or something but now has been converted to a dance studio. It's not a professional studio with mirrors adorning all the walls, but the brick walls have at least been painted white and the wooden floor-boards are suitable for dance practice. There are some more old hessian bags hung over the exterior windows that do the job of concealment. A shortish but fit looking lady looking about mid twenty's is instructing a small group of girls in modern jazz ballet. The group look like eight to twelve-year old's, all have leotards and dance shoes, some have leg warmers.

Beth watches for a short while then feels like she has intruded and is about to leave her possie at the door when the instructor catches her eye. She motions Beth to enter and take a seat against the sidewall, with a flash of her hand she requests five minutes wait. Beth enters and sits, taking in the class, immediately she notices that the lady is very firm and talented. She drives the kids to follow instructions, they seem to work enthusiastically at a high level as Beth watches intrigued. After about ten minutes, the lady calls a halt to the session. She gives last-minute instructions as the group catch their breath, gives

then a clap of 'Well done,' and finishes with, 'See you next week,' The kids pick up bags and assorted other items and filter out, switching off the portable C D Player she saunters over to where Beth's sitting.

'Hi, a new face in town, great, I'm Karen Rossetti, I teach dance here.' Beth immediately likes her positive vibe and responds.

'Oh yes, that was great, thanks for letting me watch, I'm Beth Duncan, I just moved here to stay with my uncle Reg.'

'For a short time or longer?'

'Well for a while I think, my parents were killed in a car accident and he's my only relative.'

'Oh, I'm sorry.'

'No worries, I used to get really upset, but now I'm just trying to get on with my life, sort of moving on. Hey! The kids were really good, you're getting the most out of them.' Karen explains, 'Well most come from the outlying area on farms, many quite isolated, so they don't mind travelling in for practice, thus you see they put their best foot forward when they get here, most have long trips on the bus just to get to school. The parents are very supportive, they understand that this small amount of artwork is of real benefit to their child's development.' Beth nods, 'I understand, I found out it's a forty-five-minute trip to school each way, I've got to start tomorrow, year ten.' Karen understands and agrees,

'Yes, it's not great, we used to have a Primary School here, but it closed down, there's no mobile phone coverage, the local police-man was moved away six months ago, all in all the towns dying. I've stayed but don't know for how long, well at least while I'm here I can provide some arts activity for the kids, what about you, do you dance?' Beth enlightens, 'No actually I was very involved in aerobics, don't suppose anyone around here teaches it?' Karen answers with a slight disappointment in her voice,

'Sorry its only me here.'

'Oh well,' Beth breathes, 'Doesn't matter.' There's a short lull while Karen is thinking, she pipes up.

'Look, how about a deal?'

'Deal?'

'Yes, if you come along and help me with the kids, I'll read up and give you an aerobics lesson once a week.' Beth's face lights up.

'I'd like to help you with the kids but I couldn't afford to pay you anything for my aerobic work, I've got little money.'

'Don't worry', Karen enlightens, 'Helping with the kids would be enough, anyway I'd like to study up on aerobics, something new, challenging, so deal'? Beth beams, 'Deal, thanks a lot'.

'No, thank you, this'll be fun, meet here Monday at five after school.' They do a quick hand shake, with a smile Beth turns and leaves, traversing her way back through the town, there is more spring in her step, it has only taken a little positiveness to put some zest back into her life. Taking in the houses as she walks, they have a different appeal now, yes, the place is run down, but they give off an earthiness, old but distinctive, with lots of stories hidden behind their façade.

"Yes," she thinks to herself, "I can make something of this."

CHAPTER 4

Entering the door to Reg's kitchen she smells cooking, Sausages crackle in the frying pan and steamed vegetables look like they're ready. Noticing her sprightly manner, he chooses not to comment, rather raps another order.

'Teas on, wash up quickly, I'm plating up.' Zipping into the bathroom she quickly washes her hands, glancing at the hand towel she slightly recoils, it's dirty, doing the best she can she finds a less stained edge and dries her hands. Emerging into the kitchen, he nods, "Here!" directing her towards one of the chairs. She sits as he serves up, noticing him splashing the food about like he's an army cook. Although a bit taken back by the offhand brusque manner of the meal's presentation, she waits for him before she starts eating. Although they are relations the feeling in the kitchen is one of discomfort, he tries some basic conversation.

'Did you walk around the town? There's not much to see.' Noticing his effort for small-talk, she replies.

'Yes, I noticed it's a bit run down but in one old building there was a dance class going on. I checked it out and met the instructor, her name was Karen, she was really nice, she said she'd help me with my aerobics and I've agreed to

help her with her junior dance classes. I'm going to meet her this Monday after school.' This statement does not meet Reg's ideology.

'Humph, that Karen Rossetti, running around in that skimpy gear, leading the kids the wrong way, not good… not right.' Beth retaliates, 'But its art, you know dance, like ballet.'

'Dance…! Never made or produced anything, waste of time.'

'No, it's not there to make things, it's there to express, to reflect, show, you know to improve the soul, like a greater understanding.' He eyes her, then fortifies his point in a vociferous manner.

'The only thing you need to understand round here is what needs to be done to keep the place running.'

Trying to calm him down, she nods in agreement.

'Yes, of course, don't worry, I'll help round the house.'

He again barks.

'You're damn right you will now you're here, there's washing to be done and you'll be expected to cook meals and keep the place clean. This is no house for slackers, right you can start with the dishes… now.' With that order out of the way, he rises and moves to the alcove to watch TV. She looks at the dishes in the sink and those at the table, despondently she rises with the realisation that she's just become a slave. There's no way out, nothing to be done except do what's required. As she washes up, she feels the iniquity of her position but there's little she can do about it at the moment, through no fault of her own she's landed in a difficult situation. Her brain whips up various connotations to alleviate this situation but in the end her most logical conclusion is to do what's asked, stay positive plus upbeat and try to gradually turn the tide into some form of normality with respect and understanding towards her. Hopefully some kindness may enter the equation in the future, just a case of "Wait and see," she thinks to herself. With the

dishes finished, she pokes her head into the parlour.

'I've finished the dishes, I'm going to my room to read, I've got to get up early to catch the school-bus by seven-thirty.' He grunts, 'If you're late don't expect me to drive you down.'

'No,' She replies, 'I've been brought up to be punctual.' Glancing a look at her little dig of endorsement to her late parents he grunts.

'Right, 'Well... Night.' Entering the bedroom, she shuts the door and lies on the bed. Picking up her diary on the bedside table she opens it and begins to write. Time passes, footsteps are heard from the passageway, then a door closing, assuming that Reg has gone to bed, she closes the diary, places it back on the bedside table and starts to get undressed. Clothes are hung on hangers or put in drawers, she is about to take off her underwear when a strange feeling comes across her like she is being watched, the feeling invades her psych. She glances round the room at the paintings and tapestry but notices nothing, hesitantly she continues to get changed, puts on a nightie and climbs into bed. Drifting off to sleep she holds the second pillow to her chest like a security blanket.

CHAPTER 5

Monday morning breaks and Beth's running around the house trying to get organised. She is wearing a blue checked high school dress, blue jumper tied round her neck, white socks and black shoes, her hair is combed and tied into a pony-tail, the basic requirements for a high school girl. The fridge is raided for a bread roll and an apple plus a health food bar. Racing to her room, she stows them into her bag along with folders, books and writing utensils. Dashing out she calls on the way, "By uncle Reg, see you tonight round five." A quick glance at her wristwatch tells her that time is of the essence, so the walk to the bus stop accelerates from a brisk walk to an easy jog. Rounding the corner into the main street she spies other kids at the stop and breathes a sigh of relief that she hasn't missed the bus on her first day of school. The bus trip is similar to the one in to town, the other children on the bus all seem of primary school age, one or two she believes she saw at Karen's dance group, because they don't know her acquaintances are reserved and besides a shy smile she is left to her own countenance for the trip.

After about forty minutes or so the bus enters the township of Rosenbury, a sign announces a "Rosenbury

pop1560." Watching the direction of various students, she follows like a sheep, "One of the flock" she thinks to herself, turning the corner, a large red brick fronted building emerges into her view. The High School is similar to many of the country ilk, reddish-brown brick front with cream columns either side of the main entry. Various portable classrooms are scattered around the nether regions of the grounds. The original building is the stand-alone structure with classrooms feeding off from the main corridor. All the rooms have heavy wooden doors and glass windows, entering she moves to the main administration window. Approaching it a middle-aged receptionist looks up from her desk.

'Yes, Miss can I help you?'

'Thank you, I'm new, today is my first day, I'm Beth Duncan, I believe someone rang you regarding me starting today, year ten.'

'Right,' is the business-like reply. 'I have your timetable and this is a map of the school... here.' She places the sheets into Beth's hands.

'You'll be right, there are two floors and the classroom doors are all numbered. It's easy to find your way around, thank you.' With that discourse finished, she turns and heads back to her desk, Beth is a slightly bit flummoxed, she gathers her senses, a thought flashes into her head, "When you're by yourself you really are by yourself... definitely growing up time." Taking a breath, flicking her hair she refocuses and walks down the corridor. Just as the admin lady said the rooms are not difficult to find, the logical sequence of numbering leads her quickly to the room of her first period, other students are filtering in, following suit she enters and moves towards the teacher. The lady is about forty, her fair hair with a smidgeon of grey on the side is tied back, she is wearing a white blouse and black pants. Expecting pleasantries and a class introduction Beth is surprised again by the business-like attitude.

'Beth is it, yes new, right… ahh there's a seat over there by the window, right everyone settle down, okay we have a new girl with us, Beth, she'll be here a while, So where did we leave it last week?' That's it, that's the introduction, Beth glances round the room and is met by noncommittal looks, she reservedly moves to her seat feeling slightly deflated, not the bright warm start to a new school environment. Books are distributed from the front desk by the few students in the front rows, pages are opened as the teacher starts, Beth has a quick glance at her timetable, "English – Mrs Jenkins," as the session continues, she has time to dwell with her thoughts. She is slightly mystified regarding her introduction to her new environment. It's not that it's unfriendly just slightly baffling due to the clinical nature of the situation. "Still," she thinks "No point to ponder," and again with a short breath and a flick of her hair she looks at the given text. The realisation is obvious, just a case of "Get on with it." Life is different now and it's up to her to handle it, change won't come from the outside, she'll have to make it happen and application plus forward-thinking will obtain its justified result, a steeliness bonds in her eyes reflecting the strength of her soul. Each period is of a similar vein, no-one really introduces themselves but that she believes regarding the students is true to form 'cos teenagers are that extremely insular. The school itself is an integrated one, like an extended Central School. It caters for students from Prep grades to Year Twelve, the kids from the bus headed in the same direction as her. Although the Primary School is positioned slightly apart from the Secondary campus, some of the senior primary children come to the canteen to buy food or drinks. A primary girl of about twelve years of age notices Beth by herself in the canteen's surrounds during the lunch break, she moseys up to her.

'Excuse me, but weren't you the girl who popped into our dance class the other evening?' Beth is obviously relieved to

have someone to converse with.

'Yes, I'm, new to Luina, I spoke to Karen, your teacher, she's going to help me with my aerobics and I'll help her with your dance work.'

'Great,' the young girl beams, 'I'm Shelly.'

'Beth.'

'You don't dance?'

'No, just aerobics but I know something about dance.'

'So, what's aerobics like?' A conversation emerges and Beth finds Shelly really bouncy and alive, after a long chat they part, Beth ponders a thought her mother used to say,

"If you want interest and enthusiasm look no further than primary children if you want insecurity and awkwardness go straight to High School, don't pass go and don't collect two hundred dollars." The reminisced thought brings a smile to Beth's face, she thinks, "Such a wag my mom." The bell for the afternoon sessions breaks her train of thought, she raises and moves off to the first of her afternoon classes.

At the finish of the day, Beth wanders out of the main building and down the block to the bus stop on the main street. One thought is obvious to her, "at this present time this year ten level is behind what she came from." She thinks, "I better keep on my toes and be careful not to slip behind. Might have to occasionally call a few old friends from the old school just to check that I'm on course and working at the right level. Next year VCE starts, geez this is important when it comes to setting up for university courses, hmm... don't want to stuff this up." Approaching the bus stop, she notices Shelly, who gives her the excited wave and beams."Hi," she calls. Again, easy conversation starts flowing, they all board the bus, Shelly acts as "Master of Ceremony" and gets all the kids to introduce themselves. Beth recognises some from the dance class they all seem a lively bunch and in no time at all, they are babbling away as the bus grinds its way back to Luina.

CHAPTER 6

Round five after dropping her bag at home Beth enters the dance studio, she still has her school uniform on. The young girls are stretching, Shelly is one of them, she spies Beth's entry and gives her a wave. Beth responds with a wave as she moves across the floor to where Karen is positioned. Karen looks up.

'Hi, glad you're here, I'll introduce you to the kids.' She claps her hands.

'Come forward everyone, I want to introduce you to a friend of mine who's going to help me in the classes.' The children all move in a semi-circle around, Karen and Beth.

'This is Beth, she knows some dance and is really good at aerobics, come forward and introduce yourselves.' All move forward, shake Beth's hand and introduce themselves, Shelly is the last one, she comes closer and with a wry grin on her face says.

'Hello, I'm Shelly, pleased to meet you, I hope you have a very enjoyable stay in our little town, anything you want, please feel free to ask.' She bows, there is a slight pause, all the other girls start giggling, Karen has this confused expression on her face, she looks at Beth, who is also caught up with the

giggling, she raises her shoulders in a sign of not understanding, Beth gains control of herself and explains.

'I've already met Shelly at the school and most of the others on the bus.' Laughter breaks out, Karen rolls her eyes and shakes her head.

'Oh, god, girls! Tsk, tsk, tsk.' She joins in the laughter, they all continue to chatter, watching Beth's easy manner with the kids she realises that she'll be fine. Clapping her hands, she orders.

'Okay everyone let's go through what we know so Beth can gauge where you're at, come on places.'

The kids disperse to areas in the room and wait while Karen switches on the CD Player. The music starts, they begin moving to it, Karen is at the front dispersing instructions by tilting her head and calling out over her shoulder. While the action is in swing, Beth walks around the periphery surveying the scene, she's impressed by the work effort and the standard achieved, especially as the kids only come in once a week. With the first part finished, Beth walks amongst the group and gives a few comments, mainly positive, Karen nods to her and the session continues with Beth watching and getting a feel for it.

After an hour and a half, the whole session finishes, Karen gives them some feedback plus what she wants them to practice at home in preparation for next week's class. The girls all listen, nod in agreement, disperse to their gear and start to filter out, as they leave, they call good-bye to Beth and wave, showing they like her and are happy for her to be involved, Karen sits, has a swig from her drink bottle and addresses Beth.

'I had a look on the internet, also found some old books on aerobics, it's very interesting, regimented like dance but much more gymnastically orientated, lots of strong jumps and movement. You've got to be stronger than a normal dancer especially ballet but with almost as much flexibility and the choreographer has to be really inventive with lines and

formations'.

'Yes,' replies Beth, 'It's real team work whether two or ten, look I brought a CD, I'll show you what I know.' She lifts a CD from her bag and gives it to Karen to put on, while Karen loads the CD, Beth slips on some dance sneakers. She positions herself in the centre of the room and starts moving once the music starts, Karen watches, studying her and her actions closely, the music finishes, Karen expounds. 'That was great, I get the idea, what you need is extension work that'll lead to more challenging routines and involved movement, I can adapt this to the two of us. Go to the centre of the room, I'll put on the chorus part and join you when we are in unison on that, then I'll get you to try a few different things.' They start working on the part, occasionally Karen halts proceedings to clear up something, change or add on. Time passes, both are sweating, Karen checks her watch and calls a halt to their session.

'Okay, take five.' They rest on the bench.

'Look,' Karen continues, 'I now know much better what you're on about, give me a few days to research some things, how about we meet back here in two days?' Beth beams, 'Okay, that sounds great.' They take off their dance shoes, shut down the CD Player, slip on some street clothes, switch off lights and exit the building, Karen locks the side door then they both walk through the car-park and onto the street.

CHAPTER 7

Being interested in finding out more about Karen and the town Beth asks.

'So, do you like the small town atmosphere?' Happy to relate information, Karen replies.

'Well, when I was growing up, it was good I knew lots of people, there were kids my own age to play with, tons of open space, so yeah, it was good. But we all grow up, I finished High School and got a placement in College in Launceston, well and like everyone else I got a taste for the larger city life. You know more people, more things, an array of different sorts at college, parties, everything done at a faster pace. Just as I was finishing my course my mum got sick and I had to return home to look after her and nurse her through her final months. Coming back was difficult, I realised just how small and introverted everything and everyone was. I had to do something to occupy my spare time, well… I decided to open a dance studio and surprisingly lots of kids wanted involvement, thus lessons, also I met Geoff and we've become an item.'

'Oh, so there are still some eligible young men in the town'?

'Ha!' Karen laughs. 'Not many, Geoff was the last

reasonable one, very reasonable if I must say, all the others left, only the dregs stayed, truthfully the towns dying, no school, no police, no mobile coverage, it's disintegrating.'

'That's too bad,' responds Beth. 'Sometimes a small community can be really supportive, warm and friendly.' Karen now carefully digs.

'Like your uncle Reg?' Beth feels she has someone to confide in and is happy to explain.

'Well it's not quite what I expected, my father was an outgoing person with a lively personality, uncle Reg is almost the opposite he...' She breaks off as a mid-eighty's Holden Commodore slows down next to the two girls. The driver winds down his window, he has a cigarette hanging out of the side of his mouth, he looks a poor imitation of a "Cool Dude" and calls out in an overtly masculine way.

'Hi girls, what's happening, want a ride to where you're going?' Beth's unsure how to handle this situation and turns to Karen who replies.

'No thanks, Johnny.' Johnny dismisses Karen with a sneer, then directs his next question to Beth.

'Hey you, forget her, wanna lift? The boys will make room for ya, won't cha boys?' Beth's looks down politely answers, "no thanks." Karen buts in again but this time more aggressively.

'Look Johnny we're being polite, no thanks.' Johnny's sneer becomes more intense.

'No thanks, no thanks, what the fuck's no thanks, get in, live a little, put some fun in ya boring little lives.' Karen now attacks vehemently.

'Listen, dropkick, no means no in any language, so piss off and leave us alone... go play with your little friends or whatever you morons do.' Johnny's not happy being verbally assaulted by some young girl, especially with his friends in the car.

'Fuck you ya big-headed bitch, walk and get blisters, see if I care.' But Karen's up to it and in full flight.

'Better on the feet than on the brain listening to you idiots, piss off and go play with yourselves.' At this point, the girl in the back seat sitting in between the two weedy youths leans over to the window and vindictively barks.

'Hey, we'll play with ya sometime ya tart, come on Johnny let's go.' With that she gives Karen the "Bird", Johnny hits the accelerator, the wheels spin in on the bitumen and they tear off.

'What was that?' Beth asks Karen explains.

'You know before I said only the local dregs were left in the town, well that was them, the guy driving was Johnny Holden.

'What!'

'Yep, and he drives a Holden, weird eh? The weedy one next to him was Philip Pilson, "Pills" to everyone, in the back was Terry "Tatts" Smith and Billy Surso, they're scrawny dickheads, harmless; however, the girl in the middle was Nancy Clements, everyone knows her as "Noogs." Beth's mouth drops open, "Noogs!"

'Yep, and, unlike the others, she's a nasty piece of work but don't worry if they hassle you just give it back, I know them all, spineless and harmless, more bark than bite.' Beth's still not sure.

'If you say so, boy, you sure were tough on them.'

'No probs I went to Primary School with them, well Noogs and Johnny, but they were never in my group of friends, we actually used to tease them but hey, they all dropped out by year nine and did, I dunno what, nothing really, just hung around the town. If they tried anything my boyfriend, "Ha ha, almost fiancé," would kick their butts big time, he's very big and strong plus his nephew works with him and he's big also, so... no problems there. Hey, why don't you come around for

dinner after next practice and meet them, they're really nice.' Beth's happy to return to polite normality.

'Oh yes thanks, that'd be great.' They arrive at an intersection on the end of a block, Karen inquires.

'I've got to go a couple of blocks this way, do you know which way to go to get to Reg's?'

'Yes, I'm okay, I'm getting orientated, just down here then turn left and then a right and it's just down a bit.'

'Great,' says Karen, 'I've got to go this way, see you for dance in a couple of days and dinner after that.'

'Okay, see you then and thanks.' They give each a short hug and move off in different directions.

CHAPTER 8

Johnny's Commodore is headed towards the back blocks, Noogs starts bitching.

'Fair-dinkum, that bitch has always pissed me off, always walking around actin' better, doing that dance crap, shakin' her little butt, bloody tart.' Johnny amused at her discomfort, tries to bait her.

'So, ya pissed, what're gonna do?' Her eyes darken, reflecting a tormented soulless being inside.

'I'd love to organise the boys to make that bitch scream.' Tatts has livened up and joins in the thought process.

'Hey, we'll help.'

Billy's not to be left out.

'Yeah, I'd love to g-g-give her one, j-j-just say the w-w-word and we'll be "In like Flynn." Johnny's smirking, but decides to throw a spanner in the works.

'One slight problem lads, her boyfriend Geoff the plumber and his apprentice Rod. Remember she lives with them.' Pills pipes in with some remanent of logic.

'Shit that's right, and he's big, I couldn't take him.' Johnny's pulling the strings of these puppets, they're not very smart, he knows they need idea feeding.

'Mate you're so scrawny you couldn't take anyone by yourself... but with others, now that's a different story.' Noogs starts to pick up his drift.

'So, your point?' Johnny's now in his stride preaching to the congregation in his own eloquently serene way.

'Well, we got no police, right? Plus, no mobile coverage, the town's isolated.' Tatts is confused.

'Is... lated, what's islated?'

'Isolated not islated, it means cut off, didn't you learn anything at school?'

'Na... only that Mr Jacks hated me guts and belted me all the time, the cunt.'

'Well me boy, things are a-changing, no fuckin' school now an' no one to belt us, actually 'bout time that we did the belting, cos round here now we got the power.' Noogs vicious smile deepens, she vehemently snarls.

'And I know who to start with.' Johnny pulls the reins in slightly.

'Na na, settle, let's just see what people we're dealing with, like who's the new girl?'

'Dunno, friend of the dance tart's,' helps Noogs.

'Well,' continues Johnny. 'Let's do a bit of investigating and find out.' Noogs really starts firing.

'Find 'em and fuck 'em I say.' Billy's into it.

'Yeah, me old man always said I was fucked, so I reckon that's me, a fucker.' Johnny leans across to Billy.

'That's you, Billy, a machine, a fucking machine'. Billy jumps on Tatts and starts pretending to hump him, everyone laughs, Noogs yells.

'Go machine, go machine'... ha ha... Yeah.'

CHAPTER 9

Wandering home Beth's in deep thought, various images and thoughts swill round her head. "New town with a variety of personal, polite, enthusiastic also the dull and antagonistic, some making the best of their situation, others with a chip on their shoulder. Best not to dwell just get on with it and see where the voyage takes me." She enters the front-gate, walks to the door and down the passageway into the kitchen. Reg is at the sink making a cup of tea, he grumpily barks.

'You're late! I'm not waiting for kids who are gallivanting around the town at night, your dinner's in the oven, what's left of it.' Beth doesn't react, it's been a good day and she's made new friends, although his attitude is annoying, she tries to disarm him.

'No worries it'll be fine.' Taking the meal out of the oven, she sits at the table, before Reg can go on the attack, she beats him to the punch.

'Don't worry I'll do the dishes, oh and by the way where's some cleaning stuff, I want to have a shower and need to clean the bathroom first.' Reg is slightly taken back by this flurry of interest in domestic cleanliness that he hasn't directed and is unable to be caustic, he answers straight forward in a

clinical way. 'Some cleaners under the sink here, some in the cupboard in the laundry.' Beth smiles at him and with a slight vibrancy answers, 'thanks.' He grumpily leaves with his cup of tea in his hand and settles in the alcove, although not dwelling on it, she feels she's had a small victory. Finishing her meal, she rises to the sink and washes the dishes, grabbing some cleaning detergents and brushes she heads to the bathroom. Entering the bathroom with bucket and equipment she stops and stares, it looks like it's not been cleaned for a long time, with a slight grimace and a shrug of the shoulders she rolls up her sleeves, organises herself and starts scrubbing. After about an hour or more she stands and admires her handy-work, the room is much improved, a feeling of satisfaction and contentment enlivens her psyche, a smile emerges.

Replacing the cleaning materials, she enters her bedroom and starts to get changed for a shower. Stopping halfway through she looks round the room, it's drab and if not dirty then at least dusty, running her finger on the underside of the bedside table proves the point. Pondering the fact that this room will also need a "Spring clean,' she starts to get changed. With a towel around her, she heads for the bathroom but stops in the kitchen, turns to the alcove where Reg is watching TV, moving across near him she plants herself in the doorway and asks.

'Uncle Reg is there a vacuum cleaner in the house?' Looking up Reg is taken back by the image of a pretty young girl wrapped only in a towel addressing him in his house. He's flustered but gathers himself enough to splutter.

'Vacuum... err, no, only brooms and a dust-pan.'

'Oh, that's okay I think I know where I can borrow one, thanks anyway.' Turning she moves off towards the bathroom. Reg is in deep thought, he hears the shower water running, gets up and moves to outside the bathroom door, after a pause, he stealthily opens the door a little and peeks in. He can see

the outline of Beth in the shower behind the frosted glass, he watches for a short time then closes the door and returns to the kitchen and starts to make a cup of tea but still in deep thought. Beth exits the bathroom with a now wet towel wrapped around her, as she passes through the kitchen she calls out.

'Goodnight uncle Reg.' Reg having his tea in front of the TV, grunts a reply but turns his head to watch her disappear. Entering her room, she slips on her nightie and starts to dry her hair. Whilst involved in the drying procedure she gazes round the room, a determined look comes across her, she knows that if this is to become habitable and take on the semblance of herself with her feel and personality then it'll be up to her to make it happen. The acerbic thought reflects her attitude to the whole situation. "It needs improving and it's up to me to shape it... and shape it I will." Climbing into bed, switches off the light and drifts off to sleep, this time she doesn't clutch the pillow.

Morning breaks, Beth's running around getting organised, already dressed in her school uniform, she zips round the kitchen, grabbing food from the fridge, stowing that and various folders into her bag she heads down the passageway towards the front door, as she passes Reg's door she calls out.

'Goodbye uncle Reg, see you tonight.' Because she now knows the bus schedule, enough time has been allowed, so the walk to the stop is a relaxed one. No one is at the stop, thus allowing her to wait contentedly. A few minutes tick by, the quiet is broken by the sound of a car moving down the street, it passes the stop and slows. It's the eighties Commodore, and Johnny is at the wheel, but this time he's alone, noticing her, he slows the car even more and tries to give her a superior glare. She feels intimidated and is about to drop her eyes to the ground when she remembers what Karen said, raising her head she stares back at him with a penetrating look. This look

of defiance slightly shocks then annoys him, he spits out of the window then accelerates away. Soon after other kids are dropped off at the stop, with most of the kids coming from the outlying areas a parent has to be "Mom's Taxi." The kids have told their parents about Beth, the new girl who's helping them with their dance classes. The parents drop off the children give them a kiss goodbye and wave to Beth, happily she reciprocates, this sign of normality and polite manners wipes away in her memory the recent interaction with Johnny and his disgusting display. The girls all chatter away and continue after boarding the bus.

Although expecting the same situation at school, things start to change, a couple of girls in a number of her classes start chatting to her also, boys who are friendly with these girls join in. Just basic teenage "chit chat", but Beth is relieved to be included. Come lunch-time she is waved over to sit with the group, she spots Shelly who gives a small wave but doesn't come over, she is with a group. With a quick glance Beth notices one of the girls give Shelly a subtle acknowledgement wave which is reciprocated with a cheeky grin. Obviously, they know each other, Beth grins inwardly knowing that somehow Shelly has set this up, as Shelly's group disappears Beth glows from the kindness shown. She thinks to herself, "what a difference Shelly to Johnny" a small shake of her head and she returns to her new group's conversation.

CHAPTER 10

Late that afternoon Beth arrives home from school, walking into the kitchen she drops her bag and calls out.

'Hello, uncle Reg, I'm home.' No answer is heard, taking a glass from the draining board she fills it with water, sits at the table and ponders. Finishing the drink, she goes to the fridge, takes out some mince and vegetables and places them on the cutting board, glancing down she notices her schoolbag lying next to the table. Not wanting uncle Reg to have any excuses to admonish her for untidiness, she picks it up, walks down the passageway and drops it in her room. On the way back she slows outside Reg's room, cautiously knocking on the door she calls.

'Uncle Reg, are you there.' Like before, no answer is heard, stealthy she opens the door and switches on the light. The room is almost identical to hers, a painting on the wall, an ornamental tapestry above the bed like hers, there's a wardrobe, a bedside table, a chair and a chest of drawers, the wallpaper is a brown ochre, it feels depressing to her as her room is. Her gaze and thoughts are broken with the sound of a car moving down the driveway at the side of the house, switching off the light, she gently closes the door and bolts back to the kitchen and

immediately starts cutting the vegetables. Reg enters the back door and sees her working at the dinner preparation, he grunts "Gidday," and moves down to his room. Holding her breath, she waits, soon he returns, grabs a beer from the fridge, faces her and asks.

'What'r making?'

'Rissoles,' is the polite reply, 'They'll be ready in about thirty minutes.'

'Humph... okay,' is the noncommittal answer. Moving to the alcove he switches on the TV and settles into his chair, sighing with relief she continues with the dinner preparation. Being quite content to do it, allows her mind to wander when she'd help her mom with the evening meal and chat about the days "doings," it's her reflection of happier times, life in a normal family. 'Maybe,' she thinks to herself, "This preparing and serving of dinner will soften uncle Reg's attitude, 'cos really he's only had himself to look after all these years." Her mind is ticking over with positive endorsement with her head nodding with subconscious agreement, she serves up, and calls out, 'It's ready uncle Reg.' Standing he moves to the table, noticing his movement has a slightly tragic effect on her. He must be only five or six years older than her father, but he acts and moves like a worn-out old man, way older than his years.

"What happened to him?", she wonders. Sitting down with the discomfort of age, he nods with appreciation of the prepared meal and digs in. The only conversation emanating forth is the comment, 'Mmm... not bad... pass the sauce... ta.' No "how was your day," or even the basic pleasantries, the meal is quaffed quickly, with accelerated eating. Watching him devour his food, her thoughts are piqued, "etiquette is not at the forefront at this table." She is still eating in a pleasant unhurried manner when he rises and blurts out.

'Yeah, that was okay girl.' With that acknowledgement of appreciation, he withdraws to the parlour, back to his TV

and beer, she's left to finish her meal by herself. Although the meal was not quite the family get together, she does have time to think about the day and reflect on developments regarding her fitting into the school, the town and her interaction with various people. Time just drifts, flowing with her casual thoughts, reality jolts her daydreaming as Reg gets another beer from the fridge. With a shake of her head, she slips into action mode. Dishes need attending too, she rises and sets to the chore. They're soon cleaned and stowed away, moving to her room she gathers various books returning to the kitchen plonks them down on the table, opening them she starts to work. Hearing the sound Reg glances over his shoulder, noticing that she is obviously starting her home-work, twigs his curiosity, he asks.

'Homework... eh!' 'What you working on?'

'Maths,' she answers. His reply is strong in agreement, 'Good... useful.'

'And literature.' He turns back to the TV with an offhand comment.

'Humph... waste of time... no practical use.' There's no point in responding, it would just bait him, so she continues with the work. Time moves along, finishing she, tidies up her books and rises to leave the room.

'Goodnight uncle Reg.' She begins to move off when she suddenly stops remembering something.

'Oh, and Karen invited me to have dinner with her tomorrow night after aerobics practice... err... if that's alright.' He starts to become cynical.

'Getting all friendly with that arty Karen, are you? This is what brought your family down, mixing with them arty types, out all night, no good will come of it, mark my words. Good honest work is what you need, that's what'll get you through life.' Beth's now getting a bit fed up with his preaching on the attributes he profounds is the way to live, she fires up and responds.

'Works okay, being a slave to some male, not so.'

This generalised dig in his direction fires up his antagonistic nature.

'What! I'll thank you to keep a civil tongue in this house miss, especially to family who have agreed to take you in when they didn't have to.' His response jolts her back into a clear understanding of her situation, she's definitely overstepped the mark.

'Yes, sorry you're right, it's very kind of you to take me in, I do appreciate it… I'm sorry uncle Reg… umm I'm tired, I'll see you in the morning, goodnight.' She exits the room, head down slightly, however, as she departs the kitchen, she doesn't notice Reg watching her, he has a different look on his face as if his admonishment has hurt himself also. There is a softening, a confused look in his features, this new situation with a border, especially this bright pretty young girl has changed his lifestyle and he's having difficulty coming to terms with it, his tranquil lifestyle has become irrevocably complicated. Beth lies on her bed with a disconsolate look, she gazes round the room and spies her aerobic gear, gets up undresses and holds the leotard in front of the mirror. Staring at it held in front of her body enlivens her, yes, she looks fit and this aerobics activity combined with a diligent work ethic has got her to this position. This realisation brightens up her demeanour, a smile returns to her face but there is still something in this room that intrudes upon her soul, she can't put her finger on it. Glancing round again she takes in the surrounds, but nothing stands out in this bland place. What has constituted this feeling at the moment cannot be solved, unwilling to ponder this problem any further she places the aerobics leotard on the chair, changes into her nightie and climbs into bed. The light is turned off and as she drifts off, she's not sure if a faint sound was coming from the room next door or just her imagination.

CHAPTER 11

The morning rush is on again, with Beth zipping round trying to find food and getting other items organised for school. Stowing everything in her bag she heads down the passageway, slowing next to Reg's door she calls.

'Goodbye uncle Reg, don't wait up I'll be late.' There's no answer, she beats a hasty exit out of the house. Walking down the street expectations of the evening ahead puts a spring in her step. Somehow the worn buildings don't seem as tired, the trees and foliage have a greener hue about them, life is on the move. Shelly and some of the others are at the bus stop all bright and bubbly with the effervescence of youth, they're a welcome diversion from the sullenness of her home-life. The bus trip begins and continues with all and sundry babbling on about irrelevant things. Someone mentions a video clip they saw on U-Tube and discussion on dance becomes the major topic of conversation. Year ten has also evened out, Beth has found her friendship level, the natural pecking order of the species has been affected. Beth's quickly twigged that these new friends are very much in line with her, regarding interests, attitude and manners, thus her settling in process has been smoothed out resulting in her feeling more at home in this

school environment.

The main problem, is that these friends come mainly from the school's area, none live in or near Luina. So, with a forty-minute or more trip to the school she will only see them during the day. No chance of a sleepover with uncle Reg picking her up in the morning, plus Shelly and her friends although younger are mainly from the outlying farms, few live in town. A couple of very young ones do, but she can hardly see herself hanging round eight-year-olds especially with her almost sixteen and on the cusp of senior teen years and all the aspects and problems that encompass that difficult passage of time in one's life. This situation leaves just Karen who at about twenty-five has at least experienced all those things that lie ahead for Beth, she acknowledges that Karen will probably become the "go-to", person regarding any growing problems that will rise. At least in this constricted environment she will have an experienced female to confide in, uncle Reg will definitely not fit the agenda of the helpful adult.

That evening at the dance studio, Karen is setting up the room as Beth enters.

'Hi.'

'Hi Beth, how was your day?'

'Oh, the days are okay, I've settled in at school and made some friends, only two problems, they all live round the Rosenbury area and the bus travel takes forever.' Karen grins.

'I know, I did it for years, ended up doing my homework on the bus, I was practically the last one on it over its final stretch.'

'Yes, I can see that, but I'm travelling with Shelly and the "giggling gerties," with their carry on doing my homework might be a tad tricky, but I'll try it, how was your day?'

'Shrinking like the town. I don't work at the store anymore, well I do, but it's only if I want to, that is gratis. They don't make enough money to pay anyone so if I go in its

only to keep myself occupied. Geoff has work, but he's got an apprentice who has to be paid, I really can't see us hanging on for much longer, we need a larger place with a more viable income.'

'I know what you mean but uncle Reg seems settled here, don't think he's moving.' Karen shoots a sharp reply but quickly recovers herself.

'Yeah, he would like… well, anyway let's get these aerobics happening.' She organises the music on the CD player while Beth gets her gear ready for activity. She pulls out and slips on a two-piece crop top and sports nicks. Ties up laces on her dance shoes and fixes a band round her hair, with the pony-tail in order, she stands upright, Karen glances, Beth gives her a nod of "Yep, ready for action."

They start with Karen following Beth's actions, their combination improves as they become more familiar with the others style arriving at the part that Beth hasn't developed yet Karen tells her to watch a variety of actions she's developed, then comment on which ones she thinks are more suitable. Karen replays a variety of moves, rewinding the player and showing the variations, Beth is impressed, this lady has definitely done her homework. Finishing, they discuss the movements and settle on some that they believe are the most logical and artistic compatible. Work then starts on these, they move, stretch and sweat over the new movements. An hour or so, Karen checks her watch and calls a halt to proceedings, Beth's thankful and gasps getting her breath back, she manages to comment.

'That was great, thanks, the new moves look fantastic especially as you haven't done this sort of thing before.' Karen smiles acknowledging that her time and effort have been appreciated.

'Well, thanks, I've taken it as a challenge, I know I'm punching out of my weight division, but If I can get this

together then I can add another string to my bow and down the track I will be experienced enough to teach this as well. You could say I'm using this to gain experience to add to my CV, okay enough for today, let's pack up and go, I'm hungry.'

'Me too,' Beth agrees.

They both towel down for a short while, Karen puts on an old track-suit while Beth slips back into her school uniform, lights are switched off, door locked and they move into the evening. Walking the same way as last time they come to the point where they separated, Karen turns left directing Beth to follow away from Reg's house. The walk continues as they chatter occasionally changing direction but always moving further from Reg's house. After about three blocks have been negotiated, Karen stops outside an old weatherboard house. It's not dissimilar to Reg's. There's a ford utility parked in the driveway, Karen explains in an almost apologetic way.

'Home... mm... not much.' Beth helps, 'Similar to uncle Reg's.' With animated efference Karen bubbles.

'Yeah, but it's not what it is, it's what you make of it, come on.' Walking up the front path, they climb the steps and enter the front door, moving down the passageway they pass some doors, Beth reflects, "It really is the same as Uncle Reg's, bet this leads to the kitchen," entering the kitchen, Beth smiles to herself, "Yep". Karen calls out.

'We're here.'

A tall man of more than six foot is working at the bench preparing some food. He looks about thirty with an extremely strong physique but is very casually dressed in old jeans and a worn flannelette shirt, turning he smiles an infectious grin. Beth immediately recognises him as the man who said "Mornin' Miss" on her first day here and gave her directions. In an instant she realises he has a warming personality. "Ah ha... She thinks to herself, so he was the last reasonable male in town', she takes him in, impressed and

agrees "Hmm… yes, he is very reasonable." Karen rushes up to him and puts her arms around his neck and gives him an affectionate kiss, then breaks away.

'Hi honey, how was your day?'

'Oh, not to bad', is the reply, 'Yours?'

'Good', she beams, 'My work passed Beth's inspection.' Cheekily he responds, 'Oh we have an inspecting officer, do we?'

'Yep and this is her,' Beth this is Geoff. Beth smiles, 'Hi.' Geoff continues, 'Gidday miss, so how's the teacher going, she passed inspection, did she?' Beth definitely warming to him plays along.

'Oh, I think so, I'll put my report in later.' He laughs, 'Ha sounds good, I'll have someone else to help keep her in line, anyway, it's great to meet you.' Beth smiles internalising, he is the polar opposite of uncle Reg. Geoff yells, 'Rod where are you, we've got visitors.'

"Coming", is the muffled reply from down the hall, a young lad of about seventeen enters the kitchen, he is also wearing a checked flannelette shirt and jeans plus sneakers. His fair hair is longish but combed and his face is pleasantly alive "He will grow" she thinks, "into being a very handsome young man, maybe Geoff wasn't the last eligible man in town." Karen addresses him. 'Hi Rod.'

'Hi Kaz,' he replies. She continues, 'Rod, this is my new dance helper, Beth.' He turns and smiles then his face slightly freezes, he blinks simultaneously with a small opening of his mouth, standing in front of him is one of the prettiest girls he has ever seen and at a quick glance she is about the same age as him. He immediately becomes self-conscious and shy. Beth feels his discomfort and retreats into her shell, slightly dropping her head. Geoff looks at Karen and winks, then nods his head as if to direct her to get the teens more socially relaxed, Karen's right onto it, pushing Rod forward she orders.

'Well go on shake hands, be polite.' He moves up to Beth and looks at her, then in a manner that only awkward teenagers can manifest puts his hand out and fumbles to hers. She's no help either, normally confident she's become reticent and doesn't handle this polite handshake situation with any dexterity, they both have become hopelessly introverted. Geoff has been watching this display of adolescence gaucherie and is quietly laughing to himself. Eventually, Beth regains enough composure to hold Rod's hand and shake it, they look admiringly at each other and while continuing shaking Rod attempts politeness.

'Umm... Hi... how you going.' Beth attempts to follow this polite formality.

'Ahh yes, good... umm okay, thanks.' Suddenly Rod realises.

'Oh, you're the girl I saw at the bus stop.'

'Yes,' she answers, 'That was my first day here.'

'Oh, really.' Giggling, Karen buts in, 'Hello, you can let go hands now.' They realise they have shaken hands too long and immediately drop hands and blush, Karen looks at them in a caring way reflecting on the naive but loveable manner of teen youth, she slips an aside to Geoff, "ahh, youth." Geoff takes hold of the situation in a humorous way.

'Okay Rod stop gawking, you've seen a pretty girl before, get the lady a drink, the girls have been working hard.' The offhand comment drags Rod back to normality.

'Umm, what would you like?'

'I don't know', she responds, 'What have you got?'

'Well come over to the fridge and I'll show you.' They move to the fridge, Rod opens the door, they peer in at the assortment of drinks, Geoff already has a Gin and Tonic ready for Karen, as he hands it to her, he whispers.

'Yep, nice girl, good one Kaz.' With drinks all sorted, everyone sits at the table and begins general conversation

about the day's events, Geoff has to keep an eye on the dinner, so he's up and down from the table with Karen joining him at the bench for the final preparation. Rod and Beth are now hitting it off and are talking in a relaxed manner, Karen can catch snatches of their conversation. He's interested in her aerobic activity and listens intently as Beth explains the intricacies involved in training and performance. She smiles to herself thinking, "Good lad, don't just talk about yourself, show interesting her and what makes her tick." She's happy that they seem to have "clicked", especially as they are of similar age. Dinner is served, its nothing grand just a stir fry of meat and vegetables, but the meal is irrelevant to the personnel present, everyone eats and chats, conversation flows. Beth occasionally watches and reflects, it reminds her of the family life she once had, noticing her internalising Rod asks.

'You seem far away, what are you thinking?'

'Not really thinking, just this situation, it reminds me of having dinner with my parents and well... you know home-life, it's been different since they died and this is, well nice.' Geoff pipes up.

'Well no problems there, we'll be your family away from family now.' Everyone laughs, Karen starts to act like a matriarch, speaking with sternness.

'Now I've told you no laughing at the dinner table will be tolerated.' Rod joins in the acting. 'Why, it's her fault she always makes me giggle.' Beth enjoying this banter adds, 'tis not, it's always you getting me into trouble.'

'tis not.'

'tis so.' Acting also Geoff interjects.

'Silence children, now is that the way to act at the dinner table?' Everyone ceases their play-acting, Rod puts his hand to his chin acting as if in deep thought then answers, 'Yes.' Everyone laughs, Beth comments.

'Oh, I wish uncle Reg's house was like this.' Geoff looks

and inquires.

'Reg, Reg Duncan?'

'Yes,' she reply's, 'He's my father's older brother, my uncle, I'm staying with him. It's strange 'cos we never had any contact with him over the years but he's my only relation.' The conversation stops, Beth notices the tension.

'Why, what's wrong?' This time Karen answers, her tone is more serious.

'Nothing really, it's not our place to repeat idle gossip.'

'But I live there now', continues Beth, 'Is there something I should know about him?' Karen glances at Geoff who returns with a nod, she continues in a serious vein.

'Look you're obviously sensible, so I'll repeat what I know and leave you to make up your own mind. A while back, Reg was questioned by the local policeman, when we had one, about why he hung around the local Primary School watching the kids play, especially when he didn't have children of his own. No charges were laid, but tongues wagged, basically he was told to keep his distance, then the school closed down, so problem solved.' Through this discourse, Beth listens intently.

'Thanks, that's interesting, I'll keep my eye out at home. You said that the school closed, I've seen the old building on the far side of town, I guess that's why so many of the young ones catch the bus to Rosenbury, but no police also?'

'Yep,' Rod chips in, 'he got moved on and also there's no mobile coverage, the mountains never helped.' Geoff expands, 'Good thing we've got the land-line, at least we can use the normal phone and our computer.' Beth's thoughtful expression changes to a grin as she adds an offhand comment.

'So, it's not a complete back-water.'

'Close enough to it,' answers Karen, small towns die if they lose their school, next will be the General Store. If that goes, then it's a forty-minute trip to Rosenbury for supplies, as you already know.'

'Gosh,' mutters Beth. Geoff quips with a sly smile on his face.

'Thank god the last thing to go will be the pub.' The comment lightens the conversation as Karen continues.

'All jokes aside, the town is dying, maybe the store might stay for the farming community, but that'll be about it.' Geoff enforces the situation.

'I used to be quite busy, that's why I took on Rod as an apprentice, but now it's getting leaner, pretty soon we'll have to leave, the only ones left will be Johnny Holden and his gang.'

'I've seen them', enlightens Beth. 'Karen gave them a real send off the other day, what's their story?'

'Well', responds Karen, 'Just dropkicks, brain dead dropouts, small-town mentality, what's to know?'

'But I saw a girl with them, why does she hang out with the lowlife'?

'You mean Noogs.' Beth's manner responds incredulously, 'Yes Noogs, Noogs, is that a name?'

'Yep, Nancy Noogs Clements,' vindicates Karen. 'Shocking isn't it and unfortunately as bad as it sounds, she's probably the worst of the bunch.'

'Why?' Geoff now continues.

'Her dad, if he was, was the town drunk, till he staggered out, her mum, if you can politely call her that was... err, I guess she was the local town bike.'

'Oh, I hate that expression.'

'I know,' agrees Karen. 'But in her case, it was true, poor Nancy never had a chance, she had to fight for everything, couldn't compete with the local girls at school or on any level, thus she just slipped down, losing her soul on the way. Now she's just negative, hates everything and everyone, she's impossible to have a normal conversation with.'

'And the others?'

'Billy's had a similar home-life, he's destined for a life

of petty crime, Pills and Tatts are mindless followers, Pills is supposed to be inbred, not sure but looking at him you'd probably believe it. Tatts just isn't smart, plus they're all very weedy, no good at school or sport. You can see why they conjugate together, a nice little bunch of half-wits. Johnny's the obvious leader, he had more to offer but is lazy, he keeps them round to reinforce his ego. He wants to be the big guy in town but the towns shrinking, so pretty soon he'll move on but not with the others, really Noogs is the one with the chip on her shoulder.'

    'You said they were harmless?' Geoff takes over. 'They were when we had a police presence and strong community, but as the town has disintegrated, they've become more aggressive.'

    'So, should I be worried?'

    'Naa… They know if they tried anything Rod and I would kick their butts.' Karen sensing Beth's unease adds.

    'Actually, that's very true, if they know you're our friend then you're safe, except for the occasional swear word and insolent stare.' Beth's relieved. 'Phew, thanks… small town's eh…!'

    'Yep,' Geoff beams, 'Everybody knows everybody and everything.' They all laugh, the conversation continues to flow across the table. After dinner has finished and coffee and tea has been poured the talk starts to dwindle, Beth feeling warm and fuzzy after hours of chatter announces.

    'Well this has been great, but I'd better be getting back home, it's getting on dusk.' Geoff gives Rod a nudge under the table, who returns from the contact with a questioning look, Geoff has to give him a look of "well, come on," with his eyes, he twigs.

    'I'll walk you back if you want?'

    'Oh thanks, that'd be nice.' She stands then remembers.

    'Oh Karen, I'll be there on Friday to help with the kids.'

This sparks an idea in Geoff's head.

'Hey, when you are finished, why don't you come here for "Take-away." Beth's confused, 'But there's no "Take-away" in town."

'Private "Take-away," he grins. She laughs, 'Okay done, and thanks again for dinner, it was great.' Everyone stands, she moves to Geoff and gives him a hug, then to Karen, finishing the hug she exits the kitchen with Rod in tow. Geoff starts clearing the dishes from the table, turns on the tap and plonks them in the sink, he looks at Karen and humourlessly quips.

'He might not have his mind on the job tomorrow.' Karen chuckles but answers in a more serious vein.

'Well, it might be good for her as well to have someone her own age to confide in, plus a little developing romance wouldn't hurt a young girl, it might take her mind off the past.' Geoff nods.

CHAPTER 12

It's early evening and although the sun has just set there is plenty of dusk light to see where one is going. The reddish infusion of the last remnants of sunlight on the horizon and sparse cloud cover with its greyish outline makes the scene picturesque. Beth and Rod amble down the street in no obvious hurry to get to their destination.

'So, do you like working for your uncle?'

'Oh yeah, he's great, I've got friends in other towns doing apprentice-ships and some of them get quite a hard time but Geoff's not like that.'

'Oh right,' he seems really nice, you know, open, relaxed.'

'Ha, unless I do something wrong, or don't think logically, then he stirs me'.

'Stirs, with what?'

'He'll tap me on the head and say, "Rod, use the nod."

'The nod, Oh dear!'

'Well, I deserve it most of the time.' Beth gets playful and moves closer to Rod, she starts patting his head, commenting, "Poor Nod." He doesn't withdraw his head from her patting which is almost caressing and is about to comment

when Johnny's Commodore slows next to them, the five are inside, Pills half crawls out of the window and calls out.

'Hey mate, found a root for the night. Feel like sharing? Beth's dropped her head, she and Rod ignore the lewd comment and just continue with walking straight ahead, Johnny accelerates the car slightly, so it keeps pace with them as Pills continues.

'Hey I done been brought up proper, I've been taught to share. I don't mind slops.' He turns his head forty-five degrees and comments to the others in the backseat.

'What about you guys?' Raucous laughter emanates from inside the car, Rod is getting fed up with this antagonistic baiting and is about to answer back when Beth grabs his arm and whispers, "don't." With Beth holding his arm, he calms down and turns his attention to her, this act of calming him down seems to ignite the gang, Noogs buts in.

'Hey tart, you can hold something better than that, why don't you go downstairs and really get ya teeth into the job... or are you too precious.' This tirade has an effect and gets under Beth's skin, she gets a steely look in her eye and starts to arc up, showing annoyance, Noogs sensing this annoyance continues.

'Hey precious, do ya want me to show ya how?' This comment now really gets under Beth's skin, she turns her head and is about to give a reply when Rod feeling her angst puts his hand around her and pulls her in close, softly and emphatically whispering into her ear, "don't, let it go." His close proximity distracts her attention, she forgets the car and gazes at him, a bond is kindled, the gang realise that they suddenly have been rejected to the back isles in this play, they try a flurry of insults, Pills leads.

'Don't forget to wipe yaself after.' Tatts follows him. 'Yeah, I don't wanna catch anything.' Billy pathetically adds. 'She's t-t-too scrawny anyway.' But it's to no avail, they realise that they have lost the battle, Noogs lets rip with the last

bombastic blast.

'Probably a fuckin' bleeder anyway, you have her... let's go, Johnny.' Johnny plants the foot and the Commodore races away, however, this last round of insults hasn't even been noticed by Beth and Rod, Beth turns and faces him, noticing his other hand has slipped around her waist, she speaks softly in an unperturbed way.

'They're gone.' He's immersed in her eyes, all he can reply is. "Uhh, uhh..." Beth's also caught up in the moment, she gazes into his eyes, with a girlish softness and says 'Thanks for looking after me.' He answers in a dreamy fashion, 'you too.' They are very close and just look at each other for quite some time, very gradually their heads contract till their lips are almost touching. Holding his gaze, she smiles, then kisses him softly, slowly withdrawing they continue to stare into each other's eyes, she moves forward again and kisses him but this time with far more passion. Seconds pass and they withdraw. Continuing to stare at her with glazed eyes shows he's hopelessly smitten, she's better at restoring normality to their situation, announcing with little conviction.

'I've got to get home.'

'Uhh, uhh.' Is the best he can do. She begins to move off, grabbing his hand and leading him along, moving off down the road they hold hands and nestle into each other, closer to Reg's house, their pace slackens even more, in an effort to delay their inevitable parting but eventually they arrive at the front gate. Beth breaks the bond.

'Thanks for walking me home.' Rod's still dreamy but manages, 'No Problem.' She giggles at his emaciated mental state.

'I'll see you Friday night for "Take-Away." At last, he seems to have restored his faculties and reciprocates with enthusiasm, beaming.

'Oh yeah, great, looking forward to it.' Leaning

forward, she kisses him quickly then sprints up the steps to the front door, opening it she turns waves then enters. Watching her disappear Rod smiles to himself, allowing all these positive vibes to run through his body he turns and with a spring in his step saunters off down the road. Beth enters the kitchen, Reg is in the parlour watching TV, he grunts his normal gruff pleasantry.

'You're home... bit late.' Beth answers as if she is miles away.

'Yes, I suppose so.' He turns and eyes her suspiciously, noticing a change in her demeanour and asks.

'You alright?' The answer is as vague as her first statement, a very laissez-faire answer drifts from her.

'Yes... going to bed... goodnight.' With that, she turns and almost floats out of the kitchen. Reg is absolutely confused by her manner, this change of character metamorphosing into some sort of hippy dropout is most alarming. He looks at his watch and frowns, with deep thought he tries to come to some realisation of the change but it being just too difficult trying to understand the meandering psychology of the younger generation he gives up and returns to watching the TV. Beth returns to her room, drops her bag, takes the aerobics gear out and neatly folds them over the chair. Unzipping the side of her dress she starts to undress, stopping she looks at the picture of her parents sitting on her bedside table. Switching her view back to her aerobics gear she opens the wardrobe door and stands in front of the full-length mirror. An intense study of herself takes place, again she transfers her view back to the photo of her parents then back to the mirror. Slipping out of her school dress, she intently stares trying to visualise herself in a progressive situation but done with the acceptance of her parents. Turning she views her body, agreeing with her analysing, she nods happy that her physical stature is fine, it definitely is a fine example of a young woman, no longer a little

girl. A smile breaks across her face knowing that her parents would be very proud of her and happy with whatever decision she might make in the future. Discarding her underwear, she slips on the nightie and moves into bed, this time she holds the pillow, a soft smile ripples across her face as she drifts off to sleep.

CHAPTER 13

That evening Johnny and the gang are parked at the old quarry, lounging round the car. Johnny vents his frustration.

'You know this town really pisses me off, I mean we've been here, I dunno, how long? Doesn't matter, all we've ever got is, "What's your problem?' What're doing now?' Jeez… I'm sick of it, I really wanna stick it up them.' Noogs has been nodding her head in agreement, she's been tarred with the same brush all her life.

'… know what ya mean… been there also. Shit the way people used to talk behind me mother's back. Then they'd look at me… me … I mean I ain't done nothing wrong.' Billy relates. 'Yeah, f-f-fuckin' do-gooders, I hate 'em all. Always t-t-trying to make ya som'in' ya never w-w-wanted, I felt like a bleedin' dog at school, sit up, say please, be polite to ladies, shit n-n-none of them was ever n-n-nice to me.' Pills agrees. 'True, I got the same sorta treatment, 'cept they tried to whip it in ta me, the cunts.' Johnny nods in agreement, they are a brotherhood, interlopers together in what they believe is a biased community, their own small example of society.

'I'm with ya boys, but times are a-changing.' Showing

some surprising resemblance of knowledge Tatts interjects.

'I'nt that a song by Bob Dylan?'

'Oh yeah', responds Johnny, a tad excited by one of his gang's dawning of intelligence. 'He wrote it 'cos he was pissed off with older people.'

'Hey', Billy agrees, 'I'm pissed off with old people.'

'Yeah', snarls Johnny, 'Not just old people.' Noogs has seen the snarl in his comment, it excites her when Johnny draws the vociferous statements out of his soul, she grins menacingly.

'You mean?'

'Yeah, like who does that new chick think she is? Walkin' round with her boyfriend, thinking she's better than us. Christ she's must have only been here a short while and already she's got the snobby attitude to us, fuck, she hasn't even met us.' Pills agrees, '… Can't even have a joke with her… snobby bitch.' Billy lays down the law stammering, 'New ta town, a-a-a-actin' all high an' m-m-m-mighty, she needs a real good fuckin.' Noogs sneers excitedly, the conversation has her juices pumping.

'Yeah, and I wanna watch, have a laugh and then punch her lights out.' Everyone laughs, comments of "Oh yeah," "Fuckin' go girl," and "blood oath," are expounded amongst the laughter, it's Tatts who brings everyone back to reality.

'Yeah but her boyfriend Rod, well he's big and he works for Geoff Miller and shit he's really big, built like brick shit-house, I couldn't handle them.' Johnny's been posing this problem for a while and he believes he's devised a solution.

'No but you don't, the trick is to divide and conquer, one problem at a time, solve that then you can have all the fun you want with "Little Miss" and her friend Karen.' 'Fun,' thinks Noogs aloud. 'Now that's an interesting word, all boys like to have a bit of fun in their lives, don't ya boys? Even I'd like a bit of fun.'

CHAPTER 14

Friday morning Beth is on the bus with Shelly and the others but is far away in thought, not involved in their normal babbling conversation. Shelly notices and as the others warble on, she slides up to Beth.

'Penny for them?'

'Wha,' oh sorry,' replies Beth. 'Miles away.' Shelly grins, aware that some heavy thinking is going on behind those bright blue eyes.

'You've got something on your mind, I know, I'm reading about the psychology of the mind reflected in body positioning.'

'What… But you're only grade six?'

'Ha ha, doesn't mean I'm dumb, the teacher is giving me certain upgraded books, they're supposed to stimulate my curiosity and get me working at a higher level, sort of high achievers.' This initially surprises Beth, but with quick reflection it sort of falls into place. Shelly was the one she believed noticed her predicament of isolation at the new school during her first days there and deviously with good intent manipulated the situation. The result being she now has new friends and is relaxed in the school environment, she decides to

try Shelly out.

'You see, I met this boy round my age, the other day…'

'Boys!' Is the gasping reply, 'Oh gosh, I think I'm out of my depth already.' Studying her Beth realises, "intelligent yes, caring yes, experienced… no." She is still only young, the pondering by her, however, invites Shelly's curiosity, even if she is inexperienced in this area she asks with maturity beyond her years.

'Look I know I don't know much, you are obviously older than me, but if you need someone to well, I don't know, sort of talk to, then I'll try to be of help. You see we've only just started, Health and Human Relations at school, so I don't really know the ins and outs of the body parts yet, or how the mind is affected by the opposite sex. We haven't touched the reproductive process yet, so "mame" here is rather in nowheres-ville right now.' Beth studies her and almost cries after this disclosure, she thinks to herself. "What a most lovely person, obviously not up to my maturity but willing to put her minimal experience on the line in regard to friendship." She needs to show appreciation but let her down carefully. Picking her words, she advises.

'Oh, you are a dearest friend, thanks awfully, yes I've got a few thoughts in my head regarding my situation and yes they are more advanced than you have experienced. I guess that's the difference, yes, an age gap and a difference. I know that if I confide in you or even need a conversation, you'd be most considered in your help but it's something I'll have to work out myself, I guess it's part of growing up, that's ahead for you but if I do need someone you'll be the first port of call.' The reply satisfies Shelly.

'Okay, no worries, I sort of think I know what you're on about, so good luck stay umm… happy and do what's right for you, I'm around.' With that, she gives an emotional hug, stands and returns to her seat amongst the younger ones.

CHAPTER 15

That evening at the dance studio it's Karen who is the more bubbly of the two, she's done a large amount of background work and has arrived armed with ideas. Propelling this forward, it's Beth who doesn't quite have her mind on the job. Karen inwardly grins thinking, "I wonder if Geoff is having the same problem with Rod?" Still she presses on and her infectious enthusiasm cajoles Beth into action, they begin to attack the new movements with motivation and industry. At the finish of this intense session Beth's knackered and botches a new move. 'Oops sorry, I lost you just after the second chorus, we don't go back to the extended raises, do we, it's the side slips, isn't it?'

'Yes, side slips, I was doing the side you were doing the front, looked like mid-air jumps.'

'Ha ha, either that or I'd been drinking.' Karen agrees, 'that's a good idea, we've had enough for today, how 'bout we call it quits for now?' Beth nods in agreement, 'Yep, I've had enough.' They retire to the bench, CD player is switched off, and they change back into their normal clothes, tracksuit and school uniform. With everything packed up, lights switched off Karen locks the door and they start the trek to Karen's house,

walking down the road Beth inquires.

'I haven't had takeaway for ages.'

'Yes, it's been a while also.'

'What will it be?'

'Oh, I don't know, Geoff's always keen on making pizza, thinks he has some Italian blood in his veins, strange considering his mother's name was Anderson and his surname is Miller. If not Italian, it might be Chinese.' She giggles, 'Actually it's probably whatever the boys can rustle up from the pantry.'

'Well whatever the boys make, I'm sure it'll be fine, I need something especially after all that sweating.' Karen laughs and puts on a debonair tone. 'Ladies don't sweat, they perspire or gleam.'

'Oh yes, sorry, dearie me! I've worked so hard, all this perspiring has made me clingy, oh, dear, what can I do?'

'No problem young lady, I'll have a shower and change, you can have one too.'

'Right thanks, I brought a change of clothes.' Karen picks the subconscious tract, "Hmm, oh did you now, didn't seem to worry too much last time, want to be seen at our best do we?' Beth blushes Karen chuckles to herself, grabs Beth's arm and helps.

'Couldn't agree more, got to look our best for the boys.' They laugh and walk on arm in arm.

In the kitchen of the house, Geoff and Rod are hard at it at the bench preparing dinner. The girls enter the kitchen, Karen moves straight up to Geoff and gives him a kiss and hug. Beth is unsure what to do, Rod likewise, she pauses then with a shrug of her shoulders and flipping her head, walks up to Rod and gives him a hug. He smiles back, happy to be enveloped in the warmth of the emotion, they break, Beth walks up to Geoff says "Hi," and gives him a hug, he announces.

'Pleased to see that you couldn't stay away from

"Mill-uina's Takeaway.' Confusion reigns in the kitchen, Beth stumbles "Mill… what?'

'Mill -uina", again he proudly announces, "Miller – Luina" get it?'

'Oh'… is the unilateral chorus of acknowledgment, Beth continues.

'Well, I smelt something nice as we entered.' Geoff becomes playful.

'Nice… hmm, Oh, that'd be Rod's aftershave', then acting as if talking to himself, 'Wait is he shaving yet?' Rod gives a look of mock disdain, Geoff continues.

'Yes, no? Oh well, perhaps you girls will settle for pizza.' He starts singing with an Italian brogue. 'Oh, sol a mia …' Karen clasps her hands over her ears and interjects.

'Woah, woah, Mario, we get the idea. There was something nice going on in this kitchen as we entered. Right you boys continue going with the pizza, we need to get showered and changed, Beth you can use Rod's room, second door down the passageway on the left.'

'Okay,' she nods. The girls pick up bags and exit the kitchen, while the two boys continue with their culinary skills, the sound of a towel flapping can be heard in the background. A door creeks open, a body wrapped in only a towel bursts forth from the bathroom and scoots through the kitchen with a muffled, "'Scuse me." The boys glance up then to each other, shrug shoulders then continue working. Soon the sound of the bathroom door opening is heard again, another body wrapped in a towel zips across the kitchen, Geoff comments. 'It's getting like a Burke Street in here.' Rod laughs, they both continue with the dinner preparations. Ten or so minutes pass, then Karen enters the kitchen in a floral dress of late fifty's style, her hair is brushed and neatly free, she has the slim fit body of a dancer and doesn't carry any excess weight, her soft woman's appearance is enhanced by subtle muscle toning. Geoff looks

over his shoulder and smiles, no repour, just a look that says everything, lovingly impressed. Karen ventures to the fridge and takes out a can of gin and tonic, gets a glass from the cupboard and sits at the table. Entering the kitchen, Beth's got on her aerobics sneakers but with a light blue mini skirt and a short pink singlet top. Hair is washed and combed but unlike Karen she has made more of an effort with her make-up, not a lot but enough to enhance her already attractive features. Rod flips a glance over his shoulder at this very fit and attractive young girl, Geoff has to give him an elbow to close his mouth. Rod's not moving much, Geoff gives him another elbow, looks at him and raises his eyebrows but still Rod is slow on the uptake, he's forced to whisper to him.

'Well get the girl a drink.' Rod, gathering himself turns and addresses Beth.

'Umm... a drink? Over here see what you'd like.' He moves to the fridge, she follows, opening the door he gets a faint whiff of her perfume, it's subtle, not overpowering.

'Oh, you smell great.' This show of appreciation encourages a reply, she acknowledges with a soft giggle and a slight curtsey.

'Thank you, glad you noticed.' She runs her hand over his as he takes a can of soft drink from the fridge, eye contact is held for a fraction then released. Closing the fridge door, they move back to the table, Geoff has already put the pizza in the oven and is sitting next to Karen.

'So how did the practice go girls?'

'Good', is the enthusiastic answer from Karen, 'We're coming along well,' she glances at Beth who agrees.

'Oh yes, I mean you're so easy to work with, some of our old teachers were tyrants.' Geoff's curious.

'Yes, where was your old place?'

'Down the South Eastern suburbs of Melbourne, Waverley, do you know it?'

'Yes actually, when I was young, we lived in Ashburton for a while, down near Gardiners Creek.'

'Oh, the creek with the bike track running next to it, it went all the way into the city, it was great.'

'So, you had a bike?'

'Yes, but I had to leave it behind when I moved down here.' Rod's been listening, his thoughts have accelerated.

'I think there's a couple of old bikes in the garage, I can take them out and give them the once over, get them going and we can go out. Beth's enthusiasm rises.

'Right, oh that'd be great, you're on, we could go for a picnic.' Her eagerness is contagious, Rod nods and smiles.

'Yeah, way to go, I'm in.' Karen's inquisitive and asks.

'So, how's life with uncle Reg?' 'Oh, not too bad, he's a bit reclusive and… well strange, I'm not sure how to handle him actually, but I'm doing my best.'

'Fair enough, just float along and see what happens but if there are any problems, you're always welcome to stay here. With Reg be assertive, don't let him push you round.'

'Thanks, I won't, I just want to work out what makes him tick.' Karen doesn't want to tread too far in and put Beth offside with her uncle, she lets the offer drift.

'Something I guess, anyway our offer stands and if you had to move in Rod wouldn't mind giving up his room.' Rod slightly surprised by Karen's offer quips an off the cuff unintentional faux pas.

'Give up… I dunno, shares okay.' Raised eyebrows round the table, even more from Beth whose mouth has dropped open a tad, her eyes widen. There's a silence before Karen and Geoff roar with laughter at Beth's expression, Rod's just realised what he's said and drops his head in extreme embarrassment, looking at him she tries to diffuse the situation.

'Really, I'm not that sort of girl,' before giggling 'Well not yet anyway.' This brings hoots of laughter from all,

comments of "oh really", "oh little miss" float across the table, Rod lifts his head, looks at Beth and shakes it as an apology inferring, "oh why did I say that," she pats him on the arm and joins in the laughter. Once normality has been established again, Karen rises and careful extracts the pizza. Geoff gets a bottle of wine from the fridge, pours a glass for Karen then himself, looking at Rod he nods an invitation for a glass of wine. Rod places his hand over his glass and shakes his head. Geoff looks at Beth, knowing that she's underage but decides that she should be included. He politely offers her a glass, this relaxed family environment allows her to make a decision. Pondering she pauses then nods to Geoff to pour some wine into her glass.

The pizza is cut and served, they start dinner, as they eat, conversation flows again as it would in a normal family round the dinner table, occasionally Beth reclines back and just watches. In the back of her mind she is reminiscing on what family life used to be like. Rod has noticed her dalliance and seems attuned but rather than inquiring he just smiles which she reciprocates. Life has pushed her into a somewhat strange and different direction. She'll have to adapt, it's not any more of a problem than it would have been before, the only difference is that the process due to necessity has been accelerated. "That's fair enough", she thinks to herself," but right now this is as close as I'll get to the normality of family life, security and love". Rod doesn't quite understand that's the catalyst for the pacified smile on her face, mixed with a satisfied demeanour.

With dinner finished, Karen gets up and prepares coffee and tea, all continue to chat, no one mentions TV, their company is better. Coffee served they continue to interact, jokes are told about Rod's mistakes at work. Geoff admonishing, "Rod use the nod", which opens up a situation for Beth able again to pat Rod's head and exclaim in a pitying way, "Poor nod." Geoff thinks this is hilarious, Karen supports Beth's maternal action by also patting his head and adding, "Poor

little nod," bringing forth laughter all round again. Everyone is interested in Beth's school situation, her new friends and workload. She explains this year as a springboard to year eleven and V C E. Geoff nods in understanding in the back of his mind he is aware that if Rod and her became more friendly it would be of great benefit to the lad's maturing as she seems to be.

When Beth explains the help, she presumes Shelly made in the manipulation of her new friends, Karen is not surprised. She explains that in an interview with Shelly's parents they informed her that Shelly's IQ is one of the highest in the state and various universities have been in contact with them and her school regarding the advancement of her education. They understand that Shelly is extremely bright and is learning way beyond her year levels at school, but she is still only twelve and has the maturity of one that age. Advancement is fine but not at the expense of her social level, thus being involved in activities that she does not excel any more than the others of her age is of paramount for her balanced development, Karen's dance class fits the agenda perfectly. This appraisal is met with nod of comprehension all around the table, none more than Beth who agrees with these comments regarding Shelly. Everyone has aspects of interest to put regarding this point of discussion, whether it be from experience or just stories they have heard. The time clock ticks past nine-thirty, Karen raises her arms, stretches and announces.

'Okay guys, I'm tired, sorry to be a party pooper but I'm off to bed.' Geoff agrees, 'I'm with you.' Rod's upbeat now and tells Beth.

'I'll walk you home.' She smiles subtly with acknowledgement, and answers. "Thanks". Geoff does some of the cleaning up of the dishes then follows Karen down the passageway. Beth collects her bag from Rod's room and they exit the house.

It's well and truly into night, so they have to tread

carefully. There are no streetlights in these back-blocks or footpath. So, with the uneven surface between the bitumen road and the gravel leading up to the house's nature strips one has to be careful not to trip or fall. As they ramble along, they chat about dinner, Beth's relaxed and comfortable explaining to Rod.

'That was great, I wish uncle Reg was more like you guys.' Rod's intrigued.

'So, you don't know anything about him really.'

'No, he grew up with my dad but by the age of twenty-eight or so he just vanished up the country somewhere, Dad used to send him a Christmas card but we never got one in return. After a while, he changed address and never bothered to forward it, Dad sort of gave up the idea of being the instigator with him all the time and just let it slide. We just got on with our lives, I do know there was no disagreement or anything untoward. Dad said they got along well as children and through the teenage years but they just grew apart, I think in some ways he missed him, but well, I came along and life moved in a different direction'.

'So, you must have been expecting someone of similarity to your dad?'

'Yes, and that's shown not to be the case, it's not that he dislikes me, I just feel his obligation to look after "family" as he calls it is an intrusion to his lifestyle. Guess he had a quiet place here where nobody disturbed him, everything cruisy then I came along, I'm trying my best to fit in but still feel like I'm an intrusion in the house.'

'Well, you're a welcome intrusion here.' She looks up with that soft smile again and is about to answer when she trips and tumbles. Rod grabs her arm just in time to stop her hitting the ground hard, he levers her up still holding her arm. Looking at him now in close proximity she smiles "thanks", her hands have rested onto his hips but there is no disentanglement.

The moon glows high above them caressing them with a
soft aura, there's an easy breeze rustling the foliage hidden
in the night, the romantic mood is perfect. He leans forward
and kisses her, she reciprocates, her actions elevating their
emotions. Entwined like a romantic figurine found in a gift
shop they stay holding their passionate embrace when suddenly
a vehicle's headlights can be seen in the distance, separating
slightly she profounds.

'Damn, who's that?' He is now jolted back into reality.

'Dunno, no one really moves round here much at
night.' Cocking his head, he concentrates on the cars sound,
suddenly exclaiming.'

'Wait that's the sound of extractors on an old six-
cylinder car, maybe a Ford or Holden and there's only one car
in this area that has that set up, Johnny.' Looking at her, then
with some urgency in his voice he orders.

'Quick, back here, behind this hedge.' Ducking down a
driveway they crouch behind a squared hedge, as they wait, he
has his hands around her waist, she's squatted in front of him.
The vehicle's sound creeps closer and closer, its light beams
now are visible on the bitumen road in front of them. Slowing
it draws opposite their possie as if the occupants are searching
for something. She squirms slightly forcing him to readjust
his hold, causing his hands to slip onto and half cupping her
breasts. The tension of the situation has disguised their physical
contact, Johnny's car continues on its slow manoeuvring way,
similar to a search vehicle, it crawls on, turns the corner and
disappears, Beth exhales.

'Phew,' although still crouched she starts to giggle, Rod
looks at her.

'What?' She looks at him with a glint in her eye.
'Thanks for holding me.' He's about to reply when it dawns on
him, he's holding her left breast, standing he drops his hand
and looks flummoxed fumbling an answer.

'I was… umm… you know… umm… the car… and…'
Putting her finger to his lips as he splutters, she whispers.

'Shh, thanks for protecting me.' Taking his hand, she places it on her chest near to her heart.

'See my heart was racing you've calmed it down.' Hers may have calmed down, but now his is racing, gently she lowers his hand to his side and returns them to reality.

'I've got to get home.' It's not an order but a polite request, controlling himself he agrees.

'Yes okay, I'll take you to your doorstep, make sure those idiots don't return.' The comment doesn't bring the expected response, she starts giggling, he's confused.

'What?'

'We were like soldiers, umm what do you call them, ahh, oh yes commandoes, sneaking round trying not to be seen, so what's the mission? Do we have to rescue someone, you know someone who's captured by the enemy or do we have to blow up something?' Joining in the silliness he acts regimentally.

'Rescue… yes, I've got to rescue two things in the garage, then our mission is to explore the grassy patch down by the river, you're the guide, you know the scout, plus you have to prepare supplies.' She breaks away from him, stands to attention and salutes, "sir, yes sir, all packages will be present this Saturday morning at nine o'clock."

'Well done corporal, we'll have a briefing at your place at the nominated time.'

'Yes sir,' she exclaims falling into laughter, they move off hand in hand. Arriving at Reg's house, she turns and faces Rod.

'Thanks again Rod, it was a great night plus a bit of excitement.' She leans forward and kisses him passionately, breaking off she says, "See you Saturday," and walks into the house. Rod watches her disappear, again he's in a dream-world,

his imagination is running on overdrive, with a shake of his head, he turns and wanders off down the road. His gait is relaxed and secure, not in any hurry just allowing the night's experiences to filter through.

CHAPTER 16

Entering the kitchen, it's not particularly late, so Reg is in the parlour watching TV, he glances over his shoulder at the sound of her entrance.

'Ya home.'

'Yes, uncle Reg,' she stays diplomatic, 'Geoff made pizza.'

'Pizza,' he grumps, 'that iy-tie food.' She's on the defensive treading very carefully.

'Well not really, it was more of Geoff's concoction.' This seems to work.

'Geoff's mixture, well I guess might have tasted alright.' Looking for an opening, she's trying to exploit her timing.

'Yes, he's not a bad cook, it was fine, also Rod has asked me to go on a picnic this Saturday with him, down to the river.' Expecting a tirade regarding her age and work ethic etc. she is surprised by the answer.

'Rod, eh! Geoff's apprentice, seen him 'round working, seems an alright sort of lad, you could do worse. The weekend eh! Outside with the fresh air a bit of relaxation after a week's hard grind, yes it could be good, enjoy yourselves.' She's almost floored by this endorsement; but knows she still has to tread

carefully not overplay her hand.

'Yes, we will, thanks Uncle Reg, I'm off to bed.'

'Alright Luv, goodnight.'

"Luv," from uncle Reg, did she hear correctly, walking down the passageway thoughts emanate from her. "Is my politeness having an effect"? or "Is my association with Geoff and Rod more appeasing to his sense of correctness, especially as they are both trade workers". Too confusing to contemplate deeply, this time it's her who goes to bed slightly mystified.

Dawn breaks and Beth's up early and organising food in the kitchen, she makes some sandwiches with ham and cheese, throws in a couple of muesli-bars and two apples. They're stuffed into a small pack-back along with a towel and her bathers, hat, sunnies and everything is ship-shape. Attention now turns to her, with typical female discernment she ponders, "Now, what to wear?" Scrimmaging through the wardrobe various items are thrown onto the bed, balancing up her alternatives she dwells, "I need to be cute but interesting, not too colourful, don't want to clash with natures surroundings." The thinking process is in full flight, resolution becomes vexing, after a slight pause and with a flick of her head and a shrug of her shoulders a decision is reached, blue mini skirt and white singlet top. Finding her sneakers, she slips into them, stands, looks in the mirror, gathers her hair putting a tie around it, so that's become a pony-tail, with a nod to herself of approval of the choices for riding she exits the bedroom. Gathering the backpack, she sits at the kitchen table having a quick drink of water, soon a tap is heard at the door. Opening it she sees Rod standing there wearing a blue T-Shirt and board shorts. Glancing over his shoulder she spies two bicycles leaning on the front fence, they look old and slightly rusted, definitely no similarity to today's sporting bikes, Rod chirps up.

'They're not much to look at, but they work and the tyres are good.'

'No, they're fine,' she enthuses, 'wait, I'll get my bag it's got all our stuff in it.' Zipping back into the kitchen, she grabs the backpack and heads back down the passageway. Just before exiting through the front door she stops and has a quick thought, retracing a few steps to outside Reg's room she taps on the door and quietly calls out. "I'm off uncle Reg, be back this afternoon." Expecting no reply again she's surprised when a muffled "Righto," is heard. A quizzical look appears on her face but with no time to dwell on it she just shrugs, flicks her head and departs. Outside Rod waits, she runs up to him and gives a quick hug.

'You ready corporal,' he jokes.

'Yes sir, packed and ready for action', she replies, playing along.

'Right come on, let's go.'

They board the bikes, he wraps his towel round his waist, she slings the back-pack on and they pedal off. With the sun breaking through the clouds at various intervals and a soft breeze buffeting their motion, they journey along the backstreets. Pretty soon the houses are left behind, the sound of a few cars fade into insignificance and soon the surrounds of nature take over. Peddling along they occasionally yell "Wee", especially when the slope of the road allows free sailing, Beth notices the forest trees. Large gum trees tower over the road casting shadows across the bitumen, weaving in and out give a feeling of traversing an abstract painting, free of form but included in the myriad of colour. The environmental image has a cathartic effect on the two teens. They laugh as they pedal throwing silly comments to each other, it's the picture of youth enjoying the tranquillity of nature, freedom of expression allowing their characters to breathe. Rod pulls over and motions Beth to stop.

'Down here,' he directs, 'follow me.' The bitumen is left behind as they follow a dirt track, it meanders for about a

kilometre until they emerge into an open expanse of grasslands.

'Over here,' he nods, dismounting he walks the bike towards some trees on the far side, she follows. Pausing, he says, "Here's good," drawing up next to him she surveys the scene, it couldn't be more picturesque.

'This is beautiful,' she exclaims, 'how did you find it?'

'Oh, Geoff told me about it, the grass isn't too high and the river runs through, at this particular part the water is deep enough to go swimming. With the canopy of trees all around its pretty good and secluded, I think he and Karen used to come down here on hot days.' She has a wry smile.

'A perfect setting for a romantic lunch.' He doesn't pick up the inference.

'Donno, just nice surroundings, peaceful after a long hot day's work.' She grins and directs.

'Well anyway, let's lay our towels down here and explore the creek.' Removing his towel, he places it on the ground, she follows pulling hers out of the backpack and laying it next to his. Walking in a relaxed manner they head down, she notices that the setting is very natural in almost an artistic way. "Any landscape painter worth their salt would set up here," she thinks. The grass lines either side of the creek, the forest of trees about fifty meters away surround the grassland there's a slight drop to the water. No dirt but rather a build-up of gritty silt like refined pebbles at the edge of the bank, the creek's water flows just over it, approaching the bank she views the surrounds.

'Want to go swimming?' She enthuses. He's just a little cautious.

'Yes, but let's put our feet in first and paddle around making sure it's not too cold.' With that logical thought, they bend down and ease off their shoes, carefully she slides down the bank and places her feet into the water. Expecting the mountainous stream to be cold, she's surprised by the

reasonable temperature and calls.

'Come in, try it out, I think it's okay.' Moving to the bank, he's less stable not actually smooth on his feet, thus being a little clumber-some, instead of sliding in, he drops down with less aplomb, hitting the water with more force. A splash of water, showers her, his shorts are now half soaked and she's copped a fair splattering of water, he grins. "Oops." 'Graceful movement not a strong point?'

'Sorry, I'm a bit wet also, but hey you're right the water's fine, do you want to go back and change into bathers?'

'Yes fine,' wading back to the bank he helps her out but with their moist hands she almost slips back into the water, forcing him to cling on.

'Oops, got you,' he says, a coy giggle is returned. They move back to the towels, he's been swimming here before but this situation is different, again he's a little slow on the uptake. Whipping off his T-Shirt, he naively remarks,

'You right, ready?' She stands in front of him holding bikini briefs and top in her hand, with a tilt of her head she reflects a questioning look on her face. "And where do I get changed?" The look breaks down his lack of understanding of feminine requirements, glancing left and right he spies the thick wood of trees about fifty metres away to their right, the rest of the area is low grassland, he's flummoxed.

'Umm... well...over there's not too far... I mean...' There's something very appealing about youth who if they are true with their feelings have a hopeless way of showing it. His unsureness resonates with her but she takes command 'cos a little leadership is needed, grinning she orders.

'No worries, turn around, I'll be quick.' Traversing one eighty degrees, he waits. The situation now starts an escalation in his mind. The sounds from behind him intensify his already flowing imagination, a soft rasping sound of a zipper being moved, the equally sublime sound of material slithering and

landing on the grass. Another sound of cloth moving, then an elastic flip, followed by the delicate sound of feet shuffling then more again of material being slid. His ears prick up trying to identify sounds to the female movement, more subtle material movement is heard followed by her "Uhh," the sounds finish, she orders.

'Okay, you can turn around now, but I need a little help please.' Turning he's met by a vision that poleaxes him through the eyes straight to the heart. Standing in front of him is the loveliest vision of a young girl that he's ever laid eyes on. The ponytail has been released, so her hair now hangs free, but her body developed from all the movement exercise is firm with subtle muscle toning which acts as an enhancement of the female form. She has slipped into a white triangle bikini with ties on the side. On a scale of one to ten of flesh coverage this costume barely rates a two, plus the ties are very high up on her hips exemplifying taught hamstrings and backside. She is holding the strings of the two top triangles behind her back, leaving the front loose and delicately poised. His imagination has been swept aside with reality, with her loose hold of the straps behind her the front is barely doing its job of coverage. Knowing he must not stare it still provides turmoil of where does one look. His gaze moves down to her toes and up to her head, he's desperately trying not to stare at her half-covered breasts. His discomfort appeals to her, his gentlemanly aspect flames her admiration to him, coyly she asks.

'Can you help tie these please?' He swallows and with awe moves forward, she turns and he starts fumbling with the chords around her back.

'Not too tight,' she playfully advises, 'Don't want to cut off circulation.'

'Okay,' he stumbles, the fumbling continues. Throughout this process she has a mischievous grin on her face, finishing he steps back and, in an effort to reflect calmness, says "Yep,

done." Instead of turning immediately she pauses, then with an effortless motion that only dancers can exemplify she turns and faces him, placing her hands on her hips and shifting one knee diagonally across she asks.

'Well?' This is way too much for a young man to handle, his senses move into overdrive, he feels a growing in his board-shorts but is unable to slow the process. A gulp and admiring "Yes," is the best that he can do. She traverses her gaze now from his eyes to his body his torso has muscle definition of a very fit and strong young man, glancing down, she notices the induced excitement starting to display itself in his attire. "Enough of the teasing," she thinks to herself, "This isn't fair."

'Come on,' she shouts and scoots off towards the creek. 'Beat you in.' Relieved he follows energetically. Slipping into the water again with delicate poise she starts gliding across a few metres however his enthusiasm overrides sensibility, he just jumps in, causing a huge splash.

'Woah,' is the surprised cry, 'You big bomber,' jumping on him she tries to dunk his head but he's way to strong and lifts her up pitching her over his head.

'Ahh ha,' he grins, 'You've got to do better than that.' The challenge has been set, over the next fifteen minutes she constantly tries to dunk him using head-locks, arm-locks, pushing and general athletic playing around, eventually, they run out of steam.

'Enough,' she breathlessly calls. 'I give up.'

'Okay,' he laughs, 'Let's go back.' Helping her out they walk back to their spot, she drops down exhausted onto her towel. He flops down beside her, rolling onto one side, he raises his head onto one elbow and gazes at her face. Water is dribbling from her hairline in small tracks across her cheek, brushing it away he comments, "You're dribbling," returning his gaze the playful look emerges through her eyes.

'Oh really, gosh my towel won't reach.' Smiling he leans closer and flips another trickle off her eyebrow, commenting 'You've got another blob on your nose.'

'Oh dear,' is the coy reply.

'No probs,' he continues and flicks it away. Staring more intently into her eyes, he comments abstractly with a small amount of hesitation.

'There's some on your lips,' She grins a very coquettish reply.

'Oh dear, do I need help?' This playfully distressed comment now forces a smile on him, he leans forward even closer, touching with his finger again he carefully wipes the moisture off her lips, her heart is now racing she whispers.

'Almost gone.' Steadying himself, he looks into her eyes then leans forward and delicately kisses her. The response is immediate and passionate, holding the embrace, his hand nestles to the side of her chest just near her breast. He kisses again, she is respondent when suddenly with an extraordinary snap he sits bolt upright and yells.

'Ouch, what the…?' The jolting comment surprises her, she's confused.

'What, what's wrong, what is it?' His head rotates left and right then skywards.

'Something hit me', he blurts, 'in the middle of my back.'

'Hit, what…?'

'I don't know, like a …' Before he can finish the sentence, a minuscule stone bounces next to them. 'What the…?' He yells, extricating himself from her presence, standing he surveys the surrounds catching a glimpse of someone standing between them and the woods, vehemently he exhorts.

'That's Billy Surso, the little prick, what's he doing here?' Directing an order to Beth.

'Wait here, I'll teach him to throw stones the little bastard.' With that, he sprints off in Billy's direction, her cries of "Don't, let it go," fade into thin air as he sprints towards his antagonist. Billy has a nasty grin on his face as Rod sprints towards him, suddenly with a change of direction he sprints into the woods. The chase is on but Billy is small and manoeuvrable able to zip round trees and traverse the undergrowth more fluidly. He seems to know Rod's limitations, allowing him to catch up then accelerating away. After about five minutes of hard running logic dawns on Rod that this chase is useless, he slows, furiously glaring at the disappearing image but resigned to the fact that he'll never catch Billy. Turning he starts to walk back to the river. At the river, Beth had called to Rod to forgo the chase but to no avail, with a full head of steam Rod was zoned on revenge. Knowing that this chase he'd embarked on would blow itself out in due course she lay back and relaxes. The sun warms her, she ponders. "Why would Billy come here and throw stones at us?" The perplexing nature of the problem unsettles her, still there is nothing to do but wait. Footsteps are heard, Beth rolls over shading her eyes from the sun's glare and asks, "Did you catch him?"

'Not Billy,' is the unexpected weasel reply, sitting bolt upright, she stares at Pills and Tatts, their nasty acne faces pungently sneering down on her.

'What's wrong darlin,' snickers Pills, 'Ya boyfriend left ya?' A wave of unsureness envelopes her, trying to show bravado she explains the question'.

'He's chasing Billy who was throwing stones at us, why did Billy throw things at us?' Tatts shrugs.

'Billy do as Billy wants to do, like us, we do as we want ta do.' Pills leans forward and does a small tug on the neck strap of her Bikini, she brushes his hand away.

'Now now darlin', why you done that, what with youse lookin' so pretty, hey Tatts she's alright and look, ya can see

most of her.' With that statement, Beth realises she's in trouble, the nature of her predicament punches her in the stomach, she's scared but tries to bluff her way out.

'Leave me alone, I'll yell for Rod.' They both smirk.

'Yell all youse like, he bin chasing Billy whose leading him all round the jungle, be miles away by now.' It's obviously a setup, now she panics, yelling.

'Rod, Rod... help.' Tatts grins.

'Save your breath darlin', he won't hear you'. The horror of the situation resonates in her mind, never before has she experienced bullying or worse, what might lie ahead, now she's in the middle of it pusillanimously vulnerable. Swallowing nervously, she gathers some semblance of courage and stands facing the two intruders. This show of defiance has little effect except that the two intruders can view her completely. It's extremely difficult to display strength of character standing in front of two inbreeds dressed in nothing but a string bikini. The look that envelopes their faces makes her recoil, their eyes drop from her head to her toes then up again. She swears that Tatts is starting to drool out the side of his mouth, Pills focuses on her breasts, forcing her to raise her hands in front of her chest. The two inbreeds inch forward to either side of her, pushing their moronic heads close to her cheeks. She can smell the stench of bad breath and unkempt body odour wafting around them, the repulsiveness of the situation is only enhanced by Pills sneering question, tugging at her Bikini top strand he leers.

'So, Miss Precious, what're you hiding under here?' Tatts starts to fiddle with the tie at the side of her briefs. He smiles and quotes.

'When the ship comes in, it ties up; when it goes out, it unties.' With a swipe of her hand, she tries to brush his hand away, pathetically pleading. 'Don't please... please leave me alone.' The two halfwits look at each other and connect with

evil eyes.

'When we've seen and tasted all there is to be seen and tasted missy.' Tatts pulls at the string, it falls loose, exposing her thigh. Beth doesn't have enough hands to cover her private parts. Tears well in her eyes, again she begs Pills.

'Please… don't.' The effect is synonymous of a red cape to a bull, he reaches behind her grabs her neck strap and starts to pull the tie apart when a voice is heard from the edge of the wood.

'Hey!' Rod has returned into the grasslands and has spotted the two hovering around Beth, he starts sprinting towards them.

'Shit', blurts Tatts, 'he's back early, let's go.' Pills nods and leaves with a final threat.

'Another time, Princess.' They belt off, Rod arrives and can see that Beth is in a state of near shock, her hands are wrapped around her chest, tears dribble down her cheeks, she is shaking having endured the ignominy of the penetration of her personal, looking at her his heartbreaks, carefully he inquires.

'Are you alright?' She nods and croaks a "Yes", in between her intermittent breaths and crying. Placing his hand on her shoulder and tenderly inquires.

'They didn't do anything, I mean, did they?' Raising her head, she sniffles.

'They were leering at me and touched me.' Glancing down he now notices her bikini briefs untied on one side exposing the side of her thigh, deftly he reaches down picking up the two ties and reconnects them.

'There we go,' he tries to enlighten, 'can't have you wandering round a spectacle for everyone to see, you're not that sort of girl.' This delicate attempt at humour to try and diffuse the situation works, she looks up at him, still whimpering but manages a smile. 'That's better,' he comments, 'Don't worry, I'm here to protect you.' Placing his arms around her, he holds her

tightly, she nestles in, the security of his presence elevates her discomfort. Standing in such a comforting embrace she realises that's the single thing she has been missing since her parents passed away, security. Wrapped in his arms she feels safe, his presence providing the warmth like a parent nurturing a young child. They stay huddled together for many minutes, he can feel by the way she stays nestled against him that at this moment, he is the rock on which she can stabilise her emotional turmoil. Gradually calming down she starts to relax in his arms, raising her head, she looks into his eyes, smiles and with youthful honesty says, "Thank you," then kisses him. But this time not passionately but with a caressing manner filled with love. This is a new sensation for him, the transmitting of feelings from the soul through the lips, the feeling inside him is indescribable, a warmth that envelopes his whole body, they stay like that until, she whispers.

'Can we go home?' With understanding, he agrees.

'Of course, I'll pack things up.' Moving round, he places the towel into the backpack, she's redressed back into the mini-skirt and singlet top, handing him the backpack, he surmises.

'Bugger, they spoilt a really good day.' Eying him up and down as they pick up the bikes she responds.

'Interrupted, they can't spoil this… us.' Nodding in agreement, he puts his arm around her and leads her across the grasslands.

CHAPTER 17

Back at the house, Reg is surprised by her early return, on her entry he can tell something is amiss.

'You're early, what's up?' By now, she has regained her composure and although uncomfortable images cross her mind, she decides to unburden herself to him.

'We were out of town about two kilometres on the grassland by the creek when three boys started throwing rocks at us. One hit Rod in the back but he's strong and chased them away.' Reg's face frowns.

'Three boys, which three boys?'

'Some of those that hang around with Johhny, one was Billy Surso.' His eyes narrow.

'That lot, scum useless layabouts, inbreeds.' Then with a more intent look at her noticing her discomfort, he starts to put two and two together and asks.

'You alright?'

'Yes" she answers with marginal confidence, 'Rod chased them all away, he's much bigger and although there were three of them, I think they were scared to face him.'

'Not surprising,' he scorns, 'Cowards the lot, well as long as you're okay then no harm done.' She looks at him

intently, wishing she could go to him, maybe a hug, some TLC, but that's not on the cards in this house at this particular time.

'I'll have a shower and rest', she mumbles, the words barely sliding out.

'Alright Luv, take your time,' is the response. Slanting her head in surprise, she notices, "Luv", there it is again. Although not a hug it's this starting point that gives her hope that these surrounds might still fashion itself into some semblance of a family home. Displaying half a week smile she shuffles out of the kitchen, entering the bedroom, the backpack is discarded on the floor, unzipped and the towel extracted. She whips off the singlet top and unzips the skirt allowing it to drop to the floor. Reaching across she deftly opens the wardrobe door so she can view herself in the mirror. Standing there with her bathers still on a curious expression manifests itself on her face. Her brain races with questions. "What was so enticing about my image that caused their behaviour? I'm nothing special, certainly not overly tall." The studying continues, she unties the bikini straps and lets it flop to the floor, bending over she slips out of the briefs. This time a more investigative process of her personal takes place. "Yes, I'm reasonably fit plus my breasts are reasonably firm from all the exercise, my legs, especially my hamstrings and my backside are taught, shoulders square and diaphragm tight, not a six-pack but definitely tight, yep there's a subtle muscle definition there". The questioning of herself regarding her physical form continues, she turns and inspects her rear image in the mirror but it's all to no avail, no conclusions can be derived, the "why me," still inhabits her head. Still one thing is now obvious, there are nasty elements around in this town so in future she'll need to make sure of where she's going and with whom. This last thought passage brings Rod's image to the surface, plus how he handled the situation, his manner in protecting her modesty and comforting actions was of a gentleman, standing up for

her when in need. The thought of him plus his actions brings a smile to her face, grabbing a towel she drapes it round her and is about to leave the room when that minuscule scrapping sound is heard. Glancing round she tries to navigate to it, "Is it a mouse?" But nothing is seen, with a shrug of the shoulders she exits the room.

On the way to the bathroom, she glances at the parlour but it's vacant, assuming that Reg is outside working in the backyard she enters the bathroom, places the towel on the rail and turns the shower taps to get the pressure and temperature right. "One thing that can calm the senses is a warm shower," she thinks. Stepping in she allows the warm water to rush over her skin, its tickling-warm feel has the desired effect, tension seems to fade as the water trickles down her back. During the shower process, she doesn't notice the bathroom door move slightly, two eyes peep into the darkened bathroom. Her outline view is blurred by the shower's frosted glass, a short time passes then the door closes. Once her shower is finished, she towels off and returns to her bedroom, changes into shorts and t-shirt before re-entering the kitchen. Moving to the sink she switches on the kettle and takes a cup from the draining board, Reg enters the kitchen via the back door.

'Making a brew Luv, I'll have one thanks.'

'Alright, Uncle Reg.'

As he moves to his room and she prepares the extra cup, her thoughts redirect to his speech. Again, he used the word "Luv," also the request for a cup of tea wasn't the gruff command he normally projects. "Why the mellowing manner?" she questions herself. "Well there's nothing different in the household situation and well, while we're not the embodiment of domestic bliss thing there is a slight change." The logical thing to do she realises is to continue on and carefully negotiate the changes as they arise, mentally she scolds herself, "Do not rock the boat, subtle steering required." He enters the kitchen,

she politely orders.

'Sit down uncle Reg, it's almost done.' He pulls open a chair and sits, commenting, "Righto." Placing the two cups on the table, she joins him and sits.

'Feeling better now Luv?'

"There it is again," she grins to herself, answering. 'Yes thanks, the shower worked a treat.'

'Good.'

'I've got a bit of homework to do so I might get stuck into that.'

'Righto,' he nods, 'I've got work in the back-garden, be in at six.'

'Okay', she responds, 'Do you want me to prepare anything for dinner?'

'Oh, right, umm... just the vegies if you want, I'll get the meat going when I come in.'

'Fine,' she smiles at him in a more caring way, it seems to unease him slightly, he frowns in a confused manner. Finishing his tea, he stands and swishes the last remnants down the sink and stiffly says, "Righto," then exits the kitchen. With his leave she ponders, concluding. "In his own way I think he's trying to make an effort, it must be difficult for him, all these years by himself, now me, this turbulence but he is trying I'm sure." This realisation brings a smile of contentment to her face. Round six Reg enters, Beth is at the bench peeling potatoes, he looks but instead of grunting exclaims.

'Got them going, righto, I'll wash my hands and get the chops on.' Disappearing to the bathroom, he emerges quickly and moves to the fridge, taking the meat chops out, he places them in the frying pan switches the gas on and lets the heat do its magic. Returning to the fridge he grabs a can of beer, pops the ring top and takes a swig exclaiming, "Ahh, that's better" and is about to take another drink when he focuses on Beth, pausing he asks.

'Do you want a drink Luv?'

Now, this question is ambiguous, to say the least, she's not sure how to answer. "Does he mean an alcoholic drink"? A very delicate move forward is needed here she knows.

'Oh, I used to have a small wine occasionally with my parents, they said I should be getting used to it 'cos it was the social custom.' She waits with bated breath, he's thinking, tension mounts inside her.

'Yes,' he replies in agreement, they were right, you're young but soon will be of age, you should be introduced gradually through the family home.'

"Agreement, with her parents!" Her jaw almost hits the ground. He continues, 'What were you allowed?'

'Umm, just a white wine, I think it was called Pino Gris.'

'Pino Gris, yeah I've heard of it but I don't have any of that here.'

'Don't worry,' she jumps in, 'Water will do fine.' He's thinking again.

'Look I've got to go into town tomorrow morning, do you want to come with me, as well as getting some supplies I'll see them at the pub. They'll steer me in the right direction.' Beth's flabbergasted, this show of interest and consideration is overwhelming, she stutters.

'Oh... umm, err yes, thanks... ahh what time will we leave.' 'After breakie, round nine-thirty, pub won't be open till ten, right get those vegies happening these chops are almost done.' Draining the vegie pots, she serves them onto the plates, he places the chops down and they sit to enjoy the evening meal.

'How was the ride?' he inquires, 'Like the countryside?'

'Yes,' is the answer as she starts recalling what they saw on the ride. The meal continues with harmonious conversation for the first time since she arrived.

CHAPTER 18

Morning dawns, Beth slowly wakes, turning over she hears the distant clatter of cutlery emanating from the kitchen, stretching, she lays still for a moment gaining her senses then slides out of bed and exits the room. Reg is in the kitchen working at preparing breakfast, he hears her enter and speaks.

'Tea's on the table, toast is on the way.'

'Okay,' is the bleary response, 'Just going to the bathroom.' Finishing the buttering of the toast, he places pieces on plates and sits at the table, Beth re-enters the kitchen and moves to a chair, glancing up he's awestruck by her appearance. She's only wearing a fine summer nightie which is quite transparent and rather loosely fitting because he has lived by himself this type of appearance has never advertised itself ever before in his kitchen.

'Thanks,' she politely says as the tea is tasted. 'What's the time, how long before we leave?' This ordinary question has him in a turmoil, not so much the question but the apparition in front of him. At her original home, there were no restrictions regarding the manner of how one moved around the house, especially as the family consisted of the father, mother and only daughter. They grew up together and

were used to each other's physical appearance, even when Beth hit puberty, both her mother and father explained everything in a free and open way thus eventually she felt completely at ease wandering round the house in any state of dress or undress, as did her parents. This situation known to her has not been reciprocated in Reg's house. So, because of the relaxed dinner last night her casual attitude to her home environment has increased. Therefore, wandering out to breakfast in her nightie whilst normal in her original home has "Rocked his boat," somewhat. It's as if the swinging sixties revolution has landed slap bang in his kitchen, his old oligarchy is strained, he answers, desperately trying not to show any reaction to her appearance.

'Well, well... err, finish up and we'll go in about thirty minutes, that'll umm give you time to change.'

'Oh yes, I showered last night so only have to slip on shorts and a T-Shirt'. With her elbows on the table, holding the cup, leaning forward and sipping the tea, the loose nightie is almost unobtrusive in covering her physicality. The whole situation is too overwhelming for him, using discretion he rises, takes his cup to the sink rinses it and comments.

'I'll fix a few things,' then retires shaking his head in disbelief, Beth continues to sip her tea oblivious to the turmoil she has created, enriched and enlivened, she whips back to her room changes and presents herself at the rear of the house.

'Hi uncle Reg, I'm ready.' His reaction to her normal attire is relief and appreciation, with his senses returning to normal he directs.

'Righto, in we get.' The car is a very old Ford utility, made in the early nineteen-seventies. The front seat is an ancient bench-seat, dash-board has a façade of chrome work with old fashioned knobs and dials spread across it. It's a manual column gear-shift, Reg uses his left foot to control the clutch, Beth's in awe, she feels a sense of excitement, the same

as people who travel in old steam trains or antique cars. The appropriateness of the car to the town is not lost on her, the trip, although short is a pleasurable experience to her, actually fun. She grins to herself thinking, "If I see anyone should I wave like the queen", this produces a giggling fit, Reg turns his head and questions.

'You right there, Luv?' Unable to control her feelings, she bursts out.

'Oh, this car, its… It's fantastic, this is great.' Never before has anyone made any sort of comment regarding his mode of transport, he's slightly bemused.

'Well glad you like it, they don't build them like this anymore.' Beth agrees and chuckles.

'They certainly don't, this is great its… fun.' Impressed by her appreciation, he turns to her and gives a wink plus a smile then concentrates on the road, they continue driving. It doesn't take long for them to reach the main street, although not empty there's only a sparse scattering of people. They seem to be moving in and out of the General Store buying supplies or goods, whatever's needed. Reg parks the car slightly closer to the garage with the store only twenty metres away, switching off the ignition he tells Beth.

'I've got to see Mick at the garage first, then mosey to the General Store, once I've got that all sorted, I'll nip across to the pub and see if they've got any of that wine, meet you soon near the store.'

'Fine', she replies. They exit the car, he moves off in the direction of the garage, Beth ambles in the direction of the store. Being a pleasant day with a hotchpotch of cloud cover and deciding to catch a bit in the warmth of the sun, she moves to a community seat diagonally opposite the store. Gazing round she enjoys watching the town's people moving round the street, going about their business. Like any small rural towns, she gauges they are a variety of personalities but with a

stronger element of farmers. A blue Hi-Lux utility pulls up near the store and a strong tall weather-beaten man of about forty steps down onto the bitumen. The passenger door opens and a young girl in shorts and T-Shirt exits the car, Beth strains her eyes then recognises her, its Shelly, she calls out.

'Hey Shell!' Shelly's eyes dart round looking for the source of the identification, fixing her gaze on Beth she races over turning her head as she goes, throwing a few comments to the man. He nods then climbs the steps into the store, racing over so quickly they practically collide, averting to a girlfriend hug.

'What are you doing here?' questions Beth.

'Oh, dad had to come in and get some supplies, so I came along for the ride... you?'

'Ha, the same, uncle Reg needed to talk to Mick at the garage, hey great to see you and in something other than school uniform or dance gear.'

'Oh yes, this is normal "Lil ol' me," Shelly quips with a slight Southern American drawl, producing a giggle from Beth who then inquires.

'Do you get into town much or is it just for dance sessions?'

'Well yes, mainly just for dance and being dropped off at the bus stop, there's not much to see, pretty small really but dad appreciates the company, it's a fifteen-minute drive from our farm, so it gives me time to chat and tell him things about school plus dance classes, although I think he acts polite, not really into it.' Beth agrees, 'I know what you mean, my uncle Reg thinks any form of artistic endeavour is, 'A bloody waste of time,' she says mocking Reg. The acting produces a snort from Shelly.

'Parents eh', she exclaims, then realising her error apologetically says, "Sorry." But Beth's no longer affected by these small faux pars', she just smiles.

'Uncle Reg is my parent now and hey, I think he's mellowing, becoming less grumpy, watch this space.'

'Old Reg, less grumpy, that'd be a first.' The comment produces a guff extracting a little acting also like a Southern Belle, fluttering her eyes, Beth rolls the drawl out.

'Oh, lawdy me, must be my feminine charm making him all flustered, oh dearie me.' They collapse against each other in fits and giggles, as they chatter, a car parks right in front of them, Beth glances up, it's an eighty's Holden Commodore. The door swings open and Johnny eases himself out, he's wearing jeans and a black T-Shirt with Metallica printed on the front, dark mirror sunglasses adorn his face with a pack of cigarettes stuck under the sleeve of his T-Shirt. Very much the image of "Mr Cool," Noogs gets out of the passenger door. She also has jeans on plus some sort of tank top, but the space around her midsection is bare. She's not fit therefore a roll of fat "Muffin top," hangs over the top of her jeans, not an attractive look, add to that some poorly chosen tattoos on her arms plus the spider's web on her neck her presence reflects her attitude. "Tough chick, don't mess with me." Johnny moves a couple of steps towards the girls, stopping and leans on the bonnet.

'Well, well, well, its Miss Precious,' then swivelling his eyes to Shelly, 'And who's this Princess Lea?' Selly's shocked, she's never had any involvement with the local louts before, she does her best with politeness.

'I'm not... I mean... I'm Shelly Byrnes.' Noogs steps forward and eyeballs Shelly.

'Shelly, you're no fucking sea shell, ya scrawny little cunt.' Shelly's eyes open wide, she bursts into tears, sliding across the seat she grabs Beth's shoulders and buries her head in the nape of Beth's neck. Beth now is the only one who can defend their position, quickly glancing round she can see local people moving, not involved in their situation but at least

nearby. This playing field is somewhat balanced she realises. Lifting her head from cuddling Shelly's sobs she states directly and with sarcasm.

'Very good, you know how to upset a twelve-year-old, wow you must be so strong, gosh where did you go to school to learn that? Oh wait, you don't go to school, what do they call that... umm, oh yes, dropouts.' Johnny smiles at the comment, he's enjoying the tete-a-tetes banter, something he doesn't usually hear.

'Oh, we enjoy lots of things out of school, driving round, having picnics with friends down by the river.' Beth's now on the back foot, the three louts obviously told Johnny about their encounter. She's embarrassed and quickly loses confidence.

'Tsk, tsk, tsk', buts in Noogs, 'Not playing with our friends, hey, all they wanted was fun and a fuckin, hey, you been broken in yet?' Tears start to well in Beth's eyes, the memory of those digesting louts perving at her, and man-handling her is about to bring her undone when a voice is heard.

'Shelly, you right.' Mr Byrnes stands next to Johnny's car, he's over six-foot tall with massive sunburnt granite hands the result of years of manual farm work. Shelly releases her grip on Beth and flies to him, burying her head into his stomach, he knows who the antagonists are but calmly calls, "Young Beth, come here love." She doesn't need a second invitation, slipping past Johnny she nestles into Mr Byrnes other shoulder, reaching into his pocket he pulls out a ten-dollar note and softly addresses the two girls.

'It's alright lasses, here, go to the store and buy yourselves a soft drink.' Shelly's slowed her snivelling, she nods reaches out takes Beth's hand and they wander over to the store. Mr Byrnes now turns to Johnny and Noogs, his eyes darken, his voice drops down a tone to almost a growl.

'You fuckin' useless pricks, if I had a gun with me, I'd shoot you right now.' His hands' clench, he stares at Johnny who is visibly shrinking in front of him, his cowardice flourishing in this antagonistic situation, Noogs, however, is made of sterner stuff.

'Hey we ain't done nothin… piss of leave us alone.' His vision changes direction, now directly at her.

'Nancy Clements, so this is how you ended up? I know all about your tough upbringing, okay tough it was but you're an adult now, what's with the bitterness? You want to go through life like this, with this attitude? Nancy, get out of here, change, try something different, make something of yourself.' During this helpful tirade, Noogs has been acting the spoilt school-girl, half-listening rolling her eyes, once he finishes, she vindictively echoes him.

''Make somethin' of yourself, do this do that, just like fuckin' school.' He stares but isn't drawn into an argument, 'fair enough, your choice.' Then returning his gaze to Johnny, he addresses him with forthrightness.

'Right I'll make this real clear for you lad, you ever touch, go near or upset my young Shelly again I won't think, I'll just get my twelve-gauge out and hunt you down, put you six feet under, no one will convict me 'cos I'll have the backing of the farming parents. They know all about you, you'll disappear off the face of the earth and no one will look for you 'cos no one cares.' Then with the most vehement snarl.

'I've hunted all my life round here, seen wild animals shot, bleeding to death in incredible pain, with a look in their eyes pleading for me to finish them off, if I take you down boy I won't be quick, I'll make sure you suffer more than those poor animals.' The ferocity of the statement rips into Johnny's soul. Mr Byrnes finishes.

'You savvy?' The best this coward can do is slur, "Yes sir." Byrnes nods, glares at Noogs who by now is also shrinking,

a voice is heard from behind.

'You right, Jim?' Reg has walked up behind Jim Byrnes, Jim turns his head.

'Yep, no worries here, everything as clear as glass thanks Reg.' Patting Reg on the shoulder, he nods and turns, both men walk away, involved a small discussion. Reg is driving home, Beth's in the front seat with him but unlike the amusing trip in she's reserved. After talking to Jim Byrnes, Reg puts enough of the pieces together, with an effort at being consoling he comments.

'Look Luv, don't worry about those dropkicks, you're safe here with me.' Looking at him inquiringly, she tries to fathom his character, she responds.

'Thanks, Uncle Reg, yes I can see that, but why are they like that? I mean it's one thing to be well... uneducated or just stupid, but what did Shelly do?' I mean she's never met them before and those moronic boys the other day at the river, I've never really met them, so why be antagonistic to me?'

'That's a tricky question Luv, don't have the answer, you'd have to be one of them psychologists to work them out but one thing I do know is that they're all stuffed in the head, well maybe not Johnny, I believe he was smart enough at school. The rest well basically back woods mentality, I believe in America they call them "hillbillies", half are inbred, the others just oxygen thieves.' Looking at him, she breaks out in a smile, "did he just crack a joke?" His colloquialism tickles her imagination, thus providing the catharsis for her subdued mood, she giggles.

'Oxygen thieves... haa, good one uncle.' Glancing at her, a glow ignites inside him, this alleviation of her social problem feathers a pronounced effect on his psyche, he's starting to feel an attachment to her. It's an area in his personality that has been dormant for a long time. Not since watching the kids playing at the local school, whistling he drives on.

CHAPTER 19

After the confrontation in the main street, Johnny has become very quiet, Noogs attempts to use bravado.

'Fuckin' farmer, who's he to tell us what to do, eh Johnny?' But there is no reply, Johnny's in a state of shock, the realistic threat has cut him to the bone. Unlike the school lecturing by teachers or parents, this was directed straight at him, personal, and he didn't like it one bit, a chill went down his spine, Noogs tries again.

'Ehh Johnny?' He gathers some resemblance of composure and snaps.

'Shut up, get in.' She hasn't seen him affected like this before and is puzzled by his reaction. Not being very adept at reading people she's just never understood that Johnny's a coward at heart and uses the likes of her and the other inferior types around him to build his ego. Confused at his reaction she follows his directions, gets in the car, and silently waits as he commences to drive off.

On the outskirts of town, a dilapidated house stands, two old wrecks of cars nest vacantly to the house. Various materials of waste and disrepair are scattered round, a mangy undernourished dog of some Kelpie breed sniffs at various

piles of garbage strewn around the bin. The fibro-cement is cracked and has splintered off in various places. Rotting stained curtains are visible inside the windows, showing it as an unkempt dump. Pills is sitting on an old petrol drum, throwing stones at a jam tin nestled on top of a fence post, he's in conversation with Tatts and Billy.

'Hey, we sure got up that tarts fanny.' Tatts guffs.

'We was going good 'til the boyfriend came back, hey Billy, why didn't cha lead him in real far so we's have time with her?' Billy's not impressed.

'Hey fuck you, w-w-what am I a bleeding g-g-greyhound running round for y-y-youse to have all the f-f-fun, w-w-what about me? She's a bit of a looker. When do I get to do somin.'

'Yeah, yeah, yeah, scoffs Pills, 'I get ya, but iffa we'd had another ten minutes she'd be pork bellied.' This offhand slang comment amuses Tatts.

'Ha ha... pork bellied.'

'Not in her belly ya dick', extorts Pills, 'I saw her thigh, jeez nice bit of muscle.'

'Muscle,' yells Billy, 'I want ta see m-m-more than m-m-muscle.' Pills grins.

'Well I tells ya, she weren't wearing much and from what I seen the next bit would be pretty good, better than lookin' at Noogs arse.' Nods in agreement all round.

'So, what do we do now?' asks Billy with an increased excitement in his voice. Pills shrugs, 'Donno, wait for Johnny, he'll show us when and what,' nodding in agreement Tatts adds.

'Yeah, he'll show us when with her twat.' This produces laughter all round.

Johnny's driving is erratic with speed the main essence, even Noogs is unsure regarding her safety in the car, she tries to calm him down.

'Ya going out to Pill's place?'

'Maybe,' He drives on recklessly, she tries again.

'Let's meet the boys and have a talk about that little tart.' Snapping his head ninety degrees, he vents his inner fears.

'Fuck her Noogs, I don't want that farmer prick chasing me with no twelve-gauge.' Realisation sinks into Noogs at last, she now understands that Mr Byrnes got to Johnny now she needs to think quickly to get Johnny back on-side. She knows enough that without Johnny their little gang would be rudderless, an idea surfaces.

'Hey Johnny, forget him and that scrawny daughter of his, we was never interested in her, I was just pulling her leg, you know, muckin' round, having fun. Its little miss precious who's got up our noses. Remember she lives in town, the other little fucker lives miles out of town, they hardly ever come in.' Johnny decreases speed.

'You're right and I saw her with that old guy Reg, she must be living with him, he's a decrepit old thing, one push and his bones would snap.' A smile returns to Johnny's face.

'Yeah, they got nothing to do with the farmers, although they live in town, they're the ones isolated… hey! I'm using big words again! Yeah, and I did promise you and the boys some fun, Yeah, let's go see them and chat, we got plans to make Noogs, we got plans to make.' He drives on at a reasonable speed, Noogs smiles to herself, "Yep, Johnny's Back."

CHAPTER 20

Reg parks the car in the garage, they get out then enter the house, he explains.

'I've got some wiring to fix up in the backyard, will be out there for a while.' She nods, and answers.

'I've almost finished my homework, might come outside and read a book, we've got to study it for literature.'

'Okay Luv, it's a nice day so best get to it.' He grabs his weather-beaten slouch hat from the edge of the bench smiles at her and exits to the backyard, Beth gets a glass from the draining board, half fills it with water and sits at the table, thinking deeply regarding the day's events. Weighing up the facts she nods and flicks her hair, clearly, she poses to herself, the idiots are to be wary of, but with Geoff, Karen and definitely Rod she is safe in their protection. Also, Uncle, Reg has stepped somewhat into the breach, she now feels safer in these surrounds. His developing genial attitude has propitiated her psyche, she gets up from the table with an invigoration that only security can evoke and traipses to her room.

Rummaging round in her bag she finds the literature book that's required for school, continuing to glance round she spies her swimsuit which was discarded yesterday after the

involvement down by the creek. Realising that her sunbaking was interrupted yesterday, the inclination returns to catch some rays. The lovely day with intermittent cloud cover attunes itself to her in almost a sybaritic way, "This would be a lovely afternoon in the backyard, catching some rays, reading a book while uncle Reg works. Just like the old days, well sort of but well yes a really nice afternoon." Slipping into the bikini then shorts and a loose top, she grabs a towel and heads towards the backyard. Reg is grappling with chicken wire, trying to stretch and retighten the barriers round his vegie patch. Hearing the door slam, he looks up as Beth descends the back-steps to the yard. The grass although not recently cut isn't too long, easily comfortable enough to lie on, choosing a spot she delicately lays out the towel. Lying down on her stomach she positions the book in front of her, further forward Reg is wrestling with the wire, she calls.

'Tough going?' He looks up between forced grimaces and comments in an exasperated way.

'Bloody stuff won't do as its told.'

'Do you need a hand?'

'Naa, okay here, done it many times, you just relax and read, I'll win this bloody battle.'

'All right but just call if you need an extra pair of hands, I'm going to catch some rays.' Lowering her head, she directs her attention towards the book, he glances, nods then returns his attack towards the chicken wire. Time drifts, the sun is winning the battle with the clouds of which will be the dominant element, the day heats up, Reg is gradually getting in control of the tangled mess of chicken wire, stopping to brush his brow with a handkerchief that was stuck in his back pocket. Beth has also warmed up, she decides to discard the outer shirt and shorts, standing she slips the shirt over her head and drops the shorts, at the start of her movement, the slight rustling sound is captured by Reg, as she stands, he asks.

'You right?'

'Yes, just going to catch some more rays.' With an effortless motion, she discards her outer garments, he stares in disbelief, what she believes is just a cute little teenage bikini that most teenage girls would wear down the beach or at the local pool, to him he sees the most minuscule pieces of fabric just barely covering her private parts. It's like a scene straight out of "Lolita", to make matters worse as she turns and straightens her briefs, she exposes to him that they are the new style that is almost like G-String at the back, leaving her backside cheeks completely exposed. In his conservative opinion she is practically buck-naked, stretching and then smiling at him she comments.

'It's a really nice day.' And with that, she lies face down on the towel and continues reading. He's transfixed but recovering attempts to return to the job with fixing the fencing wire, occasionally he glances up only to be met by a vision of two firm breasts being reasonably held by the bikini top but still obvious and her backsides gleaming in the sun like two whales frolicking in unison in the ocean. Trying to find the right words he is perplexed by his inability to do so, Beth rolls on her side leaning against one elbow the movement and her change of position does nothing to ease his uncomfortable disposition. Struggling with what he believes in his righteous mind is an iniquitous situation, he somehow delves deeply into his resilient character and drags his wandering eyes back to the chicken-wire and the task at hand. During the manual operation the pull of curiosity drags his eyes back to her relaxing in the sun. He's fighting to rationalise this social conundrum, which is threatening his conservative environment, as he works she occasionally shifts position, this causes their glances to meet, whereas she is relaxed in her position and returns his acknowledgment with a demure smile he has to act calm, as if this is the norm, nothing out of the

ordinary here, which is as far from the truth as is possible. His mind is not wholly on the task at hand, eventually his hand slips and the wire grabs his finger squeezing it against the post.

'Ouch, dammit,' he curses. Looking up and quickly putting two and two together, she realises he could do with another pair of hands, before he can refuse, she calls.

'Wait there, I'll hold while you nail.' Dropping the book, she moves across to his work area, it's happened too quickly for him to discard her invitation or reject it. The next thing he knows she is standing straight in front of him with that inquisitive smile like a ten-year old ready to help dad.

'Do you want me to hold this while you hammer?' He knows he needs assistance but this will be more than tricky, with her lithe almost naked image directly in front of him, he's supposed to concentrate on accuracy regarding hammering a nail in to support the wire. Concentrating he looks her in the eye then directs.

'Okay hold this still, just here, yes.' Now he directs his attention to the nail, the trouble is her breasts are directly in line with his field of vision. Swallowing he swings the hammer, "miracle upon miracles," he thinks the nail is hit perfectly. Confidence is restored he concentrates and succeeds with a second hit, the nail is three quarters in, feeling relaxed that one more hit will fix it he swings the hammer upwards to make the final stroke. She readjusts her stance, not a great deal but enough to make her breasts bobble. The movement does the job of distracting him in a minor way, he misses the nail and hits his thumb, with a scream of agony, he drops the hammer and jumps in the air.

'Ahh… jeez… ohh… bloody hell.' Grabbing his thumb, he bounds round the yard like a headless chook, without realising she is the cause of his attention wavering she springs into action.

'Ohh… ohh, Uncle Reg, ohh… ohh, heck, stay there

I'll get some band-aids.' She bounds off into the house. Flying in the back door, she heads straight for the bathroom and the medicine cabinet. Rummaging around she finds band-aids and Savlon cream. Whipping back to the yard she sees Reg in pain holding his thumb with his other hand.

'Quick uncle Reg over here to the tap, we need to wash it then put some antiseptic on it then band-aids.' Understanding the procedure and allowing Beth to take control he wanders over to the backyard gully trap and lets her turn on the tap, putting his hand under the cold water, the throbbing starts to subside.

'Take your thumb out,' she instructs sympathetically.

'Hold it still the bleedings stopped, I'll dry it, put some Savlon on it then bandage it.' Drying the wound, she is careful to be delicate especially when applying the antiseptic cream. Although sore, Reg is amazed at her delicate touch, it's more than the standard nurse's treatment, this is performed with caring, the softness of her touch and stroke in applying the cream does more than treat the wound, it pacifies his soul. Never before has anyone so cared for him in such a delicate and loving way, as she applies the band-aid she is concentrating on the task. He is in close proximity and although allowing her to tender the wound he is looking at her body. Looking up she smiles but is curious at the line of his gaze, it's almost as if he is studying her not the thumb that she is holding. A small feeling of curiosity creeps into her head but with a flick of her head she's dismissed it, with authority she states.

'Right, I think that'll fix it.' At the first word of the statement, he raises his eyes to meet hers, before any words of gratitude are admitted he holds her gaze, she does the same but reads his thoughts differently. To her interpretation there is something behind his eyes, something fighting for recognition, something that hasn't evolved for a long time like an appreciation of kindness. Her gentle touch has seemed

to broken down some internal barrier, unable to completely understand this situation she still believes that her presence and help is accelerating the mellowing of his character. But one question remains with her, "was he, looking at me that way as I tended his wound?" She was the concerned one, playing nurse tending his wound, definitely showing outward emotion directed towards his wellbeing. Confusion reigns in her head, trying to think logically she comes to the realisation that maybe she just misjudged the situation, returning from these thoughts she commands.

'Right uncle Reg, nurse Beth in charge here, you need to go into the parlour and rest in your comfy chair,' he nods weakly, this whole affair has drained him. Like a dispirited sheep being led to the slaughter, he drags himself inside and flops into the chair. She opens the fridge and extracts a can of beer, pops the ring top then grabbing a glass presents it to him.

'Here we are uncle Reg, this'll make you feel better.' Looking up, he smiles weekly, somehow gaining the strength to reply.

'Thanks, Luv.' Again, the use of the word "Luv" is a catalyst for her to show physical emotion towards him. Leaning forward and putting her arms around his neck, she gives him a hug, not noticing his reluctance or inability to reciprocate the physical show of emotion. He doesn't know where or the appropriate place to place his hands, especially when in front of him is just a palpable form of female flesh, completely overwhelmed he manages to babble.

'Umm, well… umm thanks.' Breaking away and standing taught in front of him, acting a little like a sergeant-major she declares.

'No worries nurse Beth is on hand, anything you need just ask. Now don't worry about dinner, I'll attend to that later, you just rest, I'll go outside for a while and continue reading my book.' With that, she and heads out through the backdoor,

the relief on his face at the departure of her physical presence enables him to relax. He seems to sink further into the chair, almost as if it is swallowing him, like a Joey returning to the safety of its mother's pouch. Security in stable surrounds, at last resonate through his body. The whole episode has been overwhelming but now he is embedded in his secluded peaceful domain, an air of calmness envelopes him, influencing him, he drifts off to sleep. In the backyard Beth again relaxes on the towel, picking up the book her thoughts stray from the text.

"Did he look at me while I was tending him? If so, why?" Trying to reason the information at her disposal it's rather confusing trying to gain insight into this situation.

"He went to mend the fence, I came outside to read and sunbake, all seemed normal, it got hot, he was struggling with the wire, I slipped off into my swimwear to catch more of the rays. Occasionally we'd smile, we seemed contented not intruding in the others space, he was glancing at me as I read then he jammed his finger, I rushed to help, he seemed uncomfortable at my presence but allowed me to help. It was then when he hit his thumb, I rushed inside to the first-aid cabinet came back cleaned and dressed his wound then helped him inside. But where's the connection for him looking at me? I was only... ohh, I was sunbaking in my bikini. The trouble started when I got rid of my skirt and top, maybe he hasn't been in the presence of young girls, probably for a long time and I'm flouncing around in my swimwear, he hasn't seen that sort of thing much... hey, but I'm here now, I'm family, that's different surely." The inquisition brings forth questions but no real answers, deciding there is no solution at the moment to the questions, she has posed to herself she returns to the book. Time moves on, the afternoon evaporates into dusk, Reg is drowsing in his chair, now dressed appropriately Beth enters the kitchen, a pang of remorse envelopes her as she glances at him listless in the chair, there is a worn-down look about him,

this twigs a spark of interest in her. She realises that actually she knows very little about him or his life, the only small amount that her father explained wasn't much and sparingly presented. "I need to find more information about him,' she rationalises to herself, "If not from him maybe Karen." With the sound of movement from the kitchen, Reg stirs, glancing at Beth.

'Hello, Luv, what you doing?'

'Preparing dinner uncle Reg. We're having sausages, peas and mash, you just sit there.' He smiles, 'Well done girl.' She reciprocates, 'Yep, no worries, nurse Beth is now chef Beth.' Smiling, he wonders, "Youth, how can they be so bubbly?" then answers.

'Good on you Luv.' She extends the conversation.

'Oh, and how's the thumb?'

'Much better but it'll be swollen for a few days, probably black and blue.'

'No worries,' she beams, 'I'll check it before you go to bed.'

'Thanks, Luv, oh and how's that book you were reading?' She starts to answer whilst preparing the tea, again, a warm glow envelopes her, the feeling of family, the conversation develops.

CHAPTER 21

Johnny has relaxed and is driving in a relatively normal way, Noogs sits next to him, she's also relaxed believing she has calmed him down and redirected his thoughts. However, Johnny is stewing over a number of things in his head, what Noogs doesn't realise is that the confrontation with Mr Byrnes has definitely put a chink in his armour. Not that he was the brave and adventurous type anyway but his "Mr Cool", demeanour has been somewhat tarnished in his own eyes. It's obvious to him that the town is definitely too small, really, it's time to move on but he'd like to go out with a bang, yet with no repercussions on him. Glancing at Noogs he's summed her up, overweight, unattractive and bitter, destined for jail and a miserable life, fun to be around 'cos she can antagonise situations but no way does he want to be around when the boom comes down and it will in the near future. As for the three halfwits, they're so easily led and they worship the ground he walks on, they can be manipulated to do anything he wishes.

"Yeah," he grins to himself, "they're the puppets and I'm the puppet master but caution is needed to direct them in the appropriate way so when they go down, I'll not be involved or go down with them." Smiling to himself, he has it sorted

in his brain, "Feed the cockroaches, watch 'em swarm, view the last encounter then vamoose, outa sight, outer mind, no repercussions."

'Hey Noogs, when we get to Pills place, I'll drop you off, you have a good old "pow-wow", with the boys, I got some thinking to do.'

'Thinking Johnny?'

'Yep, how we're going to put this puzzle together, so you and the boys can enjoy yourselves.'

'Enjoy, fun, love those words, Johnny.'

'Yep,' he extends her thoughts processes, 'You need it, you deserve it.' With a satisfied look of awe on her face, she thinks

'He really is a great guy, thinking about us, love being round him.'

CHAPTER 22

Next morning Beth is organising her belongings for school, grabbing and stowing some food from the fridge into her bag, she races down the passageway calling out as she passes Reg's door.

'Goodbye uncle Reg, I'm off, see you tonight.' A muffled "Righto" is heard as she zips out the front door and down the steps, enjoying the brisk walk in the crisp morning air she arrives at the bus stop with plenty of time up her sleeve, no-one else has arrived yet. Sitting on the bus-stop seat, she has time to dwell on the weekend, mainly her thoughts are directed towards Shelly. The probing question is how will she be after the awful involvement with Noogs, discretion will need to be the manner of the trip. Soon enough the "Mum's Taxis" appear and drop off the kids, Shelly's mum is the last one to deposit the child, walking up to Beth, Shelly gives her a smile, a relieved Beth greets her.

'Good to see you, Shell.'

'You too' is the honest reply.'

'Let's have a chat on the bus.'

'Yes, that'd be good.' They hug simultaneously, the bus appears and they board moving to the rear seat. All part of the

pecking order, older ones command the rear of the bus. Sitting, they place their bags next to them, Beth tries to alleviate any leftover tension by asking.

'Shelly, did you have a nice weekend?' Shelly's thrown for a second, knowing what happened, looks, then realising she's just pulling her leg, joins in the playful banter acting matter of fact.

'Oh yes, just the same old same old, nothing spesh.' Looks are exchanged, they suddenly burst into laughter, the tension is broken as they continue to giggle. The younger ones in the front seats turn with uncertain expressions, calming down Shelly comments.

'Very funny, but as you can expect I've got some questions.' Beth nods, still smiling but the discussion becomes more serious, Shelly continues.

'I've talked to my dad but he's as much in the dark as to why that horrible girl would … well verbally attack me that way, was it because I was with you?' Smiling to herself, Beth knows that this girl is no-one's fool, she's pieced it together pretty well, time to elucidate the information she has at hand.

'Look, its nothing to do with you and yes rather your association.'

'Association?'

'Yes, and actually not very much to do with me, you see our friend and dance teacher Karen went to school with Noo… umm, Nancy and well… let's say Nancy wasn't brought up in a loving household, at school the other girls, Karen included were pretty mean to her.'

'But,' buts in Shelly. 'That was years ago, Karen's in her mid-twenties now, all those little school fights and squabbles should have been left behind, as you grow and make your way in the world.'

'Correct, you're right, but remember this is a very small town, still-waters run deep.' The saying slightly confuses Shelly.

'You mean?'

'Well, very little happens here, you certainly don't grow away from your roots, everything is too close, as you grow, so the town closes in on you, it suffocates you plus your memories, there's no getting away. If you can't escape its tension, especially to do with your past, well it builds, you fester, worry, this worrying turns from defensive mode into attack, revenge. That's where Nancy is, others have moved on only Karen is around she's now the target and Nancy wants to attack anything to do with her. It's like getting revenge for the past, I've become a friend of Karen's, so I'm in the firing line as if to say, you're a friend of mine, so you got a burst.'

'Realisation dawns on Shelly.

'But I don't live in the town.'

'Correct again, so you are safe, you only come in with your dad. Uncle Reg told me that your dad had a word with them after you and I went to the store, I believe he put the fear of God in them. I'm pretty sure they won't ever say or do anything to you again, you might get a look or a half sneer but that'd be about it.'

'So,' continues Shelly, 'I'm pretty safe, what about you?'

'Well I'm not sure', I don't know her and have only spoken to her when she's been inside Johnny's car and that was only swearing and sexual innuendo, we've never really met.'

'Weird.'

'Yes, it happened the other night when I was walking home with Rod after dinner at Karen's.' Ears prick up.

'Walking home, with a boy after dinner, wow... ahh, like is he your boyfriend?'

'Well... umm...,' she becomes a little reserved, 'I guess like a friend who's a boy, sort of...'

'He is, you're blushing, oh god wait till I tell the girls.'

'No wait, please don't, it's not anything special yet, it might not work out, let it ride please, don't blab.' Stopping in

mid excitement Shelly gazes at Beth, focusing on her she thinks and starts to understand, choosing her words carefully, she discloses.

'Yes, you're right, sorry, I got carried away, that's your personal life, god I almost fell into small-town gossip. Forgive me, if there's anything you want to share, feel free but I won't mention it to anyone, not even my parents.' Beth breathes a sigh of relief.

'Thank you, you're very understanding for your years, tell you what, I'll give you some outlines but nothing specific, might be of use to you in the future, deal?' Beaming Shelly agrees, 'done deal,' now what did you say he does'?

'Shelly.'

'Okay, okay, let's talk dance, I saw a video clip...' The bus rolls on, talking and giggling carries the trip.

CHAPTER 23

Geoff and Rod are on a house a block in from the main town, Geoff glances at his watch.

'Hey, it's twelve-thirty, do you want to go down to the store for us and grab some lunch?'

'Okay', is the reply, 'What do you want?'

'Oh, a pie and a sausage-roll will do, oh and a can of ginger-beer, get what you want for yourself.' He hands Rod a fifty dollar note and returns to fiddling with a pipe connection. Rod ambles off, in a short while he's in the main street just gazing round at the minimal activity, climbing the steps to the general store, the door swings open and Johnny exits, their paths cross. This is now a one on one meeting, a level playing field, Rod eyeballs him, sticking his chest out plus a slight clenching of his fists, he's expecting a look or an offhand comment. He's really surprised when Johnny addresses him personally. 'Oh hi, Rod... umm glad you're here, look have you got a minute, umm... I need to explain a few things and, guess, apologise.'

'Apologise?' Rod's slightly taken back. 'Yes?' Johnny's relaxed and, confident, his "Mr Cool" persona is nicely motoring. He explains.

'Look, firstly, the other day with me and the guys in the car, sorry 'bout that. They're fools, I know, I should have put them in order, but I was pissed off with life and let them carry on. I've had a few things go wrong with my work and well... this town's not going to do it for me, I'm moving on reasonably soon.' Listening intently, Rod believes he notices sincerity and nods in agreement.

'Yeah, I know what you mean, our works drying up, there's just enough to keep us afloat, we'll probably have to move on as well.' Nods of endorsement come from Johnny.

'Yeah, but I'm not going to the next town, I'm going to the city to try my luck, got a mate down there and he's got plenty of building work, so I'll give that a go.'

'Fair enough,' agrees Rod, 'But what about that business with Pills and his halfwit mates down by the river the other weekend'?

'Hey, I knew nothing about that 'till they came back to Pill's place braggin' about how they upset you and the girl, look I know they're morons but it was more than dumb it was unkind.'

'Unkind', thinks Rod, 'Johnny's thinking about kindness,' he ushers a forceful reply.

'Yes, it was, she was very upset.' Johnny's really conciliatory now.

'Yep I agree, those three are well... really backwoods types they need careful handling, I guess they sort of look up to me 'cos I've got a car, anyway, I told them off and I promise nothing like that will happen again.' Rod tries to ascertain if it's an act or he's fair-dinkum, deciding on the later he agrees to take him on face value.

'Okay, fair enough, if you say that's the end of it then we'll let it rest, thanks.' A smile breaks on Johnny's face,

'Good, gotta go, see you round.' Watching Johnny walk away Rod swears he has a spring in his step, he continues

watching until Johnny's out of sight. This vexing conversation has him confused but he decides to roll with it and enters the general store.

CHAPTER 24

At the High School Beth is seated in the cafeteria with her friends, conversation is general, when one of the girls, Jenny, asks Beth how the weekend was, Beth dwells, pauses and starts thinking, the break in the answer causes a halt in their conversing. Everyone's attention is directed towards Beth, the inquisitive gazing acts as a catalyst to tension. Beth glances round noticing that she has become the focal point of their attention. A decision on how much information she will disclose becomes paramount, she edges in carefully, it's like verbally treading on eggshells.

'Well it was going to be good, Rod and I were going on a picnic…' Interjections fire from left and right.

'Rod… picnic… who's Rod… picnic, where?'

'Woah, he's just a friend from my town.' Jenny's direct, 'You don't have a picnic with just a friend from town, expand girl.' Wearily Beth tries, 'Well he might become, I mean it might become…' Jenny's in again like a hawk.

'Might means is, 'cos you're hedging, okay come on spill, gritty details girl.' This is not quite the low-key school friend's conversation she envisaged or even wants, she decides to tell a few details but watered down a fraction.

'Well we went out of town a couple of K's to this really cool spot down by the river, we went swimming and came back and were relaxing...'

'Ha,' is the vigorous retort by Jenny, 'Right!'

'Well, we were when this boy appeared and threw stones at us, Rod got really mad and chased him into the wood, they disappeared but two of the boys' friends snuck up on me while Rod was away and they sort of... umm...' Her friend's eyes are like laser beams.

'Well, sort of accosted me.'

'What!' shouts Jenny, 'accosted,' with this she completely loses the plot becoming overcome with anxiety.

'Fuckin' hell, shit... oh god, oh Beth, you're so calm... did they... oh god... I mean... oh Jesus... you okay?'

'Yes, yes I'm fine, Rod came back before anything much happened, he scared them away, so we packed up and went home.'

'Wow,' breaths Ira, another girl in the group. Jenny's more inquisitive.

'You said much, what's much?'

'Oh, nothing really, they just sort of tried to talk dirty with some minor touching.' Ira's mouth drops open.

'Minor touching, what's minor touching... oh, don't answer, don't think I want to go there.'

'It's okay,' responds Beth, trying to calm the inquisition down, 'Just hands on the shoulder, nothing more.' Leon now inquires.

'Who were they, did you know them?'

'Sort of, the one who threw the stones was called Billy Surso, the others I'm not sure of their names. Pilson and Smith, I think.'

'Billy Surso,' thinks Jenny. 'I know that name, yes, my older brother had a friend who lived in Luina for a while. Umm... he went to school with Billy Surso, now what did they

say about him? Not sure but it's something like he was some sort of half-wit maybe inbreed and they used to set him up for pranks at school. I think they were a bit mean to him, the teachers turned a blind eye 'cos they couldn't stand him. That's right, they said he smelt bad like he never washed or something, they had a nick-name for him, now what was it... umm steely, ... no, smelly... yes that was it "Smelly Surso." He hated it and dropped out by the second year of High School, no-one cared, he dropped off the face of the earth, well local area round here anyway.' Beth's adds.

'Well he's in my neck of the woods and part of a gang of half-wits, so I've got to keep my eyes open.' Consternation has enveloped the group during this conversation, they've come to really like Beth she's good company with a bit of wag about her, these discussions are worrying to all of them, they feel for her safety, Jenny pipes up.

'Look if things ever get too hot for you over there, I'm sure my folks would put you up.'

'Oh thanks,' reply's Beth, 'But I live with my uncle Reg, I told him about it and he's on the lookout, so I'm perfectly safe. Also, Rod is apprentice to Geoff and they've said if ever anything looks like going wrong, I could board with them but I don't think it'll come to that, 'cos they are both very big and strong, the weedy half-wits wouldn't stand a chance against them.' Ira agrees, 'Well it looks like you've got it covered, so that's cool... now about this Rod?'

'Ahh, no, no', implores Beth, holding her hands up in mock surrender, 'Umm later, maybe.' Eyebrows round the table are raised, eyes flash to each other, the vultures are circling for information. Beth holds her defensive mode.

'Later you guys, later.'

CHAPTER 25

On the bus trip home, Shelly inquires about her day. Beth explains that she let drop about her happening at the creek to her school friends, laughing she explains she admonished them humorously.

'Talk about the Spanish Inquisition, I was able to give them just enough info to keep them satisfied.'

'I guess they were interested and trying to help with advice, boy you sure live an exciting life.'

'Ha,' snorts Beth, 'the type of excitement I can do without.'

'Yeah, I see your point, hang in.' They chatter as the bus winds its way along the country road. Reaching its destination, the bus stops close to the general store, everyone exits, Shelly and Beth are the last out, they hug goodbye then Shelly sprints across to her mother's car. With a wave she's gone, Beth stands still for a moment perusing the main street, no sign of life at four-thirty in the afternoon, with a shrug of her shoulders she moves off. Passing the general store, she jumps slightly as the door flies open and Billy Surso with a can of drink in his hand ambles out. Seeing her he stops, there's only the two of them, the tension mounts. Her eyes narrow she

cautiously looks him but quickly notices he doesn't respond. Curious at his ambivalent nature she decides on a different tack, with warmth of tone in her voice she addresses him.

'Hi Billy... it is Billy, isn't it?' He's really unsure and uncomfortable.

'Yeah, might be.'

'We haven't really met.' His gaucherie in manner hinders his ability to follow polite conversation, the best he can do is.

'Err... nah.' Understanding a bit about him, she tries to slant the conversation to a level he can handle.

'Well you live in town and I do also, I thought I'd better say hi and introduce myself, I'm Beth.' This normal form of civility is so foreign to him it's as if he was conversing to an alien. Basically, he doesn't know how to respond, in an undignified way, he splutters.

'Yeah, well yous right, I-I-I'm Billy.'

'Great, how are you doing?'

'Alright, I g-g-guess.'

'Can I ask you a question?'

'... suppose.'

'Why did you throw stones at us the other day?'

'Dunno... somin' to do.'

'Well, when you ran off, your two friends hung around me and were rude, I was a bit frightened, do you think that was right?' He's just a simple person unable to think outside the square or even have a personal opinion. He mumbles.

'Donno, we was just m-m-muckin' round, havin' f-f-fun.' Beth presses her point.

'Did you think that I might have been scared?'

'Nah, was j-j-just fun.'

'But it wasn't for me, you can see that, can't you?' This hammering of the point gradually breaks through.

'I guess, umm... sorry.' Inwardly she breathes a sigh of

relief, thinking constructively she attempts to build a bridge.

'Okay, accepted, well we can be friends now.' However, this simple platitude does not have the desired effect, he becomes cautious showing anxiety.

'Why, why you w-w-wanna be friends with me, you're s-s-smart, I'm not, what you wanna d-d-do with me?' His aggressive response to her humble request forces her onto the back foot.

'Umm, because I live here, it's normal to be friends with people, especially when they live in a small town, it's what people do.'

'People do, people round here never d-d-done anything normal to me or me m-m-mates. You're smart, y-y-you be normal, I don't want these normal f-f-fuckers… what does Noogs call ya… precious, you go be p-p-precious to all these n-n-normal ones. I got me mates, their me f f-friends, not you fuckers, you s-s-stick with your friends an' I'll s-s-stick with mine, yeah, mine, not y-y-yours!' With that tirade, he storms off down the street, she watches him march off, she's completely perplexed, the simple attempt to build a friendship and repair some bridges has gone up in smoke. Shaking her head, she reasons to herself, "well I tried," confused by his reaction but resigned to his obdurate response she turns and heads home.

CHAPTER 26

Entering the house, she dumps her bag in her room and moves to the kitchen, getting a glass from draining board and then filling it with water she glances out the window. Reg is in the backyard working on the chicken wire again, at the sound of the backdoor slamming Reg looks up, Beth's in her school uniform walking towards him.

'Hi uncle Reg, how's the thumb?' A smile breaks across his face.

'Ahh, you're home, thumbs okay thanks Luv, how was your day.'

'Okay,' with slight hesitation, she continues. 'I bumped into Billy Surso in town, just as I got off the bus.' Reg's eyes narrow, his furrowed brow tightens.

'Yeah, and what did he want?'

'Oh, not him, more me, I tried to be friendly and get him onside, sort of amicable like a friend, well more like a friendly acquaintance.' Reg stops his work.

'Right, go on, what happened?'

'Well I thought I was getting through to him, he even said sorry for throwing stones at us down by the river, but when I suggested we be friendly 'cos we live in the same town,

well, his attitude changed. It's as if he hates the town's people, normal people he called them, it didn't work, he sort of gave me a blast ranting that his mates were his friends, not mine and to stick to my own lot, the smart ones he called them.' Reg takes it all in, nodding as she explains the intricacies of their meeting. He then explains.

'Not surprised, he never got on with the other kids here or the townsfolk. His father was an itinerant worker, therefore never around, his mother poorly educated, don't think she could read, they lived alone in the backblocks, I believe the house was squalor. She's still there, but nobody sees her, Billy runs free, has done all his life. He went to school spasmodically but looking at the gene pool don't think it was great. He's almost a sandwich short of a picnic, almost, not quite, definitely on the lower end of the intelligence pecking order, school was not his domain.'

'No,' she adds, 'I was talking to some friends at school, their older brothers knew him, I think he was teased for being backward.'

'Yep, that'd be right, not really fair but life isn't fair is it!' His last phrase is delivered in an atavistic manner, a subconscious reference to his past, the manner of the delivery tweaks her curiosity but she decides to stay on track.

'Well anyway, my effort failed, he's not interested in being friends.'

'Don't worry,' 'he's harmless.' Smiling but not a hundred per cent sure about his summation of the situation she presents a relaxed demeanour asking.

'What's for dinner?' His reply is quite positive.

'Chicken for a change, I got some in town the other day.'

'Oh, that's good,' she bubbles, 'I'll do some homework then help you with the vegies.'

'Done deal, girl, sounds good, plus a little extra.'

'A little extra', she thinks, 'What's that?'

'Well', He continues, 'Best get on with this wire.'

Stooping, he grabs the wire and starts to bend and manipulate it, Beth turns on her heels and heads into the house. Picking various textbooks from her bag, she spreads herself over the kitchen table and starts the work. Time passes and dusk descends, Reg enters with a satisfied look on his face, he strides in like a town crier ready to make an announcement to those in front. His footsteps force her to glance up, she can tell he's pleased with himself, his demeanour has an earthly radiance, he announces.

'Not beaten by that stuff, got on top of it, she's all Jake.'

'Good, well done, I'll clear this away, I'm finished anyway.' Clearing the books into her bag, she deposits them in her bedroom, Reg has disappeared into the bathroom to wash his hands, both re-enter the kitchen he orders but more in the manner of a request.

'I'll do the chicken if you like and you can do the vegies.' Beth nods in agreement, he then walks to the fridge and takes out a can of beer but before pulling the ring top, he asks.

'Do you want a drink Luv?'

'Oh thanks, I'll get a water', is the cheerful reply. He continues.

'No, I mean a drink with dinner, he reaches in again and produces a bottle of wine. Holding it like it's a prize won in a competition he proudly announces.

'It's a Pino Gris like you tried at home.'

"Oh gosh," she thinks to herself, "We are moving ahead, careful how you handle this," Replying in a polite more adult way.

'Thank you, uncle Reg, that'd be very nice.' He smiles, unscrews the top of the bottle and pours some in a glass that he's extracted from the cupboard, handing it to her he toasts.

'Cheers Luv,' and clinks his beer can to her glass, then

takes a swig. Following suit, she sips the wine, it's clear, dry but refreshing, accelerating her taste buds she has another sip.

'Slowly,' he buts in, 'Only one and it's got to last all dinner.' Grinning, she nods in understanding, places the glass on the table and returns to peeling and preparing the vegetables. The chicken doesn't take very long, her vegetables have been timed to finish at about the same time, placing a fillet on each plate, she spoons out the vegies and they sit.

'Well get stuck in, 'Looks good lass.' They start dinner, the conversation returns to their discussion earlier regarding Billy and his friends, as he expounds various details, she stores in her memory, all the while sipping at the wine. Soon she starts to feel a warm glow inside and discards her school jumper, at a few of his offhand comments she laughs, his colloquialisms tickle her sense of humour. Like many people he's quite amusing when he's displaying his normal viewpoints using his Australian vernacular. He's also noticed the extent that she is involved in the conversation, laughing at his terminology, there is a developing renaissance in the house and he believes that it's him driving it. The spark of life now is drifting through a house that it was devoid of before, although not influenced by the alcohol he also feels an inner warmth that's generated by her. They finish dinner, she explains.

'I'm bushed, I'll have a shower then go to bed.' His response echo's her thoughts.

'Yep Luv, I'm tired as well, might retire early, you go in the bathroom first, I'll tidy up here.'

'Right,' is the pleasant answer, she leans forward and gives him a hug.

'Thanks for the wine,' then giggling a fraction, 'It was yummy.' Again, he's not sure how to react, his hands hang limp by his side, breaking away she heads down the passageway to her room. There is a freedom in her movement, a relaxed detachment, the result of the wine consumed. In the room, the

wine has really broken down her polite façade, she drops out of the school dress, discards the sneakers, picks up her nightie and towel and heads out towards the bathroom. At the sound of footsteps, Reg who is washing dishes at the sink turns his head to comment but freezes as Beth swoons through the kitchen in her underwear, towel and nightie slung across her shoulder, completely oblivious to his stare.

'Won't be long, you can use it next,' is the throwaway line to him as she disappears into the bathroom, with the wine having a seductive effect, she doesn't bother to close the door. With it half-open he can see from his position all the movement inside. Beth turns on the water taps feeling the downpour for the water to reach its suitable temperature, with the water temperature feeling correct she places her hands behind her back and undoes the bra strap which is dropped to the side. Lowering her briefs, she flicks them off, so they land next to the discarded bra, then she steps into the shower, this whole process has been viewed by Reg, she has been oblivious to his gaze, he has watched the whole procedure but stands at the sink with a frown on his face. Hearing the water splashing around he walks to the bathroom and closes the door, sitting at the kitchen table he ponders, internalising his thoughts. The sound of the shower water ceases, he returns to the sink and finishes the dishes. The sound of the bathroom door opening alerts his senses, at the light flapping of footsteps on the linoleum floor, he raises his head. Beth moves across the kitchen in her nighty, bra and panties in one hand towel in the other, she slows and faces him to tell him that she's finished. He stares in disbelief, with the backlight from the rear of the kitchen, her body outline is completely visible to him, it leaves nothing to his imagination regarding the female form. He's nonplussed, rooted to the spot, she however happily informs him.

'I'm done uncle Reg, it's all yours.' With effort he

smiles, but it's a forced smile, trying the best he can muster to seem normal he answers.

'Righto, almost done here, goodnight.' Shaking her damp hair, she smiles delivers a soft "Night," turns and disappears down the passageway, he is left standing at the sink, still rooted to the spot. His household situation has changed so much that his thoughts are as tangled as the chicken wire outside. Sitting at the table he is again immersed in deep concentration, desperately trying to find a way or method not only to handle this situation but to work out just how he fits in. He's admonishing himself but is oblivious to any answers, to him the generation gap has made his house uncomfortable to live in. Although intrigued by her he must find a solution for harmony to reign in the household, just for his own peace of mind.

CHAPTER 27

Up at Pill's house, the gang is hanging around outside, the talk is general with no specific point, Noogs asks.

'Where's Billy, thought he was coming up?' The question is met with various shoulder shrugs of indifference, a distant sound of footsteps is heard scrunching thru gravel, Billy appears Pills greets him.

'Hey Billy, how's it going man?' The response, however, is somewhat subdued.

'Yeah, 'right, I guess.' Noogs picks up his deference.

'What's up Billy?'

'Nuthin' m-m-much.'

'No, where you been?'

'In town.'

'Okay, what happened there?' He becomes hesitant to disclose.

'Nuthin', bought a drink.'

'Right... so who else was there?'

'Nobody, j-j-just ...'

'Just who Billy?'

'You know that g-g-girl, like the one who's f-f-friends with Rod.'

'Okay, what was she doing?'

'Nothin', got o-o-off the school bus.' Noogs knows Billy, he's hiding something, he doesn't express himself very articulately, his limited conversation makes him vulnerable to interrogation, she continues to use leverage.

'Did she say something to you.' Slowing down what is already a limited conversation, he stumbles on with the attempt to express himself.

'She sort of... well, t-t-t, talked about the time at the creek, told me we s-s-scared her.'

'Yes...?'

'I said s-s-sorry.' Noog's teeth clench.

'Did you.'

'Yeah but she said she wanted to be f-f-friends, I didn't l-l-like that, like it was an act or s-s somin,' so I said no, I got me m-m-mates.' Noog's teeth unclench, but her eyes narrow.

'That fuckin' little minx, you know what she was tryin' to do don't 'cha.' Pills looks at Tatts, they're both in the dark here.

'What,' blurts out Tatts.

'Doin' what Johnny said, get someone offside, try to break us up.' Turning to Billy, she changes her expression to conciliatory.

'Well done mate, you held firm. So, she wants to be friendly does she, try to break us up does she, well we'll see about that. Let's go and see Johnny, he'll know what to do, oh that fuckin' little bitch, oh we gotta fix her.' Standing, she strides off, Pills looks at Billy who returns the look to Tatts, none of them really understand the logic of Noog's declaration but like tin soldiers they spring to life and follow her.

CHAPTER 28

Beth enters the dance studio, Karen is there setting up she glances up at the sound of footsteps.

'Hi, Beth,' is her sprightly greeting.

'Hi, Karen.' Karen continues, 'I heard what happened on the weekend with Rod, you okay?'

'Yes, fine thanks but good thing Rod was there.' Nodding in agreement Karen adds.

'Yes, it was, but for them to even consider doing something like that is worrying.'

'Well,' continues Beth with a sheepish manner, 'It wasn't the only problem.' Karen's raises her head to one side accelerating more than just curiosity.

'Go on.' Beth recounts the confrontation with Johnny and Noogs in the town centre on the Sunday. Karen is horrified at the part where Noogs verbally attacked Shelly, she's almost in tears.

'But why? She doesn't even know Shelly.' Explaining she has tried to nut it out, Beth discloses her reasoning.

'My guess is it's something to do with you and your past association with Noogs.'

'Me? I only knew her at school and that was vaguely.'

'Yes, but you and the other girls teased her and I guess made her school life torturous.' Although Karen recognises some truth in the accusation, she tries defending herself.

'But that was years ago, Primary School and an early bit of Secondary, she'd dropped out by year nine.'

'Yes,' agrees Beth, 'But with baggage, mental scares, now she's older I think revenge might be on the menu somewhere down the track. All the other girls either live in a different town or have left this area, you're the only one left from that era. Remember the town's shrinking, there's no police, plus she's got her little gang of half-wits.' The realisation crunches into Karen's head like a fist.

'Gosh, you could be right... oh hell and because you're my friend now, you're in the firing line as well.'

'Could be but there are a couple of points in our advantage.'

'And they are?'

'Well they're weedy, our friends Geoff and Rod are tall and strong plus Mr Byrnes put the fear of god into Johnny, I'm sure they won't say anything or touch Shelly, I believe she's safe and being on the farm and out of town she's out of the equation.'

'So,' establishes Karen, 'It's me and most likely you in the firing line?'

'Yep at the moment I guess so but with Geoff and Rod around I think we're safe, as you told me the occasional swear word or stare but that's about it, also my uncle Reg seems to be stepping up to the plate. My home life is settling into well... normality, he's softening, maybe getting used to me being around.' This information enthuses Karen.

'Great, that's a relief.' At that precise moment the girls enter the studio, Shelly is amongst them, Beth whispers to Karen.

'Psst, don't mention the altercation to Shelly in front of

the others, no-one knows, think she wants to keep it that way.'

'Okay got it, no probs but I might have a quiet word to her after the other girls have left, just to show I know and we have her back.' Beth nods in agreement.

'Yes, good one.' Karen claps her hands and beckons the girls in.

'Right we'll pick up from last week, first stretches, okay organise yourselves into space.' The girls start to discard bags and apparel then position themselves spread out in front of Karen. The session starts, Beth wanders around occasionally instructing someone on technique, the girls apply themselves vigorously enjoying the demand of physicality with control. Any time the moves are performed correctly both Karen and Beth are forthcoming with praise. The sessions are not easy or "Micky Mouse" in any retrospect, the demands produce the desired outcome and the young girls know it, they revel in the almost professional requirements. Beth has noticed whilst listening to the kid's general chit chat on the bus that because of their improvement through their studio work a number have a desire to have a crack at a higher dance level once in secondary school. After an hour or so Karen claps her hands and calls a halt to proceedings, she recounts the new work that they have done, heads nod and smile in agreement, as chests heave and perspiration flows from the strenuous workout.

'Now practice those new routines at home and we'll put it together next week, well done, you can go.' The girls move to their bags, some towel down for a few minutes all take their time in getting organised, part of the "Cooling Down" process. With the putting on of sweatshirts, jumpers and leg warmers they start to file out with various "Bye Karen, See you, Beth", Karen catches Shelly's eye and quietly addresses her.

'Shelly honey, a quick word please.' Shelly's put on her jumper plus her sneakers, she ambles over.

'Hi, Kaz... yes?' Pondering for a second choosing the

right words she begins.

'Look Beth told me about what happened in town the other day and I just wanted you to know that I'm here for you, whether you need anything or just someone to chat to.' Shelly's eyes become a little misty.

'Thanks, Kaz, umm Beth was great, we've chatted about it on the bus trip, I'm pretty good with the whole thing now. She explained it wasn't me so much as my association with her and you.' Karen laughs, 'Ha, you're right, so drop us as friends now.' Shelly's eyes open wide, she subconsciously bares her soul in an inadvertently open way.

'Oh, I couldn't do that, I love you guys.' Suddenly tears explode from all three interspaced with comments of "Me too," "Oh yes," they crush together in a defiant group hug, tears flow throughout the embrace, a few kisses are planted on cheeks, their strong bond acting as a catharsis for their problems. Breaking and wiping tears away, Karen's comment underlines their mood, "Girl Power, Yeah." Raising their hands, they all do high fives. Jim Byrnes has been outside waiting in the car-park for Shelly, after a brief time and Shelly doesn't appear, he exits the car and walks to the dance studio, entering the room he notices the three girls finishing off their high fives, he calls.

'You right, Shell?' She looks up and answers.

'Yes, dad coming,' smiles at the two girls, says a quiet, "thanks guys," picks up her gear and leaves with her dad. He escorts her through the door first, enabling him to slow and turn his head towards Karen and Beth, they hold his vision, he nods, smiles and gives them a thumbs up, they smile back. His look says it all, appreciation of their manner relating to his daughter, they glow understanding his demeanour. Karen breaks the silence.

'Well, that was an end.' A loving look comes from Beth, she beams with a truthful bearing of her soul.

'Thanks, I'm so happy to have met you.'

'Me too,' is the response, 'Look how about takeaway this Friday after our session, I know Rod would like to see you, he was a bit worried you know.'

'Yes great, I'd like to see him, he was such a gentleman the other day.' Karen grins to herself and tries a little facetious interplay, using humour, she admonishes Beth.

'Rod, a gentleman? Have you got the right person?'

'Ha,' laughs Beth, 'a gentleman and also clumsy and a bit dawkish.'

'Yep, that's him,' chuckles Karen, 'let's go.' They turn and wander out arm in arm. Dusk has descended, the girls walk together still arm in arm, chatting in a relaxed, manner, a car's lights can be seen two blocks away, Beth freezes mid-stride whispering, "Wait." Karen's confused, "What is it?" The car's lights disappear the sound of the engine recedes with the vision.

'Okay,' breathes Beth, 'Oh sorry, I thought it was Johnny's car again.'

'Again,' queries Karen, 'What do you mean again?'

'Actually, it was quite funny, it was the day before the picnic whilst Rod was walking me home. We were forced to hide behind someone's hedge as Johnny's car with the gang inside crept past. It was sort of spooky, I told Rod we were acting like commandos.'

'Commandos! Were you going to blow them up or something?'

'Well that was one of the suggestions,' giggles Beth, 'but we decided to reconnaissance the river instead the next day.'

'Oh reconnaissance,' smirks Karen, 'and what did you take for this mission?' Now Beth starts acting like a captain in the army.

'Lieutenant Rod was in charge of transport.'

'Saw that, two bikes were issued.'

'And sergeant Beth was in charge of supplies.'

'And they were ...'

'Rolls, apples and muesli bars.'

'Right but what about liquids?' Beth starting to giggle, 'forgot about that one... umm, the creek, we were going to live off the land.' The last off the cuff comment does it and the girls break down in laughter, Beth concludes.

'Started well, didn't end well, the enemy won the encounter, not too many casualties though, we'll strike back... ha ha.'

'You idiot,' cajoles Karen, 'oh we're at the break point, you go your way, now be careful it's only a few blocks but it's dark.'

'No probs,' is the confident answer, 'I'll be fine, see you Friday for aerobics practice then take-away.' They hug, before moving off in their separate directions, as Beth walks along the darkened back roads, she realises that her comments were false bravado, any bird or animal sound is magnified in her imagination. Her pace quickens, the security she displays normally when ambling along is replaced by nervous speed. Determination shapes her face, walk speed is above brisk, turning the last corner she sees uncle Reg's house with the porch light glowing. Relief floods her, enabling a slowing of her pace, approaching the house she realises that the situation over the last week or so has definitely had an effect, opening the gate she blows a breath out and admonishes herself. "Interesting how these situations can distort your psychosis, definitely more strength of character needed here... don't let them get to you." Inside the house, she drops her bag in her room and walks to the kitchen, Reg is at the sink preparing dinner.

'Giddy, Luv,' he greets her, 'how was practice with the kids?'

'Great,' she answers while at the same time thinking, 'he's showing interest in the dance kids, what's with the change of attitude?' Not dwelling on this character development too much she adds.

'They're coming on really well.'

'Good one,' is the reply with a truthful tone. 'Got the vegies going will have the steak on pretty soon.'

'Great,' she replies enthusiastically, 'I'll just wash up.' Moving off to the bathroom, she manages her ablutions and returns to the kitchen. Reg has the steaks cracking in the frying pan, the smell acts as a catalyst to her taste buds, hunger pains rumble through her stomach, he smiles invitingly.

'Do you want another glass with your meal?' Laughingly she replies, 'Okay but just one, I don't want to become an alcoholic.' Nodding knowingly.

'Don't worry lass, you're a smart filly, can't see that happening.'

"Complements on her mental strength," she rationalises, "Hmm, things are on the rise here, don't know what's happening but roll with it."

'Help yourself', he invites. 'Steaks nearly done.' Moving to the fridge, she grabs the bottle and fills about two-thirds in a glass, replacing the bottle she sits at the table taking a couple of sips. The dry soft biting liquid has the effect of soothing her nervous tension from the walk home.

"This is really nice," she thinks then mentally qualifing herself, "Now, now don't get too carried away I've just begun adult drinking." Looking over his shoulder, he questions.

'How's school going? Made any friends? Teacher's okay?' She's surprised, by the escalating interest in her circumstances, especially regarding her education, while he serves up the dinner, she answers his queries. There's a certain glow of satisfaction in her as she enlightens him regarding her studies, friends and teachers. They sit, she clinks her glass to his bottle, then with "Cheers", they start dinner, conversation again flows as she recounts the day's doings. Now with the ease of conversation, dinner carries on for longer, he is also informing her regarding his day's activities, telling her about

the new vegie patch in the backyard, what will be planted, the time scale for fruit and vegies to ripen and other horticultural relevant information. Although not overly interested she nether-less enjoys his enthusiasm in relaying information to her, definitely she notices how he is becoming more accustomed to her presence in the house. His obdurate manner is beginning to evaporate, this enhances an inner glow of serenity, the household is shaping up, with the dinner finished she announces.

'Thanks, uncle Reg, that was great, I'll do the dishes.' But he's adamant.

'Don't worry Luv, I've got it covered, you've had a big day what with school and dance classes, you relax.' His kindness touches her.

'Oh thanks, uncle Reg, actually I need a shower, I'm a bit bushed and this wine has… umm, relaxed me somewhat, I'm tired.'

'No probs, you go on, I'll fix up here.' With the announcement, she rises, smiles at him and exits the kitchen, he starts clearing the dishes from the table to the sink, turning on the water he allows the sink to fill then starts scrubbing and rinsing.

Moving down the passageway, Beth sways slightly not realising the sobriety of her has been affected, in her room she drags her shoes off and unbuttons her school dress. The wine has had an effect of lowering her inhibitions, opening the wardrobe door she stands in front of the mirror in her underwear viewing herself. A smattering of ego protrudes from her psych, "hmm," she amuses herself, "Looking fit, not bad, dance classes are working." This self-analysis is not only her primary concern, but her thoughts also turn to another. "So, I must be physically attractive to Rod, yeah, he thinks I'm alright." The introspective analysis brings a smile to her face. With her characteristic nod and flick of her hair she grabs the

towel, nighty and heads to the bathroom, moving with a 'blaze' attitude she sweeps through the kitchen, spying Reg at the sink she calls.

'Going for a shower.' Looking up, he answers, 'Okay'. With her mind state unhindered, she breezes in and, with an irreverent swish, swings the door half-closed. The normal procedure regarding the shower water takes place, the hot tap is turned on to an even pressure, the cold tap is adjusted till the water temperature is appeasing to her. Once this is established, she undoes her bra strap and hangs it over the vanity bench, lowering her panties she flicks them off to the side. As she's just about to enter the shower she deliberates, her panties lie on the floor, "Not the right place for them," she scolds herself, so with a deft movement she turns, scoops them up and is about to place the on the bench next to her bra when a breaking light from outside the door catches her eye. It was if a shadow moved past the door diffusing the light for a second. "Strange," she thinks to herself, "What was that?" With no answer imminent she steps into the shower but leaves the shower door open a smidgen, enough to view the open space of the bathroom door. Nothing seems to happen, so she concentrates on soaping herself and washing, about a minute or so later she glances at the door, the light changes again, instantly the kitchen glow is returned because of the frosted glass she is unable to specifically determine just what is the cause of the differential light. "Strange," she thinks to herself, keeping an eye on the door as she washes but there are no more changes. The light from the kitchen is of a constant nature, shrugging to herself she continues with the washing and cleansing. Once towelled, dried and dressed in her nighty, she enters the kitchen combing her hair as she walks. Reg is seated in the alcove watching TV, he has a beer in his hand, the dishes have been finished and are drying in the rack on the sink. Everything is as the status quo in the household. The shower having a

calming effect and the remnants of the wine still providing a subtle lowering of her inhibitions she walks up to the parlour and addresses Reg.

'Oh, uncle Reg.' He turns and looks at her, 'Yes, Luv.'

'This Friday Karen asked if I could go to her place after aerobics practice, she wants to show me a few things, she said I could have dinner there.' The answer is relaxed and easily reciprocated.

'Righto, that's fine, Luv.'

Watching his eyes as he answers, there is nothing untoward, they seem to view her as a whole being, not like those disgusting boys at the creek who leered at her then ogled her breasts. Slightly relieved she reply's "Thanks," turns and walks off thru the kitchen. At the entrance to the passageway, she slows and turns, he's still watching her, he must have tracked her movement from the parlour to the passageway, smiling she waves, he tips his hand to the side of his head as in a mock salute then turns and continues watching TV. There is just the smallest segment of doubt and curiosity creeping into her head, climbing into bed she dwells on these minor infractions. The thought process has too many implications, unable to come to any real truths regarding this ambiguous situation she drifts off to sleep.

Friday morning Beth's up, packing her bag, raiding the fridge as usual, with everything stowed she heads out the door calling as she passes Reg's door.

'I'm off uncle Reg, going to Karen's tonight, be back later.'

'Righto,' is the muffled reply. Skipping down the steps, she starts the walk to the main street bus stop. The brisk morning air is invigorating, a few birds chirp, the dew on the grass strips enliven the houses with a shining sheen announcing the morning, the day's beginning. Walking along her brain ticks over with questions immersed in her head, the

clarity of the morning is still not having any effect in clearing her questions. Arriving at the bus stop, some of the kids have already been dropped off, she's met with a variety of "Hi Beth's," which is happily reciprocated. A Hi Lux drives up and Shelly exits it, her mother noticing Beth gives a hand wave which is returned, then she drives off, Shelly approaches.

'Hi Beth, how are you?'

'Good,' is the reply then a question, 'you went to the local Primary School here, until they closed it down, didn't you?'

'Yes, that was two years ago.'

The bus rolls up to the stop, everyone boards, Beth and Shelly head to the rear seat, Beth continues.

'What was school like?'

'Oh good, you know everyone, small schools are like that, teachers are relaxed, things get done on a whim.'

'Like what?'

'Oh, I don't know, maybe go outside for a game whenever the teacher felt like it, you know do things as the mood entails. Definitely not organised by a strict timetable. I remember one time our teacher was tired and she took us out for a spell of cloud gazing, you know like you lie down and stare at the clouds and let your imagination run riot, it's real fun.'

'Right,' answers Beth, then more inquiringly.

'Did people of the town get involved in the school, I mean did parents or whoever come in to help out?'

'Oh yes, different people came in and did various tasks. We had mums come in and hear reading, others worked at the small canteen, on sports day we had helpers, the town was involved.' Beth nods, then prods.

'Did my uncle help out?' Shelly isn't dumb, she has spotted the crux of the questioning immediately.

'No, he never actually helped out but seemed to hang

around watching the kids play, any open sports days he'd be there but well… seemed a bit of a loner. I don't think many of the other parents associated with him much, donno why, so what's with the questions?' Beth knows Shelly's sharp but she tries to keep it ambiguous.

'Oh, just filling in background info, trying to work out what makes him tick.' Dropping her head slightly Shelly eyes Beth intently.

'Right and what's brought on this desire for information, anything happened at home?' The response from Beth is carefully constructed.

'Look no, not really, just a feeling sometimes, maybe I'm imagining things, I think I'll try a few ideas and see what evolves'. Curiosity vibrates through Shelly's head.

'Okay, well let me know if anything develops, you know an ear is worth a thousand voices… hey, that's good, I made a proverb, wow…am I smart.' Grinning Beth retaliates.

'Oh, I don't know, maybe scratching above average.' The offhand reply incenses Shelly.

'Scratching! Hey, I punch above my weight,' and with that she wacks Beth on the shoulder.

'Oww, mistake miss,' is the sharp reply. 'You're out of your weight division,' she wacks her back.

'Right you'll see,' is the humorous reply, she lunges at Beth trying to get her in a headlock. Beth grabs her arms a wrestle develops on the back seat. The younger ones on hearing some minor commotion turn their heads and view the wrestling match, one boy starts the chant.   "Fight, fight, fight…" soon everybody joins in, 'Fight, fight, fight…" Suddenly a booming voice blasts out from the bus's internal PA.

'Hoy, you two at the back, settle down or I'll put you both off now.' Beth and Shelly break apart and stare at each other, then explode in fits of laughter, the rest of the bus join in the laughter, they know it was just a case of play-acting.

'I win 'cos I'm older,' preaches Beth.

'Ha, wait till I grow,' responds Shelly, 'my time will come.' They look at each other grin and hug as the bus rolls on.

CHAPTER 29

That evening at aerobics class, Karen is busy setting up when Beth enters the room.

'Hi,' greets Karen, 'how was your day?'

'Oh, pretty normal,' Beth's replies, then with a mischievous grin on her face 'besides getting in a fight and almost getting kicked of the bus.'

'What!' Explodes Karen, 'You, a fight on the school bus, who with?' Acting coy, Beth strings it along.

'Oh, actually a girl from this area, umm... I think Shelly is her name.' With this announcement, Karen knows she is pulling her leg, and shakes her head.

'God, you had me going for a second, what really happened?'

'Nothing really, we were mucking round on the backseat and it turned into a wrestling match.' Karen grins and shakes her head disapprovingly.

'Girls, I don't know, muckin' round with boys, wrestling on the back seat of the bus, where will it end?' They eyeball each other and get the giggles, when some sort of composure is gained Karen orders.

'Right to work... where we up to? I know the left

slides and kicks, let's start at the beginning and work our way there.' Switching on the CD player, they move to their starting positions, the music thumps out, they start the appropriate movements to the beat. The session continues occasionally they lose themselves in the movement they're trying to perfect. After about an hour Karen calls a halt to proceedings. 'Phew', I think that'll do it for today, jeez we really ploughed thru, we must be getting fitter.' Beth breathing heavily agrees.

'Yeah, that was a workout, thanks.' Moving to the side they squat next to their bags, extracting drink bottles they each suck the cool liquid, now with composure gained Beth comments.

'That really builds an appetite, I'm hungry.'

'Yep,' Karen agrees, 'me too, let's throw gear on and go.' Pulling on sweatshirt tops, packing their gear in the bags they vacate the premises, walking along the back blocks, Beth discloses to Karen.

'You know I'm very lucky to have you and Geoff as friends.'

'Great but what about Rod?'

'Oh yes, he's really nice what you hoped a young man would be like,' dependable, courageous and with a sense of humour, plus strong from all the outside work. He's great.' Karen listens intently, smiling, she agrees.

'Good, I'm glad you're getting on, especially with someone close to your own age, it's good to have friends.'

'And you, you're more than just a friend, I feel like an attachment, not like a sister but… Oh I don't know just really caring.' Karen smiles and locks elbows easing her in close almost snuggling in close.

'Absolutely correct, love you too.' She leans forward and gives Beth a peck on her nose. Beth looks for a second then bursts out giggling and pecks her one back on her nose, they both laugh and continue down the street with arms locked,

Beth continues.

'Yes, you and the others are great and especially with those dropkicks around, you need strong friends.' Chuckling Karen advances a different notion.

'Like Shelly?' Beth pulls a face of careful consideration.

'Well, maybe a bit stronger.' They laugh. 'I don't think Shelly's got anything to worry about, Mr Byrnes has the matter in hand, I mean he's really nice but he exudes that, "Don't mess with me," look about him. Karen adds.

'I knew someone who played football with him years ago when I mentioned his name like this guy's a farmer now, he just said two words, "Hard, man.' Agreeing with her analysis, Beth adds.

'Yep, way above Johnny in the tough stakes.'

'You know,' continues Karen, 'Johnny's only a couple of years younger than me, he went to the same Primary School. At school, he was as meek and mild as water, almost timid, his "Mr Cool" persona is I believe just an act to cover his fragile nature.'

'Could be right,' agrees Beth, 'Shelly did say that when her dad told him off, the best he could offer was, yes sir.' Laughing, Karen extends the comment.

'Just like you corporal, sir, mame sir, yes sir.' She turns and mimics a salute. Beth stops and standing to attention returns the salute with the order.

'Well done, dismissed private.' They break up in fits of laughter then move on. The house lights soon become visible, Karen agrees with Beth.

'Hey, come to think of it I'm very hungry also, hope the boys have prepared something yummy?' Pushing through the gate, they climb the steps and enter the house, arriving in the kitchen they spy the two men working away at the bench, Rod is chopping up vegetables, Geoff preparing some sort of meat, they turn at the sound of the girls' entry.

'Hi,' beams Geoff, Karen immediately makes a bee-

line to him, kisses and hugs him. Rod and Beth are now more accustomed to showing affection in front of the others, she walks up to him with a "Hi" and gives him a warm hug plus a soft kiss on the cheek, Karen breaks in.

'Well chef Antonio, what do we have?' Or is it chef…?'

'Ahh so,' returns Geoff in a pathetic attempt at an Asian dialect. 'Ve have, chow-mein tonight.'

'Ahh,' responds Karen also attempting the Asian dialect and bowing, 'Velly good.' Rod looks at Beth, they both roll their eyes, Beth breaks the nonsense by asking Rod.

'Can I use your room, I need to change.'

'Yep,' is the response, 'No probs.' She continues.

'I'll have a shower first.'

'Okay,' he answers, 'We're still preparing stuff here, be a while, feel right at home.'

'I need one also,' calls Karen, she breaks from Geoff. 'Won't be long,' then to Beth,

'Come on, race you in,' the girls zip out of the kitchen. Beth grabs her bag from the passageway and rushes to Rod's room. Unzipping the bag, she extracts a small towel, whips off the sweatshirt, rips open the Velcro tabs on her shoes kicking them off. Grabbing a skirt and singlet top but still in her aerobics gear she slings the towel across her shoulder and heads to the bathroom, as she exits Rod's room the next door opens, Karen is in her underwear also with a towel across her shoulder, they stop, look at each other, then the race for, the shower.

The boys are hard at work in the kitchen, hearing the sound of trampling feet they look up to see two bodies with arms flailing to get in front go flying thru the kitchen towards the bathroom, with a startled look Rod glances at Geoff and questions, 'Was that an indoor race'? Geoff shrugs, shakes his head and returns to his vegetable's preparation, in the background giggling can be heard emanating from the

bathroom. In the doorway of the bathroom, the two girls have been jostling for first position, Karen muscles her way past and squeezes thru thus entering first, with the wrestling match finished Beth enters and announces with a grin.

'Okay, I guess, you're first.' Karen chuckles and winks.

'Right I'm in.' Before Beth can move Karen's whipped off her top then lowered and flicked her panties away. Standing buck naked, she gives Beth another smile and opens the shower door. Beth watches in amazement, she's never been in the presence of a naked lady before. Yes, she'd been round her mum at home at various times but that was family, different and she was younger, sort of innocent. This is way different, she feels unsure and vulnerable plus the shower glass allows her a view the same as looking through a window, nothing is hidden. Karen is working on turning the knobs in an effort to get the correct temperature, eventually satisfied she turns and giggles a request to Beth.

'Room for two, I don't mind.' Now Beth is really out of her safety zone, thinking to herself, "Am I being seduced?" With too many questions ricocheting thru her head, she stumbles a reply.

'It's okay, I'll wait.'

Karen, although wet, cocks her head looks at Beth and then steps out she's dripping water onto the floor, she walks a couple of paces straight up to Beth and stops right in front of her. Beth is rooted to the spot not knowing what to say or where to look, Karen looks directly into Beth's eyes.

'Okay, I know what you're thinking... well I think I do, let me clear this up a bit. One I am not a lesbian, I love Geoff, he's great in bed but when I shared a room in college, my room-mate was a young gymnast. Boy, she was so fit and had a boyfriend, loved him big time but sometimes we'd shower together, she said it was a woman's touch, so soft and sensual, different from a strong man, I was unsure like you at first but

eventually agreed to share and well… it was great. We both loved making out with the boys but this was different, sensual, amazing exhilarating, I loved caressing her body, it was great but it was only an exercise in sensuality, not sexual intercourse, I leave that to Geoff. Look, sorry flirting with you so, you are young, I guess to the world, I'm not pressuring you feel free to wait, hey, I'm wet gotta get back.'

She smiles and turns, Beth realises that she's sort of seducing her, weighing up her options she is relaxed how her brain accepts the situation in a mature way. Thinking to herself, "Life, love, experiences, a new door has opened do I step through, my dad would have, yes live it.' Karen is about to re-enter the shower when Beth's voice is heard.

'Wait.' Slowly Karen turns, looks, raises an eyebrow, flicks her hair and grinning says.

'Waiting.'

Beth's heart is beating, adrenalin is pumping through her veins, she steps forward close to the dripping Karen. The water on her gives her an ethereal glow, she's investigated her own personal appearance in her bedroom mirror, now she can compare. Placing her hand on Karen's neck, she runs it down Karen's arm, the muscles are firm and strong, she has biceps that show definition. Sliding her hand up to Karen's neck she begins tracing her body, moving down she runs her hand in between Karen's breasts. Stopping she cups the left breast in her hand, it's firm, sliding upwards her hand circles the nipple, as she rotates, she can feel the nipple harden, delicately squeezing it her hand movement transmits a feeling inside her, licking her lips causes nervous energy to flow arousing her. Continuing on she moves her hand downwards over Karen's diaphragm, the sensation is one of strength, noticing that Karen almost has a six-pack, definitely there is muscle definition, more than hers. Lifting her eyes from Karen's body they connect, eye contact is held, the saying that "the eyes are

the window to the soul," was never truer with slight deviation. Karen's eyes are inviting, Beth's inquisitive, both have a cloud of desirability hanging over them that aches for release. "The time has come to experience another facet of life," Beth coerces to herself, withdrawing a step she smiles almost giggles and agrees.

'Oh well, in for a penny...'

Putting her hand into her crop top she eases it over her head, following this she turns one eighty degrees and deftly lowers her aerobics briefs. Looking over her shoulder at Karen, she smiles and in a naughty gesture wiggles her bottom, the coquettish movement excites Karen who moves forward and sensuously wraps her arms around Beth's breasts instigating bodily contact, whispering.

'Okay, shower time,' holding Beth's hand she leads her into the shower. On entering, Beth shuts the door turns and faces Karen, her heart is exploding in anticipation, as the water cascades over them they feel each other's body. Beth is aware of the differences, she runs her hand over Karen's skin its plain she is fitter, there is much more definition in all departments of her body. Reaching behind Karen she notices that her buttocks are firm, she can feel the hamstrings tightly immersing into the gluts. Returning to the front she drops her eyes down towards Karen's mound, it's completely bare of pubic hair, she has a "Brazilian," running her hand over the smooth skin on the top of the clitoris, induces a gasp from Karen, she whispers.

'Turn around.' Beth follows the order, Karen picks up a bar of soap and begins to wash Beth's back. The feeling of soft hands joined with swishing rotation of the soap on her back makes her senses tingle. She starts to purr like a cat, humming, mmm... mmm. Karen leans in and massages Beth's back with her breasts. The feeling of the suds being swirled around with Karen's firm but buoyant breasts intensifies the stimulation of Beth's senses. Karen now moves her soaped hands down to

Beth's buttocks rotating round the in wide arcs. She gets to the cheeks division and runs her hand down Beth's crack over her hole and across her vagina. Beth gasps, this is a new sensation unthought-of before and never experienced. She is now in the area of sexual desire, her breathing becomes heavy, her senses tingle, desire overcomes caution leading her to want more. Turning her head Beth whispers, "lower," then bends forward so that her vagina is open to touch. Karen runs her hand over it projecting her middle finger slightly, so it splits the clitoris hood divide. Beth has never progressed this far before in her sexual experimentation, she's looked at herself in the mirror with an occasional touching or raising of her breasts as if her hand was a push-up bra plus some experimenting with a girl-friend but this whole new sensation it envelopes her, desire is erupting forging through her body.

'Oh yes, that's beautiful,' she moans.

Karen continues rubbing, Beth's murmuring increases to whining, then Karen slows her hand movement. Raising her hands to Beth's breasts she feels the nipples, they're hard and large. With more soap applied to her hands she washes Beth's front, from her face, across her breasts, down the diaphragm, around the vagina, down her legs and finishing with her individual toes. Beth stands transfixed, Karen's touch is just as she said it would be, soft, caressing sybaritic. The whole experience has aroused feelings in her that had just surfaced before, it has been an overwhelming and wonderful experience. Finishing Karen turns off the taps, they both exit the shower, still dripping wet Beth asks with excited trepidation.

'Oh, that was unbelievable, my first sort of sexual experience but it was with you, a girl, and well... I want it more, does that mean I'm a lesbian'? Karen laughs.

'No sweetie, look women are sensual creatures, I love Geoff but I also adore a soft woman's touch, it's, well, different. We won't be like this all the time but occasionally after dance

practice, however this for me was the build-up, now I'm ready for Geoff and something different tonight. You're still young, that lies ahead but I guess I was giving you your first sexual experience', she grins, 'Hope you enjoyed it'.

'Oh yes, yummy.' They both giggle. Beth looks into Karen's eyes.

'Thanks awfully, it was real umm... fun.' She leans forward and kisses her on the mouth, the kiss is returned, not in a passionate way but with loving, they part and smile, Karen leads.

'Okay, let's get ready for the boys.' Wrapping towels around them, they sprint out of the bathroom.

The boys are involved in the finishing touches of the meal, with the sound of footsteps on the linoleum floor, they glance up. The two girls move thru the kitchen with their towels draped around them, Geoff does a wolf whistle causing them to slow, Karen curtseys slightly then pulls Beth towards the door. Just as they are exiting the kitchen Karen unhinges the tie of the towel surrounding her. It's still held in her hand but flips open displaying her buttocks for just an instant before they disappear down the passageway. Behind them Beth hears Geoff's voice, he laughs, "Ha." They walk down the passageway, Karen turns into her room and has a quick aside to Beth.

'Don't worry, just setting the scene for later,' then she departs into the room. Entering Rod's room, Beth dries herself with the towel and rummages thru her bag. Taking out her underwear she views it, the style is different from her normal schoolgirl style. The briefs are the string bikini kind. The back part is not quite G-string but very high cut, slipping them on there is a sensual feel reflected in the cut. There's a mirror in Rod's wardrobe just like hers at home, opening it she views herself. Unlike the normal positive smile of assurance, she gives herself at home, this time the vision is enticing, her smile has a mischievous sense to it, picking up the bra again she views

149

it and smiles, it's a push-up kind. For a young girl of her age her proportions are quite womanly, feeling her breasts she nods in satisfaction. She likes them, their size is about thirty-four bust, not small but not too large, certainly able to make an impression with any low-cut tops. Engaging the straps, she turns the bra and settles the cups under her breasts, then picking up the string singlet top she carefully squeezes it over her head, does some adjustment and views the result. The mirror reflects the image she has desired, her breasts have been forced upwards, they rise with form very similar to the fashion of society in the seventeen hundred's. Grabbing the blue mini-skirt she attaches it, pulls on the sneakers, a quick comb of her hair, a little lip gloss and looking in the mirror again she smiles to herself. "Presto, done… ready for action." With a confident smile and air, she exits the room, wandering down the passageway she slows at Karen's door and knocks, "come in," is the answer, entering Karen stands with her underwear on, Beth notices it's the same type as hers, Karen smiles and asks.

'Can you help with the zip on this dress,' nodding to a floral pleated dress on the end of the bed.

'Yes sure,' is the upbeat reply, she moves behind as Karen wrestles the dress over her head. Once positioned, Beth zips it up, turning Karen grins.

'Well, will I do?' Laughing, Beth answers in an admiring way.

'Very well, he's a lucky guy'. The response is a slight curtsy followed by an appreciative comment directed towards Beth.

'Yep, and you look great also, hey, I never realised, great boobs, definitely worth showing off.' Normally Beth would blush at such a compliment, however, with this new development of her personality through recent experiences she is maturing quickly, looking directly at Karen she answers confidently.

'Thanks, I'm happy.' Then with a grin, they take hold of each other's arms and exit the room. On entering the kitchen, the boy's lookup, again Geoff comments.

'Alright, looking good girls.' This time Karen acts up a bit foxy walks up to him gives a kiss and asks with a suggestiveness of tone.

'What's to drink?' He's straight up with the reply.

'One G and T, there on the sideboard ready for her highness.' Watching the interplay Beth notices how Karen uses her feminine charm, she's enticing him, it's like being involved in a play, thinking to herself, she rationalises.

'This is the maturity of being in love or at least being involved with someone.' Studying Rod, she smiles, he returns the smile but his body language suggests he's struggling with himself not to drop his eyes and ogle her especially as her breasts are prominent, he says with conviction.

'You look great.' Her effort in presentation has been acknowledged, with animated coquettishness she replies.

'Thank you, anything to drink?'

'Yep', he smiles, 'Coming right up.' Going to the fridge he grabs a can of "Bacardi and Coke," fills up two glasses, hands one to her politely toasting, "Cheers," they both sip, Geoff interrupts proceedings.

'Dinner's ready, everyone to the table.' With everyone seated, he takes the wok from the stove and plants it in the middle of the table, ordering. "ladies first". Plates are handed to him as he serves the Chow Mein, once all are served, he orders, "Dig In.' They taste, nods of appreciation show from round the table, Karen comments.

'Oh, velly good Mr Dim Sim.' Beth follows.

'Nice work Mr Curry Puff.' The boys grin and answer in unison.

'Tank you oh honourable ladies.' Their mimicking draws laughter from the girls. Geoff redirects the conversation.

'Hey Beth, Rod told me you had a run-in with the idiots down by the river.' She nods and answers with a slight grimace on her face.

'That wasn't good but there was something else on Sunday.' Slightly confused Geoff inquires.

'Sunday?' Beth retells the story regarding the confrontation between Noogs and Shelly in town, Geoff yells.

'What! Little Shelly, she's only twelve or so, still at Primary School,' his rage intensifies, 'they need shooting, wait no, put 'em in the stocks.'

'Easy,' buts in Karen, 'calm down.' Continuing, Beth eases his concerns.

'Yes, it's okay, Mr Byrnes had a word with them after and I think he put the fear of God in them, they're unlikely to step out of line again.'

'Jim Byrnes, ehh,' dwells Geoff, 'Hmm, hard man, yep that'd do it.' Breaking in Rod expounds his information.

'I have news too,' eyes turn to him. 'I bumped into Johnny outside the store the other day.' Geoff raises his eyebrow.

'Did you, you didn't mention it to me.'

'No, I forgot, you were working me too hard.' This brings gaffs and chuckles plus off-hand comments of, "Oh diddums," "Poor you," "Yeah, hard life," he grins and continues. 'Well anyway I was ready for an altercation but he was different, I mean nice.

"Nice!" is the unison chorus.

'Yep, and get this, he apologised for their behaviour 'round the town and also said he told off the other three half-wits for their actions down by the river, reckons he knew nothing about it, then get this, he said he's leaving town soon. Said his works dried up and he's got a better chance in a large city.' The other three stare at him in amazement, Rod finishes.

'He said, no hard feelings and shook my hand, I agreed

and well I guess we parted friends, well if not friends at least friendly.'

'Well, beat that,' says a gobsmacked Geoff. Karen's not so sure, "I don't believe it." Beth's even more unsure.

'Are you sure it wasn't an act?' Shaking his head, Rod is not a hundred percent on the validity of the conversation.

'Look I'm not sure either, I guess we'll have to take him on face value, but he seemed adamant that he was leaving town.' Pondering, Beth asks the question.

'So, where does that leave the others?'

'Rudderless,' Geoff confirms, 'they'll lose their captain, they don't drive or have cars, betcha Noogs who does have some sort of brain, a nasty one, though, will follow, without him even she will get sick of hanging round with the half-wits.'

'And the half-wits,' asks Karen, 'What about them?'

'Lost,' explains Geoff, 'they'll stay out on the outskirts of town doing nothing, maybe a bit of fishing in the river but that'll be it. They don't have the gumption or drive to do anything either positive or negative.' Karen generalises.

'Well, our problems might be solved.' But Geoff's weary.

'Yes maybe, let's just wait and see.' They all agree with an assortment of nods and knowing half-smiles, changing the subject Karen asks Geoff.

'How's work? Aren't you doing some adjustments to the Phillips house?' Answering for Geoff Rod buts in.

'Yeah, underground and new downpipes, and guess who's doing all the digging?' Eyes light up round the table waiting to throw a remark in, Beth's first.

'Lil ol' you.'

'Yep, the poor apprentice.' Karen leans across the table and chiacks him, feeling his arm.

'Oh, but what strong muscles you are getting.' He groans.

'Yes, but they ache at night.' Beth's got the answer.

'Well we'll have to rub some lineament or something in, you need it to relieve the tension.' Karen's eyebrows raise.

'Will we?'

'Yes, when I get my physio degree, umm in about five years', they all laugh, more general comments flow at Rod's expense. "You'll be dead by then," "remember patience brings rewards," Rod groans, "I'll be a broken-down wreck by then." He laughs and smiles at Beth, the smile says everything, conversation drifts from Geoff and Rod's work to dance classes. Beth's intrigued by the fact that Rod shows interest even though it's not really "his thing." It's this manner that enhances his appeal to her. As conversation continues, Geoff gets up and pours a wine for Karen, noticing that Beth has finished her Bacardi and Coke he asks.

'Do you want a wine?' Pondering she's aware of what her uncle Reg mentioned about being careful, to get gradually used to it.

'Just a half,' is the reply, then jokingly, 'Don't want to get tipsy,' guffs all-round, Karen bursts. 'Oh yes, half a glass, be careful.' Then more seriously, 'actually good on you, to know your own mind and limitations', Beth answers, ambiguously.

'Oh, I do like to push the boundaries now and then, you know experiment, try new things.' Karen smiles.

'Yep, that's what life's about, new experiences.' They share a quick, unobtrusive smile and continue eating, once the meal is finished Geoff calls.

'Right who's for coffee?'

'Yes please,' responds Karen, Rod and Beth shake their heads. Boiling the water, he stirs in the instant coffee and hands a mug to Karen, sitting down he yawns.

'Hmm, been a big week one way or another.' Karen agrees.

'Actually, I'm bushed I think I'll retire,' at the same time

throwing a subtle glance at Geoff who adds.

'The dishes can wait till the morning.' Beth's in immediately.

'Oh, don't worry, we'll do them.' Rod's in agreement, 'Yep, then I'll walk you home.'

'No complaints here,' remarks Geoff, 'Thanks guys.' He stands, gives Beth a hug and holding his coffee heads off, Karen also stands and gives Beth a hug, during which Beth whispers into her ear.

'Thanks for everything, and I do mean thanks, it was exhilarating, real fun.' Karen smiles with contentment.

'No probs loved having you here, catch you next week.' And with that, she turns and follows Geoff. Rod and Beth clear the table, placing the dirty dishes and cutlery in the sink, half filling the sink with warm water, she starts washing, Rod's taken over the drying duties. During the work a few soap-suds are flicked about, he's butting in and washing some dishes both are washing and mucking around. Giggles and comments abound. 'Careful," "oops, sorry," fly from one to another, by the time they've finished both have wet tops.

'Tricky business this washing,' he grins. 'Think you're a sloppy washer.'

'Me, you were the one flicking excess suds around.' Acting with a slight indignant act.

'Me... well, maybe just a little bit.' Laughing she pats him on the shoulder.

'Anyway, I have to go.'

'Okay', he agrees, 'I'll walk you home.' 'Thanks, my bags in your room.' They exit the kitchen, walk down the passageway and enter Rod's room, finding her bag, she starts remerging through, telling Rod.

'I'll need to find a dry top.'

He has already had the same idea and is searching thru his wardrobe for a new t-shirt. Finding one, he slips off the

damp one and is about to pull on the dry one when he turns his head, noticing Beth staring at his bare torso. His skin is smooth, hairless but with strong muscle definition, he stops, she looks away from his gaze focusing on her reflection in the wardrobe mirror, following her gaze he holds her image. Traversing her eyes, she meets his again, then slowly with subtle a coquettishness she tries to lift her top, with the dampness it's become clingy, difficult to get off, quietly she asks.

'Can you help?' Swallowing, he takes a shallow breath and moves to her, placing his hands either side of her top, he eases it upwards and over her head. With her push up bra performing its requirements her breasts stand out in close proximity to him, this time he allows his eyes to drop. The roundness and firm structure succulently enticing, his diverted gaze also has an effect on her, it increases her sensuality. Standing upright she makes her physical presence more inviting. Being now very close Beth initiates contact by running her hand over his bare chest. He follows by rubbing her neck forcing her to nestle the side of her head into his hand, this continues for a minute or so till he slowly lowers his hand down to the side of her breast, she gasps, inhaling with an excited breath. Looking up their eyes meet, he lowers his head and kisses her, a short kiss allowing them to break, again they stare into each other's eyes. Coming together again they embrace more passionately, the force causing them to fall backwards onto his bed, the kissing evokes a desire to touch and explore each other. Whilst continuing to kiss her hand travels from his head and neck to his chest, then to his torso and hips. Traversing round the top of his jeans she feels the material tighten, running her hands over his crutch his hardness steels a desire in her. She stops and sits up, calculatingly looking at him, her thoughts run. "He hasn't forced himself on me at all, it's been me making the advances." Gazing at him she reconciles with herself. "He really likes me,

if I said we need to stop now, he would comply, I know he wouldn't do anything to compromise our relationship. Yes, if I said I have to go back now we would stop."

Whilst she is contemplating, he's watching her, half expecting these comments. Thinking of Karen and these new sensual experiences, they've woven their way into her psych. Decision time is at hand, with a quick nod, flick of her hair she returns her gaze to his, meeting his gaze smiling an impish smile she lowers her hand to his belt. Fiddling with it, it soon becomes loose, moving to the foot of the bed she tugs on the trousers, helping them to slide off, tossing them aside she moves back to his side. He now only has his jocks on, the bulging in them is obvious, with a tender touch she strokes the outside of the jocks. She's like a young girl playing with her dolls, he moans quietly, with a deft touch and sublime movement she slides her hands inside, feeling his penis she is amazed how warm and taught it is, she can almost feel the throbbing of excitement pulsating through it. A strangely humorous look transcends his face as she handles him. It's an ecstatic look, not of humour but directed at the sensuality of the moment, as she handles his member, she reflects on the feeling transmitted to her from Karen's touch round her vagina when they were both showering. "It must be similar," she thinks, a pleasing feeling sweeps across her knowing that they are sharing the same feeling.

Withdrawing her hand, she again focuses on his eyes, then stands and moves to the foot of the bed, the movement is slow and methodical with a subtle flair that only dancers can replicate, he's watching fascinated. Carefully with discretion she puts her thumbs into the top of her skirt and ever so sublimely lowers it a few inches so it just hangs on the edge of her cheeks and hips, turning, she wiggles her backside, so it has to give in to the gravitational pull forcing it to slide to the floor. Glancing over her shoulder she places her hands behind her neck, the

excitement she's creating is causing his penis to expand more than is possible. As she turns, he can see her complete physical structure which is exemplified by the push-up bra and string bikini briefs, he mumbles.

'You look fantastic.' Sensuality takes over she is now in the complete mood and answers.

'I can look better.' With that, she unclips the last strand at the back of her bra, letting it slide to the floor, he swallows. Using her thumbs, she hooks them onto the side of the bikini briefs. Smiling the most mischievous smile, they are slid to the floor, now standing in front of him stark naked she strikes a pose and asks.

'Well?' His eyes are open wide, this time he moves his eyes, directing them over her whole body. She's already had a compliment from Karen regarding her breasts, so deciding to enhance the vision for him she places her hands behind her head and delicately wiggles them, his astonishment is reciprocated by his answer to her.

'Oh... you're fantastic.' The comment brings a smile of satisfaction to her face, appreciation at this most momentous time in their lives is paramount. They both need positive acknowledgement for this first coming of sexual experience, although not a Brazilian like Karen, she has shaved her pubic hair in a small "V". The hair is blonde and sits prettily above her vagina, being so young, the surrounds of her vagina are smooth and hairless. He glances at it, she watches his eyes noticing the direction, this appreciation of her female form and genitalia has on her, she desires to show off.

'Look,' she directs, then parts her legs and rubs her fingers over her hair and vagina. He is overcome with emotion and starts rubbing the bulge in his jocks, the moment is so sensually engaging she doesn't want it to end, certainly not too quickly.

'Wait,' she calls, forcing him to cease his movement,

crawling on the end of the bed, she inches over his toes allowing her breasts to slide across them. Moving almost on all fours she works her way up his legs, stopping at his crotch, with an impish smirk she lowers his jocks down his legs finally sliding them off, this is the first time she's seen close up a male member. It's such a strange muscle compared to female genitalia, hers is a slit with nothing to really take notice of but here in front of her is this muscle with veins protruding and this different kind of knob-like top. Having read magazines and talked about sex with her parents she has a fair idea what oral sex is about, knowing that it is meant to be reciprocated she decides to lead. Carefully she licks round the muscle, he groans, "yes, yes," The taste is overwhelmed by the feeling of sensuality, it's transmitted between them, she becomes embroiled in the experience. He pleads, "Take Me, in your mouth," excited by the prospect she lowers her mouth over the knob.

'Suck, lick,' he implores. She's beginning to get really excited, following his directions thrill cascades between them, he grabs her breasts and squeezes them, the whole sensation reverberates between them. Suddenly he calls.

'Wait … you.' Raising her mouth from his member, she looks at him, slowly working her way up his body, kissing his diaphragm and torso as she goes. Reaching his neck, she rises and kneels in front of him, legs astride of his chest. Leaning forward they kiss passionately, levering her back a smidgen he's able to raise his head and start kissing and licking her breasts. The sensation is intense, she is lost, wrapped up in the emotion, she calls with breathlessness.

'Lick me, suck me.' He responds, the feeling to her is of sublime ecstasy, a feeling similar to that when Karen washed her breasts in the shower. Wanting more she commands, "Lower." Grabbing hold of her shoulder he flips her over, so she's now lying on her back arms diagonally apart, legs astride, inviting his seduction. Placing his head in between her legs

he starts licking, there is a slight salty taste, now he's caught up in this sensation of giving pleasure. He continues kissing all around her vagina, she starts groaning in desired pleasure, completely caught up in the moment she directs.

'Inside, with your tongue.' Using his hands, he parts her vagina, he notices the pinkness on the inside placing his head over her slit he forces his tongue to protrude inside her. She moans, "Yes, oh yes," as he continues to drive his tongue in, the response from her is a quivering with sensation. Suddenly she pulls his head up and with fire in her eyes, orders.

'I want you now.' He looks at her and speaks earnestly.

'I haven't done this before.'

'Neither have I,' she responds, 'I'm still a virgin.'

'Do you want to go on.' She stares lovingly at him, their eyes meet, with truthfulness she answers.

'With you... yes.' His eyes moist over, she notices and lives in the tender moment for a short while.

'I have some protection,' he quietly announces. Leaning over, he opens a side drawer and gets a condom out but he's not sure how it all works, ripping it open he stares at it, Beth comes to the rescue.

'Let me help.' Taking it, she gets him to lie on his back then delicately rolls it over his penis and down using the palm of her hands, satisfied she lies back next to him, quipping.

'Thank god for "Girlfriend" magazine.' Moving on top of her, he is ready, but she knows the feeling has to be right, she is excited but needs to be open, ready for his penetration.

'Stroke me a little first,' she asks. Obliging, he moves his hand across her vagina, the sweeping stroke gives pleasure.

'A little higher,' she directs, trying to find her "G" spot. As he continues, she is squirming and moaning more, he realises she is becoming moist also her vagina is loosening up, now she's in the zone, anticipation and desire are at their highest, she stares and pleads.

'Come inside me, now, I want you now, even if it hurts.' Taking his penis in her hands, she opens her legs even wider and guides him in.

'Careful, go slowly is the request.' He pushes in and out but not too deep, just near the top of her vagina, this miniature penetration builds her sensuality, knowing this will hurt her desire overrides it. With his movement, she can feel his penetration pushing against her hymen, she's lost in ecstasy and cries. 'Yes, yes, go, go.' He pushes in, she gasps with pain as he breaks thru, as he moves in and out, the pain subsides and a glowing feeling replaces it. The performance gets more intense she can feel his penis stiffening even more, they're both caught up in the emotion. She starts rubbing his chest, her hands flay at his back, the euphoric feeling wells up inside of her drawing an emotional, "Yes, yes... more, more." Joining in, he emits, "Oh yeah, yes." Enraptured in the total sexuality euphoria takes over, she is lost in her first experience of sexual intercourse. To her it's like an out of body feeling, she is oblivious to anything in the total agony of her ecstasy, losing control she cries,

'Fuck me, fuck me, hard... hard... hard.' On the last word, he releases and ejaculates into the condom, at the same time she climaxes in her orgasm. This is a feeling never experienced before, it's a monumental release of ecstasy thru her whole body, she shudders with the release of euphoria, letting the feeling envelope her, it stays for a moment then dissipates. He is exactly the same, slowing he collapses on top of her, they stay in that position for a minute, both feel the pleasure of being entwined and still connected. Gradually he pulls out and rolls to the side, twisting heads they gaze into the other's eye, hugging her she nestles in close.

'So that was sex,' she grins. Smiling back, he agrees, 'Yeah, I guess so... wow.' They both giggle, he pulls the sheet over them, kisses her and they drift off to sleep, wrapped in each other's arms, both sublimely relaxed.

CHAPTER 30

Morning breaks, Rod and Beth are drowsing in his bed, the sound of footsteps is heard coming from the kitchen. They are now both awake, looking at each other smiles are exchanged, footsteps close in down the passageway, the door opens and Karen sticks her head in.

'Rod are you…' The vision of Rod and Beth in bed together halts her sentence, her voice trails off, with a shocked look on her face, she panics, closes the door and runs to Geoff's room, Rod sums up the situation.

'We could be in a spot of trouble here, any regrets?' She grins and kisses him commenting, 'None at all, but be ready for flack.' The next footsteps are stronger and heard pumping down the hallway, the door opens, Geoff's head pokes in, with a forceful tone, he orders.

'Right you two, get your clothes on and come out here immediately.' He slams the door and thunders back down the hallway, Beth and Rod look at each other, grimace and start to comply. Once presentable, they walk down the passageway and enter the kitchen, Geoff points to the lounge and sternly orders.

'Through here.' Moving to the lounge they sit on the sofa, Karen and Geoff are pacing in front of them, silence

reigns, tension builds, Geoff starts.

'Rod we're happy that you two have become friends, but friendship means walking her home, talking about the future, being thoughtful, not... umm mate, you're only seventeen.' Karen takes over.

'Beth how old are you?'

'Sixteen and about three months.'

'Sixteen'... she turns to Rod, 'You're seventeen, what you've done is illegal... I think.' She continues but there seems to be a lingering of doubt or guilt behind the reasoning. 'Beth, you were invited into this house because we believed you were responsible but this is not the behaviour of a responsible person.' Geoff nods in agreement and extends.

'Mate you can't just rush off and do what your emotions tell you, life's about being sensible, I mean I don't get you two, you've only just met and within a couple of weeks, you're... well... ahh, you're just not being smart.' He transfers his gaze to Beth.

'Look you are obviously a well brought up girl, I'm surprised you let yourself get caught up in this, I mean, you know the right thing.' Karen cuts in and out as they both try to explain responsibilities, it's not a rant and rave, it's more like a lecture, Beth and Rod sit like two school kids being told off. Watching and listening not interrupting, taking it all in, Beth watches in admiration, these two people are carrying on because they care really care, not like old uncle Reg. Although copping a blast she feels a real warmth emanating from them, instead of feeling picked on she feels wanted and relaxed, Karen mentions Reg and what the implications will be when he finds out. As she talks Beth feels that the strength of her argument is a slight façade covering a minor amount of guilt hidden inside, they continue the parental style lecturing but eventually peter out, Geoff asks.

'Well, have you got anything to say?' Nodding, Beth

politely says 'Yes.' Choosing her words very carefully and distinctly, she begins.

'Firstly, you both have been so kind to me since I arrived, my new home life has been difficult whereas you have treated me like a sister I would never do anything to jeopardise our relationship but everybody has to experience life and all it entails at some stage.' Continueing, she notices that Karen has subconsciously bitten her lower lip.

'Half the girls at my old school had experienced sexual relations to some degree, I had discussed this with my parents, they were very positive and said they would support me when I decided to make that decision, their only stipulation was that I make it wisely. They said when I decided to become involved that they would talk to me about contraception and also fill in any gaps or questions that I might have. Nothing was off the board, they were completely open regarding my sexual education. They were wonderful, then I met Rod, my age, strong but caring as I said to Karen before a young gentleman, well, the time was right for both of us, it was our first time and a beautiful experience, like you said Karen, one that you never forget.' Rod now sees that it's his turn to state his feelings.

'I agree, it was the best thing that's ever happened to me in my life, she's the most beautiful and understanding girl that I have ever met.' With these comments, Beth glows inside and places her hand on his knee, softly smiling at him. The truthfulness and honesty of these statements seem to pacify Karen and Geoff, she can see them subtly melt in front of her. It's as if they have reverted back to their past, their first time, Karen has mellowed, she's now relaxed with less deep-seated anxiety and comments.

'You'll still have to tell Reg something, I suggest not everything but at least something that gives him the general idea that you're growing up, not a little girl anymore, I'll walk you home and apologise for keeping you out overnight without

telling him. I'll make up some excuse.' With a less brusque manner, Geoff orders Rod.

'Alright Rod, get dressed into work gear, we've got a long drive today, got to pick up some digging equipment.' Karen gives less of an order, more of a request.

'Beth you go to and get your gear together.' They both exit the room, Geoff looks at Karen and shakes his head.

'Teenagers.' She comments to him but with a forlorn sentiment, she believes there is an element of her involvement in this situation, she needs to solve this dilemma.

'Tell me about it but one thing we need to do is get them together and explain a few things, we'll have to work a few things out from our end I guess like standards and expectations.' Geoff nods in agreement.

'Hmm... didn't expect this one, good thing is that they are both level headed kids, I'm sure we'll work something out.' Agreeing, Karen smiles. 'Yeah... christ when did I become a parent, I'm too young.' This causes a laugh from Geoff. She continues, 'But I need to have a girl on girl talk to Beth.' Geoff nods in understanding saying, 'I'll need to do the same with Rod.' Rod is first out of the room, he's immediately collard by Geoff and beat a hasty exit. Beth follows, entering the lounge room, Karen gives her a smile, she returns the smile with a slight sheepish grin. 'Let's go,' quips Karen, they leave the room.

CHAPTER 31

Walking down the street Beth notices Karen is a study of deep concentration, she starts generating conversation.

'So, umm, Karen... when did you get it on for the first time?' The style of the open, intimate question jolts Karen back into reality, she relaxes, smiles and thinks to herself. "This is a lovely girl's first time, who am I to ruin it." Her answer immediately shifts the generation gap from older younger to two young friends in discussion.

'Oh, it was years ago, actually when I was in college.'

'Do you remember him?'

'Oh yeah, he was a dish, a Phys Ed major, very fit, a little painful but something you never forget, no matter what happens thru life, you never forget the first.'

'Yes,' agrees Beth, 'It was special and now I feel liberated sort of.' Trying to interpret the response Karen asks.

'...cos of the death of your parents, like you need to grow up more quickly?'

'Well not need to, I'm still a young girl at heart but want to, I've already watched you and Geoff, you guys have a beautiful mature relationship. I'm limited in the area of sexuality but will try and go with the flow, it's time to move on

and experience the next phase of my life. Where that takes me, I don't know, I'll do my best at school and continue with my aerobic fitness exercise, so at least I'll be prepared for whatever lies ahead.' Karen's impressed with Beth's analysis. 'Actually, that sounds pretty mature to me.'

'Well I know I'm young and inexperienced but I do want to learn how to enjoy life as well as work. The other night with you in the shower was a beautiful experience, I loved it, I'm sure you'll show me more.' Studying her as she speaks, Karen gets a lump in her throat commenting. Look I didn't mean to lead you, umm I sort of feel responsible for what happened.'

'Responsible!'

'Well, I sort of drew you out of your comfort zone and well introduced you to areas that you hadn't investigated before, by doing that I felt that I'd led you into your involvement with Rod. I mean it was a pretty big step for one night, especially when you hadn't experienced anything of that nature before.'

'Look you didn't, I wouldn't have involved myself in anything I didn't desire.'

'Yes, I know that you're a strong personality but I did lead you in the shower, not quite forced but sucked you along.'

'Ha ha, very apt choice of words.' The comment makes Karen blush a tad.

'Yeah right… but still maybe I shouldn't have.'

'No, it was great, I loved the experience, plus you did rather set the scene for me to extend it with Rod, a big thank you for that.'

Stopping Beth looks at Karen who continues to have a doubtful look, leaning forward, she moves closer to Karen's face only about two centre meters away, with a tender smile she leans in the last bit and kisses the tip of Karen's nose, then withdraws a little.

'Look you've opened the door, not forced, you've

engineered excitement in me.'

'Yes, but I feel a bit guilty because of your inexperience.'
With a coy smile, Beth answers.

'Well, not completely.'

'How's that, you said you've never had a boyfriend
before?'

'Yes, true but I also said I came from an open family.'

'Yes, I remember you saying that but I didn't dwell
much on the aspect of open, umm... should I be going here?'

'Oh yes no problems at all, I'll explain.' They begin
sauntering on as Beth starts her revelation.

'When I said inexperienced that was true, certainly
from a male-female point of view but regarding the
understanding of sexual encounters I had a very interesting
introduction. Firstly, my family was very open with regard to
sexuality, my father and mother loved each other dearly, very
active sexually and never tried to hide any aspect from me, that
was of no consequence when I was young, I mean Primary
school age. However, when I turned twelve or thirteen, I hit
puberty like all the rest of the girls at school, you probably
remember how it knocks you around. You lose confidence,
become insular, your bedroom becomes your sanctuary. The
only ones you feel you can confide in is your friends who are
experiencing the same changes, although one might think
that'd help it really doesn't. Most young girls are so introverted
they won't talk much or discuss it. When it came up at school
during health and human everyone just clammed up, so I had
no one really, or so I thought but I'll come to that later. My
parents were great thru all this, they didn't pressure or hassle
me, just let me work my way thru it, puberty I mean, they still
continued with life as normal but, well, I became quieter and
embarrassed, especially if I bumped into my parents in the
bathroom and they were naked. At ten I was part of the family,
I'd bounce into mum and dad's bedroom on weekend mornings,

didn't care what state they were in, sometimes they would be resting quietly and the next thing they'd have "Pumpkin Pie" joining in and bouncing all over them, it usually produced fits of laughter and mayhem.'

'Pumpkin Pie?'

'Yes, that was my dad's nickname for me.' 'Pumpkin Pie… ha ha… very cute.'

'Yes, and I loved it, still do, but puberty hit and I changed psychologically, they didn't, I did, this went on for about two years. I didn't turn away or get rude like some of the other girls at school, I was just naive and confused. But round fifteen I connected with one of the other girls in our group. Her name was Maddie, when the other girls would bag their parents, brothers or sisters, I noticed that she never really agreed and I believed gave a few comments or facial mannerisms to act like she was part of the group, I was sort of the same. I didn't agree with the other's snide comments regarding their families, but like Maddie I laughed or acted as if I agreed just to save face. I mean I loved my parents, it wasn't their fault that I was unsure in fact they were very tactful in offering advice, no pressure but an ear to talk too if ever needed.' Nodding in understanding Karen admits.

'Well, that sounds pretty normal, actually rather lucky they were so sympathetic but you mentioned your friend Maddie?'

'Oh yes, well, here goes, I was about fifteen and a bit and was doing some shopping at the local mall when I bumped into Maddie who had just come out of a shop. We exchanged pleasantries, spying the bag I asked a harmless question of "Oh what did you buy?" Her response was slightly guarded, something like "Oh nothing, just something for my brother's birthday." I knew she had a brother he was about two years older than us. I'd never really met him just a smile or a few basic pleasantries, so I asked "Oh right what does he

need?" She was offhand and dismissive again with the "Nothing really." Then she changed the topic questioning me with a directness she never really showed at school. She asked, "Hey Beth do you really agree with what the others say at school, I mean regarding their parents and family." The look on her face showed me she was serious, also I realised that if I gave the normal answer, she'd be polite but the conversation would trail away. I remember looking directly at her trying to read her, my head buzzed, "What does she want, what do I say." It sounds easy now but at fifteen this was a big moment. I remember being incredibly unsure but something in her attitude drew a conviction from me, so I answered truthfully. "No, I don't like it or agree." She eyed me and smiled with respect to my admission and said, "Thought so." Following that she asked, "Do you love your parents?" Since I was being truthful and believed that suddenly I had a sister in arms I replied, "Yes, they're great, it's not their fault that I'm... you know a bit unsure about myself." Suddenly I felt like a weight had been lifted off my head, the way she looked at me I believe she felt the same. She said, "Have you got time for a chat?" I did so we went into a café and sat.

She started explaining that she understood why the other girls were arcing up at home against their parents but she didn't want to follow their path. I asked her "Are you happy at home?" "Oh yes," she replied, "My parents are great." This admission was so refreshing I felt a wave of joy infiltrate thru me. Then I said with a grin, "Even your brother?" The reply floored me, "Oh yes, I love my brother, he's so cool and understanding." I mean at fifteen soon sixteen to admit that, well I was amazed. Then she continued, "I mean my family has always been so open regarding everything." I realised where she was going, well I thought where she was going and joined in. "Yes, I know what you mean, so has mine." So, we started on a conversation regarding our family's, especially our parents, the

similarities were amazing. Their open attitude to everything but how she'd drawn away from them 'cos of hitting puberty." I couldn't believe it, I was the same in all aspects, I felt like I was talking to a kindred spirit, I was so relieved and happy not just for her but me as well. I had been unburdened, so naturally, I asked how she was now. There was a pause, she reached over and held my hand tenderly and exclaimed "free." I don't know if it was the physical contact or the word free but I felt a tingle all over my body".

She explained that when she was a little girl, she'd run into her parents' bedroom with her brother on weekend mornings and bounce into her parents' bed, many times their parents would have arms wrapped around each other, they became a hilarious distraction. I laughed that I'd done exactly the same thing, we both agreed that its part of the joys of youth. Also, she shared a room with her brother and until puberty hit, they'd been very happy together. I explained I was an only child so I hadn't had that experience of sharing with someone, the way she bubbled on telling me about her brother, it almost made me envious. Anyway, I asked her when did they separate, and get this, she said once she hit puberty and started periods. She was so open and trusting of me I felt a sort of camaraderie, this must have been reciprocated 'cos she expanded that when her first periods hit, she asked her parents about changing rooms. They were fine with it and explained that they'd explain it with her brother. Now here's the interesting bit, she sat down also to talk to him, she explained that she was going thru changes, both physically and mentally and needed space. He agreed but stressed that he also was affected by changes, she asked him about his changes curious that he should respond in such a manner, he talked about starting shaving, hair growing in different places plus the effect girls were having on his psyche. So, she says to him "girls... but I'm a girl," and get this he explains that round fifteen and later girls start having

an effect and that boys have a thing called wet dreams and basically, it's like having sexual intercourse in your sleep. You ejaculate and have an orgasm, in the morning your sheets and P J's are wet and sticky, didn't she ever notice? Shaking her head, she proclaimed that she was oblivious to his situation and fired back that she'd started having periods, was using tampons and pads, hadn't he ever noticed? "Not really," he replied just that she'd developed up top and seemed to be growing by the month.'

'Okay Karen, here's the really lovely part, Maddie said they sat on the bed and just held hands, he was so understanding and open she just melted inside. He was nothing like the bitchy stupid girls at school. When he said he'd move out to the other room to give her space it showed understanding and caring, well something glowed inside of her, it was love thru respect. Anyway, he moved out and she tried to get used to being alone in her own room it was different but she got used to it. Well a year or more went passed they were still relaxed around the other, it was recently that a new era as she called it started. It was one morning she was bursting to go to the toilet which is situated in the bathroom, she bursts in and he's there trying to shave, seeing him in there she was about to turn and leave when she remembered the openness they had before, so courteously apologising to which he answered "no probs," she dropped her panties and does her business. Flushes, cleans herself then her hands and is about to leave when she hears "Oww." Asking what's wrong he replied "unsteady hands." Walking up she offers "let me", and with female tenderness she runs the razor over his face.' 'Now this is interesting, he plays football, always has and she's heard he's pretty good, the training over the last few years has stepped up, more running, push-ups, weights etc. as she shaves him her hand rests on his bare torso. Concentrating on the task at hand she has to manoeuvre to different standing positions not

noticing that her free hand has rested on his hip. Finishing she notices a bulge in his PJ's, well she's a bit confused and asked." What caused that?' He just smiled gives her a peck on the cheek and answers "Girls, but a very nice one thanks," and walks away. Now being young but not completely naïve she realises that she has caused his reaction, slightly mystified she follows him to his room to explain that she didn't mean anything by it. However, on entering his room he's getting changed, about to put on his jocks, thus she completely views his nakedness, says "sorry" and is about to turn when he replies "no probs, hey we're brother and sister we've got no need to hide." Well "Boom" a penny drops, she looks at him and smiles thinking "Yep he's dead right, I don't want to be like those neurotic girls at school, I want to be free and open like our family used to be," so she said to him. "Let's just be open and relaxed around each other sort of like it was when we were kids." He agreed that would be nice but things had changed, they had changed and couldn't go back, that they'd both have to adapt." They hugged and agreed.

'Well Karen that got me thinking, she'd grown into this new era as she called it, I needed to do something as well. That night I started talking to my parents about various aspects of my life, I think it slightly surprised them but they let me roll with my questions and thoughts. They were great, no preaching just listening and trying to understand where I was coming from as I tried to work my way thru the unsureness over the last few years. That night while I was in the bathroom cleaning my teeth, I heard them talking in bed. They were discussing me, their main points were that I was a sensible girl who had a difficult time dealing with puberty but they felt I was starting to come out the other side. The thing that really struck me was how much they expressed to each other their love of me. Listening, it almost brought me to tears, I thought to myself, "How understanding, they love me even though I've been off for a while, just like Maddie's family." So

that night I opened the bathroom door and stepped in, said
"Goodnight" to them in their bedroom which I hadn't done for
quite a while then kissed them both, they acted as if this was
the normal situation but I could tell they were really chuffed
at my effort to restore normality into the family regime'. 'Over
the next few weeks I revised my attitude to family life, I left my
door open again, started wandering around in my nighty and
underwear, entered the bathroom regardless of who was in
there and basically initiated a return to normality, all I needed
was the final piece to be put into place. That weekend I woke
early and went into the bathroom to do my ablutions, hearing
sounds from my parents' bedroom, I opened the door, my
father was lying next to mum. It was a warm morning, so they
had nothing on, I could see my mum's breasts full and still firm,
they noticed me standing there and slowed their interaction,
mum asked "Yes sweetie?" I looked and desired to be part
of the family unit again like the old days. Dad followed and
asked "What is it pumpkin pie… do you want to jump in?" I
was relieved but needed to make a point. "Yes, I think I'd like
that but one thing I'm not a little girl anymore." Mum was just
so wonderful and said, "We know that darling but to us you'll
always be our little girl." She lifted her arm in a welcoming
movement, said "Come on," and with that I clambered into
the bed between them snuggling in like I was ten again. They
wrapped their arms around me and kissed and cuddled me, it
was a wonderful feeling being part of the family again. From
then on, the household was back to normal, one thing I noticed
was how I seemed to have instigated an increase in affection.
They showered me with hugs and kisses, dad would give me a
wrestle and playful slaps on my bottom plus it had some effect
on their sex life. I mean they had always been active but now
I notice they seemed to lift to a new level. Many nights and
weekend mornings they'd be going at it hammer and tongs,
Mum was fantastic, explaining things, it was a great learning

experience. So, feeling more settled I mentioned to them that I had a friend at school, Maddie, and that we had been chatting about life and sex and stuff and that I'd been invited over to her place. They agreed that it was good that I was discussing things with friends and believed she and I sounded mature enough to handle new developments especially in the sexual area. They did stress that any information that I might need to know they were happy to be the "go-to" people, they were so understanding, just like Maddie's parents. The next day at school, I got Maddie by herself and said I might come over, she was very happy and said she had something to show me anyway.'

CHAPTER 32

K aren nods. "Okay... I see, so what happened when you went over?'

'We met after school and walked to her place, it wasn't that far from my place actually. Once there she introduced me to her mum, I was surprised how close in age her mum was to my mum, after some basic small talk Maddie and I moved to her room. Sitting on the bed she explained that she was really excited that I had agreed to come over and wanted to show me some new clothes she had bought. Girls like fashion so I was interested, she directed me to close my eyes, while I had them closed, I could hear sounds of draws opening and closing then footsteps exiting the bedroom. I opened my eyes and waited about ten minutes, soon she returned and again asked "Close your eyes". I could hear her enter the room, she called "Open", I did and what a sight, Maddie had transformed herself, she had combed her hair allowing it to flow freely applied a little lipstick and was wearing a black dress with matching black three inch block heeled shoes with an open toe. But Karen the dress, gosh it was brilliant, black with silver threads running through it, very low cut at the front and an open back, tight round the bodice and flaring out just below the hips, it just

covered her backside. The thing is she carried it off so well, little Maddie from school was gone replaced by this elegant sensual young lady, I sat amazed. Staring at her I was taken by her figure, I mean the top was enhancing her boobs and what boobs, I'd never taken much notice of her figure at school, I mean you don't with everyone in school uniform. If you'd asked me to describe her, I'd have replied, tallish, about five foot eight, blonde hair blue eyes and a pretty, no more attractive face. I knew she was in the swimming team and did movement classes so was reasonably fit but now in front of me was this most glamorous mature looking girl. She struck a pose and asked "Well?" 'I answered "Amazing, you look so attractive", my comment seemed to please her 'cos she commented, "I also got accessories, do you want to see?" 'Now I thought she meant jewellery but to my surprise she grinned at me and carefully unzipped the side of the dress and let it slide to the floor. There in front of me she stood in heels all five foot eleven with the sexiest underwear I had ever personally seen. The bra was a minuscule black push up bra, the briefs were nothing more than a G-String with a mesh front, both pieces left nothing to the imagination that this was one very attractive female. Her sport and exercise had given her a most sublime figure, I tell you Karen she was ten out of ten.' 'She asked, "You like?" I stammered something along the grounds of unbelievable, then she invited me to feel the material. Boy was my heart racing, I stood up and felt the material, as my hands ran across the bra and G-String they also ran over her body, she started murmuring "Mmm", then looked at me and asked.

'Can you see yourself wearing something like this in the future?' My heart was pounding but I answered truthfully.

'Yes, I'd like to.'

'Karen, she looked me in the eye and declared. 'Yes, I thought you would, I've watched you at sport, you're really fit you would really show this off let's compare now.' She leant

forward and kissed me on the lips then started to unbutton my school dress, I could have said stop but I was too excited, truthfully Karen I wanted to compare, I guess I was sensually aroused. She helped me discard the dress I stood there in front of her in my normal basic white bra and panties. She ran her hands over my body and whispered "beautiful" then she leaned forward and kissed me again. Karen I was enthralled, captivated, something inside of me glowed with excitement, I couldn't help myself I said. 'Let's really compare.' She looked at me and grinned and replied, "Yes lets, I'd love to."

'Stepping back a step she loosened her bra and flipped it aside, I could only stare, she had magnificent breasts they looked about a thirty-four and taught with beautiful large rosy nipples, she gave me a wink and a nod to follow suit, which I did. This allowed her to reach out and fondle my breasts, I tell you Karen it was the most wonderful feeling I was so excited. Then she stepped back and slid her G-String down, I gasped, her groin was completely hairless and silky smooth, major waxing and moisturising must have gone on there. She enticed me, "Feel", Oh, it was beautiful, so soft and smooth, following she asked "You.' 'By now I wanted to join and show off, recently I'd started trimming my pubic hair so not to be too bushy, because of that I looked young and fresh, not succulent like hers but cute. She gushed how lovely it looked then suggested we lay back on her bed, lying back we nestled into each other and started kissing and canoodling. It was lovely Karen, we didn't go further sexually just stayed like that enjoying each ones presence. After about half an hour I explained I had to leave, I rose and got dressed, as I dressed, I asked her.

'Are you getting ready for boys?'

'No,' she replied. 'Just putting my toe in the water with girls first but they must be open for experimentation… like you are, can we meet again sometime soon?'

'Yes,' I told her. 'I'd really like that.' Then I opened up

my soul explaining.

'Maddie you are a beautiful girl and you're moving ahead, you're not a lesbian, are you?' She nodded no, then I explained.'

'Neither am I but we can help each other I really love what we experienced today I'd love to be involved more maybe delve a little deeper.'

'Me too,' she answered and still lying on the bed she moved to lie on one side resting her head on her hand she mischievously smiled blew me a kiss and waved bye I answered "beautiful, later" and exited the room.'

'Gosh,' exclaims Karen. 'I really want to get together with you again, you've really excited me but tell me did you get together again?'

'Only once and we just did the similar sort of thing, then my parents died and I moved down here, at first I thought that sort of thing was finished but I met you, I'd love to have fun with you." Holding hands, they walk towards Reg's house as they move Beth divulges some inner thoughts.

'You realise, I've got to take some responsibility for myself, I can't live with uncle Reg for the rest of my life.'

'Can't or don't want to?' The statement gets an uncertain smile reciprocated back to Karen, arriving at Reg's house Beth's already worked out how to handle Reg, she tells Karen.

'Thanks for the walk and the chat, look there's no need to come in, I'll talk to uncle Reg and clear the air, it'll be alright.'

'Okay if you're sure,' responds Karen, 'Come over to our place tomorrow night and we'll all sit down and see if we can come up with something that is mutually agreeable to Geoff and I and you and Rod.' Beth agrees and beams, 'Okay and thanks you and Geoff have been so understanding, not so much parents, but real friends.'

The acclimation touches Karen's heart, she melts a bit, they hug, Karen turns and with a "Love you," moves off, smiling Beth waves then enters Reg's house.

CHAPTER 33

Entering the kitchen, Beth can see Reg at the sink preparing some breakfast, as soon as he sees her, he fires up, the old Reg is back.

'So, you decided to show your face at last, what do you think this is miss, a hotel? I expect some decency to be informed by you as to where you are at night, you could be off gallivanting round to well… I don't know, so what have you got to say for yourself?' She's stayed calm during his tirade, treading carefully tries to explain and appease him. 'Yes, uncle Reg you're right to be cross, I didn't mean to stay out all night, but by the time it was to leave Karen's everyone was dead tired so they offered me a bed and it was too late to call you, you would have been asleep. Karen walked me home this morning and was going to apologise but I said I'd explain and hoped you'd understand'. He starts to wind down.

'Well, no harm done, but make sure you do call in the future, I don't want you wandering 'round the place at night like some of those other losers round this town.' Emphatically Beth agrees,

'No, I won't, I've seen them and have no intention of turning out like them.'

'Yes, well fair enough, you do seem to have a level head on your shoulders, so we'll leave it at that.' Beth breathes a sigh of relief, 'thanks uncle Reg for being so understanding.'

'Well, umm… that's alright, alright then,' he mumbles. With a spring in her step and avidity of tone, she tells him.

'I'm going to unpack my things and have a shower, I'll have a cuppa with you when I'm finished if you want?' He nods in agreement, picking up her bag she bounces out of the kitchen to her room. Unzipping the bag, she takes out dirty gear, bundles it up and heads to the laundry. Re-entering the bedroom, she slips off shoes, skirt and top, grabs a towel, toilet bag and heads for the bathroom. Reg is pottering round in the kitchen as she moves thru, she calls out, "showering now.' He looks up noticing she is wearing just her underwear, with a studied look he answers "Righto.'

In the bathroom, Beth closes the door but it's not sniped, taking a small hand mirror out of her toilet bag she rests it on the top ledge of the shower. Flipping off her underwear she enters the shower but before turning the water on she aligns the mirror so she can see the reflection of the door although her back is to the door. Turning the shower taps on and getting in, she picks up the soap and begins washing. Halfway thru her washing she glances at the mirror noticing door slightly opening, Reg's eye can be seen peeping in, the shower screen is frosted glass but the intrusion is annoying, the effect is one of questionable irritation rather than being scared. After a few minutes the door closes, she finishes washing and steps out, dries herself, wraps a towel around her and heads back to her bedroom. Travelling back thru the kitchen Reg is at work at the sink, he doesn't look or make a comment just head down. Back in her room, laying her underwear down and still with the towel draped around her she glances round the room, nothing but those few paintings and that oriental tapestry hung above her bed. Standing on the bed she attempts to move the

tapestry, it slides to the left, "Bingo," a five-centimetre hole is in the wall, behind it is Reg's tapestry, however with only one in place a person can clearly see thru to the other room, obviously the reverse applies. Footsteps are heard in the passageway, sliding the tapestry back into position she sits on the end of the bed and starts drying her hair with a spare towel, desperately trying to work out how to handle this situation. A determined look strengthens her face, putting down the spare towel she walks to her bag and takes out a comb, returning to the bed she starts combing her damp hair. That soft rustling sound is heard as she continues to comb her hair concentrating on making it straight and manageable. Then delicately the comb is placed on the bedside table, undoing the towel she allows it to fall to her waist, her back still facing the tapestry, suddenly she whips her torso and head round and winks at the tapestry. There is the sound of a thud from Reg's room next door then footsteps almost running down the passageway, with a determined look, she throws a skirt and top on and storms down the passageway, entering the kitchen Reg is sitting forlornly in a chair, Beth storms up to him and demands.

'Uncle Reg, why are you watching me, or should I say peeping at me?' He's been sprung and has no reply except.

'I dunno.' She looks at him, sixtyish but more like eighty, a decrepit old man slowly broken down with time, a new emotion sweeps across her, this situation is so surreal. A sixteen-year-old girl who's just had he first major sexual experience with a boy as well as a sexual encounter with a member of the same sex is now about to play parent to an aged sixty-something year old uncle. Losing her aggression, her heart metamorphoses itself into compassion, pity ekes out of her, she tries a different tack.

'Please uncle Reg talk to me, I'm understanding, we can work this out.' He looks at her, his eyes dimmed with shame, thinking to himself, "How do you talk, explain yourself to

this young person, she practically comes from another planet.' However, he knows he must at least try, she deserves an explanation no matter how pathetic, summing up some small semblance of courage he tries.

'You mightn't understand this but it sort of comes from your parents, you see when I was growing up your dad and I, even though I was a bit older well, we were poles apart, he was good at everything, I was just a plodder and especially with the girls he was popular, I guess you would say he was "Cool," well in their eyes anyway. I was interested in girls also but went about it, I donno, the wrong way, so to them I was a bit strange. Therefore hardly any dates and the ones I had were a mess, at eighteen it was out to work, I didn't fit into any sporting clubs, so I learnt to keep my own company, my job at the water-board moved me round a fair bit, so I got to know the country. I found this place and decided to stay, no one bothered me and I was out of the rat race. Listening intently, she questions.

'Fair enough, but what about that business down at the local Primary School?' Shaking his head, he answers, 'Just intrigued, I'd never hurt anyone especially a child, they're so small and fragile, yet there was an example, a microcosm of society, all different personalities being formed, there in the playground. The loud, the soft, insular, bullies, quiet ones… fascinating.' There is a lull, he continues but changes track.

'You arrived, I'd never had anything to do with girls especially teenage ones, here you presented yourself, an attractive confident young lass, a cute young thing not so down after the death of your parents but picking yourself up, still retaining a zest for life… I lost that a long time ago. The way you do things, like dress and comb your hair, it's like art, I've never seen anything like that before and in my house… I mean our house. I'm too old to love you but not too old to admire you, I know it seems strange or even worse to you but it really is only admiration plus a little curiosity.'

He looks into her eyes, tears well up, he croaks, 'My child I'm sorry.' She's overcome with his honesty, the baring of his soul has stripped away any resentment that shadowed her, looking at him, she feels so saddened for him, his lonely tragic life. Raising to look at his eyes with tears running down her cheeks she declares.

'You're my uncle and now my only family and no matter what I'll always love you. Especially for taking me in, I have no-one else.' Studying her tears roll down his cheeks also he reiterates his feelings again.

'You lovely child, I'm so sorry.' His honesty breaks her, she rushes into his arms and hugs him with ferocity, at first, he is overcome with this open display of affection towards him but then holds her fast emitting equal love. They hold the position for quite a while then gradually release, she explains.

'We both have to learn to live with each other, It'll take time but It'll be alright.' He agrees, 'Yes, Luv, you're right, time.' They brush their tears away and view each other, their expression shows a desire for a new start, she opens.

'I've got to get homework done.'

'Yes,' he answers, 'And I've got work to do outside, best get on with it.' She grins, 'Best to.' Turning Beth walks back to her room, he watches her depart, a tender smile softens his face. In her room, she sits at the side of the bed looking at the photo of her parents then at herself in the mirror, smiling she knows that her parents would be very proud of her, a small tear trickles down her cheek.

CHAPTER 34

Another school day morning arrives, Beth's rushing round getting her school stuff together, opening the fridge, she spies a brown paper bag with her name on it. Taking it out and peering inside she sees an apple, sandwich and health bar. He's made her lunch, a glow warms her, heading out of the kitchen she stops at his bedroom door and raps on it, "Yes, Luv," is the answer, opening the door he's still in bed, "Uncle Reg, I've got to see Karen tonight after school, I'll go straight there and probably have dinner with them but will definitely be home tonight just after tea, if that's alright?'

'Fine, no probs,' he replies.

'Great, gotta fly, see ya.' He smiles and rolls over in bed. Beth arrives at the bus stop as Shelly is being dropped off, they exchange "Hi's," then board the bus moving to the back seat as normal, Shelly asks cheerfully, "How was your weekend?" Beth's answer is vague, "Oh, not too bad yours?" A basic conversation rolls on till Shelly still only being polite asks.

'What'd you do?' Beth hesitates then answers. 'Had dinner at Karen's.' The answers fine, the problem is the hesitation in her manner of answer, it has raised Shelly's curiosity, she digs a bit deeper.

'Oh, who was there?'

'Umm, just Kas, her partner Geoff and his apprentice nephew.' Shelly poses a look like she's thinking.

'Hmm, two boys and two girls, that's a nice foursome, Umm, did you sleepover or go home after?' Beth's back peddling and Shelly knows it.

'Oh, I sort of slept over.'

'Sort of... what's sort of?' She inquires, continuing to smile, her curiosity drives her forward. "Hey, all those houses in town are similar, they only have two bedrooms, so where did you sleep'? Beth looks out the window pretending to view the scenery, acting as if not taking too much interest in the conversation, Shelly gives a, "Uhh uhh?' Turning towards Shelly Beth thinks to herself, "Another step in life, owning up," she looks directly at Shelly and with authority states, "I shared." Shelly digests the information, returns her gaze to Beth following up with, "With who, with him?" No answer is immediately forthcoming but with a nervous self-conscious motion, she licks her lips and murmurs, "Well sort of..." Shelly's worked it out, her eyes open wide, astonishment floods thru her.

'You didn't... I mean, you didn't... like...? With a serious expression, Beth lowers her head and her eyeballs fire directly into Shelly.

'Oh, you did, Oh my god, Oh my god, what, what did...' Snapping at her Beth forcibly whispers, "Shh, shh... close your mouth, shh..." Shelly's still in amazement land, half in shock, Beth deftly smacks her across the mouth just with enough force to snap her back to reality, it does the trick, Shelly settles this allows Beth to speak distinctly to her.

'Shelly, the only reason I told you this is because I believe you're old and mature enough to handle it, if you want to discuss anything I will but like I said before I'll not go into specifics with you.' This statement to Shelly regarding a trust

in her maturity does the trick, she smiles and in a slightly embarrassed way apologises.

'Yes, you're right, this is deeply personal, I was acting like a little school girl.' Smiling, Beth agrees somewhat but qualifies.

'Well, you are a little school girl but a smart and maybe a mature one.' The compliment brings a smile and glow to Shelly, she contemplates, diving into her psych, trying to find the right question, knowing this, Beth waits, eventually, Shelly asks.

'Umm, was it good, like enjoyable?' Relaxing now Beth answers.

'Yes, Shell it was beautiful but I feel different now, sort of like my own person, it's given me… umm, sort of confidence like I've grown up.' Listening and thinking Shelly asks.

'Do you think maybe 'cos you've lost your parents you subconsciously felt the need to grow up?' Nodding to the mature type question she agrees somewhat.

'Perhaps, but I've still got a lot of learning to do, and different situations to experience. However, I am a forward-thinking person and will stay open-minded to whatever life throws or develops in front of me. I guess you could say I've taken my first step, let's see what's next.' Watching Shelly take in this discourse, she decides to change track.

'So, how's school going, you said you've started Health and Human, how's that going?'

'Funny you should mention that,' answers Shelly, 'we've just done the reproductive system and the body parts, so I sort of know a bit about what you experienced.' Now Beth starts to question her.

'Oh yes, and how did they do that?'

'Well, we had two teachers in the room, Mr Blandstone and Miss Theron, well they laid a sheet out on the floor and got us to all sit around it. The sheet had an outline of

a man and a woman. "Right", nods Beth. 'Yes, and after some general chat they asked us to name the body parts, they started with the woman's outline.

'Okay, go on.'

'Well some offered breasts and Miss Theron drew them in, I glanced around noticing some of the other girls getting embarrassed. Then they moved to the lower part of the body near the groin and asked what it was called. Boy, it got really quiet, one girl whispered vagina and Miss Theron drew a slit in. Then they moved to the man's shape and Mr Blandstone asked similar questions. The boys now got a little quiet but one boy said penis and Mr Blandstone drew it in, then he asked about the sack that hangs below the penis, like what was it called, someone said testacies and he drew that in.' 'Well,' comments Beth, 'That sounds pretty normal.' 'Yes, yes,' says Shelly but now with more urgency, 'Mr Blandstone then said everyone has slang names for these parts, he said a lot is used in swearing. He asked us all if we knew what they were, and that Miss Theron would write them in next to the correct name, boy, that sure was a way to get silence in the group. Miss Theron started, she asked for the slang name for woman's breasts, no one muttered a word, eventually Mia Perkins whispered "Tits,' then Sally said "Boobs," and Miss Theron wrote them in. She pointed to the vagina and asked for the slang name but this was way too deep for anyone, no one said boo. However I remembered the altercation we had in town with that Nancy girl and what she called me, so I spoke bravely and told them "cunt," Miss nodded and wrote it in, I noticed everyone staring at me but I thought if others can use it why can't I, so I did.'

'Well done,' agrees Beth admiringly, 'Okay what happened then?'

'A lot of the girls were staring at me except Sally Dickson she smiled at me and gave a nod also one boy nodded.'

'Who was that?'

'Jimmy Zenotti, he's from Italian parents.'

'You know Jimmy?'

'Oh yes, he's been thru most grades with me.'

'So, what's he like?'

'Actually, he's a really good soccer player, he plays at a higher league over on Launceston, maybe under fourteens.'

'He's not a friend?'

'Oh no, but he's very nice, umm polite oh and smart, we've been battling out on the tables races all year.' The antenna rises in Beth's psych, she starts digging.

'Have you beaten him in anything else?'

'Funny you ask, we had sports races the other day during Phys Ed, anyway we both got in the final, it was a close race but I won.'

'Did you?'

'Yes, I guess I'm reasonably fit and fast 'cos of all my dance work.'

'I've noticed that you look good for your age, so when you beat him in the sprint race, did he say anything?'

'Not really, we just shook hands, he patted me on the shoulder and that was that.'

'Hmm… back to the Health and Human lesson, you said he didn't stare at you like the others or Sally.'

'No, he just looked at me with I don't know maybe respect that I made the comment.'

'Okay, go on.'

'Then Mr Blandstone took over and went thru the boy's parts.'

'I see, did anyone mention the slang names for the boy's parts?'

'Well a couple half-whispered, cock and dick, everyone was embarrassed again.'

'Okay, I can understand that, what happened next?'

Shelly pauses, thinks and continues, 'Mr Blandstone talked about how babies are made, like the boy's penis getting hard and entering the girl's vagina, like moving in and out till sperm comes out and it's this sperm that fertilises the girl's eggs, that's the start of a baby growing. Beth nods but continues to look at her in a prying manner. 'So that was it?'

'Not quite, then Mr Blandstone wrote down the words, "Sexual Intercourse" 'cos that's what it's called, he continued on and asked if anyone knew the slang word for it. Again, it was very quiet, no one was game to use the F... word, until Jimmy called out "Fuck", he was very calm, the girls were shocked, I think some boys smirked but most were embarrassed like the girls.'

'And when he said it, Shell, did he look anywhere?'

'No, but after a while, as Mr Blandstone was finishing up, he looked at me and well sort of nodded, well I think it was a nod'. Beth smiles.

'Shelly girl I have news for you.'

'What!'

'Don't open your mouth, but he likes you'. Shelly does just that, opens her mouth very wide and with a gasp exclaims.

'No, no, no, I don't even know him.'

'Do you say good morning?'

'Well, of course, but that's all.'

'Okay time to try something more.' Shelly's really confused.

'More, what more.' Rolling her eyes, Beth almost starts preaching.

'Ask him about his soccer on the weekend, his team, what position he plays, how he's going, his aims.'

'But I don't know anything about soccer.'

'Yes, I know but that's not the point, it's all about showing interest if you do, oh and not while the others are around either, I'll bet he asks you what you do.' Shelly's very

unsure.

'But I don't want any of that, you know sex stuff.' Laughing, Beth agrees and explains.

'Neither does he, trust me, but developing friends, especially boys who are mature enough to talk sensibly is a great advantage. I mean a boy who is a friend, not a "boyfriend", as such.' Deep in consternation, Shelly looks at Beth.

'But why me, I'm nothing special.' Grinning Beth administers a small dose of ego building.

'Ha, don't sell yourself short, you've already told me you're doing extension work at school, you're mature for your age with a fun personality and physically fit. He's similar, thus he's impressed plus both of you showed strength of character to use those strong swear words in front of the others, he was impressed.

'Okay I might be fit but really I'm just a little girl, you've got a woman's body, I'm not even in the ballpark.' Reassurance flows from Beth.

'Doesn't matter, he's not interested in that, you're probably the first girl who's tweaked his senses, just go with the flow, try and become friends.' Shelly nods, the advice sounds reasonable. They sit, occasionally smiling at each other watching thru the window as the bus rolls on.

CHAPTER 35

Its late afternoon, the school bus has finished its run, Beth is walking thru the back streets, the sun is declining but there is still a shallow warmth generated by it, walking in a relaxed and carefree manner she enters Karen's front gate, climbs the stairs and knocks on the front door. Footsteps are heard, the door opens Karen stands and beams at her, "Hi come in." Beth's relieved that Karen's bubbly manner seems to have returned, they walk down the passageway and enter the kitchen, Geoff and Rod are sitting at the table, they both rise. Geoff walks over to her and gives her a hug she can sense he's also in a relaxed mode. With a smile, he greets her, "Hi sweetie," reciprocating the greeting she returns with "Hi Geoff," they break and Rod walks forward and gives her a hug, she can feel the relaxation in the room, everything seems settled and calm. Geoff opens up and starts acting as master of ceremonies.

'Thanks for coming, Beth, have a seat and we'll all discuss this stuff'. Everyone sits round the table, Geoff does a quick look at Karen then starts, it's obvious they have been discussing the situation.

'Okay, well first Karen and I are glad that you two have struck up a friendship, you're both great kids... well not kids

but young people, however you are not yet adults, well not legally yet so we're going to have to work something out that appeases both parties. Regarding your uncle Reg, whatever he has decided regarding this situation is up to him, but in this house, we want certain rules to be followed if possible. Karen takes over.

'We can't condone sexual relations between minors but we also understand it's a case that you'd probably sneak off somewhere and become involved, we don't like that idea at all.' Geoff follows up.

'Rod you have work and a bit of schooling once a fortnight for your apprenticeship.' Karen adds.

'Beth, you have a lot of school time and homework so you won't have that much time to see each other during the week.' Geoff continues.

'The weekend is obviously yours, so Beth if you want to stay over sometimes then that's okay but before you agree Karen wants a good girl to girl talk with you and I need to do the same with Rod, we'll do that in a second, well what do you say, do you agree?' Beth has listened intently, taken it all in, she's the first to respond.

'Yes, I believe that's the answer my parents would have come up with.' Rod breaks in.

'Look I know we're underage and that puts you guys in an awkward position, so I reckon that sounds fair. ' Backing up his summation, Beth agrees.

'Yes, you've both been very reasonable.' Geoff looks at Karen and sighs.

'Phew, we've passed the parenting test, god I need a drink.' Everyone laughs, Beth then addresses them.

'I just want to say one thing. I know you're not my parents, more like best friends and I would never have done anything to upset you. No matter what you'd have decided, I would have complied with it and if not happy, well... Rod and

I would have had to work something out that suited us but didn't upset you, so thanks for being so understanding, umm there's one small problem…' Geoff quips, "Couldn't be you've just started… Owww.' Karen's given him a wack on the arm for being facetious.' Beth continues acting with a very worried look.

'I umm… haven't told my uncle yet, that I have a boyfriend.' Rod exclaims. "What?" Geoff's eyes bulge, "Oh no!" Karen's stuck for words, "Oh… oh dear." Recovering enough composure, Geoff exclaims.

'Well, I'd like to be a fly on the wall when you drop that little bombshell.' Laughing he announces directing towards Rod.

'And you haven't even met him yet.' Doing a quick aside to Karen, he quips.

'Does he still carry that shotgun?" Karen's eyes bite at him, "Don't." Raising his hands in mock surrender, he apologises, "Sorry… just thinking aloud." They all look at Rod, who is starting to feel uncomfortable, smiling at him Beth tries to alleviate the developing tension in him.

'Oh, and uncle Reg and I had a talk, we've moved a long way to working things out, the home front is now much more relaxed and open, we're on the improve.' Geoff quips in again.

'Until you mention the boyfriend… oww!' Karen has clipped him again and is staring daggers, this brings laughter from Rod and Beth who are enjoying their comic tete-a-tetes, Karen gains control and orders.

'Right I want some time with Beth for a girl to girl chat.'

'Yep says Geoff and I want to clear some things with Rod so we'll walk down the street to the pub, leave you girls to it we'll be an hour, that should be enough time.'

'Yes great,' answers Karen, 'See ya.' The boys rise and leave the kitchen. Karen also rises and gives Beth a nod

indicating she wants her to move to the lounge room, she sits and addresses Beth speaking in a friendly way.

'Look there's a few things to clear up, most importantly if you are to become sexually active.'

'Become,' grins Beth. Looking at her, she shakes her head and continues.

'As I was saying, there's one very important thing you have to consider and that's contraception.'

'No problems,' answers Beth, 'He has condoms.'

'Ahh well actually, yes they're good but not foolproof, they can rip or break you need more, well better.'

'Better?'

'Yes, you need to go on the pill.'

'Oh gosh I know it, what's it entail?'

'I'm on it, there's nothing to it, I take one pill a day, however, you must be vigilant and thorough, you mustn't miss a day.'

'But are there any side effects, like getting drowsy or putting on weight or anything plus how do I get it?'

'Okay, these days it's completely harmless, actually by stopping your cycles you'll no longer have periods, therefore, less uncomfortable pains, I never asked how you were with P M T?'

'Oh, I was lucky and not too bad, some girls at school well it was just awful, still, I wouldn't miss it, what do I do?'

'Okay I have a lady doctor in Rosenbury, she's young and great, we'll, make a time and go and see her. You'll find she's easy to talk to plus being young she can advise you on other aspects of a developing sexual relationship, I love her we're lucky to have someone like that in the district believe me.'

'I know what you're saying, I wouldn't have fancied going to a man to get all this information.'

'No, it's not like the old days, thank god, I'll drive you over and come with you, I think I might be more comforting

and knowledgeable, rather than having Reg with you. Beth sighs with relief.

'Oh yes, please, gee… another new experience another hurdle.'

'Yes, but I'll have to explain why I'm there and not your legal guardian but I know her really well and it'll be fine, one thing however sometime you'll have to tell Reg, its only right and proper that he knows'.

'Yes, you're right I'll handle that, try and pick the right time'. Beth glows inside and smiles radiantly at Karen.

'Oh, you have been so kind I love you so.' With that she leans forward and kisses her on the lips, stepping back she admits.

'Really I've been so lucky to have met you, you're so full of life, helpful and exciting.' Karen grins, 'Exciting … hmm, never thought of myself as exciting, hard-working yes, considerate yes, exciting … hmm as much as your other friend?' Smiling, Beth gives an honest answer.

'Oh yes just as much even more. I know we've just started having fun together but I haven't asked if you've done experimental stuff before? You mentioned the gymnastic girl at college, what did that entail?'

'Yes, it was fun, not really experimental, maybe could have been but as I said I had to come home to tend my sick mother, so nothing eventuated further than what I've already told you'.

'Well I've told you my story so far from what you've heard have I been more involved or experimental than you?'

'Sort of, Geoff and I are great, he's up for things, I love showing off in front of him, it creates sexual desire but he's a man, and as I said with the girl in college, it was different, just as it was with you, you know you really are an intelligent girl, I'll return the compliment, I've really loved meeting you.'

'As have I,' returns Beth. 'I know you're older but I'll

love learning things off you.'

'You mean sex,' confirms Karen.

'Of course, but also the way you attack life and general living, you're about seven years older than me with way more experience, truthfully, I can learn a lot, hey what about the sex stuff what do we do?'

'Oh easy, stick with our normal routine as friends but if we feel the urge, we'll run with it remember we've both got boyfriends, they'll take up some of the sex time.'

'Yes of course,' admits Beth. 'But I really enjoyed our time in the shower I think I want more, does that mean I'm developing into a lesbian?'

'No, look who did you enjoy more me or Rod?'

'I don't know, both situations were different.'

'Correct, as I said before both have their points the key is to feel comfortable and enjoy both.'

'Yes,' agrees Beth. 'I'm young and pretty inexperienced, Rod and I will find our way and when I'm with you I'll let you guide me.'

'I don't know about that, one in all in' quips Karen.' Both laugh, reach forward hold the others hand and kiss.

The two girls are relaxing at the kitchen table with cups of tea as the boys return from the pub. Karen quips.

'Here they are staggering in from the pub, ahh... relationships.' Geoff plays along.

'Hello darlin' I'm home, where's my supper?'

'You would be so lucky', is the playacted response.'

'Ah well' he grins, then changing track in a more serious vein comments, 'You girls sorted?'

'Yes', agrees Karen, 'a few things to work out but basically all good here.' Changing her direction, she tells Beth.

'I'll give you the info at dance practice this Wednesday.'

'Okay,' answers Beth, 'That'd be great.' Rod buts in, "I'll walk you home.' Rising Beth speaks earnestly.

'Thank you, guys, for everything, I guess I'm taking new steps and experiences, it's great when one has the support and love of friends.' With that, she turns and follows Rod out of the kitchen, Geoff smiles at Karen, she grins back, moves to him and hugs him.

CHAPTER 36

It's late morning, the main street is its lean self with not much action to be seen, Karen is working a shift at the General Store. She's busying herself loading shelves when she hears the sound of the front door opening, finishing placing the last few items on shelves she turns to serve the customer. Standing in front of her is Noogs, she's placed a can of Coke on the counter, with a disregard for politeness she briskly asks, "How Much?" trying her best to be polite Karen answers

'Oh hi, that's two dollars fifty, thanks.' Noogs reaches into her jeans pocket and draws out a five-dollar bill, with an aggressive touch she puts it on the counter. Karen picks it up, rings the amount on the cash register and withdraws the change, expecting Noogs to hold her hand out to receive the change Noogs does nothing. It's a statement that she wants no physical contact with Karen, in no uncertain terms. Placing the money on the counter, Karen looks at her then realising that no-one else is around so this is a perfect opportunity to try and clear the air, she initiates.

'Look, Nancy, umm I know that we're not the best of friends but can we try and get along a bit, I'm quite willing to let bygones be bygones, the town's too small to hold petty

grievances, remember we did go to school together.' Noogs studies her then vehemently returns serve.

'Yeah, I remember school with you, you and your smart-arse friends, puttin' me down, ya reckon I liked that? Na you wouldn't even know.'

'But that was long ago,' states Karen, 'we're grown up now, time has moved on, we've left that silly little school girl bitchiness behind.' Noogs is having none of it.

'No, well they say an elephant never forgets, I don't never forget, maybe you silly little bitches had your day but this dog's going to have her day, I tell you.' Karen suppresses an urge to grin, thinking to herself, "Elephants remember, dogs have their day, is she going thru the animal kingdom? What's next, attack like a leopard?" Controlling herself, she tries acting conciliatory.

'Look I understand that you're aggrieved but let's try to forget it, we're older now we can still be normal acquaintances.' By this time Noogs is really fed up, she wants no part of a friendship or even normal acquaintances, she spits out the last remarks.

'Normal acquaintances, you be normal, no one was ever normal to my mum and me. Hey and your little "Miss Precious" friend who's tried to be friendly to Billy, tell her to piss off also, we don't need no-one to be friendly with us. We got our gang, that's our friends, don't want any of you normal people trying to act friendly, we know what we got, and yous will get what you deserve in the long run.' Karen's tried her best but now she's sick and tired of the preaching, she fires back. 'Oh right, you're going to get revenge for something that happened at school over ten years ago, come on get a life, grow up.' Noogs stares her eyes flare with unadulterated hate, for a second Karen thinks that she's about to jump the counter and attack her right there on the spot, however, Noogs grabs her can of soft drink and with a final burst, exits the store. 'Fuck

you miss normal tart, just wait and see who won't grow up.'
Karen stares after her as Noogs slams the door shut, thinking
"Well, that went well, hmm... just like Beth and Billy, a job in
human relations might not quite be suitable for me."

Later that Wednesday evening, Karen is in the dance
studio preparing equipment. Beth walks in and calls with a
vibrancy, "Hi Karen, I'm here." Looking up, Karen smiles, "Oh
hi Beth, how are you?"

'Fine,' 'looking forward to this, need to burn some
calories off after sitting all day, don't want to get a fat arse, Ha
ha, not like that Noog's girl.' Stopping her work Karen looks up,
her face hardens slightly from the pleasant original greeting to
something deeper, as if something is troubling her, Beth picks
up the vibe.

'What, what did I say, you look pensive almost
worried.' Karen starts.

'The other day I was working at the store when Noogs
came in.'

'Oh yeah, and...?'

'Well, I tried to pacify her you know make amends,
become civil but she was having none of it, she even brought
your name into the conversation.'

'My name? In what context?'

'Basically, it was to do with you trying to be friendly
with Billy, she took offence at that like we were trying to
intrude on their little gang as she called them.'

'Intrude, but surely she'd realise that we'd have no
interest in being involved with that group, I was only trying to
be friendly maybe stop this antagonism towards us.'

'Yes, and I was on the same plane, but unfortunately
I crashed and burnt just like you. The thing that worries me
is the deep-seated aggression she's venting towards me and
I guess you. I think we'd better be a tad careful for a while,
try and keep out of their way, sort of let sleeping dogs lie.'

Pondering the statement Beth agrees adding.

'Look I don't get around the town that much anyway, mainly walking home from the bus stop, and getting here twice a week, so I guess I'm a pretty low profile.' Agreeing Karen says, 'Probably I'm more obvious with my part-time work at the store so I'll be extra careful to not tread on any more toes and where possible also keep a low profile, I hope it'll blow over in time. Okay, enough of that let's do something more positive, let's start and blow some of those cobwebs out.'

'Okay, grins Beth, Let's get stuck in and have some fun.' They discard some outer clothing and move to the centre of the room and start stretching.

CHAPTER 37

Noogs is storming along on the gravel beside the road, she's on the back blocks heading towards Pills place, as she tramps on, she mutters to herself. "Fuckin' bitch, bloody tart..." A branch from a tree lies across part of the road instead of stepping over it she kicks it out of the way, misjudging the weight of the branch she catches her toe on it, pain sears thru her foot, she jumps up and down from the shock of the force screaming, "Bloody hell, ya bitch you caused this, all in my mind, fuck you, fuck, fuck, fuck you." Rubbing her foot, she calms down, with a lift of her head she smells something, walking over the other side of the road a rabbit lies dead in the grass just off the road its rotting corpse has been ravaged by various rodents, the smell is of death and decay, she stands there gazing at it and mumbles.

'You got yours, soon she'll get hers.' Resuming her journey, a sly smile has developed, after about another fifteen minutes of walking she spies Pills house. Johnny's Holden car is parked near the house, she can hear voices, her mood sharpens full of built-up aggression, upon entering the dirt driveway the boys spot her and yell out, "Hey Noogs, come in." As she enters their domain, Johnny is the first to pick up the attitude

stemming from her, she's full of angst, this is more so than her normally negative self, he asks. He Noogs, what's wrong, what's got up your fanny?'

'That bloody bitch at the general store, that's what.' Johnny can read the signs, knowing he can pull her strings like a marionette he continues. 'So, what did little miss dance tart do?' She scowls back at him.

'Tried to be friendly you know "Oh let's forgive and forget, like she thinks she can wave a magic wand and everything from the past will disappear. Bloody typical, you know, "Oh forget yesteryear," even though she was an absolute cunt to me, "Let's be friendly now." I tell you my blood boiled, I wanted to jump the counter and punch her lights out." Johnny, enjoying the vehement verbal attack emanating from her however decides control is needed now.

'Okay, I can see your pissed, what do you want to do now?' Noogs is firing, 'Let's go down to the store now and give her the lot I want to see her bleed,' with that she takes a flick Knife out of her pocket and flips it open, the silvery blade gleams in the sunshine, she smiles at it. Johnny orders.

'Okay put it away, now's not the time for that.'

'Why?' queries Noogs.

'Cos you haven't done any planning yet, we said we'd take time to get things right, going off half-cocked won't help you'd only get the likes of her boyfriend Geoff and Rod onto us. We said we'd plan, lets plan, like what do you know about her, where's she living now, where's the dance place she does stuff, her little cute miss precious friend, where does she live, where does she go walkin' to and fro from school? Look there's lots of information to gather before you put plans into operation. Hey, plans into operation, I sound like a general in the army, yeah that's me.' Noogs listens and nods, she's calmed down and accepts his wiser council, all through this discussion, the boys have been silent, eventually Pills speaks.

'So, what do ya want from us?' Smiling Johnny is revelling in his newly personally formed opinion of himself as the leader of troops.

'Well,' he says with a touch of authority, 'gather round lads, oh and lass, 'this is how we'll play it.' As he feeds out the information, Noogs smiles to herself thinking. "Johnny's onto it, yeah what a great guy.'

CHAPTER 38

A few months tick by, the girls work with the younger ones on a Friday and do their aerobics session on a Wednesday evening. Most Wednesdays Beth goes over to Karen's for dinner. Beth still hasn't told Reg that she has a boyfriend and that she is now on the pill. Although they are much more relaxed at home, she's nervous regarding owning up to him. The result is that only occasionally does she stay over at Karen's on the Friday night after the girl's practice, most times with some sort of excuse but always clearing it with Reg first that she might be late or stay over. Rod seems happy with the arrangement, on Wednesdays he walks her home, they are enjoying each other's company and playful sex when time permits. He's twigged that she's a little show-off and their night sessions when time allows are bouncy and adventurous, very arousing and a lot of fun, it's definitely something to look forward to. One morning Beth's at the bus stop, other kids are being dropped off, the blue Hi Lux pulls up, Mrs Byrnes is driving, she stops, leans across kisses Shelly on the forehead who then jumps out and heads towards the stop. Shelly spies Beth and does a wave which is returned, Mrs Byrnes is about to drive off when she catches Beth's eye and waves her over.

Walking over to the HiLux Beth gives a quick aside to Shelly, "Just a min' Shell", arriving at the car she gives a pleasant, "Hi Mrs Byrnes."

'Hello, Beth, Jenny please.'

'Okay, umm Jenny can I help?'

'Look Beth you're older than Shelly but probably the closest to her age, you see this is about Shelly's development.'

'Yes...?'

'I mean, Look Shelly's just had her first period. I've had a chat with her but because she thinks the world of you as we all do, she might need someone to confide in, so if she asks you anything, please feel free to give advice, it's a tough time as you know.' Smiling, Beth agrees, 'Yep been there I understand.'

'Oh, thanks a lot sweetie you're such a treasure, by the way how do you handle it all?' Not wanting to divulge that she's on the pill Beth gives a slight white lie.

'Not to bad actually, I was talking to Karen and we both agree that fitness you know all the dance work we do, has an effect of minimising discomfort, I think it works.'

'Fitness ehh,' comments Jenny, 'I've heard that, very interesting, anyway, a slightly older girl's perspective I'm sure would be welcome.'

'Fine,' says Beth, then with a pacifying tone, 'But I'll tread carefully, don't worry.'

'Oh, Jim and I don't worry we really appreciate what you and Karen do with our girls, they look up to you so much, we really appreciate you, well gotta go, thanks again, see you soon.' With that she drives off, Beth waves at the disappearing car, then moves back to the bus stop. Shelly's there and curiously inquires, "What was that about?"

'Oh, just willing to be helpful if you want', is the honest reply.

'Helpful?' Shelly's confused.

'Don't worry,' calms Beth, 'Look here comes the bus, I'll

chat to you on it.'

The bus pulls up and all the school kids board, Shelly and Beth move to the back seat, fling bags aside and slump down onto the bench seat, Beth asks.

'Well, Shelly, how are you?' A pause follows, sheepishly Shelly answers.

'Umm... alright, I guess.'

'Just alright, anything you want to talk about?'

'Well no, umm... yes, well sort of, like you're a girl, um... how do you like handle being a girl?'

Leaning across, Beth gives Shelly a kiss on the forehead, then a hug.

'You like and trust me, don't you?'

'Yes.'

'Okay, let's be open, remembering I've been through what you're going thru and still am.'

'You still are?'

'Yep, it's part of becoming a woman and leaving the little girl behind.' Tears well up in Shelly's eyes.

'I don't know if I want to be a woman, I'm happy with what I am.' Beth grins at the comment, she's heard it all before she even mentioned it to her own parents.

'Yes, but you can't change human nature or development, what you've got to do is learn how to handle it.'

'But Beth, I bled and felt uncomfortable.'

'That's right and it continues every month, you learn to live with it.'

'Is there anything I can do to make it easier?'

'Good question, well I and also Karen agree that being fit can help minimise the difficult period of those few days. Some girls take pills to ease their discomfort, but we believe in natural remedies. Google PMT see what other girls or doctors say, you might get some ideas."

'Okay I'll try, this growing up is sure tougher than I

ever thought it would be.' Beth smiles, and tries being open and helpful.

'Anything you want to ask me feel free, or any comment you want to get off your chest do it, remember I've been there and still am, come on Shell, sometimes a big bitch session can unload and free up emotions.' Looking earnestly at Beth, Shelly reaches across and holds her hand.

'Beth, I hate these things inside me, I'm walking round feeling like I've got a cork stuck up my arse.' Giving her a conciliatory look Beth agrees.

'I know I've got them as well, we just have to live with it. I guess you get used to it, I have.' The comment does little to appease Shelly, she bleats out the next instalment.

'And also, if I use those pads, I feel like a baby again, like with a nappy on, this is what being grown up is like, for the next forty years, god save me!' Beth looks at her caringly.

'What, what,' asks Shelly. Holding her gaze for a short pause Beth decides to advise.

'Okay Shelly, I don't know if I should tell you this but let's hope you are mature enough to handle it.' Looking directly at Beth Shelly responds.

'Well I'm pouring out my feelings to you so give it to me.'

'Right', says Beth, 'You don't have to go through life feeling like this.' Shelly's eyes light up. "You don't, how come?'

'Cos there's a thing called the pill, if you use it can decrease menstrual cramps and ease the pain you might experience.'

'The pill, yes I've heard of that, its umm… to do with contraception.'

'Yes, that's right Shell, but you need a doctor to prescribe it.'

'Wow, can I get it?'

'Unfortunately, no, it's only allowed if you become

sexually active.'

'Active... you mean?'

'Yep, engage in sexual intercourse with a member of the opposite sex, plus if you're below the age of sixteen they won't give it to you, it's to stop you getting pregnant.'

'Pregnant,' gasps Shelly, 'Wow this whole thing is getting out of hand.'

'No, it's not Shell, but your first part over the next few years is to learn to manage yourself, how to live with your periods.'

'Gosh,' gasps Shelly, 'this whole business is very involved, but I get what you say, some maturity is needed here, time to grow up.' Agreeing Beth nods, 'Yep unfortunately correct.' Pondering the last comment Shelly admits.

'Okay thanks Beth, I'll try my best, gosh you sure know a lot, how come you... oh oh, you're going or are on the pill aren't you?' There's no answer forthcoming except a sly smile, all Shelly can do is stare wide eyed, then blurt out, "Wow." She continues to stare then changes her expression as she delves into her thoughts, after a short pause she says.

'Beth whoever you're going to get involved with, he's a lucky guy.' Smiling with loving sincerity Beth states.

'Well you've got your bridge to cross and I've got mine, let's stay as open friends, we've probably got a lot to talk about over the next few years.' Nodding Shelly leans forward and with tenderness kisses Beth's forehead commenting.

'Probably, but I'll really love having you as a friend, think I'll need one, god I wish I'd been born a boy.'

'Ha, no you don't Shelly, you're growing into a beautiful young girl, I've a strong feeling with your brains, attitude, fitness and looks your time at High School will be pretty special.'

'Do you think so?' Picking up Shelly's hand she rubs it and looks directly into her eyes.

'I don't think, I know.' They hug holding the embrace for quite a while, eventually breaking away Beth changes the subject and inquires.

'Shelly I'm interested in something, you stayed away from school for a couple of days.'

'Yes, mum helped me.'

'Yes, well when you returned, did anyone say anything to you like inquire about your health'?

'Well yes, Sally Dickson was away the other week for a few days so she asked how I was.'

'Right, what's Sally like?'

'Oh, really nice a bit of a tomboy, I mean very fit, best long-distance runner in the school, has played football with her older brother for years she's in the school team, I believe she's pretty good, why?'

'Oh nothing, umm... describe her to me.'

'Well she's about my height and size, blonde hair with nice friendly blue eyes and a really tanned skin, a really fun person to be around very bubbly, oh and also good at her schoolwork.'

'Okay, so you're friendly.'

'Oh yes, we sometimes go swimming at Fiona Little's place, usually on warm days on the weekend. Our farms are reasonably close together, her dads built a diving board at the edge of their dam, it's a lot of fun.'

'Right, umm... what's Fiona like?' 'Well she's very nice, got a twin brother Gary, she's taller than us, has dark hair and looks sort of more developed, you wouldn't call her pretty or cute more attractive, sort of striking. She's a bit quiet, very studious, plays netball and was in the school swimming team, lovely but quieter person.'

'Right and when you go over to her place for a swim who's there?'

'Oh, just the normal crew, us girls, Gary of course, he's

very bouncy and funny plus a couple of his mates, Edward and Jimmy.'

'Oh, the boy you mentioned to me in the Health and Human sessions.'

'Yes.'

'Ahh, did he ask about your health the other day after you were away?'

'Actually, he did, but it was just in passing, why.' Beth, tries again.

'Just one last question, when you girls go over to Fiona's for a swim, what do you wear?' Shelly's slightly confused the answer is obvious but she answers as truthfully as she can.

'We've all got Speedo's, you know for swimming on the school team.' Deliberating Beth responds.

'Right thought so, look Shelly I've got to get some things Thursday after school in Rosenbury, do you want to come with me maybe buy some stuff?'

'Well yes, I'd love to come with you but I'd have to clear it with my mum, I guess it'd be okay, can't buy anything though, like I've got very little money'.

'Yes, fair enough, look tell your mum that you're coming with me and you're thinking of buying a new swimsuit, could she lend you her card.' With a shocked look on her face Shelly says.

'That won't happen, what sort of swimsuit?' Smiling Beth looks earnestly at her and softly says.

'Time for girl's bikinis.' Shelly's mouth opens wide, she blurts out.

'Oh gosh.' Continuing Beth announces.

'Also tell Sally and Fiona the same info, see if they'd like to join us, they'd have to clear it with their parents first of course'. Shelly sits and looks bewildered, the best she can do is mutter, "Bikinis, triangles, gosh."

CHAPTER 39

Next morning at the bus stop Beth is waiting, when Jenny Byrnes drives up in the HiLux, slows and lets Shelly out. As Shelly walks towards the stop Jenny spies Beth, gives her a wave and a thumbs up then blows a kiss, Beth responds with a wave and a smile, the advancing Shelly greets her.

'Hi Beth, I'm allowed to go shopping with you and get this, I told my mum about shopping for bathers and she gave me her credit card, I mean how'd you know she'd do that?' Smiling in return Beth gives a noncommittal answer.

'Oh, just a hunch, hey anyway that's great.'

'Yes, and the other two girls are coming along as well, I'm pretty sure they've got cards as well, this is amazing.'

'Well there you go, this is the first of changes, they're starting to treat you more grown up, with responsibility.' Dwelling on this statement Shelly agrees somewhat.

'Yeah, perhaps, hmm… interesting.' The bus enters the main street and stops, everyone boards and it moves off. Stopping at the main street of Rosenbury everyone exits the bus and start walking the block to school, on entering the school gate Beth tells Shelly.

'I'll meet you all here at three-thirty.'

'Okay,' is the reply. With that the two girls move off in their different directions.

At three-thirty Beth is standing in front of the school gates, within a minute she spies Shelly walking towards her with two other girls in tow. She realizes that she's occasionally seen the other two girls around the place, they arrive, Shelly gives Beth a hug then introduces the two girls.

'Beth this is Sally,' they exchange "Hi's" and do the general girls hug, 'and this is Fiona,' the same greeting procedure follows, Beth asks.

'Did Shelly tell you what we intended to do?'

'Yes,' is the bright answer from Sally. 'You're going shopping for some stuff, Shelly's looking for some new bathers we're going to look also.'

'Right and I can give you some advice if you want it.'

'Great,' beams Sally, but Fiona in a more mature controlled polite way agrees.

'Yes thanks, that'd be really helpful.' In an instant Beth's summed the girls up, clearly Sally is the outdoors sporty type, fit looking with sun bleached blonde hair and suntan, the "All Australian Beach Girl", Fiona however is more striking in looks and manner, slightly reserved at this moment but with time and confidence Beth knows she'll grow into beautiful lady, elegant with poise.

'Right,' she orders, 'off we go.' The group move off down the road, as they move along the girls acknowledge that they've seen Beth round the school, she returns commenting that she's noticed them about also. Meandering on Sally asks Beth what she's looking for.

'Some underwear and maybe bathers,' Beth answers. Fiona is more curious and asks, 'what kind?'

'Oh, whatever catches my eye,' is the vague reply, however she says it with a subtle smile and a glance at Fiona. Arriving at a lady's boutique store Beth announces.

'There's a very good part at the rear for girls.' With nods of agreement, they enter and pass thru the lady's section to the girls' section at the back part of the store. There are racks of fashion clothing for young girls, stands with underwear and racks of swimwear, posted round the walls are advertisements for various girl's items, Beth directs.

'I've got to look for some underwear first, you girls browse thru the swimwear racks over there, I'll be with you in a tic.' The girls split with Shelly, Sally and Fiona checking out the various types of swimwear, as they browse through, they comment to each other regarding form, cut and colour, on Beth's return, she asks.

'Well have you found anything?' The girls return the question with various unsure and innocuous answers, grinning to herself Beth knows their unsureness is due to their lack of confidence, this being a big step for them.

'Okay,' she begins, 'let's get a few things straight, when you're buying swimwear it's for multiple reasons. Firstly, you must like the cut and colour, it must suit you, remember you're wearing it to catch rays and make an impression'.

'What about swimming?' asks Sally.

'Yep that too,' reply's Beth waving her hand in a slightly dismissive way. Beth knows character building and a confidence boost is needed here so she speaks directly to them.

'Look girls, you're developing into young ladies, they look at each other in a slightly embarrassed manner, Beth continues. 'This means you're leaving little girls behind, I'm standing here looking at three different girls but very attractive in your own right.' The girls grin sheepishly, 'You're all getting figures, admittedly young girl's figures but figures definitely… guys time to let loose a bit and show yourselves off.' Fiona points out seriously.

'But you're older and more mature with a better figure.'

'Yes,' agrees Beth, 'but I'm not trying to impress young

boys of your age, you are.'

'Impress,' pleads Shelly, 'we're not trying to impress.'

'Yes you are,' grins Beth, 'everyone likes to be admired, if you didn't you wouldn't be here, you're all starting a new era, time to get mature and confident, look around you at all these advertising posters, look at these young girls, they're models, admittedly a little older than you but they show confidence, you're all fit and I must say very attractive with great young figures, let's go and show off a little.' Fiona looks at Beth and asks.

'Who are you buying to show off too?' With a grin Beth answers, "a certain young man." They split and move to their different positions, time moves on, Beth returns to the girls, Sally is intrigued, she inquires.

'So, what'd you get?' 'This" answers Beth and pulls out of a bag a red G-String underwear.

'Oh god,' whispers Sally,

'Jeez,' adds Fiona. 'I could never wear anything like that.'

'Well,' confirms Beth, 'actually you probably will in the future when you're ready but that's years away, right now our task is to find something that'll work for you, that you feel enhances you and that you'll wear confidently. Okay girls time to get aggressive, Shelly and Sally look in the size six rack, Fiona try the size eight rack, come on attack.' The girls again start mingling thru the racks. Shelly holds up a bikini with red and black briefs and a red tie round top. Beth nods.

'Not bad, hold it and keep looking.' Fiona calls, 'What do you think of this?' She holds up a bikini with black briefs and a yellow bra like top.

'Mmm...'good, hold that and keep looking.' The girls keep browsing occasionally holding up another item, after twenty minutes has elapsed, they gather round, Beth orders.

'Okay I'll stay here, you go change and come out and I'll

see how they look.' Doubtful looks are exchanged between the three, Beth again orders.

'Go on, go on, come on show some confidence.' It's Shelly who leads the charge exclaiming.

'Oh, come on you guys, Beth's the only one here.' Nodding to each other a few grins are exchanged and they move off to the fitting rooms. Time lapses, Beth thinks to herself, "Hmm, I wonder who'll be the first one out"? It isn't long before Shelly appears, with hesitancy she almost tip toes out wearing the black and red bikini. She cautiously moves up to Beth with her hands protectively placed across her chest.

'Well,' asks Beth, 'come on show.' With slight trepidation Shelly removes her hands, the swimsuit fits perfectly, her fit young body is exemplified, although not big in the bust she exudes a fit young girl.

'Lovely,' smile Beth, 'Oh so perfect that's you.' Although lacking in confidence Shelly smiles at the positive response, soon after another figure appears, its Fiona, immediately Beth can tell she's more mature, she fills out the bra styled top, her breasts obviously quite full for a young girl her age. Walking up cautiously, she stands in front of Beth, placing her hands on her hips she asks.

'Is this alright?' Beth smiles and answers.

'Fiona you look wonderful, stunning, you're growing into a lovely young woman.' The compliment tweaks something in Fiona's psyche, she stands more upright staring straight at Beth she answers.

'Thanks Beth, I think they're alright also.' Turning her head Shelly calls, "Oh here comes Sally". Sally walks up in a blue and white mottle coloured bikini, standing in front of her friends she looks up and says.

'Umm… I like this.' Everyone is wide eyed including Beth, what she has chosen is a bikini of stringed triangles. What's so amazing is the tantalising effect, her whole package

has on them. The bikini is brief, parts are very small with just a minuscule triangle at the front and rear, both are held on the hips by string ties. The top triangles also are smallish held by a string across her chest and tied around her neck, with no join or clip at the front her breasts are obvious, add to that her hip ties are reasonably high her whole side and half her backside is exposed. Although not naked she has just barely the right amount of coverage needed. The best Fiona can do is, 'Oh gosh... Oh Sally.' Shelly adds with a stunned comment, "Sally, your umm... your umm...' It's Beth who brings the correct word to the fore.

'You're stunning.' The other girls nod in agreement, Beth seizes the moment.

'Sally you have a fantastic fit figure that can show anything off, you know it and so will everyone else, okay everyone, it's the start of enjoying yourselves, take a look at each other, you all look great.' The girls' glance at each other, because the other two look more intently at Sally she suddenly decides to throw a pose, putting her hands above her head and bending her knees slightly, she goes, "Yeah." They all laugh, Beth comments.

'Oh, we have a potential model here do we?' Grinning Sally reply's, "perhaps," everyone giggles.

'Right,' orders Beth, 'go change and we'll fix the payment up.' Laughing and giggling the girls rush off, once quickly changed back into school uniform they arrive back at Beth who nods them towards the counter, the service lady is an older woman and politely inquires.

'Right girls are we ready to pay?' They all nod, as they start to pay the lady mentions.

'Oh, what lovely choices, what I'd give to have your figures again, and to be able to wear these, you girls are so lucky. I had a squiz while you tried them on, you're all so beautiful and fit you'll look brilliant, oh you girls are going to

break some hearts.' With the final packaging finished she says.

'Thanks girls, well done, you are going to have such fun.' The gushing honesty has an effect of really invigorating the girl's confidence, as they walk down the street Fiona comments.

'You know this growing up mightn't be so bad.' Shelly agrees, 'Yes, you could be right.' With a grin Sally adds.

'Yeah, wait till the boys see us this weekend, oh wow.' Squeals of laughter break out and continue as they walk down the street. Trailing behind them Beth is grinning to herself thinking, "So cool, they've taken their first step, my mum and dad would be so proud." The introspective thought brings a small tear to the side of her eye, wiping it away she glows and trails the girls.

CHAPTER 40

Beth enters the dance studio in her school uniform, Karen is already there fiddling with the C D Player.

'Hi,' calls Beth.

'Oh, hi Beth,' is the lively answer, 'how are you, I heard you won some brownie points.'

'Brownie points, what do you mean?'

'Nothing just a joke but I did get a phone call from Jenny Byrnes.'

'Oh yes.'

'Yep she said she wanted me to pass on big thanks for what you did with Shelly and the girls. She said Sally's mum rang her and told her that Sally came home bubbling with excitement and wanted to show her what she had bought, when she showed her, well she said she just glowed with pride and affection. She wanted Jenny to pass on to you, thru me, big thanks. The girl's attitude to themselves has taken a huge boost from unsure to positive, Jenny says the same has happened to Shelly, girl I think you've kicked major goals with these parents.'

'Oh, it was nothing, just a bit of shopping.'

'Ha, don't sell yourself short, it was more than shopping, it was a psychological turn around, you read it and

produced it.'

'Well maybe, I was just glad to be of help.' Karen stares at her, moves forward and kisses her delicately on the lips, backing off she says. 'You know you are a beautiful thoughtful girl, the kids realise it, the parents realise it and I definitely know it, that's why I like you so much, as you say "Inside and out." Slightly blushing Beth replies softly with sincerity.

'Well if you can't help people on planet earth what's the point of being here.' Agreeing, Karen nods and adds.

'Yes, good point, however those who help must be helped themselves at times.' Looking up Beth admits.

'You've helped me a lot, I'm a different person now, alive enjoying everything life has to offer.'

'Yes, but the reciprocal right is also true, you've helped me, I've also found a new zest for live and well new experiences.'

'Laughing Beth quips, 'Ha is this the mutual feel good association?' Walking forward Karen again kisses her on the lips agreeing.

'Yep it is and I love it, let's do some practice.' They move to the centre of the room and start doing their stretches, after a short period Beth calls, "Hold on this is getting in the way." She moves to the side and unbuttons her school dress, stepping out of it she places it on the bench near the wall. Resuming her place, she is now wearing a crop top and short bike pants, they continue their stretching till Karen calls a halt.

'Right,' she announces, 'warm ups finished let's start, I'll get ready.' Moving to the side she slips off her trackie-pants and sweat-shirt top, Beth glances at her, she is wearing new gear a much smaller crop top and quite small sports bikini briefs, a smile breaks out on Beth's face.

'Oh, who's the cute one now, where'd you get those?'

'From a dance shop in Hobart, lots of girls use them, you like?'

'Oh yes,' Beth gushes.

'No probs,' says Karen, 'I'll let you check them out closer at the end of our session.'

'Wow, great thanks.' They move to the centre of the room, Karen has turned on the CD Player, as the music starts, they begin their movement. The style of aerobics is very gymnastically orientated, they perform everything from jumps, bridges handstands to push-ups and cart-wheels. The workout is intense, added to that they must keep in time with the music and each other thru the movements. The whole session is a complete workout, after fixing mistakes and a couple of complete run throughs they stop, Beth crashes to the floor gasping,

'God what a workout, I'm bushed.' Karen has her hands on her knees, she's breathing heavily, sweat is dribbling off her head forming puddles around her, standing she places her hands on her hips and agrees.

'Wow, yep that was some workout, gee we pushed it, well done.' Leaning onto one elbow Beth asks.

'Boy these workouts are great, I think we're getting fitter and well stronger, what do you think?'

'Yes definitely,' is Karen's answer, hey you said you wanted to try on this new sport gear I got, do you want to try them on now and also have a look at ourselves, let's see if we really are getting fitter?'

'Okay,' Beth grins let me have a go at them.' With that Karen stands up places her thumbs into the top band of the briefs and lowers them to the floor, underneath she has a white G-String, with a poorly executed wolf whistle Beth says.

'And the top, that's much cuter than what I've got.' Smiling Karen squirms out of the crop top revealing a very bright pink small but tight sports bra. Handing them over Beth looks at them admiringly before she can move Karen walks over to the door and snips it with the comment, "Privacy

needed." Laughing Beth says, 'Okay I'll try them on, ooh they're a bit damp.'

'Sorry,' is the answer, 'I've always been someone who sweats a lot.'

'No probs,' is the answer, 'I love the smell of you close to me.'

'Really!'

'Oh yes, you're very umm… sensuous.' Grinning at Karen she continues, with a little playacting, she sets the scene.

'Well here goes.' Lifting her crop top over her head she flicks it away, under that she has on a normal white bra, with a slight wiggle of her top making her boobs shake she then transfers to her bike pants. Because they are also slightly damp, she rolls them down displaying normal white bikini briefs, Karen's now lying on her side on the ground, her face being supported by her hand and arm.

'Well let's see,' she grinningly demands. Getting a twinkle in her eye Beth answers.

'I think they're a bit damp, they'll get caught up in my underwear, don't worry I'll fix it.' With that she reaches behind her back and undoes the bra clip. The bra is allowed to fall away, then she reaches down and slides the briefs off, standing naked in front of Karen she comments in a very provocative way.

'Let's see how they look on "lil 'ol me." Firstly, she steps into the briefs and lifts them up, with a slight squiggle she has them firmly in the right place, then picking up the crop top she lifts it over her head and wriggles her boobs into place. Standing in front of Karen with her legs slightly astride and her hands on her hips she inquires.

'Well, how do I scrub up?' Karen's eyes have opened wide she stares then admits.

'Gosh, hey, you really are getting fit, gee you look like one of those middle-distance runners in the Olympics. I

can see your diaphragm muscles, not a six pack but definitely muscle definition and your hamstrings go right up into your gluts, hardly any fat deposits at the top of your thighs, boy your legs have great definition, you've got quads, I tell you Beth you really look something.' Smiling at the comments Beth explains.

'Actually I think a few others at school have noticed, in gym classes we wear t-shirts and shorts but we're having swimming lessons at the moment and in the changing rooms, well I've only got my sports bikini briefs and crop top not a pair of Speedo's, they're okay, not revealing like to catch rays or anything but a couple of girls have made comments, I mean I wasn't showing off but I guess some of them noticed my fitness.'

'Oh, and what about the boys?'

'None of them said anything or made comments but I did notice a few of them glancing at me, especially if they thought I wasn't looking, guess they don't know anything about peripheral vision.'

'Right, and how'd that make you feel?'

'Actually, it was a bit of a buzz, umm… I think I like being appreciated physically.'

'Yes, you do, especially here in the sessions.' Smiling and with a small coquettish grin Beth admits.

'Oh yes, I love showing off to you, its umm… exciting.'

'You do, hey that's nice, well I'm happy to view, you look great in that sports gear.'

'Oh, I do, thanks I really like it, might try getting some like this soon.' Turning Beth squeezes out of the gear and redresses herself, handing them back to Karen she admits.

'You know you look really attractive in this gear, you were complementing me but I'm very turned on by your physical presence, it must be respect and admiration driving our sexual appetites, I mean we both understand how much work and effort has gone getting into shape like this.'

'Yes,' agrees Karen. 'You're right we appreciate each

other for our work ethic the end result is our physicality it all moves to stimulate us, well I guess our desires, gosh all this talk about desires is getting me excited, time to go, ha… Geoff better watch out, miss on the loose here.'

'Lucky him,' quips Beth.

'Don't worry I'm certainly not forgetting you,' Karen coyly responds.

'Oh, thank you miss,' is Beth's flirtatious answer. Grabbing bags, they turn off the lights and exit the room.

CHAPTER 41

Johnny's sitting on the front porch of his house, his domain is similar to Pills place, it's a run-down dilapidated heap, old car parts are strewn around the yard, fence posts that have been long overdue for a coat of paint are rotting away. There is a resigned disconsolate air infiltrating his mind, disturbing his thoughts.

"Look at this dump, here's "Mr Cool," living in this shit hole, Christ I wasn't made for this fuckin' town and its inhabitants, what a bunch of losers," then remembering Karen and Beth. "What's wrong with those two, they're actually pretty good, better than the dickheads that hang around me, why piss me off?" Then almost answering his own question, "Guess we didn't approach them right, but jeez they could have played along, ahh… suppose we came on a bit strong… fuck it who cares. Looks like they'll get theirs, geez why's Noogs so pissed off with them, ahh… she's pissed off with the whole world, guess I would be too with a mum like that, friggin' whore. Not much chance of lookin' better than normal, actually she's not good lookin' at all, shit just a fat tart with attitude and her so called mates, jeez not a brain between them, shit a half wit, and in bred and one who smells and stutters, Christ what am I

doing hanging round them?"

He gazes round the ramshackle house and yard getting more depressed by the minute. Spying the family dog chasing a rabbit gives him some relief. "Shit he hasn't got a chance in hell catchin' that thing, yeah but he keeps trying. He's either dumb or determined, but he's going about it the wrong way, doesn't corner the thing, hmm... not able to plan." A light has gone off in his head, his thoughts turn to a more positive vein, he starts to resolve his issues.

"Yeah, when I spoke to Rod, I was acting but hey, it must have been my subconscious talkin' to me, right, so as soon as Noogs and the boys have had their so-called fun I'm out of here. Yep smart move, those dick-heads have no idea about the repercussions, if they hurt the girls bad, they'll end up inside for years, shit I don't want to be involved. So, got to get my actions and story straightened. If down the track anyone asks or questions me I gotta be in the position that I can say I didn't know anything about it, yeah, thought they were just shootin' the breeze, anyway I'll be long gone by then. Right that's me, plan, direct but keep an actual distance from the action, hmm... maybe not initially want a bit of fun myself but definitely near the end when things hot up, okay, sounds good but I've got to have my alibis right, hey I'm smart I can work this out, yeah, cover my back." He's pondering these thoughts when a sound is heard.

'Coo-wee,' breaks thru the quiet of the bush, glancing up he can see the form of the three boys and the swagger of Noogs tramping down the road, descending on his place. He gazes at the gaucherie of their style, nausea fills his soul at their grotesque laconic and bogan style of movement, readjusting his attitude he quickly admits to himself. "Okay here come the tin soldiers at my disposal, yep games start now let's have a bit of fun," a smile breaks across his face, lifting his arm he waves.

'Johnny mate, how's it going,' asks Pills in his usual

unsophisticated way.'

'Great,' he says sarcastically, have a seat boys… oops and girl, let's see what we know.' The group sit round using various broken chairs and boxes to relax on.

'Right,' starts Johnny, 'I'll ask the questions and you guys tell me what you've found out.' They all nod with naive enthusiasm.

'Firstly, where does the dance tart Karen live?'

'Easy,' replies Tatts, 'they, I mean her and her boyfriend Geoff plus Rod got a house over on Edwards street, a couple of blocks to the North.'

'Good,' smiles Johnny, 'and where does the tart do her dance stuff?'

'I-I-I know,' stammers Billy, 'it's that old factory n-n-n near the edge of town, you know, Mc H-H-H Hendries.'

'Yeah,' agrees Johnny, I know it.'

'So little miss precious where's she livin?' Pills is excited to be involved, it's like he's in the army, he's practically wetting himself with enthusiasm to deliver his information.

'Hey I've followed her a number of times like when she gets off the bus and when she goes to do dance stuff, she never saw me geez I was like one of them detectives.

'Yes, well?' pries Johnny already getting bored with the halfwits attitude.

'Oh, yeah, well she lives with that old guy, you know old Reg over nearer the south part of town its 28 Peers street, and get this both on Wednesday nights and Friday nights, like that's when they have a lot of kids at the factory, well she goes with the other tart to her place, I guess for dinner, then later Rod walks her home, usually at night.' Johnny's a bit impressed, for halfwits they've done a pretty good job, at least now he's got all the information he needs. Leaning back on his chair he smiles and looks at Noogs then glances around all their faces.

'Have to admit you've done well me hearties, let me

think about a course of action and then we'll get moving.'
Noogs buts in, 'you mean have some fun Johnny.'

'Oh yes I'm lining this all up for you, remember what you said Noogs, "all boys must have their fun in life, hey and you guys deserve it, leave it to me, how about we meet back here in two days' time and I'll outline our plan of attack.' Noogs is beside herself, she smiles thinking.

'Geez, Johnny's going to all this trouble just so we can get those bitches and have some fun, what a guy, wish he'd want to fuck me, don't know why, hey but friends are friends, this is almost better.' She smiles at him, Johnny's taken back slightly by the image of Noogs actually smiling.

"Christ what's she smiling at me for, careful son, don't want to get involved here, keep your distance, shit Noogs, Christ run a mile, don't even think it." He sheepishly smiles back then quickly transfers his gaze to all of them.

CHAPTER 42

At the dance studio Karen and Beth are setting up, the sound of the outside door opening is heard, Karen comments, "some ones early," the inside door opens and Shelly enters.

'Hi Shell,' calls Beth, 'How are you?' 'Umm… okay,' is the reply, she's lacking her ordinary bubbly nature, although not showing signs of displeasure Beth knows she wants to chat, something's on her mind. Beth digs a bit. 'How was the weekend? Oh, you girls went swimming at Fiona's place, how'd everything go?' 'Ahh, sort of good, umm… well interesting, look Beth can I ask you some things?'

'Sure, but is it about swimming at Fiona's?'

'Yes.'

'And were the boys there?'

'Yes.'

'Okay, I'm getting the drift, tell me what happened.'

'Well the three boys were there and they were outside mucking round, Fiona suggested changing in her room and well sort of make an entrance, we got changed, slung towels across our shoulders and went outside to join them. We got to the dam and Gary yelled "Come on," so we dropped our towels and walked to the edge. Beth, the boys stopped swimming and

stared at us, I thought they were going to laugh but Gary did a wolf whistle and yelled "wow," even reserved Ed called, "Gee Whiz," and Jimmy sort of looked at us then I saw him gazing more at me, he grinned and sort of winked, like saying "very good." Beth I can speak for the others here, we all laughed but deep down inside we glowed, it was like what you said, we made an impression and a very good one at that.'

'Okay that sounds great, so you all went swimming, all good?'

'Yes, sort of but some things changed.'

'Like what?'

'We girls jumped in and started splashing round as we normally do, the boys splashed back then Gary jumped on Sally trying to dunk her and Jimmy followed suit jumping on me trying to push me under, I think Fiona and Ed were wrestling seeing who could dunk who.'

'Right, so you're all mucking round.'

'Yes, but as we splashed and wrestled Sally got out, ran to the board and jumped in trying to bomb Gary, she landed right next to him with a big splash so he attacked her sort of and they were like half wrestling and laughing, Jimmy and I had been carrying on but he ducked down and I had vision and well saw Gary holding Sally and his hands were like near her top, I mean her breasts and she didn't seem in any hurry to move away. Eventually she pushed him away and waded up the bank but when she was half way up she stopped, turned and squeezed the water out of the top triangles of her bikini.'

'Yes, so?' 'Well scrunching them up and the rearranging them, like she gave Gary a perfect view of her breasts.'

'Gee, was he watching?'

'Oh yes, and he had a big smile on his face.'

'Mmm… anything else?'

'Yes, she then straightened her briefs part, but pulled the side straps up so the back triangle went right up her

backside, I tell you her two cheeks were open.'

'Right, and Gary's watching?'

'Oh yes, but this is something else, as she straightened her rear triangle, she looked over her shoulder at him and gave a smile, Beth it wasn't a happy smile, it was a… a… I don't know.'

'Like a playful smile?'

'Yes, sort of a playful smile, I'd never seen her like that before.' Half commenting to herself Beth mutters.

"Might have created another minx, hmm… a mini minx."

'What did you say?' Questions Shelly.

'Oh nothing, go on please what did Fiona do?'

'Well as you can see, I'm intrigued with all this, goings on so I turned my attention to Fiona who has been mucking round with Ed, he's studious like her. Anyway, I'm watching and she starts to walk out of the dam to go to the diving board, but at the edge she slows, turns around sort of facing Ed and flicks her hair round, brushing it with her fingers.'

'Well that sounds normal, lots of girls with long hair do that exiting water.'

'Yes, but again it was the way she did it, as she moved her arms up her body sort of stretched and her boobs wobbled.'

'And did Ed notice?'

'Boy did he, I looked at them and I'll swear she was standing, stretching and flicking her hair, showing off to him, like I could be wrong but it looked that way to me.'

'Woah, things are going on here,' exudes Beth, 'what about you?'

'Beth, I don't know what happened, I think Jimmy might have been watching the things going on like me, anyway he jumped on me trying to dunk me and I came up spluttering and jumped on him. We were laughing and grappling, he sort of turned me round and grabbed me round the waist sort of

tighter, so I wriggled and well his hands sort of slipped up to my breasts, and Beth this is so weird, I didn't try to break away I donno I felt sort of nice and without thinking I turned round and faced him in the water like he's still got hold of me and I said, "Careful," and in a sort of cheeky way kissed him on the nose.'

'Gosh, what did he do?'

'Well he relaxed his grip on me and I swam to the edge, as I got out I turned and he was watching me with a smile on his face, Beth I don't know what came over me but I wiggled my bottom at him and gave him a grin, he looked at me and did a duck dive.'

'So how did the rest of the time go?'

'Oh, after that it was pretty normal, you know jumping in and out bombing each other, just fun. Sally and I had to leave so we called "Bye, grabbed our towels and left, Fiona also came with us to change.' Beth's in deep concentration, she eventually opens up with.

'Hmm... I think the new bathers had more of an effect than I might have thought.'

'Yes, you could be right.'

'Not all, why what happened?'

'We got into Fiona's room and started towelling off. Fiona started chatting, she said.

'Wow that was different, I mean we all got noticed big time.' And Sally commented.

'It was fun, I liked it.' I butted in.

'So, I noticed, you and Gary.' Well she looked at me, smiled and fired back.

'Yes, and I saw you wiggle your bottom to Jimmy.' I mean I blushed big time but the girls came across and gave me a long hug, we smiled at each other then Fiona brought our thoughts out in the open, she said.

'Look girls we are or have been changing, like Beth

said both physically and mentally, I mean we're not little girls any more but not grown up teens yet. The boys have noticed it and so have I, time we started acting more mature, not old but young teens, back ourselves, begin to act more mature.' I asked "What do we do now?" Fiona sort of took control and explained.

'Stay friends, talk about these new experiences in life, stay open and discuss.'

'New experiences,' I answered. 'New life eh! Boy this is going to be interesting.'

'Ha ha,' laughs Beth, 'you bet.' They move away as others start to enter the room.

CHAPTER 43

Dance practice has finished, Karen and Beth are walking down the road, Beth brings up the information regarding Shelly and her friends, thinking to herself that another lady's perspective might be needed.

'Karen there's something I want to discuss with you.'

'Oh yes what's that?'

'It's about Shelly and her friends.'

'Oh yes.' The shopping trip, it brought on other connotations.'

'Connotations, like what?'

'Well I believed that the girls subconsciously wanted to grow up become more mature.'

'Yes, that's normal for young girls, always wanting to act older.'

'Right as you know I took them into town after school and helped them buy new swimwear.'

'Ha ha, and what did they get, I've got a feeling the old Speedos might not have been the choice.'

'Correct, 'cos they are all fit with either figures or developing figures they weren't hard to lead to buying bikinis.'

'Okay, I'd gather as much, the problem was?'

'Right, that's one part, what about if they umm... sort of experiment on each other?'

'Oh, you mean physical touching each other sort of exploration.'

'Well not much more than just looking and discussing but in the future, I don't know perhaps more'

'Again, not a problem, if they are lucky enough to be at ease with each other, and I'm gathering they have agreed to be open with each other.'

'Yes, definitely, they'll stay friends, open to discussion.'

'Then let them go, actually much better being open than a demure, shy and introverted person, especially thru these formative years, they're lucky they've got each other, you know, healthy body and healthy mind leads to contentment, good luck to them I say, lucky to have such friends in this day and age.' Beth smiles at Karen's analysis that has had a cathartic effect on her, she leans across and kisses her on the cheek commenting.

'Oh, you're so wonderful, experienced, knowledgeable plus down to earth, thanks so much I feel completely at ease with myself now, I want to umm...'

'Scrub my back?' is the inviting reply. With a grin Beth agrees, 'Oh yes, 'mame here is at your deposal.'

'Well let's hoof it, the boys will be waiting anyway.' They move off arm in arm at a brisk pace. Entering the kitchen, the boys are working at the sink preparing some sort of stew for dinner, they look up as the girls enter and grin. Both girls move to their respective partners giving them a kiss and hug, Beth and Rod are now relaxed being able to connect with a more open show of emotion in front of the others, breaking away Karen announces.

'We're going to have a quick shower then we'll join you.' Geoff grins, 'Have fun.' Karen looks at him with an inviting smile then transfers a glance towards Beth coquettishly

answering, "Always try." Beth realises Geoff's in on their sexual shenanigans, instead of blushing she feels a glow inside that their interacting has an appeal to the opposite sex. Leaving the kitchen, she quickly pats Karen on the backside it's an ebullient playful gesture. From behind she hears Geoff laugh, "Ha." Changed with a towel wrapped around her Beth walks thru the kitchen to the bathroom, Karen is already in there, looking up she asks, "You ready?" Dropping her towel Beth smiles then thoughtfully says.

'We've had a hard workout with the kids I just want to relax and enjoy you, come in and I'll wash you.' Karen nods.

'Yes, that'd be lovely I'm pretty tired also.' They step into the shower and snuggle up to each other allowing the warm water to soothe them. Beth picks up the soap, traverses Karen around one eighty degrees and starts applying the soap and suds over her back. With her soft feminine touch Karen relaxes and drifts into a euphoria, the sensation dissipating any tension. She purrs then comments, "Lovely, hmm... I think I need my front done." Turning, she faces Beth, the soaping has done the trick her nipples are standing out breasts full and firm with expectation, Beth takes a step back and admires.

'You have the best body, I love washing it and admiring it, gosh it's almost more enjoyable me doing this and admiring you than having sex, I love your physic so much.' The words strike a chord in Karen's psych, she responds.

'You don't know what a subtle soft feminine touch you have its so exhilarating, I just get lost in the euphoria, thank you for letting me enjoy you.' Smiling Beth acknowledges, "Its mine to give, stand there, enjoy the experience I'll get you ready for Geoff tonight." With that she commences washing and pampering Karen's front, once the washing procedure has finished, she orders Karen out and grabs a towel commenting.

'I'll play mum.' She starts drying Karen who is amazed, she calls.

'Gosh, no-ones done that since I was a little girl, you're drying my hair, Oh that surreal feeling, beautiful.' The drying continues with Karen exacting all sorts of exuberant comments, at the conclusion she stands and gazes directly at Beth.

'That was just the best I'm so alive and turned on, god do I want action with Geoff tonight, oh thank you, you are so kind, gosh all that for me, I really love you so.' She leans forward and kisses Beth passionately on the lips, withdrawing she starts to leave the bathroom dragging the towel behind her, Beth calls out. 'Hey don't forget the towel.' With a half turn Karen shoots back.

'No way, I'm giving him something to fire him up for tonight.' Disappearing thru the door, Beth laughs and starts drying herself, a playful smile breaks across her face, thinking what's good for the goose...' Heading out the door completely naked she mosies thru the kitchen pretending to dry her hair. Looking up Geoff's eyes bulge, with the most playful coquettish smile she gives him a little wave and walks on, again she hears a laugh emanating from him. On entering the bedroom, she looks in Rod's mirror, studying herself she smiles and admits to herself.

'Thanks mum and dad but you made me and well... I'm such a little minx, oh boy life is becoming fun.' Starting to get changed she moves into smart but cute casual clothes finishing off with just the miniscule amount of make-up, viewing the final image in the mirror she admits to herself.

'If you're fit and healthy you don't need this extra stuff much.' With a quick nod, and a flick of her hair, she exits the bedroom. Upon entering the kitchen Karen is sitting, drinking something that looks like a Gin and Tonic, she looks up and asks.

'Do you want something, maybe a small wine?'

'Yes thanks,' Beth answers, 'that'd be nice.' Rod's on his toes and moves to the fridge, 'I'll get it, sit down, take a break.'

Pouring an amount into a glass he hands it to her, quietly complementing her.

'Gosh you look great... here.' Returning his look, she coyly looks away then back to meet his eyes and softly answers, "Thank you, you're so nice.' Smiling with a gracious nod he returns to the food preparation, Karen who's witnessed this small interaction speaks.

'You know we're actually so lucky to be here and involved with these two wonderful guys,' then with a louder voice, 'here's to you two boys, we're so grateful to be involved with you and love you both, cheers.' The two girls clink glasses together. Beth adds, "And you too," they smile touch hands and take another sip. The meal is just a stew but with a little amount of alcohol and good company the dinner flows, conversation easy, time drifts. Round eight-thirty Karen mentions she's a tad tired, the comment not lost on Geoff who received her eyes slightly gleaming in anticipation. Rod raises and says, "I'll walk you home," which Beth gratefully agrees. Hugs and kisses are exchanged Beth thanks them for the meal, and Rod and her depart, as they leave Karen calls. I'll see you at aerobics on Wednesday evening, going to show you stuff.'

"Righto," is Beth's answer, drawing a little vernacular from the Reg Duncan book on verbalisation.

CHAPTER 44

The backstreet is dark as Rod and Beth walk along holding hands, Rod asks.

'What was the stuff Karen was going to give you at dance practice on Wednesday?'

'Oh, just dance theory stuff,' then thinking to herself she opens up to him.

'I've been meaning to tell you I went with Karen the other week to her doctor in Rosenbury, the lady is very young and lovely to deal with. Karen came in with me, I explained that I had a boyfriend and that we'd become sexually active and that I wanted to go on the pill, just to be absolutely safe.'

'Wow,' gasps Rod, looking at her he exclaims, 'you're so understanding and mature, gee you did that just for us, unbelievable. Look can I help in any way like the cost involved?' Smiling back, she realises why she loves this boy so much.

'Well that's awfully kind, I might need a little financial help in the future but I'll let you know, it wouldn't be much.' He stops walking looks at her and says, "Anything, I don't mind." Returning his gaze, she reaches up and kisses him on the lips then breaks away, grabbing his hand, they continue walking and chatting, she thinks out loud.

'You know Karen and Geoff are so understanding.' Rod smirks.

'Yeah, even for adults.'

'Oh no I don't think of Karen that way, I mean she's older sure but not that much, I feel more like a friend, sister companion. I can share anything with her and do plus she's showed me so many things, many that relate to you and I.' He looks with intrigue, she continues.

'Well truthfully with sex stuff, she's been amazing I've developed so much knowledge in that area in such a short time and its with you that I can put it to the test.' He's got the gist of what she's saying.

'So, you sort of experiment with her and then use it with me?'

'Yep, she's great, she's really brought me on in that area, haven't you noticed?' Thinking he agrees.

'Yes, I can see what you're saying, I mean we were both green as grass to start with, I had feelings and so did you but to become more involved we need openness to try and discover, if she can show us stuff then all the better. You know I've lived with them for over a year now and she's been absolutely delightful and understanding to me, I agree, she's more like a sister plus Geoff, he's my uncle and boss but I feel more like a younger brother to him, yeah he's wiser but still a friendly and dependable work mate.' Beth nods in agreement, Rod continues.

'You know it must have been hard for them to make that decision regarding us.'

'Oh yes, put yourself in their position, I don't know what I would have done.'

'I guess that's what comes with the territory of being an adult.' She grins, 'Guess so... think I'll put it off for a while.' He laughs, 'Me too, I want to enjoy my irresponsible teenage years.' Looking directly at her. 'Especially with my girlfriend.'

Snuggling into him she agrees.

'I'm happy to go along with their guidelines, it'll make our time with together more special.' Just then the sound of a car is heard in the background, they look round and see Johnny's Holden Commodore, but it doesn't move close to them, just continues on in another direction. They ignore it and walk on.

Johnny's been cruising for a reason, like foxes around a chicken coop they've been circumnavigating the town's back blocks waiting for a sign of life, he spots Beth and Rod walking.

'Okay there they are, he's walking her home, we'll just cruise on and wait till he's by himself, on the way back after he's dropped her off at old Reg's place.' Inside the car the others are sniggering like rats.

Beth enters the kitchen, Reg is watching TV, he turns his face lighting up.

'Hello darl, how'd it go, everything alright?'

'Yes, uncle Reg, all fine, I'm going to have a shower.'

'Right I'll put the kettle on.' She goes to her room, undresses then stops and thinks, picking up a towel she heads down the passageway. Reg is putting cups out, Beth enters the kitchen in her underwear with the towel slung across her shoulder, slowing she addresses him.

'Uncle Reg I've got something to tell you.' He raises his head and looks at her, realising that she is trying to make a connection, an effort to be comfortable, free and easy in the house, just like her old family home. Wrestling with his thoughts he concludes she's attempting to break down his inquisitiveness by allowing him to be comfortable with her physical presence. He nods and inquires, 'Yes luv?'

'Umm... I've got a boyfriend, its Rod, Geoff Miller's nephew.' He now has a better handling of his composure and comments in an unperturbed way.

'Young Rod ehh... so that's why you've been going over

there so much, ha, sounds alright.' She blushes but is relieved, the exoneration being the catharsis of her slight guilt.

'Would it be alright if I brought him over to meet you?' Her request goes straight to his heart, she's treating him as a parent, with tenderness he tries to control his emotions and answers.

'Meet young Rod eh, He's doing that plumbing apprenticeship, good job that, he seems an alright sort of young fella, yep sounds good, get him over.' She beams relief, moves forward and gives him a hug saying, "Thanks." He's finding that freedom in the house has developed, he's now feeling more relaxed in her presence he gives her a pat on the backside and quips.

'No worries, get along now.' Scrunching her nose plus a coquettish grin she turns and starts to exit the kitchen, watching her leave he realises that she is very fit looking, he calls out.

'Tell you something girl, you look pretty fit, that dance stuff must have something in it.' Turning she smiles and performs a curtsy replying.

'Thank you it does.'

Continuing to the shower she breaks with a little mischievous grin to herself and wiggles her bottom a fraction more than normally, she's taken a subtle leaf out of Karen's book, just planting a seed in his brain that she is no longer a little girl. The gesture is a sybaritic symbol that she has moved into womanhood and has the womanly confidence to accompany it but still with youthful impishness. Behind her she hears a chuckle, realising that her coquettish display has tickled his fancy she is satisfied that her efforts to try and smooth out the intransigent nature of the house to something open, liveable and loving is working. Entering the bathroom she puts the towel on the rack and turns on the shower, starting to take off her bra she slows, turns and looks at the door, it's been left

half open, a beat passes, her face breaks into a smile, with a flick of her hair and a shrug of her shoulders she drops the bra, steps out of her panties and enters the shower, there is a relaxed confident freedom during her washing. Once dried she's about to wrap herself in the towel when again she smiles, nods and shrugs her shoulders, throwing the towel across her shoulder she exits the bathroom, moving across the kitchen she calls.

'Finished, won't be long.' Reg looks up, his eyes open, he breathes out a whistle and shakes his head with the realisation that his household is definitely changing, pausing he dwells then nodding whispers "So be it," and continues with the preparation of the tea. In her room she grabs the second towel and begins drying her hair, during this process she glances at the tapestry, no scrapping sound is heard, relaxing her shoulders the hair towel is discarded, the covering towel is also dropped and her nighty slipped on plus some white knickers, with a few brush strokes to the hair she exits the room. In the kitchen Reg is sitting at the table sipping his tea, there's already one on the table for her, sitting she sips at the tea, it's fresh and hot and brings a satisfied warmth to her. Reg starts.

'Now tell me about this lad.'

'Well firstly he's a real gentleman, I told you how he chased those dropkick boys away when we were down by the river. Even though there were three of them he was brave and strong coming to my defence...' Their conversation continues over the "cuppa." Time passes easily, the conversation relaxed eventually she yawns and announces.

'That's great, I'll organise it, well I think its bed time, I'm tired now.'

'You go luv,' he says. 'Don't worry about the dishes I'll finish them off, see you in the morning, off you go.' Standing she moves to him and gives him a soft kiss on the cheek.

'Thanks again uncle Reg, see you in the morning.'
She's moving off thru the kitchen when a loud knocking

sound emanates from the front door, Reg frowns, and rises commenting.

'What the dickens… I'll go.' On opening the front door, he sees Geoff and Karen standing on the porch, both looking very perturbed.

'Geoff, Karen, what are you doing here at this time?' Karen is nervous but trying to stay calm, she asks in an agitated voice.

'Hi Reg, umm… is Beth in.'

'Yes,' he answers, picking up the worried vibe, 'I'll get her.' He calls loudly, 'Beth, Karen's here.' Beth arrives at the front door and realising something is wrong asks.

'What's wrong?' Karen asks with concern.

'Rod hasn't come home, did he walk you home and drop you here?'

'Yes, we came straight here, he turned and left to go straight back to you guys.' Geoff asks.

'Did he mention about going to see anyone?'

'No, not to me.'

'Well did you see anyone on the way here?'

'No… no wait we did see that Johnny Holden's car cruising round but it stayed away, it didn't come near us.' Geoff ponders.

'Probably 'cos you were close to Reg's place, I don't like this, Reg can you get your car, I've got mine, the town's not that big, if you can look round the South I'll do the North, hit your horn if you see anything.' Reg is right onto it, he can feel their anxiety.

'Righto, will do.' They all split, Geoff moves quickly to his Ute with Karen beside him, he speeds off. Beth runs to her room and returns in jeans, sweatshirt and sneakers, she bounds down the front steps to where Reg has backed the car out, jumping in they move off. The minutes tic past, Beth is craning her head out the window trying desperately to notice

anything thru the bleak darkness. Reg has a torch and shines it out the driver's side window which has been wound down, he's travelling slowly with one hand on the wheel, suddenly Beth calls.

'Stop, did you hear that?' Reg sticks his head out the window listening intently, they both catch the faint sound of a car horn, Reg nods.

'Right, let's go.' He accelerates towards the North part of the town, Beth has her head out of the window trying to guide him in the direction of the horns sound, soon they see a car's headlights beaming, Reg pulls up sharply next to Geoff's Ute. His car's lights are shining on a body slumped on the side of the road, Geoff and Karen are crouched next to it, Karen is bent over examining it. Jumping out of the passenger door Beth screams, "Rod," and sprints towards the body, Karen is carefully analysing Rod's slumped body, there is blood all over his shirt, head and trousers, as Beth runs up Geoff grabs her, refraining her from rushing in, he cautions her.

'Careful, he's alive but badly beaten up, we need to get him home and check him thoroughly.' She nods and composes herself with an understanding regarding the severity of the situation. Raising her head Karen says.

'I've checked his arms and legs, I don't think there's anything broken, so if we're careful we should be able to lift him into the back of Reg's Ute, there's too much stuff in Geoff's. Get around him and lock arms underneath if we're careful we'll get him in the back with little intrusion to any internal injuries.' They gather round and scoop hands under Rod's crumpled body, once hands are joined with the opposite person Karen orders.

'One, two, three up, and carefully does it.' Placing him with delicate care into the back of the Ute, they leave the tail flap down so his body can lie straight, his feet dangling slightly out the rear, Karen jumps in the back to make sure his body

doesn't roll or move round too much during the trip. Beth gets in the front with Reg, carefully he pulls out from the side and drives delicately along the bitumen road, Geoff following in his ute. Arriving at Geoff's house Reg slowly backs his ute in the driveway, allowing room for everyone to be around Rod's limp body. With as much care as possible they repeat the same lifting strategy as before and move him into the house laying him very carefully onto his bed. Beth switches on the light, they all stare, he's a real mess. Geoff looks hard at him his demeanour turning from worried to anger, he starts verbalizing aggressively.

'Bloody cowardly bastards... dropkicks all of them, they need more than a good hiding.' Karen's perturbed by the tone of his voice, she's never seen him upset like this before. She can tell his manner is increasing in ferocity, she's tending Rod but tilts her head to one side pleading, "calm down." Geoff's really lost the plot by this stage, he's becoming unreasonably aggressive.

'Calm down, I'll show 'em calm down.' With that last tirade he storms out of the room. Karen turns to Beth.

'I don't know how to check for internal injuries, you stay here, I'll call a friend of mine who's a nurse at Launceston Hospital, she'll help us, thank god we've still got landlines.' She rushes out of the room, Beth holds Rod's hand, Karen's muffled voice can be heard from the kitchen.

'Geoff, Geoff don't.' The front door is heard slamming, then the sound of Geoff's Ute starting up and accelerating down the road, Karen's dials the number.

'Hello Elaine, its Karen Rosetti here, yes thanks okay... well actually not so... yes... look I need some advice. We have a boy here he's about seventeen years old and has been badly beaten up, I've checked his limbs and don't think anything's broken but I don't know how to check for internal bleeding... oh... okay.' She returns to Rod's room with the hand held phone and sits on the bed telling Beth.

'Go to the kitchen and get some scissors please.' Beth disappears then returns with some large household scissors, Karen keeps talking on the phone relaying the messages to Beth.

'Cut his shirt off him, up the arms first, then his pants, straight up the legs, we need to see his skin.' Beth does as she's told then carefully removes the shirt and jeans, throwing them on the ground she nods "all done" to Karen who continues.

'Now feel all round and across his ribs to check that they're still in line.' Feeling with delicate touch, she's not sure but something doesn't seem right. Transferring her hands to his abdominal region she deftly feels round his torso, it has a puffiness to it. Remembering what looked and felt like when they were together, it seems different, with a worried look she reports back to Karen.

'There's something wrong with his ribs and his diaphragm is umm… sort of swollen and puffy.' Looking at his face she starts to feel sick, it's scratched with dried blood covering much of it, his mouth and chin are swollen, there are also cut marks on his body, with dried blood staining many parts. The vision has turned her stomach, however Karen's next order brings her back concentrating on the task at hand, she mentally steadies herself.

'Check out his mouth, nose and ears, try to see if any blood has run out of those crevices.' Following the instructions, she feels round but no trace of blood or moisture can be found, so they seem at least to be normal. From her limited observation it looks like the blood that is situated found those crevices has splattered there from the cuts on the outside of his body, thus she tells Karen.

'He seems clear there, although there is a lot of blood, I don't think it's come from those areas.'

'Right,' responds Karen and reports back to Elaine, continuing she listens and asks Beth.

'Cut off his jocks and see if any blood has dripped out of his backside.' Realising this is no time or place for faint hearts, Beth does as instructed, cutting his jocks at the side she carefully feels under his backside, it all seems dry. She shakes her head indicating that there is no moisture there, Karen relays Elaine the information.

'Okay we've done all that and it seems to be clear, what do we do now?'... uh, uh... okay, I'll call back if there are any changes... yes, we'll bring him in soon, yes, a mattress in the back plus pillow... right... of course travel smoothly, okay thanks Elaine.' Switching off the phone she turns to Beth and explains.

'Right we've got to keep an eye on him, also he needs to be cleaned and any deep cuts carefully washed with antiseptic and dressed. Use a clean soft cloth from the laundry then carefully dab him dry, once done put a clean sheet and blanket over him.' Beth acknowledges the information answering directly, "yes will do," and leaves the room. Karen now turns her attention to the problem of Geoff, she looks up at Reg who has been quietly standing in the background, his senior presence is a comfort to her with a tremble in her voice she says.

'Reg, Geoff's got a rifle and has gone to Johnny Holden's place, we've got to get there and stop him before he does something that he'll regret.' Reg understands, he has a concerned look but takes charge.

'Right, let's get there now, come on.' They exit the room and head down the passageway towards the front door, as they leave Karen calls out over her shoulder.

'Look after Rod please, we're going to get Geoff.' A reply is heard in the background, "Okay, will do." They jump into Reg's Ute and accelerate away, speeding thru the back blocks Reg glances at Karen, she has an extremely worried look on her face, she tries to explain.

'Geoff's not normally hot headed, but seeing Rod like that well it must have really got to him.' Reg nods in understanding and tries to calm the tension.

'He's got a good head on his shoulders he won't do anything silly.' He tries to smile but realises that this false bravado is doing little to pacify Karen's fears he accelerates even faster. As they close in on Johnny's house, they can see a group of people silhouetted by Reg's headlights, his car comes to a screeching halt. Johnny and his gang are standing round a body slumped on the side of the road. Its Geoff and the gang are yelling out insults and laughing. Karen jumps out of the passenger door and rushes up to Geoff's stricken body, kneeling she screams, "Geoff," he's unconscious, his legs have blood all over them, Johnny mouths off insolently.

'He should watch out where he's goin', walkin' round in the dark with a rifle.' Karen shouts accusingly.

'What's happened, what have you done?' Johnny acts incredulous.

'Me... I ain't done nothin, but poor Pills there didn't see him in the dark till the last minute and ran over the poor guys legs, a terrible tragedy... tsk... tsk.' Karen strains her eyes at him then transfers her gaze to Geoff's legs, realizing that they are broken she screams at the gang.

'You bastards, first Rod and now Geoff, are you animals?' Noogs leans forward and draws a knife, as she flicks it across Karen's face, she speaks menacingly.

'Who you calling bastards miss stuck up, you need a right good fuckin' and the boys know how to treat your type... stuck up bitch... oh you gonna get it but good...' As she speaks the boys in the gang move slowly forward when a sound of "click," is heard. It's Reg who's armed and cocked his shotgun. They all freeze and look up, Reg is pointing the gun straight at them, he speaks slow and with authority.

'I think that'll do for tonight... right Karen stand, you

four very carefully load his body in the back of my Ute, Karen hold his feet, try to keep them straight.' They do as they're told, like a pack of scrounging hyenas, they almost snarl as they perform the duty, Karen gets in the back to support Geoff's head. Even though Reg has the shotgun Johnny's surrounded by his gang and starts to show some mettle, he speaks with conviction.

'You don't scare us old man, we rule this town now, you can't hide or stay awake forever, we'll get you soon.' Changing his gaze towards Karen he makes a snide aside remark.

'After we've sorted a few problems.' Noogs reiterates. "Yeah, sorted.' Reg looks at the gang and scoffs.

'Week as piss by yourselves… you need each other… piss week.' With that final comment he spits on the ground in front of them, turns and climbs in the Ute, starts the engine and drives off, as he accelerates away Johnny yells after him.

'We'll show you who's piss-week, you old fart.' Then turning his attention to the other gang members, he grins.

'But other things first.' His comment produces and escalation in their smiles, a feeling of power and invincibility spreading throughout the gang. Adrenaline's pumping thru his system, everything is going as planned, gone is his unsureness, his vociferous ego is in full flight.

CHAPTER 45

Reg is carefully negotiating the backstreets, there's a grim look on his face, Karen calls from the rear of the Ute.

'Reg we've got to stop at our place first, I'll need to get some things and also explain to Beth what's happened.' he shouts back, "Righto." A few minutes pass, he sees the light on at Karen's house and pulls up in the driveway, Karen jumps out of the rear and rushes up the steps and through the front door. She runs into Rod's room just as Beth has finished cleaning Rod and is in the process on covering him with a sheet. Her head whips up, Karen is breathless and distraught, she bursts out.

'Geoff's had his legs broken by the gang, Reg and I will have to drive him to the Launceston Hospital, you okay to stay and look after Rod?' Beth gasps at the surreal information but controls herself enough to nod, Karen keeps ordering.

'I'll call you on the landline when I get there, once I've got Geoff sorted then I'll come back stopping into the police at Rosenbury, sorry got to go.' Running to the closet she grabs some blankets and a pillow then rushes down the passageway, out the door and jumps into the back of the Ute. Throwing a blanket over the unconscious Geoff she calls, "Go Reg", then settles next to him supporting his head with a pillow, Reg

drives off knowing it'll be a long, slow, careful drive.

Sitting in the chair next to the resting Rod, Beth drifts off, at various times she wakes, goes to him and checks his pulse, satisfied she returns to the chair and watches. Thinking brings no answers but does induce sleep, the body's natural mechanism to ease fear, she's jerked awake by the landline phone ringing, rushing to the kitchen she picks it up and speaks.

'Hi Karen, how's Geoff?' The reply is that the doctors in emergency are looking at him right now, they believe that one leg is broken but are unsure about the other one, X-Rays have been taken and they are just waiting proof. Listening intently Beth tries to act mature and sound positive she replies.

'Okay, well try not to worry I'm here and Rods still calm and resting.' Thanking her Karen hangs up, replacing the handset Beth walks to the bedroom, stopping outside Rod's door she faces the front door, a worried expression develops on her face. Being in the house alone starts to escalate her fear, walking down the passageway she checks the lock on the front door then moves back thru the kitchen and does the same with the lock on the back door, returning to the kitchen she opens the cupboard and grabs a mug, switches on the kettle and sits. Gazing round the empty kitchen a chilly feeling of solitude and isolation envelopes her, trying to stay in control she, flicks her hair and moves to the kettle and pours her tea, once done she retires back to Rod's room.

Morning arrives, Beth is snoozing in the chair in Rod's room, she stirs. There is a sound of a key in the front door lock, followed by the squeak of it opening and footsteps in the passageway a hand taps Beth on the shoulder, looking up she sees the vision of Karen's face, a very worn and tired Karen.

'How is he?' She asks. With a soulful pragmatism Karen answers.

'He'll be alright, one leg is broken but the other is only

badly bruised, he'll be confined to a wheel-chair for a while,' gesturing towards Rod.

'How's he?'

'Resting, still sleeping, I've been checking his pulse it seems steady, like normal'. Karen smiles weakly in a resigned way, then says.

'Come on let's have a cuppa, I told Reg I'd take you home.' 'Oh thanks, alright.' Entering the kitchen, Beth gets some mugs out of the cupboard while Karen fire up the gas and puts the kettle on. Moving to the pantry she gets some tea bags out and places one into each mug, sitting at the table she is almost speaking to herself.

'I can't believe tonight, what a disaster, it started out so well.' Finishing her comment Beth adds.

'And ended in a nightmare, the boys didn't do anything to deserve this, I mean Rod was saying how Johnny and he parted on friendly terms but when we got to them, he was so antagonistic towards us.' Karen's been thinking.

'You remember when Rod said after their meeting, he wasn't sure if Johnny was fair dinkum or if it was an act but thought it best to take him on face value, well I guess we now know… it was an act.' sNodding in agreement Beth asks.

'How's Geoff feeling?'

'Oh, he's pretty drugged up, they operated and said it was successful so he'll recover, however he'll be in hospital for a week then confined for months in a wheel-chair. Once the legs mended it'll be months of physio… god what a mess, how's Rod?'

'Just the same, sleeping.'

'I spoke to Elaine, she said to check his bones and stuff when he's awake but by the sounds of it, she thinks it's probably broken ribs and collarbone which given time will heal themselves, however he also will be laid up for at least a month. I dropped into the police station and they said they'd come

down and have a word with Johnny and his friends, but with no witnesses plus the fact that Geoff was carrying a rifle it'd be hard to make any charges stick. They'll take statements then all they can do is warn them to stay away.

'Fat chance,' scoffs Beth. 'In a small town like this.'

'I know, they'll only keep a low profile for a short time but one thing I don't understand is why the boys?'

'I know I've been asking myself the same question but still don't have any answers, like you said Rod had an agreeable conversation with Johnny the other day, what changed his attitude? Beth shrugs her shoulders, they continue to ponder the why's but come up with little, half an hour passes, Karen stands and says.

'Okay time to move, got to get you home'. They exit the kitchen.

Reg is sitting at the table pondering over a cup of tea, Beth walks in despondently his heart goes out to her.

'Come on luv, sit down I'll make you a cuppa.' Not really wanting one she nonetheless sits at the table, Reg gets up and pours some more tea into a mug, hands it to her and resumes his seat. Beth explains the situation to him.

'I've been talking to Karen, she's just returned from the hospital, oh of course you know, he's got a broken leg we think Rod's got broken ribs and collarbone, they'll both be laid up for a month or more, Reg pats her hand.

'That's not good luv but it could have been worse.'

'I know, small mercies eh! But one thing we don't understand is why?'

'Donno luv, small town mentalities.'

'Small, fair enough but vindictive and violent.' He tries to explain.

'Well upbringing or lack of it is a reason, probably a violent home-life, it breeds narrow minds, especially regarding people like you.'

'Me?'

'Yep jealousy but with the lack of proper grounding they have no tools to handle life in normal circumstances, so I guess all they can do is resort to violence, it's the only thing they know. Low life, morons, drop-kicks all of them, should have seen them when we went to get Geoff, they acted like a pack of wild animals, no social aspects at all.' Still unsure Beth ponders but exhaustion starts to seep into her.

'Jealous… oh I don't know, I'm tired, I think I'll go to bed if you don't mind and uncle Reg thanks for all your help, I don't know what would have happened if you hadn't been there.' Appreciating her response, he replies.

'No problem young'un, off you go and have a lie down, try and forget tonight.' Leaving the kitchen Beth enters her bedroom and lies down. Reg is still pondering the day's movements, after a while he rises and walks to her room, carefully opening the door he looks in, she's asleep on top of the bed. His demeanour is one of a concerned adult, shaking his head he pulls the blanket over her, switches off the light and leaves.

The morning breaks, the house is very quiet, Reg moves down the passageway and knocks on Beth's door, she mumbles a reply allowing him to open and speak.

'I've got tea and toast going, take your time, come down when you're ready.' She nods sleepily then dozes again, after another twenty minutes she struggles out of bed, entering the kitchen she disconsolately sits at the table. She's wearing the same clothes she had on last night but not really conscious of that fact. Looking at her he tries to think of something to say that might pick her spirits up but with nothing coming to hand just states the obvious.

'Morning luv, pretty rum do last night.' The best reply she can give is a dispirited nod, he continues.

'What are you going to do today, school?'

'Not sure but I'd better check on Karen and Rod.'

'Yep fair enough, have a shower, the breakies ready, get a bit of that into you and I'll take you over.' With him taking command to an extent, it brings a brief smile to her face, she reiterates her feelings to him.

'Thanks again uncle Reg… umm for everything but especially last night, I really don't know what would have happened if you hadn't been there.' He smiles, "No worries luv." Rising she moves towards him and gives a loving hug, this time he puts his arms around her responding in a sanguine way. He relaxes, 'Alright off you go to a hot shower, that'll make you feel better.' Exiting she's still dragging her feet in a desolate way, he returns to his tea, thinking, contemplating thoughtfully. At the front of Karen's house Reg pulls up in his Ute. Beth's in the passenger seat, she kisses him on the cheek opens the door and steps down from the car, with a wave Reg drives off. Climbing the front steps, she rings the doorbell, the door opens a very tired and drawn Karen stands in front of her, on viewing its Beth she brightens a bit obviously pleased to see her.

'Hi, great to see you, thanks for popping over, come in.' Entering the kitchen, Karen sits at the table and motions Beth to follow, she shakes her head and exclaims.

'What a horrible night.'

'I know, unbelievable… how's Rod?' Karen's now holding her chin in her hands, elbows on the table in a dispirited manner, she answers.'

'He was alright when I checked him a while back, go and have another look.' Moving to Rod's room, she knocks on the door, there's no answer, she quietly enters. He's resting peacefully, gazing at him she notices he doesn't look as bad as when he was brought home last night. Her Florence Nightingale's effort has humanised him to a degree so that now he looks like a patient in a hospital ward, not a soldier's remains left on the battlefield. Touching his arm and caressing

softly round his biceps she leans forward and gives a tender kiss on his forehead. Continuing to observe him she takes in all his wounds and bruises, the picture is a disturbing one, with a deep breath she exits the room and returns to the kitchen. Karen explains.

'I'll have to go and visit Geoff, would you be able to stay here for a few hours and watch Rod?'

'Of course, no problem'.

'Also, we are meant to have dance next week so we'll have to cancel and pick up sessions the following week.' Beth replies with a positive answer.

'Okay, I'll help with whatever you need.' Having Beth's proactive attitude picks up Karen's spirits, she starts to move into organising mode.

'Right I need a shower first.' She exits the room with just a tad more liveliness in her step, while she's in the shower Beth busies herself by doing the dishes. Once showered and changed Karen re-enters the kitchen quickly noticing its fresh renewed state.

'Look I'll be away at least six hours, if Rod wakes up see if he wants any food but try to get him to slowly sip some water, there's food in the fridge for a sandwich. Also the names and numbers of the dance kids is on a sheet stuck to the side of the fridge, could you call them and put off dance practice next week, explain that Geoff's had an accident try not to go into details just tell them we'll make it up over the next few weeks.' Nodding in understanding Beth complies.

'Leave it to me, I'll get thru to all of them.'

'Thanks Beth, you're being such a trooper.' Then moving forward, she gives her a kiss on the forehead, withdrawing she looks caringly into Beth's eyes, smiles, turns and exits the kitchen. Beth turns and places the last few dishes away then goes to the laundry finding a broom plus a brush and pan she returns and sweeps the floor, once that job is

completed, she starts the phone calls to the various parents. Taking a break, she transfers to Rod's room to check on him, sitting on the side of his bed she lightly touches his arm, he stirs slightly, she addresses him in a caring tone.

'Hello, you're home Rod, how are you feeling?' Gradually opening his eyes, he tries to orientate himself, confused he questions.

'Home... how'd I get, ohh... I feel... ohh... like...'

'Take it easy,' she tenderly commands, 'here have a little water first.' Picking up the glass she pours a minimal amount into his mouth, then speaking in a soothing manner.

'You'll be sore but okay, do you want something to eat?' he nods and mumbles, "Okay."

'Right I'll make you a sandwich, stay still, take your time try and get your bearings.' After she's left the room, Rod starts to feel himself, he becomes aware of the bruising in various parts of his body plus his rib cage is extremely tender, any slight movement radiates a surge of pain thru him, soon Beth arrives back with a sandwich on a plate and a cup of tea. Trying to raise himself he quickly realises that the action is too painful. Placing the tray on the bedside table Beth gets a second pillow from the wardrobe and carefully slips it behind the first pillow thus giving him some semblance of sitting up. Cutting the sandwich into small pieces she orders, "open up," then grinning starts placing the pieces in his mouth, as he chews, she explains.

'You'll have to be careful we think you've got broken ribs and collarbone, umm... do you remember much?' His voice is fragile but he tries his best to recollect his thoughts.

'No, not much, after dropping you off I was walking home, I came across Johnny and Pills looking at the engine of the car, the bonnet was up, they asked for some advice so I bent over looking at the engine when I felt a sharp wack at the back of my head... well the rest is just a blur.'

'Right, well It seems like you were attacked by the whole gang and badly beaten up. Luckily you came out of it with cuts, bruises and probably broken ribs and collarbone.'

'Wha… why me?'

'Don't know, but my job is to make you better,' she starts acting in a business-like manner announcing.

'Fear not nurse Beth is here, eat this then I'll wash you.' This little bit of playacting brings a tentative smile to his face. The sandwich is finished, she takes the plate back to the kitchen then grabs a large bowl from the laundry, half-filling it with warm water she takes a washer and returns to the bedroom announcing.

'Alright patient, time for a bed-wash, stay still,' pulling back the sheet she views his battered body then adding a bit of playacting she rubs her hands together in a villainous way exclaiming.

'Ha ha… ve start.' As the hand-wash takes place he grimaces at various times but nods for her to continue. Playacting is forgone as she concentrates on the task at hand, he's obviously delicate so care is her major concern. Watching her perform the wash task, even though he is extremely tender he is transfixed by her touch, the way she traverses her hands across his body is a serene experience, he relaxes and tries to enjoy it. Only when she has finished and takes the pillow away allowing him to lie back in a state position does he feel pain, he grimaces, she responds.

'It'll be uncomfortable for some weeks but you will mend, better rest now.' Agreeing, he nods, "Thanks," she bends over him kisses his forehead then exits the room. Waiting in the kitchen she finds a book on the edge of the bench, to kill time she begins to read. Hours later she hears the sound of the front door opening, Karen enters the kitchen, Beth looks up from her reading and says.

'Oh, you're back, I'll put the kettle on, how's Geoff?'

Sitting, Karen is less despondent but still reserved.

'Not too bad actually, it's a bit better than we hoped, one leg is broken but it's a clean break the doctors said so it'll mend with no real repercussions, and the other leg is just badly bruised with cuts, this means he'll probably have less time in a wheel-chair.' Beth smiles, "Well that's better."

'Yes, probably the best we could hope for, how's your patient?'

'Sort of similar, he's awake and had something to eat and drink so that's a good sign.'

'Guess so, looks like we're making the best of a bad thing.' Turning Beth nods with a dour smile, then explains.

'I called all the parents and tactfully explained that Geoff had an accident and had been taken to hospital, they were very understanding and all sent their best wishes, I said we'd talk to them later next week regarding catch-up times.'

'Okay that's good, one thing we don't have to worry about for a while. Look thanks awfully, it lessens the load a bit but I'll need to do those make-up classes 'cos that's the only money I'll have coming in for a while.'

'Yes, it's not like there's any part-time work around here.'

'Nope, this is it, so it'll be tight for the next few months, the most important thing is to get Geoff home and to nurse both him and Rod back to health.' Beth understands and agrees but still holds a nagging question.

'Yes, and I'll help as much as I can but what about Johnny and his gang?'

'Well I had a talk to the police, they said that they'll have a word with Johnny but the reality is they come, talk and leave thus not seen again until something seriously goes wrong. Johnny's not dumb, he'll lie low for a while but his general demeanour will now be really cocky, I think we'd better tread carefully over the next few weeks'. Because she's experienced

the gang first hand Beth's worried, however she also knows
that a strong façade is needed, she agrees with an attempted
strength of character.

'I can see what you mean, no probs we'll be right.' Her
conviction behind the comment is very shallow, to Karen
however the comment shows resilience which picks her spirits
up.

'Yes, we'll be okay, well I'd better take you home.'
Attempting to continue this front Beth says with calmness and
strength.

'No, it's alright, its light and I'd like to walk, fresh air,
you know good to clear the mind.' Being tired both mentally
and physically Karen hesitantly agrees.'

'Well okay, I guess it is daylight and not too far so I
suppose it's alright, again thanks for holding the fort, donno
what I would have done without you.' Moving to Beth she
gives her a hug, then a kiss a smile of appreciation is a tired one
but open, her eyes showing the strain. Taking Beth's hand, she
walks her to the door, opening it she gives her another hug and
lets Beth leave, as Beth's walking down the steps she calls.

'We've got no kids, how about you and I get together
and do a session later in the week?' Beth replies, "yes lets," then
a wave, she heads off down the road.

The air is warm, a few birds twitter away unaware
of the turmoil that has surrounded the girls, Beth saunters
along, she fluctuates between thinking about the problems and
enjoying the therapeutic catharsis provided by the countryside.
Her ebullient manner suddenly changes, turning the corner
she spies Johnny and the whole gang, his car is parked across
the rough grass area that substitutes as a footpath. The car's
parked in such a position that walking down the street she
would have to veer around the car. Thinking of what she said
back at Karen's sounded good there, however the reality facing
her right now has ebbed that façade away, although worried

she breaths in and decides to show a bold front but this will mean walking around the car. "Best to do it and ignore any comments," she thinks to herself. Sticking her chest out she stands upright and moves towards them, as she approaches Noogs straightens up from leaning on the car and steps onto the road. Beth readjusts her direction to a wider sweep around the car, Noogs steps to her right blocking her direction, forcing her to stop, Noogs addresses her with a sneer.

'Hello schoolie, been playing nurse?' Beth doesn't answer, her inner fear intensifies but she tries to show strength by not answering and standing more upright, Noogs continues her verbal assault.

'Shame about your boyfriend.' Still no response is forthcoming from Beth.

'Dear me, you will get lonely... but don't worry, I'll look after you, I'll arrange for the boys to drop round and give you a nice good fuckin.' What'd you say?'... maybe after one of your dance practices, hey we'll even throw in a freebee for Karen, now how kind are we, come on what'd you say?' She stares at Beth and leans in very close to her face, "Mmm...?' Although scared Beth has had enough, she moves her head sideways and does a visual sweep of the boys, then directs her comments to Noogs, in an offhand manner.

'No thanks I'll wait, I don't want to lower my standards.' Noogs animosity increases, she takes the comment in, her eyes widen, teeth clench then she raises her hand as if to hit Beth, glancing over Noog's shoulder Beth calls out.

'Uncle Reg, here!' Everyone looks across the road in the direction of Beth's call, while their heads are turned Beth ducks around Noogs and sprints off down the road, Tatts is the first to notice Beth's disappearance.

'Hey!' Pills although slow on the uptake yells.

'She's gone!' Billy however sees a chance at playing hero and yells.

'Not yet, I'll g-g-get her.' Pushing off the car he begins to give chase, Noogs fumes

'Lower her standards, that fuckin' little bitch, just wait, she'll get a lowering of her standard, so low that she'll scream for mercy.' Looking at Pills and Tatts she growls with absolute venom in her voice.

'Boys you are gonna have some real fun very soon.' All through this discourse Johnny has been sitting on the bonnet and leaning on the windscreen, he slides to the pavement and addresses Noogs, teasing her a little bit.'

'Cute little schoolie getting up your fanny?' She's not in the mood for his sarcasm.

'Butt out, this is my action, you've had your fun.' Putting up his hands in mock surrender he appeases her.

'No problems, yours to give, yours to take away, have fun.'

'Oh, we'll have fun, I'll make sure the boys enjoy themselves.' Billy returns from the chase puffing in an exhausted manner.

'She g-g-got away… gee she's p-p-pretty quick.' Grinning, Johnny's enjoying this sideshow, he quips.

'Yep, a sight too quick for you, me 'ol son, might be too quick for all of you.' Aggressively Noogs directs.

'Well, we'll just have to slow 'em down, you know confine 'em for a bit…' Pricking up his ears Johnny exudes.

'Confine…' Oh big words… mmm, this'll be worth seeing but be careful we don't want the cops down here anymore, just lay low for a while, here's a go, why don't you plan a strategy. Hey! That's two big words in one day, it's all happening here, come on you root rats these big words are making me thirsty, I want a drink.' They all pile into Johnny's car, he hits the accelerator spinning the back wheels, rotating the steering wheel back and forth the car does "Wheelies", spurred on by screams of "Yeah" and "Go Johnny" inside the car.

CHAPTER 46

Reg is in the kitchen making dinner, he hears the front door open then slam shut followed by rushed footsteps down the passageway, Beth bursts into the kitchen, he notices she's out of breath.

'Hello luv, out of breath, been running?' For a second she doesn't want to burden him with her problem, then realising he's now her parent and should be treated as such she opens up.

'Johnny and the gang stopped me just two blocks down the road, Noogs was getting really aggressive but I was able to duck around them and sprint home, I'm quicker than them.' Listening to her account Reg's worried look intensifies.

'Maybe so but I don't like the sound of this, they're getting really cocky, stopping people in the street in broad daylight, not good, not right, look luv sit down we need to work a few things out.' Sitting at the table Reg ponders, inadvertently tapping his fingers on the table, his thinking is unfettered, as he rationalises the situation to her.

'It looks like things in town are going to get worse, there's no law and the ordinary people are easily intimidated. The strong ones like Jim Byrnes live out of town so they're sort

of out of the equation, unless those half-wits decide to pick on the younger ones like at your dance class, naa... after his run in with Jim, Johnny's smart enough to leave well alone, now that Geoff and Rod are out of the way you girls, Karen and you are possible targets.' Listening Beth agrees with his logic, putting her point, she almost ponders aloud.

'I can see that, but it seems that Noogs is the one with her nose out of joint it looks like she's the leader now, Johnny is... well sort of disinterested.'

'Not surprising, Noogs has always had it in for Karen, ever since early High School. She never really let it drop or put it behind her, it festered then your entry and becoming friends with Karen only made things worse.'

'But why? Okay Karen and some of the others were a bit unkind at Primary School, but people move on. I mean they'd grown up Karen's never done anything to upset her, I believe she's made attempts to be friendly or at least civil when they've bumped into each other round the town, it's Noogs who has been offhand or worse, Karen just gave up and let sleeping dogs lie.' Thinking hard Reg tries to explain what he believes is the background that has caused this escalation in vengeance.

'Look luv, it's not really Karen or you, it's what you stand for, as you know Noogs... let's give her real name for a change, Nancy was dragged up. Her dad was the town drunk, absolutely hopeless, he cleared out when she was in Primary School. Her mum was almost as bad with the drink and was renowned for taking anyone home after closing time and believe me some awful creatures paid a visit. Well it didn't take long for the local people to start looking down on her, of course Nancy would be with her hearing the snide comments the offhand remarks. By the time she got to High School she had a handling of her situation, this shaped her quickly into a real negative person. She'd give it back verbally to any person

who dared to look at her, therefore at school she was involved in many fights with other girls. Her ferocity quickly put her offside with her peers and the general public in town. The only ones she could side with was the local scum, that's the gang, they're her friends. Unfortunately, when you arrived and befriended Karen... well that was the last straw, you ask why you? Well because you're everything that she's not. Intelligent, fit, kind and attractive plus you've worked hard to get to where you've got and will do in the future, basically you tick all the boxes, she doesn't, thus she despises you and what you stand for.' Beth nods in understanding but is still perturbed as to what she and Karen will have to do to survive this tumultuous situation.

'So, if we are the next targets, what do we do? Do we hide, not walk the streets, have you pick me up all the time?'

'Well possibly, 'cos after the other night I'm a bit of authority round here so I'm likely to be on their hit list also.' This admission smacks Beth straight in the face, her now loving uncle threatened, tears well in her eyes, the hopelessness of their situation is overwhelming. She reaches out and holds his hands, her care is transmitted to him, he looks at her kindly then returns in thought searching for an answer, trying to look ahead for information he asks.

'When will Geoff be out of hospital?'

'I'm not sure, he's only got one broken leg, Karen said he'd be confined to a wheelchair for up to two months but because the doctors say the mending will probably go well, I think he's expected home at the end of the week, why?' Reg has somewhat pieced some idea together he explains what for the next week will become their "Motus operandi."

'Right, once Geoff comes home, we need to get together and discuss this problem, till then I'll drive you to the bus stop and pick you up after school. I'll always have my rifle behind my seat, also I'll take you to and from dance practice

unless Karen is able to give you a lift home now Geoff's car is free. I'll give her a call, we'll go around to hers tomorrow night and work out times plus a time to get together once Geoff's home.' Relief floods into Beth, she has an adult taking charge, moving to him she hugs him and kisses him lovingly on the cheek.

'Oh, uncle Reg, you're so kind thanks.'

CHAPTER 47

Johnny's car is parked near the old quarry, Johnny is leaning against the door, Noogs is propped up leaning on the bonnet, he's explaining the situation to her, trying to calm her down and plan, not go off half cocked.

'I know you want to get at them bitches but use ya brain, if ya go off half-cocked that'll bring the fuzz down on us, we need to lay low for a while, you know, plan some things.' Although not overly intelligent Noogs is still the only one in the gang that can at least commute some semblance of a logical conversation, she's curious about his thought process.

'Plan, what plan, like what things?' He enjoys being questioned, the way they look up to him for ideas and direction, it feeds his ego, he explains.

'Well for a start the old man, we need to get him out of the way.' Agreeing in a vociferous way.

'Yeah, hate that old prick, fuckin' old pervert that's what he is… but like how do we do that?'

'Okay give it a rest for some time, say ten days or so, let things subside hmm… subside… nice word, anyway after that the boys will go and pay him a visit in his backyard. I know he likes working in his vegie patch, gotta be careful working in

them gardens, accidents can happen, very dangerous places them gardens.' Smiling in agreement with his malicious plan Noogs laughs and comments.

'Yeah, nice one Johnny, hey you're so good at working things out, you know I'm really appreciative.' He's immediately picked up her drift and is mentally trying to find an escape route.

'Hey if ya can't do things to help ya friends what's the point of being here. Look I just want you and the boys to get what you deserve, I mean, all those years you took shit. It's your turn now make the most of it, me, I'm just happy to help, well gotta move I've some things to work on at home, let's go.' Getting in the car he breaths a sigh of relief, thinking to himself, "shit it's getting hot around this camp, let's just do this and get out of here, fuckin' Noogs," a shudder goes through his body.

CHAPTER 48

The days pass, Reg drives Beth to the bus stop as well as picking her up, on the Wednesday he drops her at the dance studio agreeing to pick her up in a couple of hours. Entering the studio Beth spies Karen sitting on the bench, the CD Player looks like it hasn't been switched on yet. She notices how dejected Karen looks, it's not the bubbly personality she usually exudes, walking up Beth tries to enhance the mood, with a lively, "Hi Kaz." Looking up Karen gives a smile, "Oh hi, you're here". Picking up the vibe Beth sits next to her on the bench, with a conciliatory tone asks.

'Penny for them?' The responsive look says everything, it's that "little girl lost and alone." She stares at Beth and says.

'I don't know if I'm up to dance but I would like to hold you, quite truthfully I need TLC.' There's no need to question motives Beth feels exactly the same, they embrace and hold the hug for over a minute. Karen whispers, "Oh thank god I've got you here with me, I need support and love so much right now." Releasing their grip Beth gazes lovingly at her and agrees.

'We've got caught up in something neither of

us wanted, we're being pulled in a different direction, I hate this, I don't like, in fact I hate violence, that's why my sport is aerobics, you know positive and fitness based. Those idiots have tried to destroy that plus our friendship. Well no way, actually to quote a stupid rock song…'. She stands and starts singing.

'We're not going to take it, no we're not going to take, we're not going to take it any more…' Karen looks on in amazement, the ridiculous nature of the act is so stupid of spirit that she bursts out laughing. "Ha… ha… ha…." The release is just the tonic she jumps up from the seat and joins in. They continue singing the chorus refrain from the song twice more then collapse into each one's arms, looking into Beth's eyes Karen speaks with unfettered truth.

'You are so lovely, thanks for the pick me up, just what I needed,' with that she kisses her passionately on the mouth, Beth withdraws slightly and earnestly says.

'It may be putting our loving and experimenting on the back burner but it can't last forever, we will get through this, then we can have fun again.' Listening Karen nods, she leans forward again and kisses Beth then clenches again in a emotional hug, the gesture a symbol of bonding, showing resolute strength thru love and appreciation, they stay entwined that way for many minutes.

CHAPTER 49

Reg returns to the dance studio at the appropriate time, the girls exit the room, as Beth climbs in his Ute Karen calls.

'Geoff will be home tomorrow, we'll see you guys on Saturday morning.'

'Righto' is his reply. With that he accelerates away, driving down the street Beth quips.

'Mum's taxi, on time as normal.' This tongue in cheek comment causes him to grin it's another step in his assimilation to parent-hood. Beth has noticed that this premonitory situation has brought about a changing of his character, he's now needed and is growing more personable, not just to her but the others as well, her presence has enlivened and opened him up to the general community. Faded is the gruff exterior, replacing it is a genial and somewhat ebullient rural gentleman.

On the Saturday morning Karen is busying herself in the kitchen, she hears a knock on the front door, opening it she sees Reg and Beth standing on the front porch, her pleasant manner is something like her old self.

'Hi, thanks for coming, come in.' She gives Beth a hug, Reg puts out his hand in the normal manner of adult greeting but Karen bypasses it and envelopes him in a hug. He's a bit

taken back by this new outward show of emotion but returns the gesture awkwardly, Karen grins at him.

'Great to see you Reg, come on in the boys are here.' Moving down the passageway they enter the kitchen. Geoff's in a wheelchair and Rod's sitting at the table with his arm in a sling plus bandages round his chest, they both look up at Reg's and Beth's entry and smile, Karen quips.

'Welcome to the war zone.' Surveying them Reg quips, 'More like the aftermath.' Everyone laughs at his dry wit, Beth walks up to Rod gives him a kiss then turns and addresses Reg.

'Oh, over all this business uncle Reg, you've never had a chance to meet Rod.' Rod tries to be personable, to make a good impression, with direct politeness he says.

'Hi good to meet you Mr Dunc... err... Reg.' Reg studies him for a short while and doesn't answer, he's thinking, the pause in the greeting starts to increase Rod's anxiety, everyone waits, Reg eventually comments but in a studious way.

'It was Johnny's boys who did this, right? I mean Beth didn't have to come heavy handed 'cos you overstepped the mark, did she?' Reg's question has him treading water, he's nervous regarding which way to answer, Beth knows Reg's pulling Rod's leg and butts in.

'Yes, uncle Reg you noticed and if he ever tries anything again, I'll break his other collarbone.' Geoff's enjoying this banter, Karen starts to giggle, Geoff's grinning Beth's half laughing. Rod looks around at them realising he's the reason for their mirth, breaking out in a smile Reg offers his hand.

'Just pulling your leg son, pleased to meet you.' Rod nervously smiles and takes Reg's hand, he glances at Beth who is still quietly laughing, she gazes at him and shakes her head. Geoff breaks in and steers the conversation towards the reason for the meeting.

'All jokes aside we do have a problem, so let's sit down

and discuss it.' Karen offers, "Would you like a cup of tea?' Reg nods in appreciation saying.

'That'd be great, thanks Karen,' Beth nods also. They all sit round the kitchen table while Karen busies herself making cups of tea, Geoff starts.

'Well we all know the situation, as the authority in the town has lessened, the police have gone and the local "hoons" or in this case Johnny and his friends have risen in confidence with anti-social behaviour. It seems that Johnny wants to be boss of the town and I guess he's sort of achieved his aim, 'cos with Rod and myself out of the way the rest of the town's folk are too old or too timid to stand up for themselves. Not so the farmers of the district but he's already learnt that lesson, strangely Johnny's not our problem so much, its more Noogs and her stooges'. Beth agrees.

'Yes, when they bailed me up in the street the other day, it was Noogs who was the aggressive one, actually Johnny seemed rather disinterested.' Reg adds.

'Reckon so, Johnny has seen the town shrink, he's proved a point to himself, he's ready to move on and most likely without the others, they're the ones with the small-town mentality.' Karen has finished brewing the cups of tea, she disperses them sits at the table and explains.

'When I came back from college to look after my mum, Noogs was the envious one, she was really negative to me.' Geoff elaborates.

'We know it's not Karen, it's what she stands for.'

'Beth nods and expands.

'That's what uncle Reg said to me, when I arrived and started a friendship with Karen, well it only exacerbated the situation.' Listening intently Rod poses the main question.

'Okay but what are they going to do and how do we deal with it or react to it?' They all pause thinking, it's Geoff who has been posing the question who leads the charge with

his solution.

'Look they've been spoken too by the police, thus they know that they're watching, so I reckon they won't do anything for a while, maybe two to three weeks and that'll be minor anyway, from there they'll escalate.'

'Why?' Asks Beth.

'Because to get courage they need to build up nerve, it won't be just us, it'll be the few people who live in town, the shopkeepers, workers any old folk. Everyone will notice a change in attitude, scoffing at any form of conservatism or authority but I agree with you all, Noogs is the real problem, she wants to prove a point with you Karen and now Beth. That being she's better than you and unfortunately the only method she knows is violence, that's what she'll use and remember she has the stooges with her.'

'Fair enough,' agrees Reg. 'I reckon you're pretty much on the money'. Karen adds.

'I agree also but to follow Rod's question, what do we do?' Silence descends on the table, everyone ponders the words. Inhaling with a deep breath Geoff announces.

'Prepare.' A slightly confused Beth queries.

'Prepare... for what?' Reg knows exactly what Geoff is alluding too.'

'For battle.' Now Karen's confused.

'Battle?' Geoff condenses.

'Well a fight.' The announcement has Karen confused, she questions the obvious.

'But you're injured?' Breathing slowly and stressing his point Geoff eyes both Karen and Beth.

'Not us... you two.' Mouths drop open with antipathy of exclamation they call in unison.

'Us...!'

'But I don't know how to fight', exclaims Beth. 'I don't even like violence.' Nodding in agreement Geoff tries to explain

the reasoning behind his statement.

'Fair enough, so what do you do? Hide and wait for them to find you… and they will like it or not, unless you prepare and do something your end result is rape and probably disfigurement. You're both lovely looking girls, see how you'd feel looking in a mirror with knife slashes across your faces and they do carry knives as you know.' He turns to Karen.

'Karen, I love you so much plus making love to you but just imagine someone like one of those revolting little stooges invading your person while others hold you, maybe they've beaten you and are holding a knife to your throat.' He turns to Beth and hammers his point. The same applies to you Beth, both of you think of the consequences, it'd stay with you for the rest of your life. When this type of thing happens it can destroy you, your confidence, loved ones, your life, do you want this to happen?' Shocked by the reality of his claims Beth answers.

'No obviously.' He finishes with a blunt demand.

'Then no option, you learn how to defend yourselves.' Everyone ponders, the first one to comment is Reg.

'I agree, it's the only way.' Regaining composure Karen tries to rationalise the direction of the conversation.

'But there's more of them and they're stronger, I wouldn't stand a chance.' She looks at a now very scared Beth. 'I mean look at us I'm not tall and Beth here is still a teenager, not the biggest girl around.' Rod can't help himself he softly blurts out.

'Not big but very cute.' Beth's head snaps round her mouth opens with a minor gasp which quickly diminishes into a soft smile.' Although an aside Reg takes up the point.

'Yep, I agree, and I want you to stay that way, so Geoff what do you propose?'

'Look', says Geoff, 'I agree you both are not big but not strong? Don't think so, you both do dance and aerobics I've seen you with little on, Beth does a small slightly embarrassed

grin to herself, you're fit.' Pleading Karen breaks in.

'But that's fit not strong.'

'Agreed, but with a training scheme you could use your fitness to get strength, especially upper body strength.'

'Right we could train to develop upper body strength but how would we use it, we know nothing about the physical aspect of fighting.'

'Well, we can help, Rod did a little amateur boxing a few years ago.' An unsure look breaks across Rod's face, he's not sure about his ability being touted.

'A bit not that much.' However, Geoff's not to be waylaid.

'But enough to teach the girls balance and the effective use of their hands, I've got a friend who trained in Special Forces in the army, I'll give him a call and get some advice. I also did a little unarmed combat drilling in the army reserve a few years ago, like Rod enough, we can work something out.' Beth's listened her face displays worry and unsureness, she looks at Karen.

'Look don't get me wrong, I believe in working to obtain your goals. The reality is I'm no hero, when those awful boys surrounded me at the river I just froze and whimpered… look I have loved meeting you guys and starting a relationship with Rod plus I'm just getting to know my uncle who I'm learning to love also.' At this announcement Reg glows, his eyes moisten.

'But me fighting… sorry I just can't see it.' Geoff has to reinforce the situation.

'I understand and agree but Rod and I are out of the ball-game, it's you and Karen that they want, if you stick together, I believe you can come through this.'

'I agree with you Beth,' enters Karen. 'But we don't have any option, we need each other. I love you and don't want anything to happen to you or me for that matter, I believe we

need to stick together and follow their advice.' Responding with subdued understanding in her voice Beth says.

'You've been so kind since I've arrived here, you feel like a sister and more, I know we'll be friends forever... look I'll do my best to support you.' With that the two girls stand and embrace, a few tears are shed, Karen turns to Geoff and asks.

'Okay, what do we do?' Breathing a sigh of relief at their agreed commitment Geoff starts.

'Okay, Rod, can you draw up a speed and strength fitness chart to run for approximately two months. It needs to incorporate punching and the use of elbows... oh and make it tough... no really tough. Reg can you drive Beth to and from the bus stop plus the dance room and here.'

'Yep,' nods Reg. 'I've already got that in action.'

'Great, okay you girls have got dance tomorrow night, come over here after for dinner and we'll show you the plan. One thing to remember is the only one of the gang who is tough, well only actually thinks he's tough is Johnny and he's not that interested we believe. The others are weak, that's why they carry knives, also they're not very strong therefore not very good fighters. We'll make you fitter, stronger and faster, plus with more guidance and experience you'll gain enough confidence to handle them. You both work hard, very hard, you are tough actually tougher than you know, we're just going to enhance it, develop it and re-direct it for a little while, any questions?' They all look at each other, Rod breaks the silence.

'So, my girlfriend's going to become a thug!' Beth reels round with a gapping mouth.

'Wha...?'

'Well a cute thug.'

'You,' she raises her hand to hit him, he gets in with a retort and grins.

'Careful, I'm injured.'

'Oh... you wait.'

'See she's changing already.' Everyone laughs, Reg stands addressing all.

'Thanks Geoff, we'll see you tomorrow night.'

'Right Reg.'

'Come on Beth.' She stands to leave, Karen remains at the table she raises her eyes and meets Beth's, her look transmits one thing, fear. Beth tries a smile, it's weak and hollow, a façade poorly disguising her anxiety as well, she leaves with Reg.

CHAPTER 50

Next night at the dance studio Karen and Beth are putting the kids thru their dance paces. Karen calls a halt to proceedings.

'Don't forget to practice those new moves we showed you before the next session and remember to stretch at home, we'll see you in a few days, thanks girls.' As the kids move to their bags and organise themselves, Karen calls out.

'Shelly a word please.' Shelly walks back to where Beth and Karen stand, she picks up a more serious vibe from the concerned look on their faces.

'Yes guys, umm… can I help?' Trying her best at diplomacy Karen says.

'Ahh… yes, maybe, look there's a chance we might need a little help in a few weeks.'

'Right, like what?'

'Umm, nothing hard but there might be a need for you to maybe call the police, well get your dad to call them. Not this week but maybe in a month or mores time after dance class.' Although mystified Shelly has enough common sense to run with this strange request.

'Okay will do, can I mention this to my dad?'

'Just say that Karen and Beth might be expecting trouble and that they might need the police here after dance, one thing please, tell him not to intervene, we have it covered but it must be us, no-one else.' Still puzzled Shelly agrees.

'Alright but if you need any help at any-time just call, I know my dad would be happy to support you guys, he really respects you.' Smiling, Karen answers.

'And we like him also. What does everyone say... Jim Byrnes... hard man.'

'Oh yeah, big time, but to me he's just a soft teddy-bear... hey daughters get away with everything.' All laugh, Shelly turns and departs, she's the last one out, Karen and Beth put on their track pants and sweat shirt tops, switch off the lights and exit the room, Reg is waiting outside. As they walk to his car, they glance to their left a car is parked on the far side of the road. Tatts and Billy are leaning on the car smoking, as the girls climb into Reg's Ute they smile and wave, inside the Ute Reg comments.

'Yeah, I know, saw them, ignore it let's go.' Gunning the engine, they accelerate away. The three enter Geoff's kitchen, Rod is sitting at the table Geoff is next to him in the wheelchair. He looks up.

'Hi.' Moving over to him Karen gives him a kiss and hug asking.

'Hi, how are you?' Grinning he replies.

'Oh, not too bad I guess, no real cause for complaints.' Beth moves over to Rod and gives him a kiss and a soft hug due to him being bandaged up. Reg addresses Geoff and shakes hands.

'Gidday Geoff.' Gidday Reg, have a seat all of you I have info.' As Reg passes Rod, he scruffs his head.

'How are you, young fella?' Rod's now getting used to Reg's Australian vernacular, he grins back.

'Getting there, Reg.'

'Good lad.' Noticing the more relaxed interplay between the two gives Beth a glowing feeling, Karen goes to the sink and gets two glasses of water for Beth and herself, bringing them over to the table, she sits with everyone, Geoff begins.

'Okay I spoke to my friend from the army special services and he was great, he's sending information thru to us on the computer, also he gave me the names of sites that could be useful, Rod and I will check them out. I told him about our circumstances and you two girls, he was very understanding, didn't prevaricate about the "why's and what's" but went straight to the points we need to know. He stressed that firstly you two must stay on the fitness, strength timeline that Rod has written out, he listened to it and said it's perfect. Next plan your strategy so you fully utilize everything to your advantage, I told him about your dance and aerobics and that you're fit, he agreed that it gives you an advantage but it must be used in known surroundings. In other words, you'll have to do some training in the dance studio, that needs to become your home bass, you have to feel it, the wall structure, the feel of the floor. I said it's a wood floor, he explained that wood has a different feel to lino or concrete. Get to know it, how your feet grip both with sneakers and bare feet, if you have to confront them do it on your home turf where you are comfortable. He also suggested a few tricks to incorporate, right have you girls changed after dance practice'? Karen and Beth shake their heads.

'Okay show us your dance gear.' They stand and take off their track-pants and sweat shirt tops, Karen has on a blue leotard, leg warmers and sneakers, Beth has on her two-piece aerobics costume, tights and sneakers. 'Right,' continues Geoff. 'He said loose anything that they can easily grab onto like skirts, loose tops leg warmers and tights, stay with the two-piece aerobics gear and sneakers especially at the dance sessions over the next few weeks, you need to be comfortable and aware of

the feel of what you're wearing.' Reaching behind him Geoff grabs a bottle of liquid. 'You will learn to use this, it's a sort of body oil, AFL footballers have used it for years. Applied to the skin it makes you slippery, difficult to hold but and I stress but... your hands must remain dry for you to grip. By wearing the two-piece, you can apply the oil to your whole body, arms, torso, legs even your hair. Next I know you've seen pictures of girls in magazines glistening and obviously all oiled up and I know that what I'm about to say is a bit sexist sorry but he said as well as becoming slimy it will enhance your physical look. So, if you stand out and look really cute and physically attractive it'll take the boys minds off what they should be thinking or at least what they should be concentrating on, thus again it gives you an advantage.'

'Now when we start training, we are going to work on the premise that four of them will enter the dance room to attack you. One will probably stay outside and act as sentry, most likely Johnny, so we'll teach you how to get rid of two immediately so the contest becomes one on one, you need to do this at the start when no weapons have been produced, okay so far?' Karen and Beth both nod, Beth quips.

'I feel like I'm joining the army.' Geoff admits.

'Pretty close actually, more like special forces. Reg, you've got some hills behind you're place, we'll make time to use them, but you'll need to stand guard 'cos one important aspect he stressed is secrecy. We don't want them or anyone else seeing you train, we must and I stress must keep the element of surprise on our side... okay Reg?'

'Yep no probs.'

'Also, can you fill an old hessian bag with sand and old clothes and hang it in the garage so that Beth and sometimes both can use it on their workouts.'

'Yeah, no worries.'

'Well we've got our plan, and our timeline worked out,

we'll train with different people in different places, Reg's place and the hills behind him, the dance studio and here. Oh, and he's also mailing us up some practice gloves to use on the punch bag and for general practice. Well that's about it, let's start, girls, Rod is going to put you thru your paces in the next room now, Reg and I will prepare dinner, here we go... let's start.' With that Rod rises and walks to the living room, Beth and Karen follow. Rod begins.

'Right the warm ups are push-ups and squats, you know how to do them try ten.' The girls start with the push-ups, they've done two when Rod calls a halt.

'No no, wait, not girls ones on your knees I want you doing men's ones on your toes.' The girls look at each other shrug shoulders and re apply themselves. The grimace on their faces show this is harder than they expected, once finished Rod explains. That's our starting number, they need to be done twice a day plus crunches, also every day you need to add on one more, ten is our beginning today, by the end of the week it'll be seventeen.' They both nod in understanding, he continues.

'Right with punching, I'll try to show you slowly with my good arm, notice how my wrist is cocked and the hand turns over as the punch is extended. Now my legs are the most important part of throwing a punch, learn to hit within your zone, do not overstretch or you're off balance.' He demonstrates foot position with balance over the leading leg, the girls start to copy with just air punches. After a while he gets them to hit at each other's raised palms taking it in turns to hit, they seem to catch on and become more definite in their actions. Next he explains about using their elbows in close, with his careful guidance they begin to use their elbows hitting into each other's diaphragm, back and head. It's all done at a beginner's slow rate, just learning positioning and balance co-ordination, at the end of the session he produces two skipping

ropes.

'Right skipping… I presume you both know how to skip but for balance and reflex work you have to be able to move the rope extremely fast while your feet do minimal movement, none of these big steps over the rope, come on try it.' The girls begin, they are both quite reasonable, he pushes them for more speed and less foot movement, once pushed they lose control.

'You need to be able to do two minutes at that fast pace, take the ropes home practice, I'll test you regularly.' Beth grins at Karen.

'Got to improve our skipping, it's like being back in Primary School.' Reg is in the kitchen preparing the meat for the meal, glancing over his shoulder to the lounge room he can see the girls being put thru their paces, they're doing bridges with one sitting on the others tummy adding extra weight, the strain on their faces is obvious for him to see. He nods to himself at their work ethic and sanguine attitude then continues with the dinner. Eventually Rod calls a halt to the training session, even though it was a beginning the two girls are perspiring profusely, they collapse on the lounge room floor breathing heavily.

'Well done,' he compliments. 'That's your start, now we develop it.' Rolling onto her side Beth looks at Karen and mouths.

'Start!' Shaking her head Karen rolls onto her back, legs and arms splayed like someone catching rays at the beach, the only giveaway is her diaphragm heaving up and down, Geoff's voice is heard.

'Come on guys, dinners almost on.' They drag themselves to the kitchen still sweating, Karen tells him in between breaths.

'We need a quick shower first.' Agreeing Geoff orders.

'Okay but this'll be done in less than ten minutes so

be quick.' The two girls pick up their bags and exit the kitchen, they enter the bathroom, Beth giggles.

'I'm wettest so I'm first,' Karen laughs.

'Well be quick 'cos dinners almost on.' Grinning Beth slips her sneakers off, then dispenses with her top over her head and looking over her shoulder with a mischievous grin slips off her sports nicks. Taking a couple of steps into the shower she turns on the taps, stops glances over her shoulder at Karen and invitingly says, "coming?" Discarding her leg warmers Karen unclips the leotard and wriggling her hips slips it off. Flipping it aside she walks up to Beth in the shower, with a twinkle in her eye she announces "I'm here." Beth turns to face her allowing Karen to get full view of her naked body. The excitement of the view of her taught young vibrant skin glistening with the water highlighting it gets Karen's motor running. She reaches forward and cups Beth's breasts with a small rotation she lowers her hands to Beth's hips, following Karen's hands with her eyes Beth then raises them to look directly into Karen's eyes.

'Anything new?' She asks. Karen looks slightly confused, drops her eyes and peruses Beth's body a second time, then she notices it. All Beth's pubic hair has been shaved off, she has a Brazilian. Moving her hand delicately across the region she's amazed at how smooth and sensual it feels, her desire increases she softly whispers, "beautiful... sexy,' grinning back Beth claims.

'Really, mmm... thank you but right now we've got to clean up 'cos dinners almost on, I'm very tight round my shoulders can you give me a rub and try to loosen them up?' Replying with a grin Karen beams.

'Oh yes, no probs, my speciality.' With the water cascading over them Beth turns her back and allows Karen to squeeze some body lotion on her back. She starts rubbing and massaging, Beth does a slight groan and murmurs at the feel of

Karen's soft hands traversing over her back muscles. The whole experience is of sensual relaxation from Karen's touch, she opens her eyes and orders.

'My turn, round you go.' Rotating Karen now feels Beth's hands massaging her neck and shoulders, it gives her an excited lift in sensuality. She murmurs, "mmm… that's good." The washing continues for a few moments then Beth says.

'Come on, they'll be waiting.' Exiting the shower, they quickly dry themselves and their hair, change into dry clothes, comb their hair and admire each other, Karen nods.

'We'll do.' Putting her hands on Karen's neck and with a slight rub she agrees.

'Very much so.' They smile at each other and leave the bathroom. The meat stew is on the table as they arrive, as they sit Geoff asks.

'How was that, feel better?'

'Oh yes, much… thanks,' bubbles Karen.

'Yep,' adds Beth, 'very satisfying.' Rod gives her a questioning look but she dismisses it whispering to him.

'Girl joke.' He shrugs and attends to the meal, Reg has started eating, he slows, stops and says. 'Well done you two, keep it up and you'll be right, you've both got more drive than that lot, stick to the program and you'll be apples.' Beth glances at him, his Australian vernacular does something to her, it's the truthful earthiness, she imagines that forged the troops together in the world wars, the development of mateship. There is something real and unique about it, she puts her hand on top of his adding.

'Yes, you're right, we'll stick to the program and we'll be fine.' He nods encouraged by her positive attitude.

CHAPTER 51

Over the next weeks the girls secretly train at the various venues. Under Rod's and Geoff's supervision the girls have improved their punching plus their strength conditioning has increased, also they have incorporated various gymnastic and aerobic elements into the training. They wrestle then practice using their elbows to break free of any lock and flip to their feet, regaining balance. Reg is intrigued by their speed and flexibility, the hill sprints at the back of his place plus the sit ups, push ups and bag work have the effect of transforming their physic. He's noticed much clearer muscle definition on their biceps, back and chest. What he hasn't seen is their mock fighting in the studio after the kids have left. The first couple of times it was reasonably lame but with the extra aggression applied in the other workouts the mock fighting has intensified, they are now combating each other. Karen and Beth have been working out at the back of Reg's place doing hill sprints and heavy bag work, although working in an area that he knows little about he is enjoying helping. Holding a stopwatch or just positive comments of, "Good lass," "come on, drive," "a bit higher," "that's right" … etc, the girls are happy for the motivation instilling that their work is respected. All this has affected

Karen more, she's surprised, all the gossip she heard about Reg had clouded her opinion, working with him has advanced a change of opinion, she's realised that he's a caring slightly cantankerous older man with a touch of grandpa more so than uncle in his character, she's warming to him. At the finish of a session Reg compliments them.

'Right girls that'll do, good work, let's relax, I'll put a brew on.' With that he turns and walks across the backyard and into the house, the girls follow, Karen talks with enlightenment.

'You know Beth I'm beginning to understand and like Reg, he's well not what the gossip mongers would have us believe, there is a warmth under that gruff exterior.' Beth adds.

'Yes, there is, let's go in and I'll tell you some stuff.' Entering the backdoor they spy Reg at the sink preparing the tea. Beth calls out to him.

'Oh, uncle Reg we might warm down, stretch then have a shower can you put the tea on hold just for a short while?'

'Righto no probs, you girls work yourselves out and I'll have mine'. They disappear out of the kitchen to Beth's room, sitting on the bed Beth looks at Karen and speaks to her.

'Karen we've been very open to each haven't we?'

'Of course, yes.'

'Well I'd like to explain a bit to you about my home-life here, what was and what is the situation now.'

'Okay, but you did say that you'd worked it out and it was fine now, it still is?'

'Oh yes great, a lot better but I need you to be understanding when I tell you this.'

'Regarding you?'

'No, of uncle Reg.'

'Oh well you seem secure and content here now, I don't see any problems, so explain away.'

'Right, well we've had a heart to heart discussion and

he explained most of his life to me. Karen, it was quite sad, not tragic but sad, a lonely existence, not quite able to fit in leading to the development of this cantankerous old man, it really just a façade for a dispirited lonely old man. When I first arrived, I was just trying to get on with my life, but he was of little support. I thought he was just a grumpy old man, anyway I met you, Geoff and Rod, thank god, you guys picked my spirits up so my mindset quickly became more positive thus I was ready to attack this new home-life with uncle Reg.

'Okay so what did you do?'

'I tried to be upbeat in everything I did especially round the home, you know house-work, cooking and general stuff, the only problem was I noticed him spying on me.'

'Spying?'

'Yes, when I was in the shower and at other times.'

'Beth, spying on you in the shower isn't normal.'

'No, it isn't, but we also had a situation in the backyard where I helped him with some fence wire, he unfortunately got nervous and because of being overcome with my presence he wacked his finger with the hammer.

'Oww, that's not good, why did he become nervous?'
I worked it out, I think it was 'cos I was wearing my bikini catching some rays in the backyard, when I went over to help him, he became flustered.'

'Ahh ha, so were there any other times in your presence that he became flustered?'

'Yep, I think on some of the weekends when I came to breakfast wearing just my nighty, it's a bit old and loose, I felt he wasn't sure where to look. Back at my old home there were no problems but here's the thing I've realised, he's never had a young girl in his domain before probably never had one in his whole life. So "lil' ol' me" lobs and I guess I'm a bit of an anomaly, like a mystery. I think he's just been investigating me really, nothing bad or dirty just confusion that needs

investigating. We've had a chat and cleared the air, you could say become more open, it's been a big step but I'm definitely feeling more at ease.'

'So, what does more at ease entail?'

'Now I move round the house anyway I want, if I'm in nighty, t-shirt or underwear, I feel okay, he's made some positive comments about my fitness and I feel okay in the shower. I now leave the door open if he wants to have a peek then that's okay, as long as I know he's there I don't mind, I think I've got rid of the spying. Actually, we're really starting to warm to each other, he's become less craggy and more sort of parental, I've actually started teasing him a little bit. Nothing serious just being a bit flirtatious and playful, you know getting a smile out of him, I think he likes it, I guess you could say there's a change in the air.' Whilst Beth has been explaining this Karen has been in deep thought she directs with objectivity.

'Okay that sounds good, I've got an idea, do you want to go to the shower?'

'Yep I'm ready, let's go.'

'Hold on', starts Karen. 'Go with just your underwear on'?

'Okay.'

'Right take off your training gear.' Although slightly mystified Beth shrugs her shoulders.

'Good one, what underwear are you going to put on after our shower?'

'Oh, I don't know, my bikini briefs I suppose,'

'Yep,' agrees Karen, 'do that, take them with you.' With that Beth whips her sports gear off slings a towel across her shoulder and hands one to Karen, they both exit the room a mysterious look still invades Beth's face, entering the kitchen Karen whispers to Beth.

'Follow my lead, we've got to talk to Reg.'

'Okay,' is the confused reply. Reg is sitting at the

table sipping his tea, the girls enter the kitchen but instead of heading towards the shower Karen walks up to Reg and asks.

'Hi Reg, can I ask you some things?' Reg looks at Karen but Beth in just her underwear draws his attention.

'Yep Karen, what do you want to know?'

'Well there's something you need to know about Beth.'

'Oh yes, and what's that?'

'You know she came from a very open house.'

'Yes, she's explained that to me.'

'Yep I know she's a modern girl with a modern open attitude to many things, few constraints regarding her attitude to many things.'

'Okay… right…'

'Well she's now got a boyfriend.'

'Oh, you mean young Rod.'

'Yes, umm do you understand what that means?'

'Well sort of, it's the way of the world now-days.'

'Yes, it is, look can I be open with you.'

'Yep, no worries.'

'Well although she's only sixteen she's become sexually active, modern girls do these days.' Beth's eyes widen, she blushes, and looks at Reg with intense worry but he smiles back and gently answers.

'Yep, I sort of worked that one out.'

'Okay great, I also have been helping her in that area, firstly I want you to know that Geoff and I don't approve but we have to accept her decision, what do you think as her guardian?' He studies Beth, pauses then states.

'Young Beth, you're a smart girl, I've noticed how hard you work, it's not in your makeup to fly off the handle, so what-ever you choose to do lass, I'll support you.' Beth just glows, she moves to him and passionately hugs him.

'Oh, thank you uncle Reg, yes I'll be careful, it's been a difficult decision, but I'm happy with my choice, thanks for

being so understanding.' For a change he puts his arm around her and hugs her back, they break and Karen continues.

'Thanks Reg but certain things have to be considered and discussed like contraception.'

'Oh right,' is the unsure reply, 'I'm not really good in that area.'

'Yes, I'd guessed as much', then adding a slightly numerical white lie. 'Look if it's alright with you I'll take her over to see my female doctor in Rosenbury to get her on the pill, the lady is young and great and will give Beth all the relevant information she needs.' Looking at Beth Reg asks.

'Is that alright with you luv?'

'Oh yes uncle Reg, I need it.'

'Okay then that's fine.' Smiling at him Beth leans forward and kisses him on the forehead.

'Oh thanks, I really love you.'

'No probs luv,' he states then adds, 'you know you've been a breath of fresh air coming here, really love having you around, so bubbly, fit and alive, it's been like a new awakening round here.' Breaking in Karen tries to develop the thought direction.

'Reg, you know I've been showing Beth some things, sort of sex stuff so she's aware of things.'

'Right Karen, I guess you've been a help.' Now grinning Karen develops.

'Well more than a help, she had a bit of experience before she got here, she's actually shown me a few things.'

'Really!'

'Yes, and I know that she feels free and open here now, you're happy with that aren't you?'

'Well Karen its actually been a bit difficult, not used to seeing pretty girls wandering round in the almost altogether.'

'Yes, but you're getting used to it now, aren't you?'

'Yes, well I guess so.'

'Reg what do you think of her physically?'

'Physically... well I don't know, really haven't had much experience in that area.'

'No probs, give it a try.'

'Hmm... well I've noticed she's got good square shoulders plus defined muscles on her legs and arms. She stands tall, you know upright and walks well also she's got a pretty face, I guess you young ones would call it a good package.'

'Yep I agree.' Turning her head, she directs the question to Beth.

'Beth do mind explaining your feelings to Reg?' She's a bit unsure but tries.

'Uncle Reg, I've been open with you and I love you, you're happy for me to treat this as an open house, aren't you?' Reg is unsure also but manages.

'Yes luv, I'm getting used to it.' Smiling she nods as if in an agreement has been reached.

'I believe I'm fit, you've seen that and well, I am a modern girl, I have confidence in my appearance, my parents taught me that.' With that she drops the towel and strikes a pose with her hands on her hips, she continues.

'Uncle Reg this is me, as I was, as "Pumpkin Pie" in the old home. Dad used to bump into me, muck round with me, playfully slap my bottom and I loved it and them but "Pumpkin Pie" has gone and now "Young Beth's" here with you. You're my parent now, I would love an open relationship with you, have you bounce me round, slap my bottom. I want to be able to talk openly about issues and sometimes even show off a little bit, Karen says I'm a bit of a minx, if so, so be it, it wouldn't have been an issue in my old home and you're my family now so I will love you and want you to appreciate me for me'. Looking straight into her eyes Reg is almost brought to tears, he speaks directly to her.

'Young Beth you are a beautiful sprightly young thing

and I agree you've got to feel free and relaxed in this house and I will respect that and you.' Then with a grin, 'might admire you, have to admit you're worth looking at.' He grins in a loving almost parental way as if he was addressing his own daughter, the bonding is transmitted she responds with a grin.

'Well let's start now, I'm going to give you a big hug, but stay there.' She advances on him, he smiles a little nervously, to relax him somewhat she pats his leg then sits in his lap. They look at each other, she kisses his cheek he responds by kissing hers then her forehead, they hold the tight embrace a while longer, relaxing she says softly.

'Thanks, we'll be fine.' The two girls look at each other Karen moves to his side, Beth explains with sincerity.

'Uncle Reg you're my family, you will guide me and I will let you enjoy my presence, we're together now in body and soul.' She leans forward and gives him a kiss on the cheek, Karen follows and kisses his other cheek. They ease up and smile then Karen says.

'Shower time.' He laughs.

'Righto off you go, you've worked hard today.' They turn grab towels and head off towards the bathroom. After they have left Reg is still sitting in his chair pondering. A grin draws across his face, he thinks to himself, "Modern girls eh... hmm... not bad at all." The girls enter the bathroom, towels are hung on the side-rail, reaching into the shower Karen turns on the taps and waits for the temperature and pressure to reach the expectant levels. While she waits Beth moves in behind her and wraps her arms around her exclaiming.

'Oh Karen, thanks so much, you were brilliant, you've opened the door and Uncle Reg has walked thru, I know we'll have a really good relationship, you're so thoughtful and kind, I love you so much.' Putting her hand in the water to test it Karen turns.

'Beth I'm glad it worked out, I sort of had noticed little

things while we've been training here like attitude changes, especially to you and just a general warming of him. I thought that the time was right and well I guess it was, I'm happy that it all worked out.' Leaning in Beth kisses her on the lips

Later in the evening when Karen has left, Beth is drying her hair in her bedroom, she glances at the photo of her parents on the bedside table, sitting on the bed she picks it up and stares at it for a while then states.

'Well mum and dad you made me, I'm from your gene pool. I am what I am, I'll always love you, you're in me and I'll always love that, I've got a special personality, I'm alive and very much involved in life. Don't worry I'll study hard and get somewhere but my personality because of you is a bit of a minx, well that's what Karen says. If I am, so be it, I'm learning and am happy with me, I'm working hard and also having fun especially sexual fun. Life is interesting if not a tad worrying at the moment, but we'll work it out and be right plus I've brought some joy to Uncle Reg's life, I know you'd be proud... see you.' Standing she stops, open the mirror and lets the towel drop, viewing her naked body in the mirror she again speaks to the photo.

'This is me in case you'd forgotten.' She flexes her arm muscles and pushes a knee out slightly in a pose.

'Pretty good eh...? Thanks, I think so also.' Replacing the photo on the bedside table she throws her nighty on and leaves the room. Entering the kitchen, she spies Reg in his favourite armchair in the parlour with a cup of tea, he's watching TV. The water in the kettle is still hot, pouring the tea from the pot she adds some sugar and milk then walks to the parlour. Looking up Reg smiles, "Hello luv," she doesn't answer just lowers herself down, sitting on the floor, leaning against the chair and his legs. Looking up she smiles, he grins back and rests his hand on her shoulders, does a slight rub of her hair then rests it back on her shoulder.

She purrs a slight murmur of "mmm…" then nestles into him and sips her tea, they both relax and continue watching the T V.

CHAPTER 52

Reg is digging in his backyard garden, he hears a sound and looks up, Tatts and Billy are standing there. He stares, they glare back at him, Reg is the first to break the silence.

'What do you two want?' Grinning with disdain Tatts comments.

'Nice garden.' Following up Billy asks.

'I'm hungry, g-g-got an apple?' Reg feels the hairs on the back of his neck rise, he continues with a bold front.

'Not for you two, now piss off.' The mood changes, Tatts sneers.

'Now is that nice, we just dropped in to say hello, it's a small town.' Billy takes up the snide attitude.

'Yeah, a s-s-small town and we have to g-g-get to know everyone.' Finishing the banter Tatts becomes more direct and threatening.

'Yeah, let's get to know each other.' Glancing at his rifle leaning against the backdoor Reg realises he's defenceless, he raises the spade in defence as the two louts move towards him.

The school bus stops in the main street, Beth descends onto the footpath and waits for the bus to continue its journey. It splutters away, she looks up and down the main street,

there's no sign of Reg, a foreboding, washes across her, she waits, minutes pass, still no sign of Reg. Her anxiety rises as the minutes tick past, glancing at her watch and slightly flustered she hurries off in the direction of Reg's house. All the time through the back blocks she's glancing over her shoulder expecting some intervention by the gang but nothing is noticed. Arriving at the house she notices Reg's Ute parked in the driveway, her anxiety intensifies she sprints up the steps, rampaging thru the house into the kitchen she calls, "Uncle Reg... Uncle Reg," there's no answer. Glancing round the kitchen there's no indication of food or drink having been prepared, zipping into the parlour there's no sign of him, all rooms and bathroom are checked nothing. Opening the back door, she spies Reg's rifle lying on the ground, traversing her eyes she sees Reg's prostrate body slumped on the ground, the shovel is lying next to him. Rushing forward she screams, "Uncle Reg." There's blood on his face and it looks like his nose is bleeding or broken, he's barely conscious and badly beaten up, kneeling next to him she cradles his head, he regains consciousness enough weakly say.

'Bastards got me with the shovel... couldn't get my gun in time...' He collapses back into unconsciousness as she cries "Uncle Reg... Uncle Reg," but he is unable to respond. Realising he is desperately in need of medical attention she sprints into the house grabs the phone, on the answer she cries.

'Karen... they've hurt Uncle Reg, please come immediately.' Replacing the phone, she races into the bathroom and grabs a towel, then rushes back to Reg. Before long, the sound of a car is heard pulling up into the driveway, then a door slamming and footsteps running, Karen rushes into the backyard, up to Beth who is still nursing Reg's head.

'Oh Beth... Oh Reg... let me look.' Feeling for a pulse she finds one, trying to remain positive she tells Beth.

'We need to get him to the hospital and fast, we'll have

to lift him into my car, but carefully'. They both delicately manoeuvre themselves either side of Reg, carefully they lift him and put their arms under his shoulders. Walking as if on eggshells they walk or half drag him to the car, opening the back flap the lower him into the back part of the Ute, Beth flies into the house grabbing some blankets and a pillow. Back outside she jumps into the rear adjusting the blankets and pillow so as to make him as comfortable as possible and cradles his head. Karen jumps in the driver's seat and carefully accelerates off, throughout the trip she can hear Beth questioning herself.

'Uncle Reg, no... you're old... no.' Back at Karen's house Geoff is in his wheelchair reading the paper, the phone rings, he sidles across to it and answers, as he listens his face darkens.

'Right, see you soon.' He hangs up the phone Rod saunters into the kitchen.

'Who was that?' Geoff's face radiates concern.

'Karen, she's with Beth, they've taken Reg to hospital, those bastards paid him a visit when he was in his backyard and beat him up.' 'Reg, but he's old?' Geoff knows exactly the reasoning, his response is intense.

'Yes, but he was the last figure of authority now the girls are completely isolated, that's why.'

'Bastards, an old man... jeez, how is he?'

'Badly beaten, he'll live but be in hospital for a fair while, we'd better get something on for tea that will keep, they'll probably be late.'

Later that night Karen and Beth walk in, the boys are watching TV. Rod stands and looks at Beth, she doesn't respond just stands there with her head down gazing at the floor. Karen goes straight to Geoff and embraces him but Beth's intransient, she just stands in the middle of the kitchen as if immersed in a dream. Rod moves across to her and stands in

close proximity without saying anything, he feels the need to comfort her but she seems distant and non-receptive, they stay like that for a short while, eventually she raises her head and gazes into his face, her expression reflects blandness and pain, then with a dispirited move she melts into his arms. Whilst rubbing the back of her head she starts to whimper this leads to crying, Karen has been watching her disintegration, she moves across and pats Beth on the shoulder, turning her head Beth pleads.

'Why us, all of this, we never did anything wrong?' Karen can only shake her head, she has no answers, the silence is broken by Geoff inquiring.

'How's Reg?' Karen replies.

'He'll be alright, badly beaten up though, broken arm, ribs and nose, so that'll keep him in hospital for a while especially due to his age. I asked him if Beth could stay with us for a while, I think he understood, was just able to nod, so Beth will move in for a few weeks, if it's alright with you Rod, she'll have to share.' Assessing the logistics of the situation Rod answers seriously.

'Look I'm busted up, no good at the moment, it's the least I can do,' looking at Beth he admits. 'Right now, your safety's the most important thing.' Gazing at him she smiles weekly as tears well again in her eyes. Breaking in Geoff tells them.

'We've prepared some food and it's still hot, go and wash up, have something to eat then we've got to talk.' The girls exit the room, as soon as they have left Geoff quietly whispers to Rod.

'Things are escalating, we've got to get them ready.' Rod understands nodding back with understanding. The two girls re-enter the room and sit despondently at the table, Rod dishes out some sort of stew onto plates and places them in front of the girls, they look at it but are not in the mood to eat,

Geoff does some coercing.

'I know you don't feel like eating but do it, it's important for your health, listen to me as you eat.' They pick up forks and grudgingly begin, Geoff continues.

'Obviously this is terrible about Reg but at least he's being cared for and out of harm's way,' he pauses. 'So now we need to turn our attention to you two.' Lifting of forks to their mouth's ceases, they stare at him.

'You're venerable out there now, if it's alright with you Beth, Karen can drop you down the bus stop in the morning and I'll contact Jim Byrnes see if he or Jenny will drop you home here when they pick up Shelly. Karen can drive you two to and from dance practice. Beth sorry, but you'll need to take some days off school, we're going to have to ramp up your training, my guess is you've barely got two weeks to prepare.' These reality checks have a severe effect on Beth, with a steeliness not obvious before she replies to Geoff.

'Tell us what to do, we'll do it, you were right, they are soft or cowards, to pick on an old man, only the weak do that,' looking directly to Karen she admits. 'Geoff is right, we are stronger, we'll do this.' Reaching forward she holds Karen's hand, they stare into the others eyes, their love and respect forging itself into a steely bond, as they stare their grip tightens, releasing they continue eating. By the end of dinner, the girls look washed out, mentally exhausted, they excuse themselves and head to their separate bedrooms, Geoff tells Rod.

'I've got to ring Jim Byrnes and explain, after that you and I need to sit down and finalise plans, Rod returns a half smile, more like a grimace, he understands, Geoff moves to the phone and dials.

'Hi Jim, it's Geoff Miller, yes fine thanks, yeah on the mend. How's Shelly, I heard you had a bit of hassle in town a while back. Yes, oh good, well I've got a favour to ask... yes thanks. It concerns my partner and her young friend... yes

that's her young Beth. Well it seems that they've become the target of Johnny and his band of half-wits. No, I don't know why, its actually more from Nancy Clements... yes, she was the one rude to your Shelly in town. No, it's okay I don't need you to step in, you've already done plenty thanks, scared the shit out of Johnny I heard but my favour is could you or your wife give Beth a lift home here after the school bus drops them off in town, it's only a couple of blocks... right thanks, it'd only be for a couple of weeks at the most... yes we know and are preparing for that, I believe the girls will be alright... yeah... look thanks, but no need... on this one you'll just have to trust me... yes I know... sounds dangerous but believe me when I say we've got it covered... yep okay, that's right... right... well thanks again, we'll be in touch. Cheers.' Hanging up the phone he grins at Rod.

'He's something that Jim Byrnes, he knows a fair bit about what's going on, he's ready to go out and shoot the lot of them, said the other farmers are all quite happy to help.'

'Shoot them!' Rod's aghast, 'others willing to help!'

'Yep and I'll tell you what, if I had said that'd help this town would be minus five people. No one would know or care, the halfwits would disappear in a puff of smoke, no trace. Funny thing is I don't even think they know or understand how disliked are, they're actually treading a thin line and they're oblivious to it, still it's our problem and we'll have to deal with it.' Turning to Rod.

'Right, time to raise the bar and upgrade what they do, they're in the zone, we both saw it now let's direct it, I reckon we've got two weeks.' The response from Rod is direct and positive.

'Yep, got it, done.'

Next morning the girls are up early, they change into their two-piece aerobics gear, Rod has them training on the large bag they snuck in from Reg's place early that morning.

He is aware of their concerted effort and doesn't need to ask for more venom in the punches, they've turned the corner. Sweat pours off them, arms flay at the bag but not like prissy girls, each punch has depth and force, when he calls for push-ups, they incorporate hand claps in between. Crunches are performed with the hands at the free, at the top of the crunch elbows and punches are thrown repeatedly to the left and right. The bridges are now performed as if someone is on top. A fast bridge is executed with a person on top then a roll sideways causing the person to fall off, the bridge person then does a gymnastic forward spring onto their feet. The element of speed is practiced incorporating a kick to the leg or torso of the prone person. There's very little holding back, the "Thwack" sound of flesh being hit or hammered becomes the norm. The most intense change has developed in the mock fights, warm ups are practiced with gloves, however once the warm ups are finished the "ultra-fight finger free gloves" are used. Rod explains about feigning or deflecting a punch, they attack each other with almost life-threatening ferocity, terrible wacks and hits are performed and suffered. Cuts and abrasions appear on their face and body's. Karen connects with two almighty left hooks knocking Beth down, Rod fights the urge to rush up and watches as Beth rolls onto her back and flips back to her feet. The welt under her eye raises, anyone inspecting her would think she's been in an almighty blue, with a shake of her head to clear the senses she moves back into the fray against Karen. Sometimes the damage inflicted on her is almost too much for Rod to bear. He watches as elbows and blows connect, occasionally she gets the wobbles, but backs away steels herself and returns to the contest always throwing a collection of punches. As the days progress Rod notices Beth's improvement, especially at manoeuvring out of harm's way. Karen is landing less punches, occasionally she grabs Beth's wrists and a grappling tussle starts but Beth has become as strong as her

now so there's no advantage.

After a week of this sparing Geoff enters and gives them instruction regarding defence against a person carrying a knife. The girls listen and begin practice on this defence mode, they practice evasion and balance. It's a matter of knowing when to strike and effective use of their hands plus knowing one's own sphere. Each is given a soft round wooden object about the same size as a knife, one is the attacker the other the defenceless victim. Towels are wrapped round the forearm on their non-preferred side to deflect the blade. All the time they learn to use their eyes to perceive their opponents balance, or lack of, thus when to strike, as the days continue Rod can see the confidence and ability coming to the fore. He feels somewhat relieved that they have come to grips with the ability to defend themselves but the cost suffered by them has really affected him. The girl who he admires, respects and loves has taken a dreadful beating and he has had to push her on, at various time he's excused himself, telling them to have a rest, then goes out the back of the house and just lets the tears roll, his feelings are a concoction of love for Beth and absolute hate for Johnny.

Later in the week Beth and Karen decide to walk down to dance practice to take their class due to the fact that there'd be towns people about. The young girls that come in are shocked at their appearance, they perceive it as if they have been fighting each other, Shelly however is more perceptive, aware of what's going on. Karen and Beth have to hug and smile in front of the girls to quell their suspicions. Doing the best at explaining Karen tells them that they are both involved in some highly strenuous military training but that its only for a few weeks, the dance girls look relieved, the hugs seem to satisfy their concerns, at the end of the session Shelly hangs back and confronts Karen and Beth.

'I'm not sure what's going on but I think I can put two

and two together enough to get the picture.' Karen raises her eyebrows in a questioning way but doesn't respond, Shelly continues but starts to get upset, tears well in her eyes.

'You're getting ready to fight or well... maybe defend yourselves against those nasty people.' Beth looks at Karen then returns to Shelly with a half nod, this acknowledgement is the end of the rope for Shelly, she bursts into tears, bubbling thru.

'But there's a lot of them, you'll get hurt or worse, I don't want to see you hurt or worse... I love you guys.' The dam wall breaks, tears flow from all three, they grab hold of each other and hug with intensity for over a minute, then Karen takes command.

'Yes Shelly, we might have to fight. I agree with you, I don't want anything to happen to Beth or myself but well, sometimes things get out of your control and in life you have to stand up for yourself.' Shelly raises two bloodshot weepy eyes not knowing what to reply, before she can say anything the door swings open and Jim Byrnes enters.

'You right Shell...' He doesn't finish the sentence, staring he believes he knows what's going on, he walks over to the three girls. Looking Karen and Beth up and down noticing their battered appearance plus their tearful eyes he speaks directly.

'I've spoken to Geoff, he's told me you've got it under control, I won't but in but I will say this and in front of my daughter. If anything happens to you two lovely girls, myself and the other farmers will find the culprits and get rid of them, that is final, non-negotiable. We really appreciate what you have done for our kids in the district, we won't let anything happen to you, everyone around here loves you two, with the last phrase Karen and Beth go misty eyed, gaining composure Karen answers.

'Thanks, Jim, for the support... I believe we've got it covered, I guess time will tell. We've asked a small favour of

Shelly maybe in a week or so, nothing major, she'll explain. Geoff and Rod have been helping us so we think we're okay.' He listens and nods with understanding, putting his large hands on Karen's shoulders he leans forward and gives her a hug, releasing his grip he then turns to Beth and hugs her. Looking intently at both girls he appeals.

'Okay but be careful,' then turning he jokes, 'come on everyone the metre's running,' then leads Shelly out, she's still sniffling and upset. Karen turns to Beth and in an effort to diffuse the tension quips.

'That Shelly, she can get anyone to turn on the waterworks.' Adding to help ease the strained situation Beth comments.

'She'll be a script-writer when she grows up… "Chick Flicks." Laughing in agreement Karen says, "Let's go," they grab their gear and follow Jim and Shelly out to his car. Pulling up outside Karen's house Jim orders with a grin.

'Okay you two out and have a good clean up and meal, say "Hi", to Geoff and Rod.' Beth and Karen in the backseat salute and answer in unison. "Sir, Yes sir!" He looks at Shelly who playfully shakes her head as if to say… "and I have to work with these morons." Exiting his car, they call,

'Thanks Jim… see you Shel.' He waves grins and accelerates away. Entering the kitchen, they can see the boys hard at work preparing dinner, at the sound of their entry Geoff looks up, they grin at him, it's been a while since he's seen them smile, offering advice he directs them.

'You guys look like you've been thru the ringer.' Staring at him they reservedly grin, he continues.

'We'll be a fair while with dinner, go shower and soak, relax.' Looking at Geoff Karen's smile is one of mature understanding, she grabs Beth's hand commenting, "Come on I need my back scrubbed." Beth does a quick take to Geoff realising he's at ease with the situation, he smiles as she is

dragged out of the kitchen. The girls enter the bathroom but unlike before Karen hesitates then speaks in a composed manner.

'We've been hammering each other to get up to standard. I know you've been on the receiving end much more than me, sometimes when I've wacked you my heart breaks but you know it's not personal, we just have to do this to survive. You always get up, in many instances wiping blood away then continuing. I'm so scared of what lies ahead plus upset with what I've inflicted on you. I love you, yes you know I don't need to say it, but when this is over and hopefully soon then we'll all be able to put it behind us and return to our normal style of living.' As Beth listens to Karen's discourse tears well up in her eyes, Karen expects a reply but Beth doesn't she stands motionless. Then slowly she lifts her crop top off, Karen stares, in silence. Beth doesn't turn her body she just delicately slides her thumbs into her aerobic nicks and lowers them, flicking them aside, standing naked in front of Karen. The vision in front of Karen is of a fit strong young girl whose body shows the bruises and scrapes as testament of the battering she has taken. Karen is riveted to the spot, the image in front of her is the result of their training, a nauseous feeling builds in her throat, she swallows trying to say something conciliatory but is lost for words. Reading Karen's insecure internal admonishment Beth walks forward puts her hand on Karen's shoulders and with composure gently says.

'These marks are for you not because of you.' Looking deeply into Karen's eyes she leans forward and kisses her, Karen starts crying, whispering.

'But I did this, I didn't want to hurt you, I love you.' Beth moves forward and holds her as tears run down Karen's cheeks, breaking away Beth smiles, a loving look radiates from her, Karen's shoulders relax she feels the psychological weight lifted off her. Twinkling her nose, she leans forward and kisses

Beth's nose which creates an immediate giggling response, Beth questions.

'Well Tinker Bell are you coming in?' The reply needs no comment, Karen lifts her top and slides her briefs down, they admire each other for a spell, Karen breaks the ice.

'I love your body, too bad it's so battered.' Opening her eyes wide Beth offers.

'Battered for a reason, come on lets shower.' With that exclamation Beth leans in, turning on the taps.

'Okay, lets wash ourselves and have a wonderful dinner,' says a more relaxed Karen.

'Agreed,' is Beth's cute response followed by a kiss on Karen's nose. Entering the shower Beth takes a hand-washer, soaps it and begins to wash Karen's shoulders and back occasionally kissing the nape of her neck which brings giggles, they swap washing duties and continue cleaning each other. The boys are finishing the dinner preparation, they look up as the two girls enter the kitchen. Karen wears a multi-coloured spring loose mini dress with string tie straps, Beth has a singlet top and blue mini skirt. With all the physical training they have been involved in they are perfectly toned; the clothes hang on them as if they were made for them. With their hair combed they don't need the extension of make-up plus their tanned bodies all be it slightly bruised they exude femininity, both boys notice it, it's obvious, it radiates from them, Geoff breaks the ice.

'Well how's that, better?' Unable to contain herself Beth bubbles.

'Oh yes much relieved, a hundred percent better.' Rod's oblivious to the "faux par" and takes the comment at its literal sense.

'Good, warm water does the trick.' Slightly giggling Beth tries to control herself and answers his comment.

'Yes, warm water is very satisfying, very pleasurable.' A

smirk is exchanged between Karen and Geoff, he announces.

'Okay you two sit… Rod organise the drinks, here it comes.' Although in a wheelchair he is able to transfer pots from the stove to the table, the smell wafts across the table bringing reactions from the girls.

'Mmm… that smells great, what is it?' Grinning he announces with an air of importance as if he was a master chef.

'A Rogan Josh with rice and vegies… well a sort of Rogan Josh, had to use different spices.' Protruding her nose over the pot Beth breathes in.

'Don't know what you added but it smells fantastic, I'm starving.' Agreeing Rod adds, 'Yes it must be all the training.' She looks at him enjoying his honest naivety'.

'Yes, training with Karen certainly builds an appetite.' Unable to stop herself Karen adds.

'All that physical training you mean.'

'Yes,' Beth continues grinning. 'That's right, getting physical,' then she giggles, Rod looks at her confused he glances at Karen who responds with a slight quizzical shoulder rise then to ease his confusion smiles and softly says, "girl's joke." again this seems to satisfy Rod, he relaxes and announces.

'Girls first, you've worked the hardest.' Serving spoons are raised and plates loaded, everyone tucks in. After a number of mouthfuls have been swallowed Geoff feels the necessity to bring everyone back to reality but as he glances round the table with everyone eating and involved in conversation, he realises that for this short time their predicament has been forgotten or at least pushed aside. Timing is everything, he realises and now is not the time to re-steer the ship. He joins in the therapeutic meal, the conversation bounces around not establishing on any particular topic until near the end Beth mentions Uncle Reg. Everything slows, Geoff knows this is the time to re-direct them all regarding their situation, he now speaks with purpose.

'Okay let's look at the facts, you've both been brilliantly

good with your training, my guess is you'll have to use it very soon probably next Friday after dance practice. They'll know you've been lying low and in their minds they probably think you're scared, again the element of surprise will be on your side but and I do stress but you'll have to finish your training over the next few days, especially regarding unarmed combat, defending against knives one on one.' The girls have now redirected their thoughts, his words have a palpable finality about them. They look at each other, then the two men, Karen clutches Beth's hand and states.

'Soon, our time, lets finish this.' There's no answer from Beth except a forceful squeeze of her hand indicating that she's agreed, this onerous task has to be finalised.

Over the next few days training takes on a more clinical approach. Focus is directed towards the use of a wrapped towel over their fore arms and wrist and how to deflect knife attacks. The link between deflection, interception and aggression are practiced repeatedly, situations in different problematic positions are rehearsed, there is no holding back from conflicts. Blows are landed and the use of elbows come to the fore, Geoff watches as Rod pushes them thru their paces. He occasionally makes points, there is no questioning by the girls, they nod and return attempting what has been directed with efficiency, by late afternoon Geoff calls a halt to proceedings.

'Enough you two are knackered, there won't be much tomorrow either, it's now a time for body rebuilding, regaining strength. Rod and I will give you each a massage tonight, it'll be a deep one to ease the tension in your muscles but right now I want you both to hit the shower block. How-ever one at a time and you need a long soak whilst you're in there, we will use some of that oil to alleviate the muscle tension, right off you go, Beth you're first then down to Rod's room.'

They move thru the kitchen, Beth ambles towards

Rod's room, she shows signs of being tired and sore, there's no conversation emanating from her, grabbing a towel she meanders back towards the bathroom. Doing what has been ordered she soaks herself fully with very warm water, it seems to sooth and relax, she almost dozes off under the repetition of the falling droplets. Soon Karen enters the bathroom, she watches as Beth is immersed in the recuperative property of the shower. Turning off the taps Beth steps out of the shower, Karen has discarded her aerobic gear, she walks up to Beth and stops in front of her, they hold their position with minimal movement, touching their fingers with just the fingertips entwined. The feeling of connection is strengthened, moving aside Beth allows Karen entry to the shower, as they move from each one's proximity their held arms stretch with the last movement the fingers break, they stop, stare into their eyes, smile and move off in different directions. Vacating the bathroom Beth has the towel draped loosely around her, she heads thru the kitchen. Geoff is preparing something for dinner, he lifts his head at the sound of her footsteps and smiles. She turns and reciprocates the acknowledgement but in a tired manner, as she turns the towel unravels and drops to the floor revealing her naked body. However, modesty has long since been dismissed, she's too tired to care, stooping she picks up the towel slings it across her shoulder, smiles back at Geoff and moves on. Watching her leave Geoff notices the bruising but more intently her muscle definition, her top torso has a "V" stature about it, where-as before she was nicely proportioned now her neck and shoulder muscles stand out with noticeable muscle definition. Her buttocks are very firm with taught hamstrings immersed right into her gluts the thigh muscles stand out forcefully. The total picture is one of strength, the young teens body fat count is replaced by hardened muscle. He's seen that type of thing before at a weigh in before a boxing title fight, although nervous regarding their impending situation a

glow of cathartic confidence emits from him, he realises that they are as ready as they can be. Upon entering Rod's room, she can see that he has draped a towel across the bed, looking at him, she has her towel slung across her shoulder that's barely performing its coverage job. Her left breast is obvious and her thigh is prominent, he gazes but in a concerned way, asking.

'How do you feel?' She doesn't answer immediately just allows the towel to drop to the floor then softly answering.

'I feel how I look... battered.' Swallowing he moves closer to her to inspect, there's no need for an in-depth analysis, the vision is obvious, bruises are all over her body, there are abrasions and minor cuts round her head, the fading remnants of a black eye are still visible, she looks like a battered boxer.

'Here lie down,' he quietly commands. 'This'll help.' Lying face down on the towel she stretches out her arms feeling a trickle of oil on her back, he's poured it down her backbone to her buttocks, then with his one strong arm he starts to push and slide round her shoulders and torso. The feel is comforting she relaxes as he glides around her body, however the softness soon is replaced by a deepening force, he is digging into her muscles with his palm and knuckles. The tightness is being attacked and loosened, but the manner like any sports massage is discomforting. Gradually he works his manipulation from her neck and shoulders down thru her lower back to her gluts, again he digs in freeing the tension from the top of her hamstrings. It's very discomforting she grimaces "Oww", but he ignores and continues. The calves get the same treatment as does the ankles and Achilles, the pain is intense but manageable, biting her lip she occasionally lets out a whimper. This causes him to glance at her and comment "not much more," with a final flourish of her ankle he states.

'Done... relax.'

'Phew,' is the reply being grateful for the break.

'Okay, turn over,' is the next order. Cocking an eye, she

squints her nose and cheekily responds.

'Oh well… if you say.' Grinning her reassures her.

'I'll try to make it less intense.'

'Hmm… that'd be nice,' is the coquettish reply. Turning over she stretches her arms above her head and spreads her legs, then playfully comments.

'When you're ready sir.' With a smirk he pours the oil over her chest and diaphragm then starts massaging. The arm muscles are worked on but there is little need for deep penetration, a grin breaks across her face, she's enjoying the sensation of the slippery liquid being smoothed over her skin. Finishing with her arms he moves to her neck and shoulders, again there is less force needed, some muscle alignment, that's all. He moves his hands to her chest, because her breasts are a major part of her anatomy, he doesn't need to apply any major work, thus deferring to meander round. As he circumnavigates her breasts she starts to murmur, this he notices is in conjunction with her nipples getting harder, she starts moving her head to and fro, the murmuring develops into words. "Mm… mm… yes… yes." Her chest starts to heave, he feels a tightening of the muscles surrounding her breasts, they have become firm, his hands start to influence himself. The softness of her murmuring accelerates his desire as well, there's a noticeable stiffening in his pants. Tilting her head, she notices the involved expression on his face, as he works on her top torso his waist is very close to her head. The appendage expansion in his jeans is obvious, she directs him "lower," as he moves his hands across her diaphragm she starts moaning. The oil is making it easy to inflate sensuality, Beth is now overwhelmed with sexual desire, her arousal intense, "go in me, go in." He's in his own world of ecstasy by watching her but forces two fingers up into her, spreading her legs she implores "yes, yes, more, more," lost in her own world of desire she starts moaning "yes, yes" and "oh god". She increases her moaning

and rhythmic squirming, her ecstasy climaxes, a shudder vibrates thru her body as she releases her orgasmic pleasure. Calming down she starts giggling. Not quite knowing what to say he stutters.

'Ahh yes… that was… umm.' With animated cheekiness she finishes his thoughts.

'Fun!' She continues. 'Wow this sex thing is really something, boy did I get carried away.' Her honesty appeals to him agreeing he says.

'Yep, me too, just watching you… wow.'

'Okay rest time, we still have to eat, lie next to me please.'

'Love to,' is the cheery response, then laying down next to her they grasp hands, look into the others eyes and grin.

A muffled call is heard from the kitchen, "Come on, food's ready." Rising Beth slips into some underwear and a skirt and T-Shirt. Standing Rod mumbles "Umm… I need help." Glancing at him she realises he's got only one good arm, grinning she tucks his shirt into his pants, adding a satisfied quip.

'There we're all done, ship shape and presentable, hey! All of a sudden I'm hungry.'

'Yeah,' he agrees. 'So am I, must be all the activity.' The comment causes a soft snort, she squeezes his hand.

'Come on time for nourishment.' Laughing they exit the room. Entering the kitchen Geoff and Karen are sitting at the table, there's a large pot of something in the middle.

'Come on you two, it'll get cold.' Sitting at the table they smile to the other two. Karen inquires.

'Do you feel better, did Rod do a good job'?

'Oh yes,' grins Beth, 'a very good job, I'm looser now.' Then politely reciprocating. 'And you, did it work?'

'Yep,' grins Karen, 'All looser and satisfied here.' Happily, Geoff comments,

'Great, glad you're both better, okay dig in, it's amazing how one can get an appetite from a simple massage.'

'Simple!' Questions Beth. 'More like sensual.' Everyone pauses then roar with laughter it's obvious that Karen has had a similar experience with Geoff, he orders, "Ladies first." The girls grab utensils and use the serving spoon to dollop amounts of stew onto their plates, the boys follow, everyone eats, for a change there is minimal conversation, food and nourishment are to the fore, once the dinner is finished Karen rises and moving to the sink starts to prepare coffees and teas. Geoff's noticed that the massages have done the trick, both girls are now relaxed and the food has been the catharsis for their impending situation, at least for the short duration. Time for another reality check, but again it needs careful directing, he begins and speaks earnestly.

'I spoke to Reg on the phone this morning, he's beginning to feel better, still in some pain but he sends his regards and Beth he said and I quote, "Look after yourself lass, don't let the bastards rub your nose in it, luv you." The final words have the effect, Beth becomes misty eyed, it's his manner with the Australian vernacular, it touches her soul. A tear trickles down her cheek, Karen and Rod reach across and hold each of her hands, Geoff raises the attitude and refocuses them for the conflict that lies ahead.

'We've done everything possible, you girls have been fantastic but it is you two that have to face this thing. I believe if you keep your heads, remembering what we've told you, you'll be alright.' The two girls nod in agreement then transfer their attention to each other, as they stare their grip of each other's hands tighten. Their strength of spirit is there, the boys can see it and feel it, they all sit holding hands for quite some while, Geoff breaks in saying.

'Let's all get some sleep, final day of training tomorrow.' Agreeing, everyone departs to their rooms.

CHAPTER 53

Morning breaks, Geoff is in the kitchen preparing breakfast, Rod stumbles thru heading for the bathroom, finishing his ablutions, he wanders back, as he travels thru the kitchen Geoff calls.

'Tell Beth to put on shorts and sneakers, she and Karen need to go for a run, nothing too strenuous, just to clear the mind and charge the batteries.' Nodding in understanding Rod mumbles a reply and wanders off down the passageway. Minutes pass, Karen and Beth in their jogging gear, enter the kitchen, Geoff addresses them.

'Go for a relaxed run but keep your eyes open we don't want anyone noticing you, do two or three k's, when you return breakfast will be ready.' Karen replies "Okay," turns to Beth and says, "Let's go," they exit the house. Rod is more alive now he wanders into the kitchen, heads for the fridge, opens it and pours himself a glass of orange juice then sits at the table.

'Right,' says Geoff. 'I've sent them on a run so we can talk, listen closely, we'll have a big job to do tonight.' Rod's slightly confused, "job?" Geoff continues.

'For weeks now they have been training for this, but what is this? Let's be clear... this will be a fight for their

lives. This is not a sporting game it's reality and an extremely dangerous reality, there's a good chance that they'll get injured or even worse, training is one thing the actual confrontation is another thing altogether. When we finish today and retire, you'll probably find doubt and fear will surface, our job tonight is to provide solace and positiveness. Fear and doubt must not take over their psyche if they are to survive, and I do mean survive, Rod here are the facts, we are sending two lovely girls to fight four nasty youths who will be armed'.

'When you say it like that I'm scared,' answers Rod.

'Yes,' agrees Geoff. 'Truthfully, I'm petrified, when no one is around and I'm by myself the thought of the whole thing brings me to tears, I understand what Shelly felt but we must be brave for them and keep up a bold positive and relaxed front. If we can keep them calm so they concentrate on what they've been shown then they have a chance. Truthfully last night when I was lying next to Karen and watching her while she slept, I was a nervous wreck but I knew I had to control myself and give off positive vibes, I'm sure they'll both need our security tonight.' Rod nods in understanding, he doesn't reply just looks at Geoff, the realisation is perfectly clear, they have a job to do. The girls return puffing, Karen announces.

'Hey I beat her in the last sprint to the house.'

'What,' responds Beth. 'Not fair you said go after you had already taken off... cheat.'

'Well it might have been a small start but I still got here first.' Looking at Beth she breaks up, they both have a laugh and collapse into the other's arms. Geoff announces.

'Right eggs and bacon almost done, wash up and let's eat.' They whip off to the bathroom and quickly return, Geoff has everything on the plates, Rod finishes buttering the toast, Geoff orders. 'Right get that into you then go over things, like the finishing bits and pieces, making sure you're on top of everything.' Grinning, the girls' tuck into the meal as Rod

disperses cups of tea. Geoff asks about their run, not that he is that interested but he wants them chatting, concentrating on superfluous topics. With breakfast finished they move outside and begin their work, just as Geoff directed, they concentrate on aspects of defence against weapons. The hours tick by, both Geoff and Rod are constructive and encouraging, giving positive feedback where possible. The girls flourish at the training, extra effort is displayed it's not a hard day there are lots of rest breaks, they continue into the afternoon. Eventually Geoff calls a halt to proceedings.

'Okay, that's enough, you've done well, time to relax.' The girls are flushed in the cheeks but by no means exhausted due to the more technical nature of their training, they hug and follow the boys into the house, Geoff directs.

'Right you two guys freshen up and we'll prepare dinner.' The girls' drift off, Geoff turns to Rod.

'Well done mate, but the hardest part is yet to come.'

'Okay, I'm with it,' is Rod's reply. The boys start preparing the dinner, the girls have grabbed towels and are heading towards the bathroom, once inside Karen asks.

'How are you feeling?' Although unsure Beth tries to answer honestly.

'Well I definitely feel stronger and more confident in being able to defend myself but the problem is that we have never actually done this sort of thing before. I'm not scared 'cos the boys have been so good with us, so I guess I'm sort of apprehensive.'

'Yes,' agrees Karen. 'Trainings fine but the real situation will be different, it always is but we are a team, I've got your back and you'll have mine and a good team will always beat a group of individuals.' Listening Beth nods in agreement and puts out her arms for a hug, Karen moves to her they clasp together. Staring into each other's eyes they repeat in unison, "Teamwork." Then Karen opens her mouth and kisses Beth's

nose which brings a giggle from her, she grins and directs.

'Shower time, hands up.' Beth does as she is told allowing Karen to lift the crop top over her head, she follows this with, "anchors away," grabbing Beth's shorts she lowers them leaving Beth standing in her sports bra and briefs. "My turn" breaks in Beth, with that she lifts Karen's top off, "now down," she lowers her shorts. This leaves them both staring at each other's body with just their underwear on. They start to feel the others body allowing sensuality to take over when a morbid faux par is inadvertently muttered by Beth.

'We will be the same after this, wont we?' Karen stops caressing her and stares, the comment has slid its negative knife in, she gathers strength and with little conviction, "of course," Beth is quick to pick up on this facade. Doubt floods both their minds, they stare at each other then move forward to a tightly clenched hug, holding it, Karen feels Beth's antipathy she knows it's up to her to straighten the ship.

'Remember... teamwork,' Beth's smile is forced but she answers, 'yes teamwork.' Stepping back, she admires Karen's body and asks, "Can I see you?" Karen knows this is a cry for attachment, her youthful insecurity needing something to hold on to, undoing her bra she lowers her panties, Beth moves forward and runs her hand over Karen's breasts then down to her groin. Withdrawing her hand, she undoes her bra and lowers her briefs, they stand and feel each other's body, knowing that this connection is important. It's not a case of sexual desire rather one of physical joining, Karen opens the shower door and turns on the taps then taking Beth's hand she leads her into the shower. They stand close together allowing the water to run over them, Karen softly asks "turn please," then grabbing a piece of soap she starts washing her. Closing her eyes Beth lets the feeling of a soft woman's delicate touch relax her and take her to that heavenly plateau, a subconscious ethereal feeling. They continue to take turns in washing each

other, just enjoying their contact, the soothing touch. The boys are in the kitchen when they hear footsteps, the girls walk thru with towels wrapped round them holding hands, they turn and smile then disappear down the passageway, Rod's unaware but Geoff is more astute, he comments to Rod.

'They were holding hands, it's a subconscious security measure, they'll need us tonight.' The girls are changed and re-enter the kitchen, Geoff acts bubbly and chats about Rod's injury and the recuperation process. He serves dinner, it's fish and vegetables as they eat the boys chatter away about various topics, in this meal however the girls are not so involved. They add monosyllabic answers or comments that singularly relate to the conversation or question. Both boys notice that at various times the girls will smile at each other but it's a forced smile, they are very much acting to hold each other steadfast, dinner finishes, Geoff tries to deviate their thoughts. Girls why don't you go in and watch some TV, I think there's a good movie on tonight', Karen agrees.

'Alright, let's see.' They rise and move to the lounge where the TV is, looking at Rod Geoff raises his eyes, there's definitely tension in the air. With the coffee's made the boys join them in the lounge, sipping the coffee and watching the movie does little to ease the girls troubled state, less than half way thru the movie Karen says.

'I don't want to see this through, I think I'll retire early, will you come?'

'Sure Kaz, no problem,' answers Geoff. They rise and depart with a general, "See you in the Morning," as they leave Karen brushes Beth's hand not a shake sort of a relaxed low five, a smile is returned, a little later Beth announces.

'I think I'll retire also, you coming?'

'Yep I'm with you,' enthuses Rod. Standing they turn off the set and walk down the passageway, walking past Geoff and Karen's room soft voices hardly audible can just be heard,

she's not sure but she thinks someone is crying, upon entering Rod's room he says.

'I'll go and clean my teeth, won't be long.' He exits, she is alone in the room, the chill of independent insecurity floods her, tears start to well up in her eyes, in her mind the room is stifling, it shrinks and with it her confidence erodes. Rod re-enters in time, he quickly picks up the vibe, she's scared, he goes to her she immediately nestles in allowing him to hold her tightly, moments pass, they break slightly, he looks down on her and with care says.

'Don't worry, you're fine, you know what to do, so does Karen, it's natural to feel a bit umm… ahh… a lack of confidence but we're with you all the way.' Tears well up into her eyes. 'I know but I'm scared, please hold me tonight.' Smiling he jokes.

'With a body like that you try to keep me away.' The offhand comment brings a slight smile, slipping off his pants and top he levers into the bed. Beth stands at the foot of the bed and looks at him, he's concentrating on her, this appeals to her sense of belonging, of being wanted. Slowly she lifts her top and lays it on the chair followed by her skirt, with her now standing in front of him in just her bra and briefs he gazes, her look is appealing, with a flick of her hand the bra is discarded then with a more playful disposition she turns and wiggles her way out of the briefs. Looking over her shoulder she inquires, "Well?' her playfulness has restored some of her confidence, resilience is creeping in helped by her coquettishness, Rod's quick to join in the fun realising that this playfulness is displacing her anxiety. 'Very impressive, like the hammies, hmm… good shoulders, what's the front like?' Grinning at the request she slowly turns, enjoying showing off, "and?" He's about to make a funny comment when there is a pause, he rises up and inspects her more closely, although not sure she feels like he is studying her diaphragm. 'Put your hands behind

your head,' he requests. Feeling slightly curious she follows his directions, the study of her torso continues, there is another pause then he suddenly bursts out.

'Blimey... You've actually got a six pack.' The exclamation from him is surprising to her, it's one thing to be admired physically but this is admiration towards awe, he adds.

'Look, go on, look in the mirror.' Opening the wardrobe door, she surveys herself in the mirror, stretching her arms upwards it's obvious not only has she lost weight but there is definitely a showing of her abdomen muscles. The realisation brings a smile to her face, closing the door and turning she faces him, the look on his face is of utter admiration, he asks.

'Before you jump into bed can you do a few stretches for me?' The request although voyeuristic in nature is taken by her as a desire to appease, to be admired, all this byplay is having an effect on her attitude. Smiling cheekily she places her hands above her head and tightens, then with exaggerated slow movement she places them in front of her torso and tightens. The result is an enhancing of definition all over her top torso, one look at his face is enough for her to desire to emit this strong image and thus a feeling of power. Unlike the sexual by play before this time she's exhibiting her advanced physical self, which in itself is a turn on as mirrored by his impressed grin, he calls. Okay my little fitness girl, you really are something now, so lovely and exciting but time to rest.' He pats the bed next to him. Releasing her pose, she walks up to the side of the bed, just before climbing in she runs her hand over herself. The understanding of what she has seen and what his comments reflect have dug themselves into her psyche, as she feels herself, the taught muscles with obvious definition, the way her breasts now stand out from the taught base of her chest. The shoulder muscles that tightly run into and support her neck and the rippling strength of her diaphragm all adds up to satisfaction

and confidence, as she lies down next to him, he comments.

'You'll be fine, you know it now also,' The earnest statement draws the required response.

'Yes, you're right, we will be.' Putting his arm around her and kissing her they drift off to sleep.

CHAPTER 54

Morning arrives, no one is stirring, there's no hurry in this household at the moment. By nine o'clock sounds are heard in the kitchen, Beth is still dozing so Rod carefully slides out of the bed and heads to the kitchen, Geoff is working away preparing breakfast, he looks up.

'Oh, hi Rod, how'd Beth sleep?'

'Not bad actually, we mucked around for a bit, she seemed to relax, so yeah, fingers crossed… Kaz?'

'A bit upset really, I did my best and eventually calmed her down, I guess wait and see.'

'That's all we can do,' says Rod with an understanding tone, turning he drifts off towards the bathroom, the clattering of dishes draws the girls out, sleepily Beth enters she's thrown on a longish T-Shirt, Geoff tries to be nonchalant.

'Morning Beth, how are you this morning?' The reply is just what he desires to hear.

'Hi Geoff, not bad, slept okay.' It's not what's said it's the way it was delivered, relaxed and confident, he smiles to himself, Karen's following, Rod greets her.

'Hi Kaz, how are you?' Her response is still tense.

'Not too bad, eventually slept a bit.' Geoff tries being

breezy.

'Well I've got the eggs going, so get in do your ablutions, 'cos breakies on the way.' The girls continue and move to the bathroom, inside Karen asks Beth.

'How are you?' The response is not quite what she expects.

'Oh, not too bad, actually okay.' Karen raises an eye slightly surprised by the relaxed and maybe even confident tone and comments.

'Well we've got a big day ahead.' The answer almost floors Karen.

'Yes, but we're under control and together, what will be will be, I'm hungry.' Planting a kiss on Karen's cheek followed by a playful slap on the backside she departs the bathroom. Karen is trying to establish control of her emotions, she opens the bathroom mirror and stares at her reflection, suddenly it dawns on her.

'Beth knows exactly the same as me, she's resigned to it has faith in me and our training, if I tense up, I'll stuff up and that could end in disaster. What I said about teamwork was true, relax... she's right, what will be will be. I'm meant to be the senior here, toughen up and lighten up girl, get stuck in, lead!' With that pep-talk finished she exits the bathroom, re-entering the kitchen she sits and comments.

'Eggs Benedict, yummy, thanks Geoff.' He reply's, 'No worries Kaz,' but deep down his mind settles, whatever was said in the bathroom has done the trick, both girls are focused and seem relaxed, inwardly he breathes a sigh of relief then asks.

'What are you girls going to do this morning?'

'Oh, I don't know answers Karen,' then turning to Beth. 'Do you feel like a walk?'

'Absolutely,' is the response. 'It's a lovely day out there.' They finish, change into shorts, T-Shirts and sneakers and exit

the house, this gives Geoff time to discuss proceedings with Rod.

'Rod, I think they are going to be alright, I don't know what you said to Beth but whatever, it changed Kaz, and its due to Beth's influence, thanks mate.' Smiling knowingly Rod understands it wasn't him just an acknowledgement of Beth's now physical image, his appreciation was comforting, from comfort came re-assurance and this led to confidence instilled again. The identification of her six-pack turned her 'round, he knows that's why they have mirrors in gyms, to gain confidence, although to some it feathers their ego but the end result is confidence and with that anything can be achieved. He is reassured like Geoff and nods, they return smiles in appreciation of a job done as best they could. The girls are away for over an hour, when they return Geoff asks.

'What time will you guys leave to go to dance practice tonight?'

'Oh, about four,' is Karen's response then turning to Beth she exclaims, 'Hey we've been so busy with ourselves we've done no preparation for the kids.'

'Right,' answers Beth. 'Let's get organized.' They stand and move to the lounge-room. The afternoon is spent with them working thru movement patterns, extensions and revising work reached at the last classes, by three-thirty they have finished their prep work and re-enter the kitchen, Karen speaks.

'We've done all our work for the kids, we'll get our gear together and mosey down to the studio.' Geoff responds with a nod and soft acknowledgement, "okay." Exiting the kitchen, the girls go to their separate rooms and arrange their gear in bags, after about fifteen minutes they reappear in the kitchen, standing at the hallway entrance Karen speaks.

'Geoff, Rod whatever happens thanks for all your effort, we've spoken and will do everything in our ability to

follow your instructions but as Beth said to me "whatever will be will be." We are nervous, that's to be expected but I believe fear has been pushed aside by friendship and teamwork, I guess time will tell, come here please Geoff.' He wheels across, Beth follows her lead saying, "come here please Rod," he walks over to her. Karen speaks loud enough for both boys to hear with empathy.

'A Kiss au revoir, not goodbye.' With that the two couples embrace and hold it for a while then the two girls break off, smile, turn and walk down the passageway and out the door. Behind Geoff is slumped in his wheelchair, Rod sits at the kitchen table, there's nothing to say, he places his head in his hands, an empty feeling invades him, Geoff wheels over to him and pats him on the shoulder. Their waiting game has now begun.

CHAPTER 55

Round five the dance kids roll in. They are their normal bubbly selves chattering about this and that, Karen takes command and orders them into position, as they move to various spots Shelly has a quick aside to Beth.

'You weren't at school today, but you're here, are you alright?' Looking at her fondly Beth answers.

'Yes Shell' fine here, all under control.' Shelly's not so easily swayed but decides not to push the point, the session starts, Karen cracks the whip, Beth shows various movements, they both are enjoying the involvement, taking their minds off what might lie ahead, an hour and a half later Karen calls a halt to proceedings.

'Right remember what we showed you, we'll start that new verse next week, see you then, well done,' The young girls smile and move to the side organising their gear, they start to drift out, Karen calls Shelly over.

'Shell' is your dad picking you up?'

'Yes,' she replies.

'Well do us a favour and poke your head outside and see if there's anyone else in the car-park besides him.' She does as is told and returns almost immediately.

'Dad's there and there's another car right at the back, I think it's those nasty people.'

'Right,' directs Karen, 'please do that thing we asked you to do a couple of weeks ago.' Shelly nods then starts to blubber.

'They're coming in here when I leave aren't, they?' Karen nods. Shelly starts disintegrating in front of them. 'But... but... there's many of them, its, it's not right, you're only two young ladies, I... I... don't.'

'Stop,' orders Karen. 'Listen you have a job to do for us as we have a job to do, we're under control, but you need to be, okay?' Slowing her snivelling Shelly despondently whispers, "okay," she lifts her bag and trudges out. Karen turns to Beth.

'So, this is it, you ready?'

'Yep,' is the confident reply.

'Right get prepared,' she throws a bottle of oil at her, they disrobe from the track suit pants and sweatshirts so that they have their two-piece aerobics gear on and immediately begin oiling themselves down.

'Put it in your hair,' orders Karen. 'So, they can't grab it.' Beth nods and works the oils through her scalp. Karen continues to organise.

'Get the towels ready,' they throw them to various spots on the floor. The outside door is heard opening, Beth looks at Karen, a determination is in her voice.

'For uncle Reg and the boys, let's fix these bastards.'

'Yes,' growls Karen. 'Remember concentrate, do what we know.' Their eyes lock in a steely resolve, the sound of the inner door opening transfixes their gaze to that, in walks Noogs, Pills, Tatts and Billy, they are wearing T-Shirts, jeans and old worn sneakers, Noogs starts.

'Hi girls,' Karen answers apprehensively.

'What do you want?'

'Oh,' continues Noogs. 'Just to catch up, we thought

you girls might be lonely, might need a good time, well we're here ta show you one, oh, look at our cute fitness gear, aren't we just the picture of health.' She walks forward with the boys supporting her, they form a semi-circle round the two girls, Pills and Billy are on the outside, Karen and Beth look worried, as they close in Karen appeals.

'Look we didn't mean anything, we don't want any trouble, why don't you just leave us alone.' Noogs now starts getting aggressive.

'Trouble, hey fuck you with your goody two shoes attitude, you don't know what life is really like. Time you learnt some fuckin' home truths ya smart arse little cunts, we'll show you trouble, a whole lot of fuckin' trouble.' Pleading Karen acts with a begging manner.

'Wait this isn't fair you out number us.' Noogs smiles, 'Oh dear we do, what do you want us to do send someone outside like playtime?' Billy finds this amusing, he guffs.

'Yeah, g-g-good one, playtime.' Karen replies to the comment but this time with more control in her voice.

'No, you don't have to do that, we'll help.' Noogs is slightly confused, "Help?" A devious smile breaks on Karen's face she yells "Now." Beth springs at Billy and crunches him in the chest with her shoulder. Billy goes flying backwards and lands on his back, at the same time Karen launches at Pills and smashes him in the face with her fist, he also goes flying backwards. Before Noogs and Tatts can move, Karen is on top of Pills and smashes his nose upwards, it shatters, he screams in agony, blood flies everywhere. Beth has jumped on Billy, she drives her foot down into his groin, he screams, she picks up his head and slams it back into the floor then picking up his head slightly she drives her fist with such force into his jaw that it shatters. Noogs and Tatts stare as if they are watching some sort of surreal movie. Beth and Karen rise from the bodies they have destroyed, Karen has blood splattered all over her torso,

Beth has blood over her arm, Karen speaks slowly.

'Now it's even, did you think we were just going to lie down and whimper, you despise us for what we do, only because you haven't got the guts or determination to try anything, you were going to fuck us, okay we're here, we're ready, give it your best shot.' Noogs is in a state of shock, she states the obvious.

'You fuckin' bitches, look what you done to Billy and Pills.' Producing a knife from her jacket she regains confidence, Tatts also digs a knife out, her attitude is restored she acts like she's in charge.

'You're gonna pay, you'll die here.' Karen again answers in a commanding relaxed way.

'Armed, we're not, you have the advantage again.' Smiling Noogs aggressively answers.

'Yeah, bad luck, come on Tatts, let's cut these bitches.' Noogs and Tatts circle round the two girls but Beth drifts away which forces the other two to split, it's now become one on one. As Karen and Beth move along the wall they stoop and pick up a towel each and wrap it round their forearm and wrist. Facing Tatts, Beth notices his feet are spread therefore he is off balance when he lunges, he jabs and swipes at her but she deftly keeps out of reach. With a subtle feint she moves back into his jabbing range. Noticing, he thinks she has made a mistake and is too close, he rams his knife at her mid-section but she knows it is coming and blind-turns like an AFL footballer, deflecting the blade with her towelled arm and grabbing his wrist with her free hand. She's now inside, close to him, raising her towelled hand she elbows him in the face, yelling with pain he drops the knife and grasps his jaw. Using her foot, she flicks the knife away, it goes spinning across the floor, now she has time to unwrap the towel from around her arm and throw it away. He also has regained some composure, screaming something he lunges at her grabbing her around the waist, but to his

amazement she turns, squiggles and slips away. The lunge has put him in an overbalanced position, before he can right himself, she sweeps his feet away, crashing down hard on the floor he is slightly stunned. Shaking his head to try and clear his senses he rises and is halfway up when she lands a knee into his side, groaning he grabs at her leg but his hands slip off forcing him to push them downwards to gain balance with the floor. Looking up he can see her in front of him and makes a grab at her ankle, holding her sneaker and low-cut sock he pulls forcing her to crash down onto the floor. Crouching he jumps at her but she rolls and does a front flip to her feet, he's amazed she's so quick and agile. Rising again he attempts to grab her but this time his movement is slow, she slams her foot into his chest with a sideways karate style kick, he collapses again. This time he's much slower to raise himself, with a last desperate effort he grabs her round the knee but she crashes her hands down on the back of his neck, he collapses again. Gaining the ascendancy Beth jumps on him driving her knees right into his back, he screams with pain. Able to roll him over she is now astride him facing him, with a look of absolute disdain she produces a flurry of punches to his face, blood splatters everywhere, he's finished, with finality she lifts his head and slams it into the wooden floor rendering him unconscious. Standing over the destroyed body she hovers looking like a lioness after the kill.

While this action has been in progress Karen has been fending off knife sweeps by Noogs. She's also picked up a towel and wrapped it round her wrist. Noogs swings and jabs wildly, she obviously hasn't used a knife much. A lot of the time she's unbalanced, Karen moves round occasionally deflecting the "swooshing" knife with her towelled hand. At last Noogs does too large a sweep forcing herself off balance, Karen turns side on and karate kicks her in the stomach. Noogs gasps, allowing Karen time to grab her arm and slam the knife hand into her

knee, "Whacking" it a few times forces the knife to drop, now with free hands Noogs grabs Karen's hair but with a twist of her head Karen slides out of her grasp. She lunges at Karen getting her arms around her in a headlock from behind but Karen elbows her in the lower chest causing her to gasp, releasing the pressure from the headlock. Spinning around she grabs hold of Noog's wrists, they come eye to eye, Noogs is half coughing, she splutters.

'You're dead bitch.'

Whipping a hand free she aims at Karen's neck with full intention to choke her. But Karen ducks under the outstretched hand and delivers a massive side punch into Noog's kidney area, causing her to scream in pain. Grabbing Noog's shoulders Karen pushes her back towards the wall, her chest and head slam into it, she's stunned, turning her round Karen can see blood trickling from Noog's nose, although unbalanced she still manages to blurt out "Fuckin' bitch." With a last-ditch effort to make some impression she now resorts to female style fighting, raising her fingers in an attempt to scratch Karen's eyes but to no avail. Karen sways back and side-kicks her in stomach pushing her back to the wall. Noogs looks half done, she's leaning against the wall, blood now streams from her face, Karen stares at her for a moment, all the months of pain, the misery she and her sidekicks have caused her loved ones builds up in intensity, anger rockets thru her, she stares and states.

'Goodbye.'

A barrage of vehement fist hits wack Noogs so intensely that her face and body seem like a punching bag. As each blow lands parts of Noog's face splits open, teeth become dislodged, the last hits flay blood all over the place, over Karen and all over the floor. The blows stop and Noog's dismantled body slumps to the floor. Karen stares coldly at her then with one almighty kick hitting the side of Noog's head she sends

Noog's body spinning sideways across the floor, sweeping thru the blood-soaked timber base. She's out cold, blood is oozing round all the bodies, the two girls stand in the middle of the room staring at the carnage. Walking forward they face each other, Karen comments on its finality.

'It's over.' Glancing round the room Beth agrees, "Yes," she looks back to Karen, the enormity of what she's been involved in starts to sink in. This is the result of what they have been training for but it stands as testament for everything she dislikes, she starts to cry. Karen draws her head into her, hugs and pats her, a sound is heard of the outer door opening, then the inner door, Johnny saunters in exclaiming.

'Hey Noogs, I just wanna see...' His voice trails off as he views the carnage, snapping his head towards the two girls standing in the centre of the room he yells.

'What, what have you done?' Karen's still patting Beth, she answers in a clam voice.

'We defended ourselves.' He's absolutely aghast.

'You two, young girls... you couldn't.'

'We did and against knives as well, your friends are in a lot of trouble, if they live, the police have been called and will be here in I'd say about twenty minutes and guess what, you're an accessory to a violent attack on two unarmed and defenceless girls, I reckon that's at least seven years minimum'. Johnny stares, the whole thing is so surreal, Karen continues.

'I'd say you've got about ten minutes to get on the road and out of town, maybe the state, 'cos they'll be looking for you, what did you do... oh yes, planning, the instigator, better hurry.' The reality of the situation as exemplified by her speech starts to sink in, however he's still perplexed.

'... but how did you...?' Beth's now recovered enough composure to answer.

'Discipline and effort, it works to overcome fear.' Karen smiles and prods.

'Clocks ticking, hmm… is that police sirens I hear?'

Johnny's now definitely worried, he turns and bolts out the door, the sound is heard of his car speeding off. Karen and Beth slump down in the middle of the floor, they share a bottle of water and wait.

In the kitchen of the house Geoff's trying to make some dinner, he's trying without the crutches, Rod's sitting at the table fiddling with his fingers, the tension is extreme. Suddenly they hear the sound of the front door opening, the boys don't know who it is, they hold their breath. Beth and Karen enter the kitchen with track pants on, even so the dried blood is splattered across their tops. They stand in the doorway, Geoff and Rod stare, the girls can see relief flood thru them, there is a long pause, Geoff breaks the silence.

'So, they came.' Karen answers, 'Yes, it's over.' They look at each other for a while then Karen walks up to Geoff and collapses into his arms. Beth walks up to Rod and stands in front of him with her head down, Rod puts his finger under her chin and slowly raises her head so her eyes look straight into his. Smiling softly at her he forces a return smile, she slumps into his body, he wraps his one good arm around her. Both couples stay standing, holding each other.

James Hand (nee Ian Handasyde)

Ian has worked for over 30 yrs as a music teacher. Currently is lead guitar player for "Turn It Up" 60's style cover's Rock Band.

Also Guitarist/singer and chief writer for Original band "Winton Central", their first CD "Moving" was released in July 2018 on I Tunes.

He has written many song's, his "I'm Trying To Get To You" won Triple J's Unearthed in 2001, for the band "No I.D."

He has written many Film scripts. His Short Film "Just Friends" was accepted and screened at Cannes Film Festival in 2006. His Feature Film "Zyco Rock" was shown at Festivals around the world.

Ian is a member of APRA/AMCOS Publishers. His first release on Amazon and Kindle in 2022 is "Luina".

To follow in the Beth Duncan series:

The Fit Girl
Shh, Secret Girl
London Bound
Two Daughters

James Hand Publishing ©
Published by Ashby's Place

www.ashbysplace.com.au